WHERE I'M CALLING FROM

Also by Raymond Carver

Fiction

WHAT WE TALK ABOUT WHEN WE TALK ABOUT LOVE

FURIOUS SEASONS

WILL YOU PLEASE BE QUIET, PLEASE?

CATHEDRAL

ELEPHANT

SHORT CUTS
selected and with an introduction
by Robert Altman

Poetry

NEAR KLAMATH

WINTER INSOMNIA

AT NIGHT THE SALMON MOVE

WHERE WATER COMES TOGETHER WITH OTHER WATER

ULTRAMARINE

IN A MARINE LIGHT: SELECTED POEMS

A NEW PATH TO THE WATERFALL
with an introduction by Tess Gallagher

ALL OF US: THE COLLECTED POEMS
edited by William L. Stull

Essays, Poems, Stories

FIRES

NO HEROICS, PLEASE

Raymond Carver

WHERE I'M CALLING FROM

Selected Stories

Atlantic Monthly Press

NEW YORK

Published simultaneously in Canada
Printed in the United States of America

SPECIAL TENTH-ANNIVERSARY EDITION

Library of Congress Cataloging-in-Publication Data
Carver, Raymond
Where I'm calling from : new and selected stories / Raymond
Carver.
ISBN 0-87113-721-6
I. Title.
PS3553.A7894W5   87-36778

Atlantic Monthly Press
841 Broadway
New York, NY 10003

98 99 00 01 10 9 8 7 6 5 4 3 2 1

To Tess Gallagher

ACKNOWLEDGMENTS

"Chef's House", "Where I'm Calling From", "Boxes", "Whoever Was Using this Bed", "Elephant", "Blackbird Pie", and "Errand" first appeared in *The New Yorker*, "Intimacy" in *Esquire*, and "Menudo" in *Granta*.

The author also wishes to thank the following publications for permission to reprint stories in this volume: *Antæus*, *Antioch Review*, *Atlantic*, *Carolina Quarterly*, *Colorado State Review*, *December*, *Discourse*, *Esquire*, *Fiction*, *Grand Street*, *Granta*, *Harper's Bazaar*, *Iowa Review*, *Kansas Quarterly*, *Missouri Review*, *New England Review*, *North American Review*, *Northwest Review*, *Paris Review*, *Perspective*, *Ploughshares*, *Quarterly West*, *Seneca Review*, *Sou'wester*, *Tri-Quarterly*, *Western Humanities Review*.

We can never know what to want,
because, living only one life, we can neither
compare it with our previous lives
nor perfect it in our lives to come.

MILAN KUNDERA,
The Unbearable Lightness of Being

A NOTE ON THE TEXT

The stories in this collection are arranged, generally, in the order of their being written. A number of them were revised by the author for the Atlantic Monthly Press edition of 1988, and in a few cases titles were changed:

"Nobody Said Anything", "Bicycles, Muscles, Cigarettes", "The Student's Wife", "They're Not Your Husband", "What Do You Do in San Francisco?", "Fat", "What's in Alaska?", "Neighbors", "Put Yourself in My Shoes", "Collectors", "Why, Honey?", and "Are these Actual Miles?" (originally "What Is It?") are from *Will You Please Be Quiet, Please?*, originally published by the McGraw-Hill Book Company, New York, 1976.

"Distance", "The Third Thing that Killed My Father off" (originally "Dummy"), and "So Much Water So Close to Home" are from *Furious Seasons*, originally published by Capra Press, Santa Barbara, 1977.

"Gazebo", "One More Thing", "Little Things" (originally "Popular Mechanics"), "Why Don't You Dance?", "A Serious Talk", "What We Talk about When We Talk about Love", and "The Calm" are from *What We Talk about When We Talk about Love*, originally published in the USA by Alfred A. Knopf, 1981, and in Britain by Collins Harvill, 1982.

"Vitamins", "Careful", "Where I'm Calling from", "Chef's House", "Fever", "Feathers", "Cathedral", and "A Small, Good Thing" are from *Cathedral*, originally published in the USA by Alfred A. Knopf, 1983, and in Britain by Collins Harvill, 1984.

"Boxes", "Whoever Was Using this Bed", "Intimacy", "Menudo", "Elephant", "Blackbird Pie", and "Errand" were first published in the USA in *Where I'm Calling from* in the section entitled "New Stories" by Atlantic Monthly Press, 1988, and in Britain as a separate collection entitled *Elephant*, by Collins Harvill, 1988.

CONTENTS

Author's Foreword[*]

I wrote and published my first short story in 1963,[†] twenty-five years ago, and have been drawn to short story writing ever since. I think in part (but only in part) this inclination toward brevity and intensity has to do with the fact that I am a poet as well as a story writer. I began writing and publishing poetry and fiction at more or less the same time, back in the early 1960s when I was still an undergraduate. But this dual relationship as poet and short story writer doesn't explain everything. I'm hooked on writing short stories and couldn't get off them even if I wanted to. Which I don't.

I love the swift leap of a good story, the excitement that often commences in the first sentence, the sense of beauty and mystery found in the best of them; and the fact – so crucially important to me back at the beginning and even now still a consideration – that the story can be written and read in one sitting. (Like poems!)

In the beginning – and perhaps still – the most important short story writers to me were Isaac Babel, Anton Chekhov, Frank O'Connor and V. S. Pritchett. I forget who passed along a copy of Babel's *Collected Stories* to me, but I do remember coming across a line from one of his greatest stories. I copied it into the little notebook I carried around with me everywhere in those days. The narrator, speaking about Maupassant and the writing of fiction, says: "No iron can pierce the heart with such force as a period put just at the right place."

---

* The "Author's Foreword" was originally published as "A Special Message for the First Edition" in *Where I'm Calling from*, The Signed First Edition Society (Franklin Center, Pa.: The Franklin Library, 1988).
† Raymond Carver in fact published his first short story, "The Furious Seasons", in 1960. See *No Heroics, Please* (Harvill, 1991).

xi

When I first read this it came to me with the force of revelation. This is what I wanted to do with my own stories: line up the right words, the precise images, as well as the exact and correct punctuation so that the reader got pulled in and involved in the story and wouldn't be able to turn away his eyes from the text unless the house caught fire. Vain wishes perhaps, to ask words to assume the power of actions, but clearly a young writer's wishes. Still, the idea of writing clearly with authority enough to hold and engage the reader persisted. This remains one of my primary goals today.

My first book of stories, *Will You Please Be Quiet, Please?*, did not appear until 1976, thirteen years after the first story was written. This long delay between composition, magazine and book publication was due in part to a young marriage, the exigencies of child rearing and blue-collar laboring jobs, a little education on the fly – and never enough money to go around at the end of each month. (It was during this long period, too, that I was trying to learn my craft as a writer, how to be as subtle as a river current when very little else in my life was subtle.)

After the thirteen-year period it took to put the first book together and to find a publisher who, I might add, was most reluctant to engage in such a cockeyed enterprise – a first book of stories by an unknown writer! – I tried to learn to write fast when I had the time, writing stories when the spirit was with me and letting them pile up in a drawer; and then going back to look at them carefully and coldly later on, from a remove, after things had calmed down, after things had, all too regrettably, gone back to "normal".

Inevitably, life being what it is, there were often great swatches of time that simply disappeared, long periods when I did not write any fiction. (How I wish I had those years back now!) Sometimes a year or two would pass when I couldn't even think about writing stories. Often, though, I was able to spend some of that time writing poems, and this proved important because in writing the poetry the flame didn't entirely putter out, as I sometimes feared it might. Mysteriously, or so it would seem to me, there would come a time to turn to fiction again. The circumstances in my life would be right or at least improved and the ferocious desire to write would take hold of me, and I would begin.

I wrote *Cathedral* – eight of these stories are reprinted here – in a period of fifteen months. But during that two-year period before I began to work on those stories, I found myself in a period of stock-taking, of trying to discover where I wanted to go with whatever new stories I was going to write and how I wanted to write them. My previous book, *What We Talk about When We Talk about Love*, had been in many ways a watershed book for me, but it was a book I didn't want to duplicate or write again. So I simply waited. I taught at Syracuse University. I wrote some poems and book reviews, and an essay or two. And then one morning something happened. After a good night's sleep, I went to my desk and wrote the story "Cathedral". I knew it was a different kind of story for me, no question. Somehow I had found another direction I wanted to move toward. And I moved. And quickly.

The new stories that are included here,* stories which were written after *Cathedral* and after I had intentionally, happily, taken "time out" for two years to write two books of poetry, are, I'm sure, different in kind and degree from the earlier stories. (At least I think they're different from those earlier stories, and I suspect readers may feel the same. But any writer will tell you he wants to believe his work will undergo a metamorphosis, a sea-change, a process of enrichment if he's been at it long enough.)

V. S. Pritchett's definition of a short story is "something glimpsed from the corner of the eye, in passing". First the glimpse. Then the glimpse given life, turned into something that will illuminate the moment and just maybe lock it indelibly into the reader's consciousness. Make it a part of the reader's own experience, as Hemingway so nicely put it. Forever, the writer hopes. Forever.

---

* "The New Stories" referred to here are the last seven in the present volume. They were first published in Britain as a separate volume under the title *Elephant* (Harvill, 1988).

If we're lucky, writer and reader alike, we'll finish the last line or two of a short story and then just sit for a minute, quietly. Ideally, we'll ponder what we've just written or read; maybe our hearts or our intellects will have been moved off the peg just a little from where they were before. Our body temperature will have gone up, or down, by a degree. Then, breathing evenly and steadily once more, we'll collect ourselves, writers and readers alike, get up, "created of warm blood and nerves", as a Chekhov character puts it, and go on to the next thing: Life. Always life.

R.C.

WHERE I'M
CALLING FROM

Nobody Said Anything

I could hear them out in the kitchen. I couldn't hear what they were saying, but they were arguing. Then it got quiet and she started to cry. I elbowed George. I thought he would wake up and say something to them so they would feel guilty and stop. But George is such an asshole. He started kicking and hollering.

"Stop gouging me, you bastard," he said. "I'm going to tell!"

"You dumb chickenshit," I said. "Can't you wise up for once? They're fighting and Mom's crying. Listen."

He listened with his head off the pillow. "I don't care," he said and turned over toward the wall and went back to sleep. George is a royal asshole.

Later I heard Dad leave to catch his bus. He slammed the front door. She had told me before he wanted to tear up the family. I didn't want to listen.

After a while she came to call us for school. Her voice sounded funny – I don't know. I said I felt sick at my stomach. It was the first week in October and I hadn't missed any school yet, so what could she say? She looked at me, but it was like she was thinking of something else. George was awake and listening. I could tell he was awake by the way he moved in the bed. He was waiting to see how it turned out so he could make his move.

"All right." She shook her head. "I just don't know. Stay home, then. But no TV, remember that."

George reared up. "I'm sick too," he said to her. "I have a headache. He gouged me and kicked me all night. I didn't get to sleep at all."

"That's enough!" she said. "You are going to school, George! You're not going to stay here and fight with your brother all day. Now get up and get dressed. I mean it. I don't feel like another battle this morning."

I

George waited until she left the room. Then he climbed out over the foot of the bed. "You bastard," he said and yanked all the covers off me. He dodged into the bathroom.

"I'll kill you," I said but not so loud that she could hear.

I stayed in bed until George left for school. When she started to get ready for work, I asked if she would make a bed for me on the couch. I said I wanted to study. On the coffee table I had the Edgar Rice Burroughs books I had gotten for my birthday and my Social Studies book. But I didn't feel like reading. I wanted her to leave so I could watch TV.

She flushed the toilet.

I couldn't wait any longer. I turned the picture on without the volume. I went out to the kitchen where she had left her pack of weeds and shook out three. I put them in the cupboard and went back to the couch and started reading *The Princess of Mars*. She came out and glanced at the TV but didn't say anything. I had the book open. She poked at her hair in front of the mirror and then went into the kitchen. I looked back at the book when she came out.

"I'm late. Good-bye, sweetheart." She wasn't going to bring up the TV. Last night she'd said she wouldn't know what it meant any more to go to work without being "stirred up".

"Don't cook anything. You don't need to turn the burners on for a thing. There's tuna fish in the icebox if you feel hungry." She looked at me. "But if your stomach is sick, I don't think you should put anything on it. Anyway, you don't need to turn the burners on. Do you hear? You take that medicine, sweetheart, and I hope your stomach feels better by tonight. Maybe we'll all feel better by tonight."

She stood in the doorway and turned the knob. She looked as if she wanted to say something else. She wore the white blouse, the wide black belt, and the black skirt. Sometimes she called it her outfit, sometimes her uniform. For as long as I could remember, it was always hanging in the closet or hanging on the clothesline or getting washed out by hand at night or being ironed in the kitchen.

She worked Wednesdays through Sundays.

"Bye, Mom."

I waited until she had started the car and had it warm. I listened as she pulled away from the curb. Then I got up and turned the sound on loud and went for the weeds. I smoked one and beat off while I watched a show about doctors and nurses. Then I turned to the other channel. Then I turned off the TV. I didn't feel like watching.

I finished the chapter where Tars Tarkas falls for a green woman, only to see her get her head chopped off the next morning by this jealous brother-in-law. It was about the fifth time I had read it. Then I went to their bedroom and looked around. I wasn't after anything in particular unless it was rubbers again and though I had looked all over I had never found any. Once I found a jar of Vaseline at the back of a drawer. I knew it must have something to do with it, but I didn't know what. I studied the label and hoped it would reveal something, a description of what people did, or else about how you applied the Vaseline, that sort of thing. But it didn't. *Pure Petroleum Jelly*, that was all it said on the front label. But just reading that was enough to give you a boner. *An Excellent Aid in the Nursery*, it said on the back. I tried to make the connection between *Nursery* – the swings and slides, the sandboxes, monkeybars – and what went on in bed between them. I had opened the jar lots of times and smelled inside and looked to see how much had been used since last time. This time I passed up the *Pure Petroleum Jelly*. I mean, all I did was look to see the jar was still there. I went through a few drawers, not really expecting to find anything. I looked under the bed. Nothing anywhere. I looked in the jar in the closet where they kept the grocery money. There was no change, only a five and a one. They would miss that. Then I thought I would get dressed and walk to Birch Creek. Trout season was open for another week or so, but almost everybody had quit fishing. Everybody was just sitting around now waiting for deer and pheasant to open.

I got out my old clothes. I put wool socks over my regular socks and took my time lacing up the boots. I made a couple of

3

tuna sandwiches and some double-decker peanut-butter crackers. I filled my canteen and attached the hunting knife and the canteen to my belt. As I was going out the door, I decided to leave a note. So I wrote: "Feeling better and going to Birch Creek. Back soon. R. 3:15." That was about four hours from now. And about fifteen minutes before George would come in from school. Before I left, I ate one of the sandwiches and had a glass of milk with it.

It was nice out. It was fall. But it wasn't cold yet except at night. At night they would light the smudgepots in the orchards and you would wake up in the morning with a black ring of stuff in your nose. But nobody said anything. They said the smudging kept the young pears from freezing, so it was all right.

To get to Birch Creek, you go to the end of our street where you hit Sixteenth Avenue. You turn left on Sixteenth and go up the hill past the cemetery and down to Lennox, where there is a Chinese restaurant. From the crossroads there, you can see the airport, and Birch Creek is below the airport. Sixteenth changes to View Road at the crossroads. You follow View for a little way until you come to the bridge. There are orchards on both sides of the road. Sometimes when you go by the orchards you see pheasants running down the rows, but you can't hunt there because you might get shot by a Greek named Matsos. I guess it is about a forty-minute walk all in all.

I was halfway down Sixteenth when a woman in a red car pulled onto the shoulder ahead of me. She rolled down the window on the passenger's side and asked if I wanted a lift. She was thin and had little pimples around her mouth. Her hair was up in curlers. But she was sharp enough. She had a brown sweater with nice boobs inside.

"Playing hooky?"

"Guess so."

"Want a ride?"

I nodded.

"Get in. I'm kind of in a hurry."

I put the fly rod and the creel on the back seat. There were a

4

lot of grocery sacks from Mel's on the floorboards and back seat. I tried to think of something to say.

"I'm going fishing," I said. I took off my cap, hitched the canteen around so I could sit, and parked myself next to the window.

"Well, I never would have guessed." She laughed. She pulled back onto the road. "Where are you going? Birch Creek?"

I nodded again. I looked at my cap. My uncle had bought it for me in Seattle when he had gone to watch a hockey game. I couldn't think of anything more to say. I looked out the window and sucked my cheeks. You always see yourself getting picked up by this woman. You know you'll fall for each other and that she'll take you home with her and let you screw her all over the house. I began to get a boner thinking about it. I moved the cap over my lap and closed my eyes and tried to think about baseball.

"I keep saying that one of these days I'll take up fishing," she said. "They say it's very relaxing. I'm a nervous person."

I opened my eyes. We were stopped at the crossroads. I wanted to say, *Are you real busy? Would you like to start this morning?* But I was afraid to look at her.

"Will this help you? I have to turn here. I'm sorry I'm in a hurry this morning," she said.

"That's okay. This is fine." I took my stuff out. Then I put my cap on and took it off again while I talked. "Good-bye. Thanks. Maybe next summer," but I couldn't finish.

"You mean fishing? Sure thing." She waved with a couple of fingers the way women do.

I started walking, going over what I should have said. I could think of a lot of things. What was wrong with me? I cut the air with the fly rod and hollered two or three times. What I should have done to start things off was ask if we could have lunch together. No one was home at my house. Suddenly we are in my bedroom under the covers. She asks me if she can keep her sweater on and I say it's okay with me. She keeps her pants on too. That's all right, I say. I don't mind.

A Piper Cub dipped low over my head as it came in for a landing. I was a few feet from the bridge. I could hear the water running. I hurried down the embankment, unzipped, and shot off five feet over the creek. It must have been a record. I took a while eating the other sandwich and the peanut-butter crackers. I drank up half the water in the canteen. Then I was ready to fish.

I tried to think where to start. I had fished here for three years, ever since we had moved. Dad used to bring George and me in the car and wait for us, smoking, baiting our hooks, tying up new rigs for us if we snagged. We always started at the bridge and moved down, and we always caught a few. Once in a while, at the first of the season, we caught the limit. I rigged up and tried a few casts under the bridge first.

Now and then I cast under a bank or else in behind a big rock. But nothing happened. One place where the water was still and the bottom full of yellow leaves, I looked over and saw a few crawdads crawling there with their big ugly pinchers raised. Some quail flushed out of a brush pile. When I threw a stick, a rooster pheasant jumped up cackling about ten feet away and I almost dropped the rod.

The creek was slow and not very wide. I could walk across almost anywhere without it going over my boots. I crossed a pasture full of cow pads and came to where the water flowed out of a big pipe. I knew there was a little hole below the pipe, so I was careful. I got down on my knees when I was close enough to drop the line. It had just touched the water when I got a strike, but I missed him. I felt him roll with it. Then he was gone and the line flew back. I put another salmon egg on and tried a few more casts. But I knew I had jinxed it.

I went up the embankment and climbed under a fence that had a KEEP OUT sign on the post. One of the airport runways started here. I stopped to look at some flowers growing in the cracks in the pavement. You could see where the tires had smacked down on the pavement and left oily skid marks all around the flowers. I hit the creek again on the other side and fished along for a little way until I came to the hole. I thought this was as far as I would go. When I had first been up here three years ago, the water was

6

roaring right up to the top of the banks. It was so swift then that I couldn't fish. Now the creek was about six feet below the bank. It bubbled and hopped through this little run at the head of the pool where you could hardly see bottom. A little farther down, the bottom sloped up and got shallow again as if nothing had happened. The last time I was up here I caught two fish about ten inches long and turned one that looked twice as big – a summer steelhead, Dad said when I told him about it. He said they come up during the high water in early spring but that most of them return to the river before the water gets low.

I put two more shot on the line and closed them with my teeth. Then I put a fresh salmon egg on and cast out where the water dropped over a shelf into the pool. I let the current take it down. I could feel the sinkers tap-tapping on rocks, a different kind of tapping than when you are getting a bite. Then the line tightened and the current carried the egg into sight at the end of the pool.

I felt lousy to have come this far up for nothing. I pulled out all kinds of line this time and made another cast. I laid the fly rod over a limb and lit the next to last weed. I looked up the valley and began to think about the woman. We were going to her house because she wanted help carrying in the groceries. Her husband was overseas. I touched her and she started shaking. We were French-kissing on the couch when she excused herself to go to the bathroom. I followed her. I watched as she pulled down her pants and sat on the toilet. I had a big boner and she waved me over with her hand. Just as I was going to unzip, I heard a plop in the creek. I looked and saw the tip of my fly rod jiggling.

He wasn't very big and didn't fight much. But I played him as long as I could. He turned on his side and lay in the current down below. I didn't know what he was. He looked strange. I tightened the line and lifted him over the bank into the grass, where he started wiggling. He was a trout. But he was green. I never saw one like him before. He had green sides with black trout spots, a greenish head, and like a green stomach. He was the color of moss, that color green. It was as if he had been wrapped up in moss a long time, and the color had come off all over him. He was fat, and I wondered why he hadn't put up more of a fight. I wondered if he was all right. I looked at him for a time longer, then I put him out of his pain.

I pulled some grass and put it in the creel and laid him in there on the grass.

I made some more casts, and then I guessed it must be two or three o'clock. I thought I had better move down to the bridge. I thought I would fish below the bridge awhile before I started home. And I decided I would wait until night before I thought about the woman again. But right away I got a boner thinking about the boner I would get that night. Then I thought I had better stop doing it so much. About a month back, a Saturday when they were all gone, I had picked up the Bible right after and promised and swore I wouldn't do it again. But I got jism on the Bible, and the promising and swearing lasted only a day or two, until I was by myself again.

I didn't fish on the way down. When I got to the bridge, I saw a bicycle in the grass. I looked and saw a kid about George's size running down the bank. I started in his direction. Then he turned and started toward me, looking in the water.

"Hey, what is it!" I hollered. "What's wrong?" I guessed he didn't hear me. I saw his pole and fishing bag on the bank, and I dropped my stuff. I ran over to where he was. He looked like a rat or something. I mean, he had buckteeth and skinny arms and this ragged long-sleeved shirt that was too small for him.

"God, I swear there's the biggest fish here I ever saw!" he called. "Hurry! Look! Look here! Here he is!"

I looked where he pointed and my heart jumped.

It was as long as my arm.

"God, oh God, will you look at him!" the boy said.

I kept looking. It was resting in a shadow under a limb that hung over the water. "God almighty," I said to the fish, "where did you come from?"

"What'll we do?" the boy said. "I wish I had my gun."

"We're going to get him," I said. "God, look at him! Let's get him into the riffle."

8

"You want to help me, then? We'll work it together!" the kid said.

The big fish had drifted a few feet downstream and lay there finning slowly in the clear water.

"Okay, what do we do?" the kid said.

"I can go up and walk down the creek and start him moving," I said. "You stand in the riffle, and when he tries to come through, you kick the living shit out of him. Get him onto the bank someway, I don't care how. Then get a good hold of him and hang on."

"Okay. Oh shit, look at him! Look, he's going! Where's he going?" the boy screamed.

I watched the fish move up the creek again and stop close to the bank. "He's not going anyplace. There's no place for him to go. See him? He's scared shitless. He knows we're here. He's just cruising around now looking for someplace to go. See, he stopped again. He can't go anyplace. He knows that. He knows we're going to nail him. He knows it's tough shit. I'll go up and scare him down. You get him when he comes through."

"I wish I had my gun," the boy said. "That would take care of him," the boy said.

I went up a little way, then started wading down the creek. I watched ahead of me as I went. Suddenly the fish darted away from the bank, turned right in front of me in a big cloudy swirl, and barrel-assed downstream.

"Here he comes!" I hollered. "Hey, hey, here he comes!" But the fish spun around before it reached the riffle and headed back. I splashed and hollered, and it turned again. "He's coming! Get him, get him! Here he comes!"

But the dumb idiot had himself a club, the asshole, and when the fish hit the riffle, the boy drove at him with the club instead of trying to kick the son of a bitch out like he should have. The fish veered off, going crazy, shooting on his side through the shallow water. He made it. The asshole idiot kid lunged for him and fell flat.

He dragged up onto the bank sopping wet. "I hit him!" the

9

boy hollered. "I think he's hurt, too. I had my hands on him, but I couldn't hold him."

"You didn't have anything!" I was out of breath. I was glad the kid fell in. "You didn't even come close, asshole. What were you doing with that club? You should have kicked him. He's probably a mile away by now." I tried to spit. I shook my head. "I don't know. We haven't got him yet. We just may not get him," I said.

"Goddamn it, I hit him!" the boy screamed. "Didn't you see? I hit him, and I had my hands on him too. How close did you get? Besides, whose fish is it?" He looked at me. Water ran down his trousers over his shoes.

I didn't say anything else, but I wondered about that myself. I shrugged. "Well, okay. I thought it was both ours. Let's get him this time. No goof-ups, either one of us," I said.

We waded downstream. I had water in my boots, but the kid was wet up to his collar. He closed his buckteeth over his lip to keep his teeth from chattering.

The fish wasn't in the run below the riffle, and we couldn't see him in the next stretch, either. We looked at each other and began to worry that the fish really had gone far enough downstream to reach one of the deep holes. But then the goddamn thing rolled near the bank, actually knocking dirt into the water with his tail, and took off again. He went through another riffle, his big tail sticking out of the water. I saw him cruise over near the bank and stop, his tail half out of the water, finning just enough to hold against the current.

"Do you see him?" I said. The boy looked. I took his arm and pointed his finger. "Right *there*. Okay now, listen. I'll go down to that little run between those banks. See where I mean? You wait here until I give you a signal. Then you start down. Okay? And this time don't let him get by you if he heads back."

"Yeah," the boy said and worked his lip with those teeth. "Let's get him this time," the boy said, a terrible look of cold in his face.

I got up on the bank and walked down, making sure I moved

quiet. I slid off the bank and waded in again. But I couldn't see the great big son of a bitch and my heart turned. I thought it might have taken off already. A little farther downstream and it would get to one of the holes. We would never get him then.

"He still there?" I hollered. I held my breath.

The kid waved.

"Ready!" I hollered again.

"Here goes!" the kid hollered back.

My hands shook. The creek was about three feet wide and ran between dirt banks. The water was low but fast. The kid was moving down the creek now, water up to his knees, throwing rocks ahead of him, splashing and shouting.

"Here he comes!" The kid waved his arms. I saw the fish now; it was coming right at me. He tried to turn when he saw me, but it was too late. I went down on my knees, grasping in the cold water. I scooped him with my hands and arms, up, up, raising him, throwing him out of the water, both of us falling onto the bank. I held him against my shirt, him flopping and twisting, until I could get my hands up his slippery sides to his gills. I ran one hand in and clawed through to his mouth and locked around his jaw. I knew I had him. He was still flopping and hard to hold, but I had him and I wasn't going to let go.

"We got him!" the boy hollered as he splashed up. "We got him, by God! Ain't he something! Look at him! Oh God, let me hold him," the boy hollered.

"We got to kill him first," I said. I ran my other hand down the throat. I pulled back on the head as hard as I could, trying to watch out for the teeth, and felt the heavy crunching. He gave a long slow tremble and was still. I laid him on the bank and we looked at him. He was at least two feet long, queerly skinny, but bigger than anything I had ever caught. I took hold of his jaw again.

"Hey," the kid said but didn't say any more when he saw what I was going to do. I washed off the blood and laid the fish back on the bank.

"I want to show him to my dad so bad," the kid said.

We were wet and shivering. We looked at him, kept touching

him. We pried open his big mouth and felt his rows of teeth. His sides were scarred, whitish welts as big as quarters and kind of puffy. There were nicks out of his head around his eyes and on his snout where I guess he had banged into the rocks and been in fights. But he was so skinny, too skinny for how long he was, and you could hardly see the pink stripe down his sides, and his belly was gray and slack instead of white and solid like it should have been. But I thought he was something.

"I guess I'd better go pretty soon," I said. I looked at the clouds over the hills where the sun was going down. "I better get home."

"I guess so. Me too. I'm freezing," the kid said. "Hey, I want to carry him," the kid said.

"Let's get a stick. We'll put it through his mouth and both carry him," I said.

The kid found a stick. We put it through the gills and pushed until the fish was in the middle of the stick. Then we each took an end and started back, watching the fish as he swung on the stick.

"What are we going to do with him?" the kid said.

"I don't know," I said. "I guess I caught him," I said.

"We both did. Besides, I saw him first."

"That's true," I said. "Well, you want to flip for him or what?" I felt with my free hand, but I didn't have any money. And what would I have done if I had lost?

Anyway, the kid said, "No, let's not flip."

I said, "All right. It's okay with me." I looked at that boy, his hair standing up, his lips gray. I could have taken him if it came to that. But I didn't want to fight.

We got to where we had left our things and picked up our stuff with one hand, neither of us letting go of his end of the stick. Then we walked up to where his bicycle was. I got a good hold on the stick in case the kid tried something.

Then I had an idea. "We could half him," I said.

"What do you mean?" the boy said, his teeth chattering again. I could feel him tighten his hold on the stick.

"Half him. I got a knife. We cut him in two and each take half. I don't know, but I guess we could do that."

He pulled at a piece of his hair and looked at the fish. "You going to use that knife?"

"You got one?" I said.

The boy shook his head.

"Okay," I said.

I pulled the stick out and laid the fish in the grass beside the kid's bicycle. I took out the knife. A plane taxied down the runway as I measured a line. "Right here?" I said. The kid nodded. The plane roared down the runway and lifted up right over our heads. I started cutting down into him. I came to his guts and turned him over and stripped everything out. I kept cutting until there was only a flap of skin on his belly holding him together. I took the halves and worked them in my hands and I tore him in two.

I handed the kid the tail part.

"No," he said, shaking his head. "I want that half."

I said, "They're both the same! Now goddamn, watch it, I'm going to get mad in a minute."

"I don't care," the boy said. "If they're both the same, I'll take that one. They're both the same, right?"

"They're both the same," I said. "But I think I'm keeping this half here. I did the cutting."

"I want it," the kid said. "I saw him first."

"Whose knife did we use?" I said.

"I don't want the tail," the kid said.

I looked around. There were no cars on the road and nobody else fishing. There was an airplane droning, and the sun was going down. I was cold all the way through. The kid was shivering hard, waiting.

"I got an idea," I said. I opened the creel and showed him the trout. "See? It's a green one. It's the only green one I ever saw. So whoever takes the head, the other guy gets the green trout and the tail part. Is that fair?"

The kid looked at the green trout and took it out of the creel and held it. He studied the halves of the fish.

"I guess so," he said. "Okay, I guess so. You take that half. I got more meat on mine."

"I don't care," I said. "I'm going to wash him off. Which way do you live?" I said.

"Down on Arthur Avenue." He put the green trout and his half of the fish into a dirty canvas bag. "Why?"

"Where's that? Is that down by the ball park?" I said.

"Yeah, but why, I said." That kid looked scared.

"I live close to there," I said. "So I guess I could ride on the handlebars. We could take turns pumping. I got a weed we could smoke, if it didn't get wet on me."

But the kid only said, "I'm freezing."

I washed my half in the creek. I held his big head under water and opened his mouth. The stream poured into his mouth and out the other end of what was left of him.

"I'm freezing," the kid said.

I saw George riding his bicycle at the other end of the street. He didn't see me. I went around to the back to take off my boots. I unslung the creel so I could raise the lid and get set to march into the house, grinning.

I heard their voices and looked through the window. They were sitting at the table. Smoke was all over the kitchen. I saw it was coming from a pan on the burner. But neither of them paid any attention.

"What I'm telling you is the gospel truth," he said. "What do kids know? You'll see."

She said, "I'll see nothing. If I thought that, I'd rather see them dead first."

He said, "What's the matter with you? You better be careful what you say!"

She started to cry. He smashed out a cigarette in the ashtray and stood up.

"Edna, do you know this pan is burning up?" he said.

She looked at the pan. She pushed her chair back and grabbed the pan by its handle and threw it against the wall over the sink.

He said, "Have you lost your mind? Look what you've done!"

He took a dish cloth and began to wipe up stuff from the pan.

I opened the back door. I started grinning. I said, "You won't believe what I caught at Birch Creek. Just look. Look here. Look at this. Look what I caught."

My legs shook. I could hardly stand. I held the creel out to her, and she finally looked in. "Oh, oh, my God! What is it? A snake! What is it? Please, please take it out before I throw up."

"Take it out!" he screamed. "Didn't you hear what she said? Take it out of here!" he screamed.

I said, "But look, Dad. Look what it is."

He said, "I don't want to look."

I said, "It's a gigantic summer steelhead from Birch Creek. Look! Isn't he something? It's a monster! I chased him up and down the creek like a madman!" My voice was crazy. But I could not stop. "There was another one, too," I hurried on. "A green one. I swear! It was green! Have you ever seen a green one?"

He looked into the creel and his mouth fell open.

He screamed, "Take that goddamn thing out of here! What in the hell is the matter with you? Take it the hell out of the kitchen and throw it in the goddamn garbage!"

I went back outside. I looked into the creel. What was there looked silver under the porch light. What was there filled the creel.

I lifted him out. I held him. I held that half of him.

Bicycles, Muscles, Cigarettes

It had been two days since Evan Hamilton had stopped smoking, and it seemed to him everything he'd said and thought for the two days somehow suggested cigarettes. He looked at his hands under the kitchen light. He sniffed his knuckles and his fingers.

"I can smell it," he said.

"I know. It's as if it sweats out of you," Ann Hamilton said. "For three days after I stopped I could smell it on me. Even when I got out of the bath. It was disgusting." She was putting plates on the table for dinner. "I'm so sorry, dear. I know what you're going through. But, if it's any consolation, the second day is always the hardest. The third day is hard, too, of course, but from then on, if you can stay with it that long, you're over the hump. But I'm so happy you're serious about quitting, I can't tell you." She touched his arm. "Now, if you'll just call Roger, we'll eat."

Hamilton opened the front door. It was already dark. It was early in November and the days were short and cool. An older boy he had never seen before was sitting on a small, well-equipped bicycle in the driveway. The boy leaned forward just off the seat, the toes of his shoes touching the pavement and keeping him upright.

"You Mr Hamilton?" the boy said.

"Yes, I am," Hamilton said. "What is it? Is it Roger?"

"I guess Roger is down at my house talking to my mother. Kip is there and this boy named Gary Berman. It is about my brother's bike. I don't know for sure," the boy said, twisting the handle grips, "but my mother asked me to come and get you. One of Roger's parents."

"But he's all right?" Hamilton said. "Yes, of course, I'll be right with you."

16

He went into the house to put his shoes on.

"Did you find him?" Ann Hamilton said.

"He's in some kind of jam," Hamilton answered. "Over a bicycle. Some boy – I didn't catch his name – is outside. He wants one of us to go back with him to his house."

"Is he all right?" Ann Hamilton said and took her apron off.

"Sure, he's all right." Hamilton looked at her and shook his head. "It sounds like it's just a childish argument, and the boy's mother is getting herself involved."

"Do you want me to go?" Ann Hamilton asked.

He thought for a minute. "Yes, I'd rather you went, but I'll go. Just hold dinner until we're back. We shouldn't be long."

"I don't like his being out after dark," Ann Hamilton said. "I don't like it."

The boy was sitting on his bicycle and working the handbrake now.

"How far?" Hamilton said as they started down the sidewalk.

"Over in Arbuckle Court," the boy answered, and when Hamilton looked at him, the boy added, "Not far. About two blocks from here."

"What seems to be the trouble?" Hamilton asked.

"I don't know for sure. I don't understand all of it. He and Kip and this Gary Berman are supposed to have used my brother's bike while we were on vacation, and I guess they wrecked it. On purpose. But I don't know. Anyway, that's what they're talking about. My brother can't find his bike and they had it last, Kip and Roger. My mom is trying to find out where it's at."

"I know Kip," Hamilton said. "Who's this other boy?"

"Gary Berman. I guess he's new in the neighborhood. His dad is coming as soon as he gets home."

They turned a corner. The boy pushed himself along, keeping just slightly ahead. Hamilton saw an orchard, and then they turned another corner onto a dead-end street. He hadn't known of the existence of this street and was sure he would not recognize any of the people who lived here. He looked around him at the unfamiliar houses and was struck with the range of his son's personal life.

The boy turned into a driveway and got off the bicycle and leaned it against the house. When the boy opened the front door, Hamilton followed him through the living room and into the kitchen, where he saw his son sitting on one side of a table along with Kip Hollister and another boy. Hamilton looked closely at Roger and then he turned to the stout, dark-haired woman at the head. of the table.

"You're Roger's father?" the woman said to him.

"Yes, my name is Evan Hamilton. Good evening."

"I'm Mrs Miller, Gilbert's mother," she said. "Sorry to ask you over here, but we have a problem."

Hamilton sat down in a chair at the other end of the table and looked around. A boy of nine or ten, the boy whose bicycle was missing, Hamilton supposed, sat next to the woman. Another boy, fourteen or so, sat on the draining board, legs dangling, and watched another boy who was talking on the telephone. Grinning slyly at something that had just been said to him over the line, the boy reached over to the sink with a cigarette. Hamilton heard the sound of the cigarette sputting out in a glass of water. The boy who had brought him leaned against the refrigerator and crossed his arms.

"Did you get one of Kip's parents?" the woman said to the boy.

"His sister said they were shopping. I went to Gary Berman's and his father will be here in a few minutes. I left the address."

"Mr Hamilton," the woman said, "I'll tell you what happened. We were on vacation last month and Kip wanted to borrow Gilbert's bike so that Roger could help him with Kip's paper route. I guess Roger's bike had a flat tire or something. Well, as it turns out –"

"Gary was choking me, Dad," Roger said.

"What?" Hamilton said, looking at his son carefully.

"He was choking me. I got the marks." His son pulled down the collar of his T-shirt to show his neck.

"They were out in the garage," the woman continued. "I didn't know what they were doing until Curt, my oldest, went out to see."

"He started it!" Gary Berman said to Hamilton. "He called me a jerk." Gary Berman looked toward the front door.

"I think my bike cost about sixty dollars, you guys," the boy named Gilbert said. "You can pay me for it."

"You keep out of this, Gilbert," the woman said to him.

Hamilton took a breath. "Go on," he said.

"Well, as it turns out, Kip and Roger used Gilbert's bike to help Kip deliver his papers, and then the two of them, and Gary too, they say, took turns rolling it."

"What do you mean 'rolling it'?" Hamilton said.

"Rolling it," the woman said. "Sending it down the street with a push and letting it fall over. Then, mind you – and they just admitted this a few minutes ago – Kip and Roger took it up to the school and threw it against a goalpost."

"Is that true, Roger?" Hamilton said, looking at his son again.

"Part of it's true, Dad," Roger said, looking down and rubbing his finger over the table. "But we only rolled it once. Kip did it, then Gary, and then I did it."

"Once is too much," Hamilton said. "Once is one too many times, Roger. I'm surprised and disappointed in you. And you too, Kip," Hamilton said.

"But you see," the woman said, "someone's fibbing tonight or else not telling all he knows, for the fact is the bike's still missing."

The older boys in the kitchen laughed and kidded with the boy who still talked on the telephone.

"We don't know where the bike is, Mrs Miller," the boy named Kip said. "We told you already. The last time we saw it was when me and Roger took it to my house after we had it at school. I mean, that was the next to last time. The very last time was when I took it back here the next morning and parked it behind the house." He shook his head. "We don't know where it is," the boy said.

"Sixty dollars," the boy named Gilbert said to the boy named Kip. "You can pay me off like five dollars a week."

"Gilbert, I'm warning you," the woman said. "You see, *they* claim," the woman went on, frowning now, "it disappeared from *here*, from behind the house. But how can we believe them when they haven't been all that truthful this evening?"

"We've told the truth," Roger said. "Everything."

Gilbert leaned back in his chair and shook his head at Hamilton's son.

The doorbell sounded and the boy on the draining board jumped down and went into the living room.

A stiff-shouldered man with a crew haircut and sharp gray eyes entered the kitchen without speaking. He glanced at the woman and moved over behind Gary Berman's chair.

"You must be Mr Berman?" the woman said. "Happy to meet you. I'm Gilbert's mother, and this is Mr Hamilton, Roger's father."

The man inclined his head at Hamilton but did not offer his hand.

"What's all this about?" Berman said to his son.

The boys at the table began to speak at once.

"Quiet down!" Berman said. "I'm talking to Gary. You'll get your turn."

The boy began his account of the affair. His father listened closely, now and then narrowing his eyes to study the other two boys.

When Gary Berman had finished, the woman said, "I'd like to get to the bottom of this. I'm not accusing any one of them, you understand, Mr Hamilton, Mr Berman – I'd just like to get to the bottom of this." She looked steadily at Roger and Kip, who were shaking their heads at Gary Berman.

"It's not true, Gary," Roger said.

"Dad, can I talk to you in private?" Gary Berman said.

"Let's go," the man said, and they walked into the living room.

Hamilton watched them go. He had the feeling he should stop them, this secrecy. His palms were wet, and he reached to his shirt pocket for a cigarette. Then, breathing deeply, he passed the back of his hand under his nose and said, "Roger, do you know any more about this, other than what you've already said? Do you know where Gilbert's bike is?"

"No, I don't," the boy said. "I swear it."

"When was the last time you saw the bicycle?" Hamilton said.

"When we brought it home from school and left it at Kip's house."

"Kip," Hamilton said, "do you know where Gilbert's bicycle is now?"

"I swear I don't, either," the boy answered. "I brought it back the next morning after we had it at school and I parked it behind the garage."

"I thought you said you left it behind the *house*," the woman said quickly.

"I mean the house! That's what I meant," the boy said.

"Did you come back here some other day to ride it?" she asked, leaning forward.

"No, I didn't," Kip answered.

"Kip?" she said.

"I didn't! I don't know where it is!" the boy shouted.

The woman raised her shoulders and let them drop. "How do you know who or what to believe?" she said to Hamilton. "All I know is, Gilbert's missing a bicycle."

Gary Berman and his father returned to the kitchen.

"It was Roger's idea to roll it," Gary Berman said.

"It was yours!" Roger said, coming out of his chair. "You wanted to! Then you wanted to take it to the orchard and strip it!"

"You shut up!" Berman said to Roger. "You can speak when spoken to, young man, not before. Gary, I'll handle this — dragged out at night because of a couple of roughnecks! Now if either of you," Berman said, looking first at Kip and then Roger, "know where this kid's bicycle is, I'd advise you to start talking."

"I think you're getting out of line," Hamilton said.

"What?" Berman said, his forehead darkening. "And I think you'd do better to mind your own business!"

"Let's go, Roger," Hamilton said, standing up. "Kip, you

come now or stay." He turned to the woman. "I don't know what else we can do tonight. I intend to talk this over more with Roger, but if there is a question of restitution I feel since Roger did help manhandle the bike, he can pay a third if it comes to that."

"I don't know what to say," the woman replied, following Hamilton through the living room. "I'll talk to Gilbert's father – he's out of town now. We'll see. It's probably one of those things finally, but I'll talk to his father."

Hamilton moved to one side so that the boys could pass ahead of him onto the porch, and from behind him he heard Gary Berman say, "He called me a jerk, Dad."

"He did, did he?" Hamilton heard Berman say. "Well, he's the jerk. He looks like a jerk."

Hamilton turned and said, "I think you're seriously out of line here tonight, Mr Berman. Why don't you get control of yourself?"

"And I told you I think you should keep out of it!" Berman said.

"You get home, Roger," Hamilton said, moistening his lips. "I mean it," he said, "get going!" Roger and Kip moved out to the sidewalk. Hamilton stood in the doorway and looked at Berman, who was crossing the living room with his son.

"Mr Hamilton," the woman began nervously but did not finish.

"What do you want?" Berman said to him. "Watch out now, get out of my way!" Berman brushed Hamilton's shoulder and Hamilton stepped off the porch into some prickly cracking bushes. He couldn't believe it was happening. He moved out of the bushes and lunged at the man where he stood on the porch. They fell heavily onto the lawn. They rolled on the lawn, Hamilton wrestling Berman onto his back and coming down hard with his knees on the man's biceps. He had Berman by the collar now and began to pound his head against the lawn while the woman cried, "God almighty, someone stop them! For God's sake, someone call the police!"

Hamilton stopped.

Berman looked up at him and said, "Get off me."

22

"Are you all right?" the woman called to the men as they separated. "For God's sake," she said. She looked at the men, who stood a few feet apart, backs to each other, breathing hard. The older boys had crowded onto the porch to watch; now that it was over, they waited, watching the men, and then they began feinting and punching each other on the arms and ribs.

"You boys get back in the house," the woman said. "I never thought I'd see," she said and put her hand on her breast.

Hamilton was sweating and his lungs burned when he tried to take a deep breath. There was a ball of something in his throat so that he couldn't swallow for a minute. He started walking, his son and the boy named Kip at his sides. He heard car doors slam, an engine start. Headlights swept over him as he walked.

Roger sobbed once, and Hamilton put his arm around the boy's shoulders.

"I better get home," Kip said and began to cry. "My dad'll be looking for me," and the boy ran.

"I'm sorry," Hamilton said. "I'm sorry you had to see something like that," Hamilton said to his son.

They kept walking and when they reached their block, Hamilton took his arm away.

"What if he'd picked up a knife, Dad? Or a club?"

"He wouldn't have done anything like that," Hamilton said.

"But what if he had?" his son said.

"It's hard to say what people will do when they're angry," Hamilton said.

They started up the walk to their door. His heart moved when Hamilton saw the lighted windows.

"Let me feel your muscle," his son said.

"Not now," Hamilton said. "You just go in now and have your dinner and hurry up to bed. Tell your mother I'm all right and I'm going to sit on the porch for a few minutes."

The boy rocked from one foot to the other and looked at his father, and then he dashed into the house and began calling, "Mom! Mom!"

*

He sat on the porch and leaned against the garage wall and stretched his legs. The sweat had dried on his forehead. He felt clammy under his clothes.

He had once seen his father – a pale, slow-talking man with slumped shoulders – in something like this. It was a bad one, and both men had been hurt. It had happened in a café. The other man was a farmhand. Hamilton had loved his father and could recall many things about him. But now he recalled his father's one fistfight as if it were all there was to the man.

He was still sitting on the porch when his wife came out.

"Dear God," she said and took his head in her hands. "Come in and shower and then have something to eat and tell me about it. Everything is still warm. Roger has gone to bed."

But he heard his son calling him.

"He's still awake," she said.

"I'll be down in a minute," Hamilton said. "Then maybe we should have a drink."

She shook her head. "I really don't believe any of this yet."

He went into the boy's room and sat down at the foot of the bed.

"It's pretty late and you're still up, so I'll say good night," Hamilton said.

"Good night," the boy said, hands behind his neck, elbows jutting.

He was in his pajamas and had a warm fresh smell about him that Hamilton breathed deeply. He patted his son through the covers.

"You take it easy from now on. Stay away from that part of the neighborhood, and don't let me ever hear of you damaging a bicycle or any other personal property. Is that clear?" Hamilton said.

The boy nodded. He took his hands from behind his neck and began picking at something on the bedspread.

"Okay, then," Hamilton said, "I'll say good night."

He moved to kiss his son, but the boy began talking.

"Dad, was Grandfather strong like you? When he was your age, I mean, you know, and you –"

24

"And I was nine years old? Is that what you mean? Yes, I guess he was," Hamilton said.

"Sometimes I can hardly remember him," the boy said. "I don't want to forget him or anything, you know? You know what I mean, Dad?"

When Hamilton did not answer at once, the boy went on. "When you were young, was it like it is with you and me? Did you love him more than me? Or just the same?" The boy said this abruptly. He moved his feet under the covers and looked away. When Hamilton still did not answer, the boy said, "Did he smoke? I think I remember a pipe or something."

"He started smoking a pipe before he died, that's true," Hamilton said. "He used to smoke cigarettes a long time ago and then he'd get depressed with something or other and quit, but later he'd change brands and start in again. Let me show you something," Hamilton said. "Smell the back of my hand."

The boy took the hand in his, sniffed it, and said, "I guess I don't smell anything, Dad. What is it?"

Hamilton sniffed the hand and then the fingers. "Now I can't smell anything, either," he said. "It was there before, but now it's gone." Maybe it was scared out of me, he thought. "I wanted to show you something. All right, it's late now. You better go to sleep," Hamilton said.

The boy rolled onto his side and watched his father walk to the door and watched him put his hand to the switch. And then the boy said, "Dad? You'll think I'm pretty crazy, but I wish I'd known you when you were little. I mean, about as old as I am right now. I don't know how to say it, but I'm lonesome about it. It's like – it's like I miss you already if I think about it now. That's pretty crazy, isn't it? Anyway, please leave the door open."

Hamilton left the door open, and then he thought better of it and closed it halfway.

The Student's Wife

He had been reading to her from Rilke, a poet he admired, when she fell asleep with her head on his pillow. He liked reading aloud, and he read well – a confident sonorous voice, now pitched low and somber, now rising, now thrilling. He never looked away from the page when he read and stopped only to reach to the nightstand for a cigarette. It was a rich voice that spilled her into a dream of caravans just setting out from walled cities and bearded men in robes. She had listened to him for a few minutes, then she had closed her eyes and drifted off.

He went on reading aloud. The children had been asleep for hours, and outside a car rubbered by now and then on the wet pavement. After a while he put down the book and turned in the bed to reach for the lamp. She opened her eyes suddenly, as if frightened, and blinked two or three times. Her eyelids looked oddly dark and fleshy to him as they flicked up and down over her fixed glassy eyes. He stared at her.

"Are you dreaming?" he asked.

She nodded and brought her hand up and touched her fingers to the plastic curlers at either side of her head. Tomorrow would be Friday, her day for all the four-to-seven-year-olds in the Woodlawn Apartments. He kept looking at her, leaning on his elbow, at the same time trying to straighten the spread with his free hand. She had a smooth-skinned face with prominent cheekbones; the cheekbones, she sometimes insisted to friends, were from her father, who had been one-quarter Nez Perce.

Then: "Make me a little sandwich of something, Mike. With butter and lettuce and salt on the bread."

He did nothing and he said nothing because he wanted to go to sleep. But when he opened his eyes she was still awake, watching him.

"Can't you go to sleep, Nan?" he said, very solemnly. "It's late."

"I'd like something to eat first," she said. "My legs and arms hurt for some reason, and I'm hungry."

He groaned extravagantly as he rolled out of bed.

He fixed her the sandwich and brought it in on a saucer. She sat up in bed and smiled when he came into the bedroom, then slipped a pillow behind her back as she took the saucer. He thought she looked like a hospital patient in her white nightgown.

"What a funny little dream I had."

"What were you dreaming?" he said, getting into bed and turning over onto his side away from her. He stared at the night-stand waiting. Then he closed his eyes slowly.

"Do you really want to hear it?" she said.

"Sure," he said.

She settled back comfortably on the pillow and picked a crumb from her lip.

"Well. It seemed like a real long drawn-out kind of dream, you know, with all kinds of relationships going on, but I can't remember everything now. It was all very clear when I woke up, but it's beginning to fade now. How long have I been asleep, Mike? It doesn't really matter, I guess. Anyway, I think it was that we were staying someplace overnight. I don't know where the kids were, but it was just the two of us at some little hotel or something. It was on some lake that wasn't familiar. There was another, older, couple there and they wanted to take us for a ride in their motorboat." She laughed, remembering, and leaned forward off the pillow. "The next thing I recall is we were down at the boat landing. Only the way it turned out, they had just one seat in the boat, a kind of bench up in the front, and it was only big enough for three. You and I started arguing about who was going to sacrifice and sit all cooped up in the back. You said you were, and I said I was. But I finally squeezed in the back of the boat. It was so narrow it hurt my legs, and I was afraid the water was going to come in over the sides. Then I woke up."

"That's some dream," he managed to say and felt drowsily

that he should say something more. "You remember Bonnie Travis? Fred Travis' wife? She used to have *color* dreams, she said."

She looked at the sandwich in her hand and took a bite. When she had swallowed, she ran her tongue in behind her lips and balanced the saucer on her lap as she reached behind and plumped up the pillow. Then she smiled and leaned back against the pillow again.

"Do you remember that time we stayed overnight on the Tilton River, Mike? When you caught that big fish the next morning?" She placed her hand on his shoulder. "Do you remember that?" she said.

She did. After scarcely thinking about it these last years, it had begun coming back to her lately. It was a month or two after they'd married and gone away for a weekend. They had sat by a little campfire that night, a watermelon in the snow-cold river, and she'd fried Spam and eggs and canned beans for supper and pancakes and Spam and eggs in the same blackened pan the next morning. She had burned the pan both times she cooked, and they could never get the coffee to boil, but it was one of the best times they'd ever had. She remembered he had read to her that night as well: Elizabeth Browning and a few poems from the *Rubáiyát*. They had had so many covers over them that she could hardly turn her feet under all the weight. The next morning he had hooked a big trout, and people stopped their cars on the road across the river to watch him play it in.

"Well? Do you remember or not?" she said, patting him on the shoulder. "Mike?"

"I remember," he said. He shifted a little on his side, opened his eyes. He did not remember very well, he thought. What he did remember was very carefully combed hair and loud half-baked ideas about life and art, and he did not want to remember that.

"That was a long time ago, Nan," he said.

"We'd just got out of high school. You hadn't started to college," she said.

He waited, and then he raised up onto his arm and turned his head to look at her over his shoulder. "You about finished with that sandwich, Nan?" She was still sitting up in the bed.

She nodded and gave him the saucer.

"I'll turn off the light," he said.

"If you want," she said.

Then he pulled down into the bed again and extended his foot until it touched against hers. He lay still for a minute and then tried to relax.

"Mike, you're not asleep, are you?"

"No," he said. "Nothing like that."

"Well, don't go to sleep before me," she said. "I don't want to be awake by myself."

He didn't answer, but he inched a little closer to her on his side. When she put her arm over him and planted her hand flat against his chest, he took her fingers and squeezed them lightly. But in moments his hand dropped away to the bed, and he sighed.

"Mike? Honey? I wish you'd rub my legs. My legs hurt," she said.

"God," he said softly. "I was sound asleep."

"Well, I wish you'd rub my legs and talk to me. My shoulders hurt, too. But my legs especially."

He turned over and began rubbing her legs, then fell asleep again with his hand on her hip.

"Mike?"

"What is it, Nan? Tell me what it *is*."

"I wish you'd rub me all over," she said, turning onto her back. "My legs and arms both hurt tonight." She raised her knees to make a tower with the covers.

He opened his eyes briefly in the dark and then shut them. "Growing pains, huh?"

"Oh God, yes," she said, wiggling her toes, glad she had drawn him out. "When I was ten or eleven years old I was as big then as I am now. You should've seen me! I grew so fast in those days my legs and arms hurt me all the time. Didn't you?"

"Didn't I what?"

"Didn't you ever feel yourself growing?"

"Not that I remember," he said.

29

At last he raised up on his elbow, struck a match, and looked at the clock. He turned his pillow over to the cooler side and lay down again.

She said, "You're asleep, Mike. I wish you'd want to talk."

"All right," he said, not moving.

"Just hold me and get me off to sleep. I can't go to sleep," she said.

He turned over and put his arm over her shoulder as she turned onto her side to face the wall.

"Mike?"

He tapped his toes against her foot.

"Why don't you tell me all the things you like and the things you don't like."

"Don't know any right now," he said. "Tell me if you want," he said.

"If you promise to tell *me*. Is that a promise?

He tapped her foot again.

"Well . . ." she said and turned onto her back, pleased. "I like good foods, steaks and hash-brown potatoes, things like that. I like good books and magazines, riding on trains at night, and those times I flew in an airplane." She stopped. "Of course none of this is in order of preference. I'd have to think about it if it was in the order of preference. But I like that, flying in airplanes. There's a moment as you leave the ground you feel whatever happens is all right." She put her leg across his ankle. "I like staying up late at night and then staying in bed the next morning. I wish we could do that all the time, not just once in a while. And I like sex. I like to be touched now and then when I'm not expecting it. I like going to movies and drinking beer with friends afterward. I like to have friends. I like Janice Hendricks very much. I'd like to go dancing at least once a week. I'd like to have nice clothes all the time. I'd like to be able to buy the kids nice clothes every time they need it without having to wait. Laurie needs a new little outfit right now for Easter. And I'd like to get Gary a little suit or something. He's old enough. I'd like you to have a new suit, too. You really need a new suit more than he does. And I'd like us to have a place of our own. I'd like to stop moving around every year, or every other year. Most of all," she said, "I'd like us both just to live a good honest life without having to worry about money and bills and things like that. You're asleep," she said.

"I'm not," he said.

"I can't think of anything else. You go now. Tell me what you'd like."

"I don't know. Lots of things," he mumbled.

"Well, tell me. We're just talking, aren't we?"

"I wish you'd leave me alone, Nan." He turned over to his side of the bed again and let his arm rest off the edge. She turned too and pressed against him.

"Mike?"

"Jesus," he said. Then: "All right. Let me stretch my legs a minute, then I'll wake up."

In a while she said, "Mike? Are you asleep?" She shook his shoulder gently, but there was no response. She lay there for a time huddled against his body, trying to sleep. She lay quietly at first, without moving, crowded against him and taking only very small, very even breaths. But she could not sleep.

She tried not to listen to his breathing, but it began to make her uncomfortable. There was a sound coming from inside his nose when he breathed. She tried to regulate her breathing so that she could breathe in and out at the same rhythm he did. It was no use. The little sound in his nose made everything no use. There was a webby squeak in his chest too. She turned again and nestled her bottom against his, stretched her arm over to the edge and cautiously put her fingertips against the cold wall. The covers had pulled up at the foot of the bed, and she could feel a draft when she moved her legs. She heard two people coming up the stairs to the apartment next door. Someone gave a throaty laugh before opening the door. Then she heard a chair drag on the floor. She turned again. The toilet flushed next door, and then it flushed again. Again she turned, onto her back this time, and tried to relax. She remembered an article she'd once read in a magazine: If all the bones and muscles and joints in the body could join together in perfect relaxation, sleep would almost certainly come. She took a long breath, closed her eyes, and lay perfectly still, arms straight along her sides. She tried to relax. She tried to imagine her legs suspended, bathed in something gauze-like. She turned onto her stomach. She closed her eyes, then she opened them. She thought of the fingers of her hand lying curled on the sheet in front of her lips. She raised a finger and lowered it to the sheet. She touched the wedding band on her ring finger with her thumb. She turned onto her side and then onto her back again. And then she began to feel afraid, and in one unreasoning moment of longing she prayed to go to sleep.

Please, God, let me go to sleep.

She tried to sleep.

"Mike," she whispered.

There was no answer.

She heard one of the children turn over in the bed and bump against the wall in the next room. She listened and listened but there was no other sound. She laid her hand under her left breast and felt the beat of her heart rising into her fingers. She turned onto her stomach and began to cry, her head off the pillow, her mouth against the sheet. She cried. And then she climbed out over the foot of the bed.

She washed her hands and face in the bathroom. She brushed her teeth. She brushed her teeth and watched her face in the mirror. In the living room she turned up the heat. Then she sat down at the kitchen table, drawing her feet up underneath the nightgown. She cried again. She lit a cigarette from the pack on the table. After a time she walked back to the bedroom and got her robe.

She looked in on the children. She pulled the covers up over her son's shoulders. She went back to the living room and sat in the big chair. She paged through a magazine and tried to read. She gazed at the photographs and then she tried to read again. Now and then a car went by on the street outside and she looked up. As each car passed she waited, listening. And then she looked down at the magazine again. There was a stack of magazines in the rack by the big chair. She paged through them all.

*

When it began to be light outside she got up. She walked to the window. The cloudless sky over the hills was beginning to turn white. The trees and the row of two-story apartment houses across the street were beginning to take shape as she watched. The sky grew whiter, the light expanding rapidly up from behind the hills. Except for the times she had been up with one or another of the children (which she did not count because she had never looked outside, only hurried back to bed or to the kitchen), she had seen few sunrises in her life and those when she was little. She knew that none of them had been like this. Not in pictures she had seen nor in any book she had read had she learned a sunrise was so terrible as this.

She waited and then she moved over to the door and turned the lock and stepped out onto the porch. She closed the robe at her throat. The air was wet and cold. By stages things were becoming very visible. She let her eyes see everything until they fastened on the red winking light atop the radio tower atop the opposite hill.

She went through the dim apartment, back into the bedroom. He was knotted up in the center of the bed, the covers bunched over his shoulders, his head half under the pillow. He looked desperate in his heavy sleep, his arms flung out across her side of the bed, his jaws clenched. As she looked, the room grew very light and the pale sheets whitened grossly before her eyes.

She wet her lips with a sticking sound and got down on her knees. She put her hands out on the bed.

"God," she said. "God, will you help us, God?" she said.

They're Not Your Husband

Earl Ober was between jobs as a salesman. But Doreen, his wife, had gone to work nights as a waitress at a twenty-four-hour coffee shop at the edge of town. One night, when he was drinking, Earl decided to stop by the coffee shop and have something to eat. He wanted to see where Doreen worked, and he wanted to see if he could order something on the house.

He sat at the counter and studied the menu.

"What are you doing here?" Doreen said when she saw him sitting there.

She handed over an order to the cook. "What are you going to order, Earl?" she said. "The kids okay?"

"They're fine," Earl said. "I'll have coffee and one of those Number Two sandwiches."

Doreen wrote it down.

"Any chance of, you know?" he said to her and winked.

"No," she said. "Don't talk to me now. I'm busy."

Earl drank his coffee and waited for the sandwich. Two men in business suits, their ties undone, their collars open, sat down next to him and asked for coffee. As Doreen walked away with the coffeepot, one of the men said to the other, "Look at the ass on that. I don't believe it."

The other man laughed. "I've seen better," he said.

"That's what I mean," the first man said. "But some jokers like their quim fat."

"Not me," the other man said.

"Not me, neither," the first man said. "That's what I was saying."

Doreen put the sandwich in front of Earl. Around the sandwich there were French fries, coleslaw, dill pickle.

"Anything else?" she said. "A glass of milk?"

He didn't say anything. He shook his head when she kept standing there.

"I'll get you more coffee," she said.

She came back with the pot and poured coffee for him and for the two men. Then she picked up a dish and turned to get some ice cream. She reached down into the container and with the dipper began to scoop up the ice cream. The white skirt yanked against her hips and crawled up her legs. What showed was girdle, and it was pink, thighs that were rumpled and gray and a little hairy, and veins that spread in a berserk display.

The two men sitting beside Earl exchanged looks. One of them raised his eyebrows. The other man grinned and kept looking at Doreen over his cup as she spooned chocolate syrup over the ice cream. When she began shaking the can of whipped cream, Earl got up, leaving his food, and headed for the door. He heard her call his name, but he kept going.

He checked on the children and then went to the other bedroom and took off his clothes. He pulled the covers up, closed his eyes, and allowed himself to think. The feeling started in his face and worked down into his stomach and legs. He opened his eyes and rolled his head back and forth on the pillow. Then he turned on his side and fell asleep.

In the morning, after she had sent the children off to school, Doreen came into the bedroom and raised the shade. Earl was already awake.

"Look at yourself in the mirror," he said.

"What?" she said. "What are you talking about?"

"Just look at yourself in the mirror," he said.

"What am I supposed to see?" she said. But she looked in the mirror over the dresser and pushed the hair away from her shoulders.

"Well?" he said.

"Well, what?" she said.

"I hate to say anything," Earl said, "but I think you better give a diet some thought. I mean it. I'm serious. I think you could lose a few pounds. Don't get mad."

"What are you saying?" she said.

"Just what I said. I think you could lose a few pounds. A few pounds, anyway," he said.

"You never said anything before," she said. She raised her nightgown over her hips and turned to look at her stomach in the mirror.

"I never felt it was a problem before," he said. He tried to pick his words.

The nightgown still gathered around her waist, Doreen turned her back to the mirror and looked over her shoulder. She raised one buttock in her hand and let it drop.

Earl closed his eyes. "Maybe I'm all wet," he said.

"I guess I could afford to lose. But it'd be hard," she said.

"You're right, it won't be easy," he said. "But I'll help."

"Maybe you're right," she said. She dropped her nightgown and looked at him and then she took her nightgown off.

They talked about diets. They talked about the protein diets, the vegetable-only diets, the grapefruit-juice diets. But they decided they didn't have the money to buy the steaks the protein diet called for. And Doreen said she didn't care for all that many vegetables. And since she didn't like grapefruit juice that much, she didn't see how she could do that one, either.

"Okay, forget it," he said.

"No, you're right," she said. "I'll do something."

"What about exercises?" he said.

"I'm getting all the exercise I need down there," she said.

"Just quit eating," Earl said. "For a few days, anyway."

"All right," she said. "I'll try. For a few days I'll give it a try. You've convinced me."

"I'm a closer," Earl said.

He figured up the balance in their checking account, then drove to the discount store and bought a bathroom scale. He looked the clerk over as she rang up the sale.

At home he had Doreen take off all her clothes and get on the scale. He frowned when he saw the veins. He ran his finger the length of one that sprouted up her thigh.

36

"What are you doing?" she asked.

"Nothing," he said.

He looked at the scale and wrote the figure down on a piece of paper.

"All right," Earl said. "All right."

The next day he was gone for most of the afternoon on an interview. The employer, a heavyset man who limped as he showed Earl around the plumbing fixtures in the warehouse, asked if Earl were free to travel.

"You bet I'm free," Earl said.

The man nodded.

Earl smiled.

He could hear the television before he opened the door to the house. The children did not look up as he walked through the living room. In the kitchen, Doreen, dressed for work, was eating scrambled eggs and bacon.

"What are you doing?" Earl said.

She continued to chew the food, cheeks puffed. But then she spit everything into a napkin.

"I couldn't help myself," she said.

"Slob," Earl said. "*Go ahead, eat! Go on!*" He went to the bedroom, closed the door, and lay on the covers. He could still hear the television. He put his hands behind his head and stared at the ceiling.

She opened the door.

"I'm going to try again," Doreen said.

"Okay," he said.

Two mornings later she called him into the bathroom. "Look," she said.

He read the scale. He opened a drawer and took out the paper and read the scale again while she grinned.

"Three-quarters of a pound," she said.

"It's something," he said and patted her hip.

He read the classifieds. He went to the state employment office. Every three or four days he drove someplace for an interview,

37

and at night he counted her tips. He smoothed out the dollar bills on the table and stacked the nickels, dimes, and quarters in piles of one dollar each. Each morning he put her on the scale.

In two weeks she had lost three and a half pounds.

"I pick," she said. "I starve myself all day, and then I pick at work. It adds up."

But a week later she had lost five pounds. The week after that, nine and a half pounds. Her clothes were loose on her. She had to cut into the rent money to buy a new uniform.

"People are saying things at work," she said.

"What kind of things?" Earl said.

"That I'm too pale, for one thing," she said. "That I don't look like myself. They're afraid I'm losing too much weight."

"What is wrong with losing?" he said. "Don't you pay any attention to them. Tell them to mind their own business. They're not your husband. You don't have to live with them."

"I have to work with them," Doreen said.

"That's right," Earl said. "But they're not your husband."

Each morning he followed her into the bathroom and waited while she stepped onto the scale. He got down on his knees with a pencil and the piece of paper. The paper was covered with dates, days of the week, numbers. He read the number on the scale, consulted the paper, and either nodded his head or pursed his lips.

Doreen spent more time in bed now. She went back to bed after the children had left for school, and she napped in the afternoons before going to work. Earl helped around the house, watched television, and let her sleep. He did all the shopping, and once in a while he went on an interview.

One night he put the children to bed, turned off the television, and decided to go for a few drinks. When the bar closed, he drove to the coffee shop.

He sat at the counter and waited. When she saw him, she said, "Kids okay?"

Earl nodded.

He took his time ordering. He kept looking at her as she moved up and down behind the counter. He finally ordered a cheese-burger. She gave the order to the cook and went to wait on someone else.

Another waitress came by with a coffeepot and filled Earl's cup.

"Who's your friend?" he said and nodded at his wife.

"Her name's Doreen," the waitress said.

"She looks a lot different than the last time I was in here," he said.

"I wouldn't know," the waitress said.

He ate the cheeseburger and drank the coffee. People kept sitting down and getting up at the counter. Doreen waited on most of the people at the counter, though now and then the other waitress came along to take an order. Earl watched his wife and listened carefully. Twice he had to leave his place to go to the bathroom. Each time he wondered if he might have missed hearing something. When he came back the second time, he found his cup gone and someone in his place. He took a stool at the end of the counter next to an older man in a striped shirt.

"What do you want?" Doreen said to Earl when she saw him again. "Shouldn't you be home?"

"Give me some coffee," he said.

The man next to Earl was reading a newspaper. He looked up and watched Doreen pour Earl a cup of coffee. He glanced at Doreen as she walked away. Then he went back to his newspaper.

Earl sipped his coffee and waited for the man to say something. He watched the man out of the corner of his eye. The man had finished eating and his plate was pushed to the side. The man lit a cigarette, folded the newspaper in front of him, and continued to read.

Doreen came by and removed the dirty plate and poured the man more coffee.

"What do you think of that?" Earl said to the man, nodding at Doreen as she moved down the counter. "Don't you think that's something special?"

The man looked up. He looked at Doreen and then at Earl, and then went back to his newspaper.

"Well, what do you think?" Earl said. "I'm asking. Does it look good or not? Tell me."

The man rattled the newspaper.

When Doreen started down the counter again, Earl nudged the man's shoulder and said, "I'm telling you something. Listen. Look at the ass on her. Now you watch this now. Could I have a chocolate sundae?" Earl called to Doreen.

She stopped in front of him and let out her breath. Then she turned and picked up a dish and the ice-cream dipper. She leaned over the freezer, reached down, and began to press the dipper into the ice cream. Earl looked at the man and winked as Doreen's skirt traveled up her thighs. But the man's eyes caught the eyes of the other waitress. And then the man put the newspaper under his arm and reached into his pocket.

The other waitress came straight to Doreen. "Who is this character?" she said.

"Who?" Doreen said and looked around with the ice-cream dish in her hand.

"Him," the other waitress said and nodded at Earl. "Who is this joker, anyway?"

Earl put on his best smile. He held it. He held it until he felt his face pulling out of shape.

But the other waitress just studied him, and Doreen began to shake her head slowly. The man had put some change beside his cup and stood up, but he too waited to hear the answer. They all stared at Earl.

"He's a salesman. He's my husband," Doreen said at last, shrugging. Then she put the unfinished chocolate sundae in front of him and went to total up his check.

What Do You Do in San Francisco?

This has nothing to do with me. It's about a young couple with three children who moved into a house on my route the first of last summer. I got to thinking about them again when I picked up last Sunday's newspaper and found a picture of a young man who'd been arrested down in San Francisco for killing his wife and her boyfriend with a baseball bat. It wasn't the same man, of course, though there was a likeness because of the beard. But the situation was close enough to get me thinking.

Henry Robinson is the name. I'm a postman, a federal civil servant, and have been since 1947. I've lived in the West all my life, except for a three-year stint in the Army during the war. I've been divorced twenty years, have two children I haven't seen in almost that long. I'm not a frivolous man, nor am I, in my opinion, a serious man. It's my belief a man has to be a little of both these days. I believe, too, in the value of work – the harder the better. A man who isn't working has got too much time on his hands, too much time to dwell on himself and his problems.

I'm convinced that was partly the trouble with the young man who lived here – his not working. But I'd lay that at her doorstep, too. The woman. She encouraged it.

Beatniks, I guess you'd have called them if you'd seen them. The man wore a pointed brown beard on his chin and looked like he needed to sit down to a good dinner and a cigar afterward. The woman was attractive, with her long dark hair and her fair complexion, there's no getting around that. But put me down for saying she wasn't a good wife and mother. She was a painter. The young man, I don't know what he did – probably something along the same line. Neither of them worked. But they paid their rent and got by somehow – at least for the summer.

The first time I saw them it was around eleven, eleven-fifteen, a Saturday morning. I was about two-thirds through my route when I turned onto their block and noticed a '56 Ford sedan pulled up in the yard with a big open U-Haul behind. There are only three houses on Pine, and theirs was the last house, the others being the Murchisons, who'd been in Arcata a little less than a year, and the Grants, who'd been here about two years. Murchison worked at Simpson Redwood, and Gene Grant was a cook on the morning shift at Denny's. Those two, then a vacant lot, then the house on the end that used to belong to the Coles.

The young man was out in the yard behind the trailer and she was just coming out the front door with a cigarette in her mouth, wearing a tight pair of white jeans and a man's white undershirt. She stopped when she saw me and she stood watching me come down the walk. I slowed up when I came even with their box and nodded in her direction.

"Getting settled all right?" I asked.

"It'll be a little while," she said and moved a handful of hair away from her forehead while she continued to smoke.

"That's good," I said. "Welcome to Arcata."

I felt a little awkward after saying it. I don't know why, but I always found myself feeling awkward the few times I was around this woman. It was one of the things helped turn me against her from the first.

She gave me a thin smile and I started to move on when the young man – Marston was his name – came around from behind the trailer carrying a big carton of toys. Now, Arcata is not a small town and it's not a big town, though I guess you'd have to say it's more on the small side. It's not the end of the world, Arcata, by any means, but most of the people who live here work either in the lumber mills or have something to do with the fishing industry, or else work in one of the downtown stores. People here aren't used to seeing men wear beards – or men who don't work, for that matter.

"Hello," I said. I put out my hand when he set the carton down on the front fender. "The name's Henry Robinson. You folks just arrive?"

"Yesterday afternoon," he said.

"Some trip! It took us fourteen hours just to come from San Francisco," the woman spoke up from the porch. "Pulling that damn trailer."

"My, my," I said and shook my head. "San Francisco? I was just down in San Francisco, let me see, last April or March."

"You were, were you?" she said. "What did you do in San Francisco?"

"Oh, nothing, really. I go down about once or twice a year. Out to Fisherman's Wharf and to see the Giants play. That's about all."

There was a little pause and Marston examined something in the grass with his toe. I started to move on. The kids picked that moment to come flying out the front door, yelling and tearing for the end of the porch. When that screen door banged open, I thought Marston was going to jump out of his skin. But she just stood there with her arms crossed, cool as a cucumber, and never batted an eye. He didn't look good at all. Quick, jerky little movements every time he made to do something. And his eyes – they'd land on you and then slip off somewheres else, then land on you again.

There were three kids, two little curly-headed girls about four or five, and a little bit of a boy tagging after.

"Cute kids," I said. "Well, I got to get under way. You might want to change the name on the box."

"Sure," he said. "Sure. I'll see about it in a day or two. But we don't expect to get any mail for a while yet, in any case."

"You never know," I said. "You never know what'll turn up in this old mail pouch. Wouldn't hurt to be prepared." I started to go. "By the way, if you're looking for a job in the mills, I can tell you who to see at Simpson Redwood. A friend of mine's a foreman there. He'd probably have something . . ." I tapered off, seeing how they didn't look interested.

"No, thanks," he said.

"He's not looking for a job," she put in.

"Well, goodbye, then."

"So long," Marston said.

Not another word from her.

That was on a Saturday, as I said, the day before Memorial Day. We took Monday as a holiday and I wasn't by there again until Tuesday. I can't say I was surprised to see the U-Haul still there in the front yard. But it did surprise me to see he still hadn't unloaded it. I'd say about a quarter of the stuff had made its way to the front porch — a covered chair and a chrome kitchen chair and a big carton of clothes that had the flaps pulled off the top. Another quarter must have gotten inside the house, and the rest of the stuff was still in the trailer. The kids were carrying little sticks and hammering on the sides of the trailer as they climbed in and out over the tailgate. Their mamma and daddy were nowheres to be seen.

On Thursday I saw him out in the yard again and reminded him about changing the name on the box.

"That's something I've got to get around to doing," he said.

"Takes time," I said. "There's lots of things to take care of when you're moving into a new place. People that lived here, the Coles, just moved out two days before you came. He was going to work in Eureka. With the Fish and Game Department."

Marston stroked his beard and looked off as if thinking of something else.

"I'll be seeing you," I said.

"So long," he said.

Well, the long and the short of it was he never did change the name on the box. I'd come along a bit later with a piece of mail for that address and he'd say something like, "Marston? Yes, that's for us, Marston. . . . I'll have to change the name on that box one of these days. I'll get myself a can of paint and just paint over that other name . . . Cole," all the time his eyes drifting here and there. Then he'd look at me kind of out the corners and bob his chin once or twice. But he never did change the name on the box, and after a time I shrugged and forgot about it.

You hear rumors. At different times I heard that he was an ex-con on parole who come to Arcata to get out of the unhealthy San Francisco environment. According to this story, the woman was his wife, but none of the kids belonged to him. Another story was that he had committed a crime and was hiding out here. But not many people subscribed to that. He just didn't look the sort who'd do something really *criminal*. The story most folks seemed to believe, at least the one that got around most, was the most horrible. The woman was a dope addict, so this story went, and the husband had brought her up here to help her get rid of the habit. As evidence, the fact of Sallie Wilson's visit was always brought up – Sallie Wilson from the Welcome Wagon. She dropped in on them one afternoon and said later that, no lie, there was something funny about them – the woman, particular. One minute the woman would be sitting and listening to Sallie run on – all ears, it seemed – and the next she'd get up while Sallie was still talking and start to work on her painting as if Sallie wasn't there. Also the way she'd be fondling and kissing the kids, then suddenly start screeching at them for no apparent reason. Well, just the way her *eyes* looked if you came up close to her, Sallie said. But Sallie Wilson has been snooping and prying for years under cover of the Welcome Wagon.

"You don't know," I'd say when someone would bring it up. "Who can say? If he'd just go to work now."

All the same, the way it looked to me was that they had their fair share of trouble down there in San Francisco, whatever was the nature of the trouble, and they decided to get clear away from it. Though why they ever picked Arcata to settle in, it's hard to say, since they surely didn't come looking for work.

The first few weeks there was no mail to speak of, just a few circulars, from Sears and Western Auto and the like. Then a few letters began to come in, maybe one or two a week. Sometimes I'd see one or the other of them out around the house when I came by and sometimes not. But the kids were always there, running in and out of the house or playing in the vacant lot next door. Of course, it wasn't a model home to begin with, but after they'd been there a while the weeds sprouted up and what grass there was yellowed and died. You hate to see something like that. I understand Old Man Jessup came out once or twice to get them to turn the water on, but they claimed they couldn't buy a hose. So he left them a hose. Then I noticed the kids playing with it over in the field, and that was the end of that. Twice I saw a little white sports car in front, a car that hadn't come from around here.

One time only I had anything to do with the woman direct. There was a letter with postage due, and I went up to the door with it. One of the little girls let me in and ran off to fetch her mama. The place was cluttered with odds and ends of old furniture and with clothing tossed just anywhere. But it wasn't what you'd call dirty. Not tidy maybe, but not dirty either. An old couch and chair stood along one wall in the living room. Under the window was a bookcase made out of bricks and boards, crammed full of little paperback books. In the corner there was a stack of paintings with their faces turned away, and to one side another painting stood on an easel covered over with a sheet.

I shifted my mail pouch and stood my ground, but starting to wish I'd paid the difference myself. I eyed the easel as I waited, about to sidle over and raise the sheet when I heard steps.

"What can I do for you?" she said, appearing in the hallway and not at all friendly.

I touched the brim of my cap and said, "A letter here with postage due, if you don't mind."

"Let me see. Who's it from? Why it's from Jer! That kook. Sending us a letter without a stamp. Lee!" she called out. "Here's a letter from Jerry." Marston came in, but he didn't look too happy. I leaned on first one leg, then the other, waiting.

"I'll pay it," she said, "seeing as it's from old Jerry. Here. Now goodbye."

Things went on in this fashion – which is to say no fashion at all. I won't say the people hereabouts got used to them – they weren't the sort you'd ever really get used to. But after a bit no one seemed to pay them much mind any more. People might stare at his beard if they met him pushing the grocery cart in

Safeway, but that's about all. You didn't hear any more stories.

Then one day they disappeared. In two different directions. I found out later she'd taken off the week before with somebody – a man – and that after a few days he'd taken the kids to his mother's over to Redding. For six days running, from one Thursday to the following Wednesday, their mail stayed in the box. The shades were all pulled and nobody knew for certain whether or not they'd lit out for good. But that Wednesday I noticed the Ford parked in the yard again, all the shades still down but the mail gone.

Beginning the next day he was out there at the box every day waiting for me to hand over the mail, or else he was sitting on the porch steps smoking a cigarette, waiting, it was plain to see. When he saw me coming, he'd stand up, brush the seat of his trousers, and walk over by the box. If it happened that I had any mail for him, I'd see him start scanning the return addresses even before I could get it handed over. We seldom exchanged a word, just nodded at each other if our eyes happened to meet, which wasn't often. He was suffering, though – anybody could see that – and I wanted to help the boy somehow, if I could. But I didn't know what to say exactly.

It was one morning a week or so after his return that I saw him walking up and down in front of the box with his hands in his back pockets, and I made up my mind to say something. What, I didn't know yet, but I was going to say something, sure. His back was to me as I came up the walk. When I got to him, he suddenly turned on me and there was such a look on his face it froze the words in my mouth. I stopped in my tracks with his article of mail. He took a couple of steps toward me and I handed it over without a peep. He stared at it as if dumbfounded.

"Occupant," he said.

It was a circular from L.A. advertising a hospital-insurance plan. I'd dropped off at least seventy-five that morning. He folded it in two and went back to the house.

Next day he was out there same as always. He had his old look to his face, seemed more in control of himself than the day before. This time I had a hunch I had what it was he'd been

47

waiting for. I'd looked at it down at the station that morning when I was arranging the mail into packets. It was a plain white envelope addressed in a woman's curlicue handwriting that took up most of the space. It had a Portland postmark, and the return address showed the initials JD and a Portland street address.

"Morning," I said, offering the letter.

He took it from me without a word and went absolutely pale. He tottered a minute and then started back for the house, holding the letter up to the light.

I called out, "She's no good, boy. I could tell that the minute I saw her. Why don't you forget her? Why don't you go to work and forget her? What have you got against work? It was work, day and night, work that gave me oblivion when I was in your shoes and there was a war on where I was. . . ."

After that he didn't wait outside for me any more, and he was only there another five days. I'd catch a glimpse of him, though, each day, waiting for me just the same, but standing behind the window and looking out at me through the curtain. He wouldn't come out until I'd gone by, and then I'd hear the screen door. If I looked back, he'd seem to be in no hurry at all to reach the box.

The last time I saw him he was standing at the window and looked calm and rested. The curtains were down, all the shades were raised, and I figured at the time he was getting his things together to leave. But I could tell by the look on his face he wasn't watching for me this time. He was staring past me, over me, you might say, over the rooftops and the trees, south. He just kept staring even after I'd come even with the house and moved on down the sidewalk. I looked back. I could see him still there at the window. The feeling was so strong, I had to turn around and look for myself in the same direction he was. But, as you might guess, I didn't see anything except the same old timber, mountains, sky.

The next day he was gone. He didn't leave any forwarding. Sometimes mail of some kind or other shows up for him or his wife or for the both of them. If it's first-class, we hold it a day, then send it back to where it came from. There isn't much. And I don't mind. It's all work, one way or the other, and I'm always glad to have it.

Fat

I am sitting over coffee and cigarettes at my friend Rita's and I am telling her about it.

Here is what I tell her.

It is late of a slow Wednesday when Herb seats the fat man at my station.

This fat man is the fattest person I have ever seen, though he is neat-appearing and well dressed enough. Everything about him is big. But it is the fingers I remember best. When I stop at the table near his to see to the old couple, I first notice the fingers. They look three times the size of a normal person's fingers – long, thick, creamy fingers.

I see to my other tables, a party of four businessmen, very demanding, another party of four, three men and a woman, and this old couple. Leander has poured the fat man's water, and I give the fat man plenty of time to make up his mind before going over.

Good evening, I say. May I serve you? I say.

Rita, he was big, I mean big.

Good evening, he says. Hello. Yes, he says. I think we're ready to order now, he says.

He has this way of speaking – strange, don't you know. And he makes a little puffing sound every so often.

I think we will begin with a Caesar salad, he says. And then a bowl of soup with some extra bread and butter, if you please. The lamb chops, I believe, he says. And baked potato with sour cream. We'll see about dessert later. Thank you very much, he says, and hands me the menu.

God, Rita, but those were fingers.

I hurry away to the kitchen and turn in the order to Rudy,

who takes it with a face. You know Rudy. Rudy is that way when he works.

As I come out of the kitchen, Margo – I've told you about Margo? The one who chases Rudy? Margo says to me, Who's your fat friend? He's really a fatty.

Now that's part of it. I think that is really part of it.

I make the Caesar salad there at his table, him watching my every move, meanwhile buttering pieces of bread and laying them off to one side, all the time making this puffing noise. Anyway, I am so keyed up or something, I knock over his glass of water.

I'm so sorry, I say. It always happens when you get into a hurry. I'm very sorry, I say. Are you all right? I'll get the boy to clean up right away, I say.

It's nothing, he says. It's all right, he says, and he puffs. Don't worry about it, we don't mind, he says. He smiles and waves as I go off to get Leander, and when I come back to serve the salad, I see the fat man has eaten all his bread and butter.

A little later, when I bring him more bread, he has finished his salad. You know the size of those Caesar salads?

You're very kind, he says. This bread is marvelous, he says.

Thank you, I say.

Well, it is very good, he says, and we mean that. We don't often enjoy bread like this, he says.

Where are you from? I ask him. I don't believe I've seen you before, I say.

He's not the kind of person you'd forget, Rita puts in with a snicker.

Denver, he says.

I don't say anything more on the subject, though I am curious.

Your soup will be along in a few minutes, sir, I say, and I go off to put the finishing touches to my party of four businessmen, very demanding.

When I serve his soup, I see the bread has disappeared again. He is just putting the last piece of bread into his mouth.

Believe me, he says, we don't eat like this all the time, he says. And puffs. You'll have to excuse us, he says.

Don't think a thing about it, please, I say. I like to see a man eat and enjoy himself, I say.

I don't know, he says. I guess that's what you'd call it. And puffs. He arranges the napkin. Then he picks up his spoon.

God, he's fat! says Leander.

He can't help it, I say, so shut up.

I put down another basket of bread and more butter. How was the soup? I say.

Thank you. Good, he says. Very good, he says. He wipes his lips and dabs his chin. Do you think it's warm in here, or is it just me? he says.

No, it is warm in here, I say.

Maybe we'll take off our coat, he says.

Go right ahead, I say. A person has to be comfortable, I say.

That's true, he says, that is very, very true, he says.

But I see a little later that he is still wearing his coat.

My large parties are gone now and also the old couple. The place is emptying out. By the time I serve the fat man his chops and baked potato, along with more bread and butter, he is the only one left.

I drop lots of sour cream onto his potato. I sprinkle bacon and chives over his sour cream. I bring him more bread and butter.

Is everything all right? I say.

Fine, he says, and he puffs. Excellent, thank you, he says, and puffs again.

Enjoy your dinner, I say. I raise the lid of his sugar bowl and look in. He nods and keeps looking at me until I move away.

I know now I was after something. But I don't know what.

How is old tub-of-guts doing? He's going to run your legs off, says Harriet. You know Harriet.

For dessert, I say to the fat man, there is the Green Lantern Special, which is a pudding cake with sauce, or there is cheesecake or vanilla ice cream or pineapple sherbet.

We're not making you late, are we? he says, puffing and looking concerned.

Not at all, I say. Of course not, I say. Take your time, I say. I'll bring you more coffee while you make up your mind.

We'll be honest with you, he says. And he moves in the seat. We would like the Special, but we may have a dish of vanilla ice cream as well. With just a drop of chocolate syrup, if you please. We told you we were hungry, he says.

I go off to the kitchen to see after his dessert myself, and Rudy says, Harriet says you got a fat man from the circus out there. That true?

Rudy has his apron and hat off now, if you see what I mean.

Rudy, he is fat, I say, but that is not the whole story.

Rudy just laughs.

Sounds to me like she's sweet on fat-stuff, he says.

Better watch out, Rudy, says Joanne, who just that minute comes into the kitchen.

I'm getting jealous, Rudy says to Joanne.

I put the Special in front of the fat man and a big bowl of vanilla ice cream with chocolate syrup to the side.

Thank you, he says.

You are very welcome, I say – and a feeling comes over me.

Believe it or not, he says, we have not always eaten like this.

Me, I eat and I eat and I can't gain, I say. I'd like to gain, I say.

No, he says. If we had our choice, no. But there is no choice.

Then he picks up his spoon and eats.

What else? Rita says, lighting one of my cigarettes and pulling her chair closer to the table. This story's getting interesting now, Rita says.

That's it. Nothing else. He eats his desserts, and then he leaves and then we go home, Rudy and me.

Some fatty, Rudy says, stretching like he does when he's tired. Then he just laughs and goes back to watching the TV.

I put the water on to boil for tea and take a shower. I put my hand on my middle and wonder what would happen if I had children and one of them turned out to look like that, so fat.

I pour the water in the pot, arrange the cups, the sugar bowl, carton of half and half, and take the tray in to Rudy. As if he's been thinking about it, Rudy says, I knew a fat guy once, a couple of fat guys, really fat guys, when I was a kid. They were tubbies, my God. I don't remember their names. Fat, that's the only name this one kid had. We called him Fat, the kid who lived next door to me. He was a neighbor. The other kid came along later. His name was Wobbly. Everybody called him Wobbly except the teachers. Wobbly and Fat. Wish I had their pictures, Rudy says.

I can't think of anything to say, so we drink our tea and pretty soon I get up to go to bed. Rudy gets up too, turns off the TV, locks the front door, and begins his unbuttoning.

I get into bed and move clear over to the edge and lie there on my stomach. But right away, as soon as he turns off the light and gets into bed, Rudy begins. I turn on my back and relax some, though it is against my will. But here is the thing. When he gets on me, I suddenly feel I am fat. I feel I am terrifically fat, so fat that Rudy is a tiny thing and hardly there at all.

That's a funny story, Rita says, but I can see she doesn't know what to make of it.

I feel depressed. But I won't go into it with her. I've already told her too much.

She sits there waiting, her dainty fingers poking her hair.

Waiting for what? I'd like to know.

It is August.

My life is going to change. I feel it.

What's in Alaska?

Jack got off work at three. He left the station and drove to a shoe store near his apartment. He put his foot up on the stool and let the clerk unlace his work boot.

"Something comfortable," Jack said. "For casual wear."

"I have something," the clerk said.

The clerk brought out three pairs of shoes and Jack said he would take the soft beige-colored shoes that made his feet feel free and springy. He paid the clerk and put the box with his boots under his arm. He looked down at his new shoes as he walked. Driving home, he felt that his foot moved freely from pedal to pedal.

"You bought some new shoes," Mary said. "Let me see."

"Do you like them?" Jack said.

"I don't like the color, but I'll bet they're comfortable. You needed new shoes."

He looked at the shoes again. "I've got to take a bath," he said.

"We'll have an early dinner," she said. "Helen and Carl asked us over tonight. Helen got Carl a water pipe for his birthday and they're anxious to try it out." Mary looked at him. "Is it all right with you?"

"What time?"

"Around seven."

"It's all right," he said.

She looked at his shoes again and sucked her cheeks. "Take your bath," she said.

Jack ran the water and took off his shoes and clothes. He lay in the tub for a while and then used a brush to get at the lube grease under his nails. He dropped his hands and then raised them to his eyes.

55

She opened the bathroom door. "I brought you a beer," she said. Steam drifted around her and out into the living room.

"I'll be out in a minute," he said. He drank some of the beer.

She sat on the edge of the tub and put her hand on his thigh. "Home from the wars," she said.

"Home from the wars," he said.

She moved her hand through the wet hair on his thigh. Then she clapped her hands. "Hey, I have something to tell you! I had an interview today, and I think they're going to offer me a job – in *Fairbanks.*"

"Alaska?" he said.

She nodded. "What do you think of that?"

"I've always wanted to go to Alaska. Does it look pretty definite?"

She nodded again. "They liked me. They said I'd hear next week."

"That's great. Hand me a towel, will you? I'm getting out."

"I'll go and set the table," she said.

His fingertips and toes were pale and wrinkled. He dried slowly and put on clean clothes and the new shoes. He combed his hair and went out to the kitchen. He drank another beer while she put dinner on the table.

"We're supposed to bring some cream soda and something to munch on," she said. "We'll have to go by the store."

"Cream soda and munchies. Okay," he said.

When they had eaten, he helped her clear the table. Then they drove to the market and bought cream soda and potato chips and corn chips and onion-flavored snack crackers. At the checkout counter he added a handful of U-No bars to the order.

"Hey, yeah," she said when she saw them.

They drove home again and parked, and then they walked the block to Helen and Carl's.

Helen opened the door. Jack put the sack on the dining-room table. Mary sat down in the rocking chair and sniffed.

"We're late," she said. "They started without us, Jack."

Helen laughed. "We had one when Carl came in. We haven't

lighted the water pipe yet. We were waiting until you got here."
She stood in the middle of the room, looking at them and grinning. "Let's see what's in the sack," she said. "Oh, wow! Say,
I think I'll have one of these corn chips right now. You guys
want some?"

"We just ate dinner," Jack said. "We'll have some pretty soon."
Water had stopped running and Jack could hear Carl whistling
in the bathroom.

"We have some Popsicles and some M&Ms," Helen said. She
stood beside the table and dug into the potato-chip bag. "If Carl
ever gets out of the shower, he'll get the water pipe going." She
opened the box of snack crackers and put one in her mouth.
"Say, these are really good," she said.

"I don't know what Emily Post would say about you," Mary
said.

Helen laughed. She shook her head.

Carl came out of the bathroom. "Hi, everybody. Hi, Jack.
What's so funny?" he said, grinning. "I could hear you laughing."

"We were laughing at Helen," Mary said.

"Helen was just laughing," Jack said.

"She's funny." Carl said. "Look at the goodies! Hey, you guys
ready for a glass of cream soda? I'll get the pipe going."

"I'll have a glass," Mary said. "What about you, Jack?"

"I'll have some," Jack said.

"Jack's on a little bummer tonight," Mary said.

"Why do you say that?" Jack asked. He looked at her. "That's
a good way to put me on one."

"I was just teasing," Mary said. She came over and sat beside
him on the sofa. "I was just teasing, honey."

"Hey, Jack, don't get on a bummer," Carl said. "Let me show
you what I got for my birthday. Helen, open one of those bottles
of cream soda while I get the pipe going. I'm real dry."

Helen carried the chips and crackers to the coffee table. Then
she produced a bottle of cream soda and four glasses.

"Looks like we're going to have a party," Mary said.

"If I didn't starve myself all day, I'd put on ten pounds a
week," Helen said.

"I know what you mean," Mary said.

Carl came out of the bedroom with the water pipe. "What do you think of this?" he said to Jack. He put the water pipe on the coffee table.

"That's really something," Jack said. He picked it up and looked at it.

"It's called a hookah," Helen said. "That's what they called it where I bought it. It's just a little one, but it does the job." She laughed.

"Where did you get it?" Mary said.

"What? That little place on Fourth Street. You know," Helen said.

"Sure. I know," Mary said. "I'll have to go in there some day," Mary said. She folded her hands and watched Carl.

"How does it work?" Jack said.

"You put the stuff here," Carl said. "And you light this. Then you inhale through this here and the smoke is filtered through the water. It has a good taste to it and it really hits you."

"I'd like to get Jack one for Christmas," Mary said. She looked at Jack and grinned and touched his arm.

"I'd like to have one," Jack said. He stretched his legs and looked at his shoes under the light.

"Here, try this." Carl said, letting out a thin stream of smoke and passing the tube to Jack. "See if this isn't okay."

Jack drew on the tube, held the smoke, and passed the tube to Helen.

"Mary first," Helen said. "I'll go after Mary. You guys have to catch up."

"I won't argue," Mary said. She slipped the tube in her mouth and drew rapidly, twice, and Jack watched the bubbles she made.

"That's really okay," Mary said. She passed the tube to Helen.

"We broke it in last night." Helen said, and laughed loudly.

"She was still stoned when she got up with the kids this morning," Carl said, and he laughed. He watched Helen pull on the tube.

"How are the kids?" Mary asked.

"They're fine," Carl said and put the tube in his mouth. Jack sipped the cream soda and watched the bubbles in the pipe. They reminded him of bubbles rising from a diving helmet. He imagined a lagoon and schools of remarkable fish.

Carl passed the tube.

Jack stood up and stretched.

"Where are you going, honey?" Mary asked.

"No place," Jack said. He sat down and shook his head and grinned. "Jesus."

Helen laughed.

"What's funny?" Jack said after a long time.

"God, I don't know," Helen said. She wiped her eyes and laughed again, and Mary and Carl laughed.

After a time Carl unscrewed the top of the water pipe and blew through one of the tubes. "It gets plugged sometimes."

"What did you mean when you said I was on a bummer?" Jack said to Mary.

"What?" Mary said.

Jack stared at her and blinked. "You said something about me being on a bummer. What made you say that?"

"I don't remember now, but I can tell when you are," she said. "But please don't bring up anything negative, okay?"

"Okay," Jack said. "All I'm saying is I don't know why you said that. If I wasn't on a bummer before you said it, it's enough when you say it to put me on one."

"If the shoe fits," Mary said. She leaned on the arm of the sofa and laughed until tears came.

"What was that?" Carl said. He looked at Jack and then at Mary. "I missed that one," Carl said.

"I should have made some dip for these chips," Helen said.

"Wasn't there another bottle of that cream soda?" Carl said.

"We bought two bottles," Jack said.

"Did we drink them both?" Carl said.

"Did we drink any?" Helen said and laughed. "No, I only opened one. I think I only opened one. I don't remember opening more than one," Helen said and laughed.

59

Jack passed the tube to Mary. She took his hand and guided the tube into her mouth. He watched the smoke flow over her lips a long time later.

"What about some cream soda?" Carl said.

Mary and Helen laughed.

"What about it?" Mary said.

"Well, I thought we were going to have us a glass," Carl said. He looked at Mary and grinned.

Mary and Helen laughed.

"What's funny?" Carl said. He looked at Helen and then at Mary. He shook his head. "I don't know about you guys," he said.

"We might go to Alaska," Jack said.

"Alaska?" Carl said. "What's in Alaska? What would you do up there?"

"I wish we could go someplace," Helen said.

"What's wrong with here?" Carl said. "What would you guys do in Alaska? I'm serious. I'd like to know."

Jack put a potato chip in his mouth and sipped his cream soda. "I don't know. What did you say?"

After a while Carl said, "What's in Alaska?"

"I don't know," Jack said. "Ask Mary. Mary knows. Mary, what am I going to do up there? Maybe I'll grow those giant cabbages you read about."

"Or pumpkins," Helen said. "Grow pumpkins."

"You'd clean up," Carl said. "Ship the pumpkins down here for Halloween. I'll be your distributor."

"Carl will be your distributor," Helen said.

"That's right," Carl said. "We'll clean up."

"Get rich," Mary said.

In a while Carl stood up. "I know what would taste good and that's some cream soda," Carl said.

Mary and Helen laughed.

"Go ahead and laugh," Carl said, grinning. "Who wants some?"

"Some what?" Mary said.

"Some cream soda," Carl said.

"You stood up like you were going to make a speech," Mary said.

"I hadn't thought of that," Carl said. He shook his head and laughed. He sat down. "That's good stuff," he said.

"We should have got more," Helen said.

"More what?" Mary said.

"More money," Carl said.

"No money," Jack said.

"Did I see some U-No bars in that sack?" Helen said.

"I bought some," Jack said. "I spotted them the last minute."

"U-No bars are good," Carl said.

"They're creamy," Mary said. "They melt in your mouth."

"We have some M&Ms and Popsicles if anybody wants any," Carl said.

Mary said, "I'll have a Popsicle. Are you going to the kitchen?"

"Yeah, and I'm going to get the cream soda, too," Carl said. "I just remembered. You guys want a glass?"

"Just bring it all in and we'll decide," Helen said. "The M&Ms too."

"Might be easier to move the kitchen out here," Carl said.

"When we lived in the city," Mary said, "people said you could see who'd turned on the night before by looking at their kitchen in the morning. We had a tiny kitchen when we lived in the city," she said.

"We had a tiny kitchen too," Jack said.

"I'm going out to see what I can find," Carl said.

"I'll come with you," Mary said.

Jack watched them walk to the kitchen. He settled back against the cushion and watched them walk. Then he leaned forward very slowly. He squinted. He saw Carl reach up to a shelf in the cupboard. He saw Mary move against Carl from behind and put her arms around his waist.

"Are you guys serious?" Helen said.

"Very serious," Jack said.

"About Alaska," Helen said.

He stared at her.

"I thought you said something," Helen said.

Carl and Mary came back. Carl carried a large bag of M&Ms and a bottle of cream soda. Mary sucked on an orange Popsicle.

"Anybody want a sandwich?" Helen said. "We have sandwich stuff."

"Isn't it funny," Mary said. "You start with the desserts first and then you move on to the main course."

"It's funny," Jack said.

"Are you being sarcastic, honey?" Mary said.

"Who wants cream soda?" Carl said. "A round of cream soda coming up."

Jack held his glass out and Carl poured it full. Jack set the glass on the coffee table, but in reaching for it he knocked over the glass and the soda poured onto his shoe.

"Goddamn it," Jack said. "How do you like that? I spilled it on my shoe."

"Helen, do we have a towel? Get Jack a towel," Carl said.

"Those were new shoes," Mary said. "He just got them."

"They look comfortable," Helen said a long time later and handed Jack a towel.

"That's what I told him," Mary said.

Jack took the shoe off and rubbed the leather with the towel.

"It's done for," he said. "That cream soda will never come out."

Mary and Carl and Helen laughed.

"That reminds me, I read something in the paper," Helen said. She pushed on the tip of her nose with a finger and narrowed her eyes. "I can't remember what it was now," she said.

Jack worked the shoe back on. He put both feet under the lamp and looked at the shoes together.

"What did you read?" Carl said.

"What?" Helen said.

"You said you read something in the paper," Carl said.

Helen laughed. "I was just thinking about Alaska, and I remembered them finding a prehistoric man in a block of ice. Something reminded me."

"That wasn't in Alaska," Carl said.

"Maybe it wasn't, but it reminded me of it," Helen said.

"What *about* Alaska, you guys?" Carl said.

"There's nothing in Alaska," Jack said.

"He's on a bummer," Mary said.

"What'll you guys *do* in Alaska?" Carl said.

"There's nothing to do in Alaska," Jack said. He put his feet under the coffee table. Then he moved them out under the light once more. "Who wants a new pair of shoes?" Jack said.

"What's that noise?" Helen said.

They listened. Something scratched at the door.

"It sounds like Cindy," Carl said. "I'd better let her in."

"While you're up, get me a Popsicle," Helen said. She put her head back and laughed.

"I'll have another one too, honey," Mary said. "What did I say? I mean *Carl*," Mary said. "Excuse me. I thought I was talking to Jack."

"Popsicles all around," Carl said. "You want a Popsicle, Jack?"

"What?"

"You want an orange Popsicle?"

"An orange one," Jack said.

"Four Popsicles coming up," Carl said.

In a while he came back with the Popsicles and handed them around. He sat down and they heard the scratching again.

"I knew I was forgetting something," Carl said. He got up and opened the front door.

"Good Christ," he said, "if this isn't something. I guess Cindy went out for dinner tonight. Hey, you guys, look at this."

The cat carried a mouse into the living room, stopped to look at them, then carried the mouse down the hall.

"Did you see what I just saw?" Mary said. "Talk about a bummer."

Carl turned the hall light on. The cat carried the mouse out of the hall and into the bathroom.

"She's eating this mouse," Carl said.

"I don't think I want her eating a mouse in my bathroom," Helen said. "Make her get out of there. Some of the children's things are in there."

"She's not going to get out of here," Carl said.

"What about the mouse?" Mary said.

"What the hell," Carl said. "Cindy's got to learn to hunt if we're going to Alaska."

"Alaska?" Helen said. "What's all this about Alaska?"

"Don't ask me," Carl said. He stood near the bathroom door and watched the cat. "Mary and Jack said they're going to Alaska. Cindy's got to learn to hunt."

Mary put her chin in her hands and stared into the hall.

"She's eating the mouse," Carl said.

Helen finished the last of the corn chips. "I told him I didn't want Cindy eating a mouse in the bathroom. Carl?" Helen said.

"What?"

"Make her get out of the bathroom, I said," Helen said.

"For Christ's sake," Carl said.

"Look," Mary said. "Ugh. The goddamn cat is coming in here," Mary said.

"What's she doing?" Jack said.

The cat dragged the mouse under the coffee table. She lay down under the table and licked the mouse. She held the mouse in her paws and licked slowly, from head to tail.

"The cat's high," Carl said.

"It gives you the shivers," Mary said.

"It's just nature," Carl said.

"Look at her eyes," Mary said. "Look at the way she looks at us. She's high, all right."

Carl came over to the sofa and sat beside Mary. Mary inched toward Jack to give Carl room. She rested her hand on Jack's knee.

They watched the cat eat the mouse.

"Don't you ever feed that cat?" Mary said to Helen.

Helen laughed.

"You guys ready for another smoke?" Carl said.

"We have to go," Jack said.

"What's your hurry?" Carl said.

"Stay a little longer," Helen said. "You don't have to go yet."

Jack stared at Mary, who was staring at Carl. Carl stared at something on the rug near his feet.

Helen picked through the M&Ms in her hand.

"I like the green ones best," Helen said.

"I have to work in the morning," Jack said.

"What a bummer he's on," Mary said. "You want to hear a bummer, folks? *There's* a bummer."

"Are you coming?" Jack said.

"Anybody want a glass of milk?" Carl said. "We've got some milk out there."

"I'm too full of cream soda," Mary said.

"There's no more cream soda," Carl said.

Helen laughed. She closed her eyes and then opened them and then laughed again.

"We have to go home," Jack said. In a while he stood up and said, "Did we have coats? I don't think we had coats."

"What? I don't think we had coats," Mary said. She stayed seated.

"We'd better go," Jack said.

"They have to go," Helen said.

Jack put his hands under Mary's shoulders and pulled her up.

"Good-bye, you guys," Mary said. She embraced Jack. "I'm so full I can hardly move," Mary said.

Helen laughed.

"Helen's always finding something to laugh at," Carl said, and Carl grinned. "What are you laughing at, Helen?"

"I don't know. Something Mary said," Helen said.

"What did I say?" Mary said.

"I can't remember," Helen said.

"We have to go," Jack said.

"So long," Carl said. "Take it easy."

Mary tried to laugh.

"Let's go," Jack said.

"Night, everybody," Carl said. "Night, Jack," Jack heard Carl say very, very slowly.

*

Outside, Mary held Jack's arm and walked with her head down. They moved slowly on the sidewalk. He listened to the scuffing sounds her shoes made. He heard the sharp and separate sound of a dog barking and above that a murmuring of very distant traffic.

She raised her head. "When we get home, Jack, I want to be fucked, talked to, diverted. Divert me, Jack. I need to be diverted tonight." She tightened her hold on his arm.

He could feel the dampness in that shoe. He unlocked the door and flipped the light.

"Come to bed," she said.

"I'm coming," he said.

He went to the kitchen and drank two glasses of water. He turned off the living-room light and felt his way along the wall into the bedroom.

"Jack!" she yelled. "Jack!"

"Jesus Christ, it's me!" he said. "I'm trying to get the light on."

He found the lamp, and she sat up in bed. Her eyes were bright. He pulled the stem on the alarm and began taking off his clothes. His knees trembled.

"Is there anything else to smoke?" she said.

"We don't have anything," he said.

"Then fix me a drink. We have something to drink. Don't tell me we don't have something to drink," she said.

"Just some beer."

They stared at each other.

"I'll have a beer," she said.

"You really want a beer?"

She nodded slowly and chewed her lip.

He came back with the beer. She was sitting with his pillow on her lap. He gave her the can of beer and then crawled into bed and pulled the covers up.

"I forgot to take my pill," she said.

"What?"

"I forgot my pill."

He got out of bed and brought her the pill. She opened her

66

eyes and he dropped the pill onto her outstretched tongue. She swallowed some beer with the pill and he got back in bed.

"Take this. I can't keep my eyes open," she said.

He set the can on the floor and then stayed on his side and stared into the dark hallway. She put her arm over his ribs and her fingers crept across his chest.

"What's in Alaska?" she said.

He turned on his stomach and eased all the way to his side of the bed. In a moment she was snoring.

Just as he started to turn off the lamp, he thought he saw something in the hall. He kept staring and thought he saw it again, a pair of small eyes. His heart turned. He blinked and kept staring. He leaned over to look for something to throw. He picked up one of his shoes. He sat up straight and held the shoe with both hands. He heard her snoring and set his teeth. He waited. He waited for it to move once more, to make the slightest noise.

Neighbors

Bill and Arlene Miller were a happy couple. But now and then they felt they alone among their circle had been passed by somehow, leaving Bill to attend to his bookkeeping duties and Arlene occupied with secretarial chores. They talked about it sometimes, mostly in comparison with the lives of their neighbors, Harriet and Jim Stone. It seemed to the Millers that the Stones lived a fuller and brighter life. The Stones were always going out for dinner, or entertaining at home, or traveling about the country somewhere in connection with Jim's work.

The Stones lived across the hall from the Millers. Jim was a salesman for a machine-parts firm and often managed to combine business with pleasure trips, and on this occasion the Stones would be away for ten days, first to Cheyenne, then on to St Louis to visit relatives. In their absence, the Millers would look after the Stones' apartment, feed Kitty, and water the plants.

Bill and Jim shook hands beside the car. Harriet and Arlene held each other by the elbows and kissed lightly on the lips.

"Have fun," Bill said to Harriet.

"We will," said Harriet. "You kids have fun too."

Arlene nodded.

Jim winked at her. "Bye, Arlene. Take good care of the old man."

"I will," Arlene said.

"Have fun," Bill said.

"You bet," Jim said, clipping Bill lightly on the arm. "And thanks again, you guys."

The Stones waved as they drove away, and the Millers waved too.

"Well, I wish it was us," Bill said.

"God knows, we could use a vacation," Arlene said. She took his arm and put it around her waist as they climbed the stairs to their apartment.

After dinner Arlene said, "Don't forget. Kitty gets liver flavor the first night." She stood in the kitchen doorway folding the handmade tablecloth that Harriet had bought for her last year in Santa Fe.

Bill took a deep breath as he entered the Stones' apartment. The air was already heavy and it was vaguely sweet. The sunburst clock over the television said half past eight. He remembered when Harriet had come home with the clock, how she had crossed the hall to show it to Arlene, cradling the brass case in her arms and talking to it through the tissue paper as if it were an infant.

Kitty rubbed her face against his slippers and then turned onto her side, but jumped up quickly as Bill moved to the kitchen and selected one of the stacked cans from the gleaming drainboard. Leaving the cat to pick at her food, he headed for the bathroom. He looked at himself in the mirror and then closed his eyes and then looked again. He opened the medicine chest. He found a container of pills and read the label – *Harriet Stone. One each day as directed* – and slipped it into his pocket. He went back to the kitchen, drew a pitcher of water, and returned to the living room. He finished watering, set the pitcher on the rug, and opened the liquor cabinet. He reached in back for the bottle of Chivas Regal. He took two drinks from the bottle, wiped his lips on his sleeve, and replaced the bottle in the cabinet.

Kitty was on the couch sleeping. He switched off the lights, slowly closing and checking the door. He had the feeling he had left something.

"What kept you?" Arlene said. She sat with her legs turned under her, watching television.

"Nothing. Playing with Kitty," he said, and went over to her and touched her breasts.

"Let's go to bed, honey," he said.

*

69

The next day Bill took only ten minutes of the twenty-minute break allotted for the afternoon and left at fifteen minutes before five. He parked the car in the lot just as Arlene hopped down from the bus. He waited until she entered the building, then ran up the stairs to catch her as she stepped out of the elevator.

"Bill! God, you scared me. You're early," she said.

He shrugged. "Nothing to do at work," he said.

She let him use her key to open the door. He looked at the door across the hall before following her inside.

"Let's go to bed," he said.

"Now?" She laughed. "What's gotten into you?"

"Nothing. Take your dress off." He grabbed for her awkwardly, and she said, "Good God, Bill."

He unfastened his belt.

Later they sent out for Chinese food, and when it arrived they ate hungrily, without speaking, and listened to records.

"Let's not forget to feed Kitty," she said.

"I was just thinking about that," he said. "I'll go right over."

He selected a can of fish flavor for the cat, then filled the pitcher and went to water. When he returned to the kitchen, the cat was scratching in her box. She looked at him steadily before she turned back to the litter. He opened all the cupboards and examined the canned goods, the cereals, the packaged foods, the cocktail and wine glasses, the china, the pots and pans. He opened the refrigerator. He sniffed some celery, took two bites of cheddar cheese, and chewed on an apple as he walked into the bedroom. The bed seemed enormous, with a fluffy white bedspread draped to the floor. He pulled out a nightstand drawer, found a half-empty package of cigarettes and stuffed them into his pocket. Then he stepped to the closet and was opening it when the knock sounded at the front door.

He stopped by the bathroom and flushed the toilet on his way.

"What's been keeping you?" Arlene said. "You've been over here more than an hour."

"Have I really?" he said.

"Yes, you have," she said.

"I had to go to the toilet," he said.

"You have your own toilet," she said.

"I couldn't wait," he said.

That night they made love again.

In the morning he had Arlene call in for him. He showered, dressed, and made a light breakfast. He tried to start a book. He went out for a walk and felt better. But after a while, hands still in his pockets, he returned to the apartment. He stopped at the Stones' door on the chance he might hear the cat moving about. Then he let himself in at his own door and went to the kitchen for the key.

Inside it seemed cooler than his apartment, and darker too. He wondered if the plants had something to do with the temperature of the air. He looked out the window, and then he moved slowly through each room considering everything that fell under his gaze, carefully, one object at a time. He saw ashtrays, items of furniture, kitchen utensils, the clock. He saw everything. At last he entered the bedroom, and the cat appeared at his feet. He stroked her once, carried her into the bathroom, and shut the door.

He lay down on the bed and stared at the ceiling. He lay for a while with his eyes closed, and then he moved his hand under his belt. He tried to recall what day it was. He tried to remember when the Stones were due back, and then he wondered if they would ever return. He could not remember their faces or the way they talked and dressed. He sighed and with effort rolled off the bed to lean over the dresser and look at himself in the mirror.

He opened the closet and selected a Hawaiian shirt. He looked until he found Bermudas, neatly pressed and hanging over a pair of brown twill slacks. He shed his own clothes and slipped into the shorts and the shirt. He looked in the mirror again. He went to the living room and poured himself a drink and sipped it on his way back to the bedroom. He put on a blue shirt, a dark suit, a blue and white tie, black wing-tip shoes. The glass was empty and he went for another drink.

In the bedroom again, he sat on a chair, crossed his legs, and smiled, observing himself in the mirror. The telephone rang twice and fell silent. He finished the drink and took off the suit. He rummaged through the top drawers until he found a pair of panties and a brassiere. He stepped into the panties and fastened the brassiere, then looked through the closet for an outfit. He put on a black and white checkered skirt and tried to zip it up. He put on a burgundy blouse that buttoned up the front. He considered her shoes, but understood they would not fit. For a long time he looked out the living-room window from behind the curtain. Then he returned to the bedroom and put everything away.

He was not hungry. She did not eat much, either. They looked at each other shyly and smiled. She got up from the table and checked that the key was on the shelf and then she quickly cleared the dishes.

He stood in the kitchen doorway and smoked a cigarette and watched her pick up the key.

"Make yourself comfortable while I go across the hall," she said. "Read the paper or something." She closed her fingers over the key. He was, she said, looking tired.

He tried to concentrate on the news. He read the paper and turned on the television. Finally he went across the hall. The door was locked.

"It's me. Are you still there, honey?" he called.

After a time the lock released and Arlene stepped outside and shut the door. "Was I gone so long?" she said.

"Well, you were," he said.

"Was I?" she said. "I guess I must have been playing with Kitty."

He studied her, and she looked away, her hand still resting on the doorknob.

"It's funny," she said. "You know – to go in someone's place like that."

He nodded, took her hand from the knob, and guided her toward their own door. He let them into their apartment.

"It *is* funny," he said.

He noticed white lint clinging to the back of her sweater, and the color was high in her cheeks. He began kissing her on the neck and hair and she turned and kissed him back.

"Oh, damn," she said. "Damn, damn," she sang, girlishly clapping her hands. "I just remembered. I really and truly forgot to do what I went over there to do. I didn't feed Kitty or do any watering." She looked at him. "Isn't that stupid?"

"I don't think so," he said. "Just a minute. I'll get my cigarettes and go back with you."

She waited until he had closed and locked their door, and then she took his arm at the muscle and said. "I guess I should tell you. I found some pictures."

He stopped in the middle of the hall. "What kind of pictures?"

"You can see for yourself," she said, and she watched him.

"No kidding." He grinned. "Where?"

"In a drawer," she said.

"No kidding," he said.

And then she said, "Maybe they won't come back," and was at once astonished at her words.

"It could happen," he said. "Anything could happen."

"Or maybe they'll come back and . . ." but she did not finish.

They held hands for the short walk across the hall, and when he spoke she could barely hear his voice.

"The key," he said. "Give it to me."

"What?" she said. She gazed at the door.

"The key," he said. "You have the key."

"My God," she said, "I left the key inside."

He tried the knob. It was locked. Then she tried the knob. It would not turn. Her lips were parted, and her breathing was hard, expectant. He opened his arms and she moved into them.

"Don't worry," he said into her ear. "For God's sake, don't worry."

They stayed there. They held each other. They leaned into the door as if against a wind, and braced themselves.

Put Yourself in My Shoes

The telephone rang while he was running the vacuum cleaner. He had worked his way through the apartment and was doing the living room, using the nozzle attachment to get at the cat hairs between the cushions. He stopped and listened and then switched off the vacuum. He went to answer the telephone.

"Hello," he said. "Myers here."

"Myers," she said. "How are you? What are you doing?"

"Nothing," he said. "Hello, Paula."

"There's an office party this afternoon," she said. "You're invited. Dick invited you."

"I don't think I can come," Myers said.

"Dick just this minute said get that old man of yours on the phone. Get him down here for a drink. Get him out of his ivory tower and back into the real world for a while. Dick's funny when he's drinking. Myers?"

"I heard you," Myers said.

Myers used to work for Dick. Dick always talked of going to Paris to write a novel, and when Myers had quit to write a novel, Dick had said he would watch for Myers' name on the best-seller list.

"I can't come now," Myers said.

"We found out some horrible news this morning," Paula continued, as if she had not heard him. "You remember Larry Gudinas. He was still here when you came to work. He helped out on science books for a while, and then they put him in the field, and then they canned him? We heard this morning he committed suicide. He shot himself in the mouth. Can you imagine? Myers?"

"I heard you," Myers said. He tried to remember Larry Gudinas and recalled a tall, stooped man with wire-frame glasses, bright ties, and a receding hairline. He could imagine the jolt,

74

the head snapping back. "Jesus," Myers said. "Well, I'm sorry to hear that."

"Come down to the office, honey, all right?" Paula said. "Everybody is just talking and having some drinks and listening to Christmas music. Come down," she said.

Myers could hear it all at the other end of the line. "I don't want to come down," he said. "Paula?" A few snowflakes drifted past the window as he watched. He rubbed his fingers across the glass and then began to write his name on the glass as he waited.

"What? I heard," she said. "All right," Paula said. "Well, then, why don't we meet at Voyles for a drink? Myers?"

"Okay," he said. "Voyles. All right."

"Everybody here will be disappointed you didn't come," she said. "Dick especially. Dick admires you, you know. He does. He's told me so. He admires your nerve. He said if he had your nerve he would have quit years ago. Dick said it takes nerve to do what you did. Myers?"

"I'm right here," Myers said. "I think I can get my car started. If I can't start it, I'll call you back."

"All right," she said. "I'll see you at Voyles. I'll leave here in five minutes if I don't hear from you."

"Say hello to Dick for me," Myers said.

"I will," Paula said. "He's talking about you."

Myers put the vacuum cleaner away. He walked down the two flights and went to his car, which was in the last stall and covered with snow. He got in, worked the pedal a number of times, and tried the starter. It turned over. He kept the pedal down.

As he drove, he looked at the people who hurried along the sidewalks with shopping bags. He glanced at the gray sky, filled with flakes, and at the tall buildings with snow in the crevices and on the window ledges. He tried to see everything, save it for later. He was between stories, and he felt despicable. He found Voyles, a small bar on a corner next to a men's clothing store. He parked in back and went inside. He sat at the bar for a time and then carried a drink over to a little table near the door.

When Paula came in she said, "Merry Christmas," and he got

75

up and gave her a kiss on the cheek. He held a chair for her.

He said, "Scotch?"

"Scotch," she said, then "Scotch over ice" to the girl who came for her order.

Paula picked up his drink and drained the glass.

"I'll have another one, too," Myers said to the girl. "I don't like this place," he said after the girl had moved away.

"What's wrong with this place?" Paula said. "We always come here."

"I just don't like it," he said. "Let's have a drink and then go someplace else."

"Whatever you want," she said.

The girl arrived with the drinks. Myers paid her, and he and Paula touched glasses.

Myers stared at her.

"Dick says hello," she said.

Myers nodded.

Paula sipped her drink. "How was your day today?"

Myers shrugged.

"What'd you do?" she said.

"Nothing," he said. "I vacuumed."

She touched his hand. "Everybody said to tell you hi."

They finished their drinks.

"I have an idea," she said. "Why don't we stop and visit the Morgans for a few minutes. We've never met them, for God's sake, and they've been back for months. We could just drop by and say hello, we're the Myerses. Besides, they sent us a card. They asked us to stop by during the holidays. They *invited* us. I don't want to go home," she finally said and fished in her purse for a cigarette.

Myers recalled setting the furnace and turning out all the lights before he had left. And then he thought of the snow drifting past the window.

"What about that insulting letter they sent telling us they heard we were keeping a cat in the house?" he said.

"They've forgotten about that by now," she said. "That wasn't anything serious, anyway. Oh, let's do it, Myers! Let's go by."

"We should call first if we're going to do anything like that," he said.

"No," she said. "That's part of it. Let's not call. Let's just go knock on the door and say hello, we used to live here. All right? Myers?"

"I think we should call first," he said.

"It's the holidays," she said, getting up from her chair. "Come on, baby."

She took his arm and they went out into the snow. She suggested they take her car and pick up his car later. He opened the door for her and then went around to the passenger's side.

Something took him when he saw the lighted windows, saw snow on the roof, saw the station wagon in the driveway. The curtains were open and Christmas-tree lights blinked at them from the window.

They got out of the car. He held her elbow as they stepped over a pile of snow and started up the walk to the front porch. They had gone a few steps when a large bushy dog hurtled around the corner of the garage and headed straight for Myers.

"Oh, God," he said, hunching, stepping back, bringing his hands up. He slipped on the walk, his coat flapped, and he fell onto the frozen grass with the dread certainty that the dog would go for his throat. The dog growled once and then began to sniff Myers' coat.

Paula picked up a handful of snow and threw it at the dog. The porch light came on, the door opened, and a man called, "Buzzy!" Myers got to his feet and brushed himself off.

"What's going on?" the man in the doorway said. "Who is it? Buzzy, come here, fellow. Come here!"

"We're the Myerses," Paula said. "We came to wish you a Merry Christmas."

"The Myerses?" the man in the doorway said. "Get out! Get in the garage, Buzzy. Get, get! It's the Myerses," the man said to the woman who stood behind him trying to look past his shoulder.

"The Myerses," she said. "Well, ask them in, ask them in, for heaven's sake." She stepped onto the porch and said, "Come in, please, it's freezing. I'm Hilda Morgan and this is Edgar. We're happy to meet you. Please come in."

They all shook hands quickly on the front porch. Myers and Paula stepped inside and Edgar Morgan shut the door.

"Let me have your coats. Take off your coats," Edgar Morgan said. "You're all right?" he said to Myers, observing him closely, and Myers nodded. "I knew that dog was crazy, but he's never pulled anything like this. I saw it. I was looking out the window when it happened."

This remark seemed odd to Myers, and he looked at the man. Edgar Morgan was in his forties, nearly bald, and was dressed in slacks and a sweater and was wearing leather slippers.

"His name is Buzzy," Hilda Morgan announced and made a face. "It's Edgar's dog. I can't have an animal in the house myself, but Edgar bought this dog and promised to keep him outside."

"He sleeps in the garage," Edgar Morgan said. "He begs to come in the house, but we can't allow it, you know." Morgan chuckled. "But sit down, sit down, if you can find a place with this clutter. Hilda, dear, move some of those things off the couch so Mr and Mrs Myers can sit down."

Hilda Morgan cleared the couch of packages, wrapping paper, scissors, a box of ribbons, bows. She put everything on the floor.

Myers noticed Morgan staring at him again, not smiling now.

Paula said, "Myers, there's something in your hair, dearest."

Myers put a hand up to the back of his head and found a twig and put it in his pocket.

"That dog," Morgan said and chuckled again. "We were just having a hot drink and wrapping some last-minute gifts. Will you join us in a cup of holiday cheer? What would you like?"

"Anything is fine," Paula said.

"Anything," Myers said. "We wouldn't have interrupted."

"Nonsense," Morgan said. "We've been . . . very curious about the Myerses. You'll have a hot drink, sir?"

"That's fine," Myers said.

"Mrs Myers?" Morgan said.

Paula nodded.

"Two hot drinks coming up," Morgan said. "Dear, I think we're ready too, aren't we?" he said to his wife. "This is certainly an occasion."

He took her cup and went out to the kitchen. Myers heard the cupboard door bang and heard a muffled word that sounded like a curse. Myers blinked. He looked at Hilda Morgan, who was settling herself into a chair at the end of the couch.

"Sit down over here, you two," Hilda Morgan said. She patted the arm of the couch. "Over here, by the fire. We'll have Mr Morgan build it up again when he returns." They sat. Hilda Morgan clasped her hands in her lap and leaned forward slightly, examining Myers' face.

The living room was as he remembered it, except that on the wall behind Hilda Morgan's chair he saw three small framed prints. In one print a man in a vest and frock coat was tipping his hat to two ladies who held parasols. All this was happening on a broad concourse with horses and carriages.

"How was Germany?" Paula said. She sat on the edge of the cushion and held her purse on her knees.

"We loved Germany," Edgar Morgan said, coming in from the kitchen with a tray and four large cups. Myers recognized the cups.

"Have you been to Germany, Mrs Myers?" Morgan asked.

"We want to go," Paula said. "Don't we, Myers? Maybe next year, next summer. Or else the year after. As soon as we can afford it. Maybe as soon as Myers sells something. Myers writes."

"I should think a trip to Europe would be very beneficial to a writer," Edgar Morgan said. He put the cups into coasters. "Please help yourselves." He sat down in a chair across from his wife and gazed at Myers. "You said in your letter you were taking off work to write."

"That's true," Myers said and sipped his drink.

"He writes something almost every day," Paula said.

"Is that a fact?" Morgan said. "That's impressive. What did you write today, may I ask?"

"Nothing," Myers said.

79

"It's the holidays," Paula said.

"You must be proud of him, Mrs Myers," Hilda Morgan said.

"I am," Paula said.

"I'm happy for you," Hilda Morgan said.

"I heard something the other day that might interest you," Edgar Morgan said. He took out some tobacco and began to fill a pipe. Myers lighted a cigarette and looked around for an ashtray, then dropped the match behind the couch.

"It's a horrible story, really. But maybe you could use it, Mr Myers." Morgan struck a flame and drew on the pipe. "Grist for the mill, you know, and all that," Morgan said and laughed and shook the match. "This fellow was about my age or so. He was a colleague for a couple of years. We knew each other a little, and we had good friends in common. Then he moved out, accepted a position at the university down the way. Well, you know how these things go sometimes – the fellow had an affair with one of his students."

Mrs Morgan made a disapproving noise with her tongue. She reached down for a small package that was wrapped in green paper and began to affix a red bow to the paper.

"According to all accounts, it was a torrid affair that lasted for some months," Morgan continued. "Right up until a short time ago, in fact. A week ago, to be exact. On that day – it was in the evening – he announced to his wife – they'd been married for twenty years – he announced to his wife that he wanted a divorce. You can imagine how the fool woman took it, coming out of the blue like that, so to speak. There was quite a row. The whole family got into it. She ordered him out of the house then and there. But just as the fellow was leaving, his son threw a can of tomato soup at him and hit him in the forehead. It caused a concussion that sent the man to the hospital. His condition is quite serious."

Morgan drew on his pipe and gazed at Myers.

"I've never heard such a story," Mrs Morgan said. "Edgar, that's disgusting."

"Horrible," Paula said.

Myers grinned.

"Now *there's* a tale for you, Mr Myers," Morgan said, catching the grin and narrowing his eyes. "Think of the story you'd have if you could get inside that man's head."

"Or her head," Mrs Morgan said. "The wife's. Think of *her* story. To be betrayed in such fashion after twenty years. Think how she must feel."

"But imagine what the poor *boy* must be going through," Paula said. "Imagine, having almost killed his father."

"Yes, that's all true," Morgan said. "But here's something I don't think any of you has thought about. Think about *this* for a moment. Mr Myers, are you listening? Tell me what you think of this. Put yourself in the shoes of that eighteen-year-old coed who fell in love with a married man. Think about *her* for a moment, and then you see the possibilities for your story."

Morgan nodded and leaned back in the chair with a satisfied expression.

"I'm afraid I don't have any sympathy for her," Mrs Morgan said. "I can imagine the sort she is. We all know what she's like, that kind preys on older men. I don't have any sympathy for him, either – the man, the chaser, no, I don't. I'm afraid my sympathies in this case are entirely with the wife and son."

"It would take a Tolstoy to tell it and tell it *right*," Morgan said. "No less than a Tolstoy. Mr Myers, the water is still hot."

"Time to go," Myers said.

He stood up and threw his cigarette into the fire.

"Stay," Mrs Morgan said. "We haven't gotten acquainted yet. You don't know how we have . . . speculated about you. Now that we're together at last, stay a little while. It's such a pleasant surprise."

"We appreciated the card and your note," Paula said.

"The card?" Mrs Morgan said.

Myers sat down.

"We decided not to mail any cards this year," Paula said. "I didn't get around to it when I should have, and it seemed futile to do it at the last minute."

"You'll have another one, Mrs Myers?" Morgan said, standing

in front of her now with his hand on her cup. "You'll set an example for your husband."

"It *was* good," Paula said. "It warms you."

"Right," Morgan said. "It warms you. That's right. Dear, did you hear Mrs Myers? It warms you. That's very good. Mr Myers?" Morgan said and waited. "You'll join us?"

"All right," Myers said and let Morgan take the cup.

The dog began to whine and scratch at the door.

"That dog. I don't know what's gotten into that dog," Morgan said. He went to the kitchen and this time Myers distinctly heard Morgan curse as he slammed the kettle onto a burner.

Mrs Morgan began to hum. She picked up a half-wrapped package, cut a piece of tape, and began sealing the paper.

Myers lighted a cigarette. He dropped the match in his coaster. He looked at his watch.

Mrs Morgan raised her head. "I believe I hear singing," she said. She listened. She rose from her chair and went to the front window. "It *is* singing. Edgar!" she called.

Myers and Paula went to the window.

"I haven't seen carolers in years," Mrs Morgan said.

"What is it?" Morgan said. He had the tray and cups. "What is it? What's wrong?"

"Nothing's wrong, dear. It's carolers. There they are over there, across the street," Mrs Morgan said.

"Mrs Myers," Morgan said, extending the tray. "Mr Myers. Dear."

"Thank you," Paula said.

"*Muchas gracias*," Myers said.

Morgan put the tray down and came back to the window with his cup. Young people were gathered on the walk in front of the house across the street, boys and girls with an older, taller boy who wore a muffler and a topcoat. Myers could see the faces at the window across the way – the Ardreys – and when the carolers had finished, Jack Ardrey came to the door and gave something to the older boy. The group moved on down the walk, flashlights bobbing, and stopped in front of another house.

"They won't come here," Mrs Morgan said after a time.

"What? Why won't they come here?" Morgan said and turned to his wife. "What a goddamned silly thing to say! Why won't they come here?"

"I just know they won't," Mrs Morgan said.

"And I say they will," Morgan said. "Mrs Myers, are those carolers going to come here or not? What do you think? Will they return to bless this house? We'll leave it up to you."

Paula pressed closer to the window. But the carolers were far down the street now. She did not answer.

"Well, now that all the excitement is over," Morgan said and went over to his chair. He sat down, frowned, and began to fill his pipe.

Myers and Paula went back to the couch. Mrs Morgan moved away from the window at last. She sat down. She smiled and gazed into her cup. Then she put the cup down and began to weep.

Morgan gave his handkerchief to his wife. He looked at Myers. Presently Morgan began to drum on the arm of his chair. Myers moved his feet. Paula looked into her purse for a cigarette. "See what you've caused?" Morgan said as he stared at something on the carpet near Myers' shoes.

Myers gathered himself to stand.

"Edgar, get them another drink," Mrs Morgan said as she dabbed at her eyes. She used the handkerchief on her nose. "I want them to hear about Mrs Attenborough. Mr Myers writes. I think he might appreciate this. We'll wait until you come back before we begin the story."

Morgan collected the cups. He carried them into the kitchen. Myers heard dishes clatter, cupboard doors bang. Mrs Morgan looked at Myers and smiled faintly.

"We have to go," Myers said. "We have to go. Paula, get your coat."

"No, no, we insist, Mr Myers," Mrs Morgan said. "We want you to hear about Mrs Attenborough, poor Mrs Attenborough. You might appreciate this story, too, Mrs Myers. This is your

chance to see how your husband's mind goes to work on raw
material."

Morgan came back and passed out the hot drinks. He sat down
quickly.

"Tell them about Mrs Attenborough, dear," Mrs Morgan said.

"That dog almost tore my leg off," Myers said and was at
once surprised at his words. He put his cup down.

"Oh, come, it wasn't that bad," Morgan said. "I saw it."

"You know writers," Mrs Morgan said to Paula. "They like
to exaggerate."

"The power of the pen and all that," Morgan said.

"That's it," Mrs Morgan said. "Bend your pen into a plow-
share, Mr Myers."

"We'll let Mrs Morgan tell the story of Mrs Attenborough,"
Morgan said, ignoring Myers, who stood up at that moment.
"Mrs Morgan was intimately connected with the affair. I've
already told you of the fellow who was knocked for a loop by a
can of soup." Morgan chuckled. "We'll let Mrs Morgan tell this
one."

"You tell it, dear. And Mr Myers, you listen closely," Mrs
Morgan said.

"We have to go," Myers said. "Paula, let's go."

"Talk about honesty," Mrs Morgan said.

"Let's talk about it," Myers said. Then he said, "Paula, are
you coming?"

"I want you to hear this story," Morgan said, raising his voice.
"You will insult Mrs Morgan, you will insult us both, if you
don't listen to this story." Morgan clenched his pipe.

"Myers, please," Paula said anxiously. "I want to hear it. Then
we'll go. Myers? Please, honey, sit down for another minute."

Myers looked at her. She moved her fingers, as if signaling
him. He hesitated, and then he sat next to her.

Mrs Morgan began. "One afternoon in Munich, Edgar and I
went to the Dortmunder Museum. There was a *Bauhaus* exhibit
that fall, and Edgar said the heck with it, let's take a day off –
he was doing his research, you see – the heck with it, let's take
a day off. We caught a tram and rode across Munich to the

museum. We spent several hours viewing the exhibit and revisiting some of the galleries to pay homage to a few of our favorites amongst the old masters. Just as we were to leave, I stepped into the ladies' room. I left my purse. In the purse was Edgar's monthly check from home that had come the day before and a hundred and twenty dollars cash that I was going to deposit along with the check. I also had my identification cards in the purse. I did not miss my purse until we arrived home. Edgar immediately telephoned the museum authorities. But while he was talking I saw a taxi out front. A well-dressed woman with white hair got out. She was a stout woman and she was carrying two purses. I called for Edgar and went to the door. The woman introduced herself as Mrs Attenborough, gave me my purse, and explained that she too had visited the museum that afternoon and while in the ladies' room had noticed a purse in the trash can. She of course had opened the purse in an effort to trace the owner. There were the identification cards and such giving our local address. She immediately left the museum and took a taxi in order to deliver the purse herself. Edgar's check was there, but the money, the one hundred twenty dollars, was gone. Nevertheless, I was grateful the other things were intact. It was nearly four o'clock and we asked the woman to stay for tea. She sat down, and after a little while she began to tell us about herself. She had been born and reared in Australia, had married young, had had three children, all sons, been widowed, and still lived in Australia with two of her sons. They raised sheep and had more than twenty thousand acres of land for the sheep to run in, and many drovers and shearers and such who worked for them at certain times of the year. When she came to our home in Munich, she was then on her way to Australia from England, where she had been to visit her youngest son, who was a barrister. She was returning to Australia when we met her," Mrs Morgan said. "She was seeing some of the world in the process. She had many places yet to visit on her itinerary."

"Come to the point, dear," Morgan said.

"Yes. Here is what happened, then. Mr Myers, I'll go right to the climax, as you writers say. Suddenly, after we had had a very pleasant conversation for an hour, after this woman had told about herself and her adventurous life Down Under, she stood up to go. As she started to pass me her cup, her mouth flew open, the cup dropped, and she fell across our couch and died. Died. Right in our living room. It was the most shocking moment in our lives."

Morgan nodded solemnly.

"God," Paula said.

"Fate sent her to die on the couch in our living room in Germany," Mrs Morgan said.

Myers began to laugh. "Fate . . . sent . . . her . . . to . . . die . . . in . . . your . . . living . . . room?" he said between gasps.

"Is that funny, sir?" Morgan said. "Do you find that amusing?"

Myers nodded. He kept laughing. He wiped his eyes on his shirt sleeve. "I'm really sorry," he said. "I can't help it. That line *'Fate sent her to die on the couch in our living room in Germany.'* I'm sorry. Then what happened?" he managed to say. "I'd like to know what happened then."

"Mr Myers, we didn't know what to do," Mrs Morgan said. "The shock was terrible. Edgar felt for her pulse, but there was no sign of life. And she had begun to change color. Her face and hands were turning *gray*. Edgar went to the phone to call someone. Then he said, 'Open her purse, see if you can find where she's staying.' All the time averting my eyes from the poor thing there on the couch, I took up her purse. Imagine my complete surprise and bewilderment, my utter bewilderment, when the first thing I saw inside was my hundred twenty dollars, still fastened with the paper clip. I was never so astonished."

"And disappointed," Morgan said. "Don't forget that. It was a keen disappointment."

Myers giggled.

"If you were a real writer, as you say you are, Mr Myers, you would not laugh," Morgan said as he got to his feet. "You would not dare laugh! You would try to understand. You would plumb the depths of that poor soul's heart and try to understand. But you are no writer, sir!"

Myers kept on giggling.

Morgan slammed his fist on the coffee table and the cups rattled in the coasters. "The real story lies right here, in this house, this very living room, and it's time it was told! The real story is *here*, Mr Myers," Morgan said. He walked up and down over the brilliant wrapping paper that had unrolled and now lay spread across the carpet. He stopped to glare at Myers, who was holding his forehead and shaking with laughter.

"Consider *this* for a possibility, Mr Myers!" Morgan screamed. *Consider!* A friend – let's call him Mr X – is friends with . . . with Mr and Mrs Y, *as well as* Mr and Mrs Z. Mr and Mrs Y and Mr and Mrs Z do not know each other, unfortunately. I say *unfortunately* because if they *had* known each other this story would not exist because it would never have taken place. Now, Mr X learns that Mr and Mrs Y are going to Germany for a year and need someone to occupy their house during the time they are gone. Mr and Mrs Z are looking for suitable accommodations, and Mr X tells them he knows of just the place. But before Mr X can put Mr and Mrs Z in touch with Mr and Mrs Y, the Ys have to leave sooner than expected. Mr X, being a friend, is left to rent the house at his discretion to anyone, including Mr and Mrs Y – I mean Z. Now, Mr and Mrs . . . Z move into the house and bring a cat with them that Mr and Mrs Y hear about later in a letter from Mr X. Mr and Mrs Z bring a cat into the house *even though* the terms of the lease have expressly forbidden cats or other animals in the house because of Mrs Y's asthma. The *real* story, Mr Myers, lies in the situation I've just described. Mr and Mrs Z – I mean Mr and Mrs *Y*'s moving into the Zs' house, *invading* the Zs' house, if the truth is to be told. Sleeping in the Zs' bed is one thing, but unlocking the Zs' private closet and using their linen, vandalizing the things found there, that was against the spirit and letter of the lease. And this *same* couple, the Zs, opened boxes of kitchen utensils marked 'Don't Open'. And broke dishes when it was spelled out, *spelled out* in that same lease, that they were not to use the owners', the Zs' *personal*, I emphasize *personal*, possessions."

Morgan's lips were white. He continued to walk up and down

on the paper, stopping every now and then to look at Myers and emit little puffing noises from his lips.

"And the bathroom things, dear – don't forget the bathroom things," Mrs Morgan said. "It's bad enough using the Zs' blankets and sheets, but when they also get into their *bathroom* things and go through the little private things stored in the *attic*, a line has to be drawn."

"That's the *real* story, Mr Myers," Morgan said. He tried to fill his pipe. His hands trembled and tobacco spilled onto the carpet. "That's the real story that is waiting to be written."

"And it doesn't need Tolstoy to tell it," Mrs Morgan said.

"It doesn't need Tolstoy," Morgan said.

Myers laughed. He and Paula got up from the couch at the same time and moved toward the door. "Good night," Myers said merrily.

Morgan was behind him. "If you were a real writer, sir, you would put that story into words and not pussyfoot around with it, either."

Myers just laughed. He touched the doorknob.

"One other thing," Morgan said. "I didn't intend to bring this up, but in light of your behavior here tonight, I want to tell you that I'm missing my two-volume set of 'Jazz at the Philharmonic'. Those records are of great sentimental value. I bought them in 1955. And now I insist you tell me what happened to them!"

"In all fairness, Edgar," Mrs Morgan said as she helped Paula on with her coat, "after you took inventory of the records, you admitted you couldn't recall the last time you had seen those records."

"But I am sure of it now," Morgan said. "I am positive I saw those records just before we left, and now, now I'd like this *writer* to tell me exactly what he knows of their whereabouts. Mr Myers?"

But Myers was already outdoors, and, taking his wife by the hand, he hurried her down the walk to the car. They surprised Buzzy. The dog yelped in what seemed fear and then jumped to the side.

"I insist on *knowing!*" Morgan called. "I am waiting, sir!"

Myers got Paula into the car and started the engine. He looked again at the couple on the porch. Mrs Morgan waved, and then she and Edgar Morgan went back inside and shut the door.

Myers pulled away from the curb.

"Those people are crazy," Paula said.

Myers patted her hand.

"They were scary," she said.

He did not answer. Her voice seemed to come to him from a great distance. He kept driving. Snow rushed at the windshield. He was silent and watched the road. He was at the very end of a story.

Collectors

I was out of work. But any day I expected to hear from up north. I lay on the sofa and listened to the rain. Now and then I'd lift up and look through the curtain for the mailman.

There was no one on the street, nothing.

I hadn't been down again five minutes when I heard someone walk onto the porch, wait, and then knock. I lay still. I knew it wasn't the mailman. I knew his steps. You can't be too careful if you're out of work and you get notices in the mail or else pushed under your door. They come around wanting to talk, too, especially if you don't have a telephone.

The knock sounded again, louder, a bad sign. I eased up and tried to see onto the porch. But whoever was there was standing against the door, another bad sign. I knew the floor creaked, so there was no chance of slipping into the other room and looking out that window.

Another knock, and I said, Who's there?

This is Aubrey Bell, a man said. Are you Mr Slater?

What is it you want? I called from the sofa.

I have something for Mrs Slater. She's won something. Is Mrs Slater home?

Mrs Slater doesn't live here, I said.

Well, then, are you Mr Slater? the man said. Mr Slater . . . and the man sneezed.

I got off the sofa. I unlocked the door and opened it a little. He was an old guy, fat and bulky under his raincoat. Water ran off the coat and dripped onto the big suitcase contraption thing he carried.

He grinned and set down the big case. He put out his hand.

Aubrey Bell, he said.

I don't know you, I said.

Mrs Slater, he began. Mrs Slater filled out a card. He took cards from an inside pocket and shuffled them a minute. Mrs Slater, he read. Two-fifty-five South Sixth East? Mrs Slater is a winner.

He took off his hat and nodded solemnly, slapped the hat against his coat as if that were it, everything had been settled, the drive finished, the railhead reached.

He waited.

Mrs Slater doesn't live here, I said. What'd she win?

I have to show you, he said. May I come in?

I don't know. If it won't take long, I said. I'm pretty busy.

Fine, he said. I'll just slide out of this coat first. And the galoshes. Wouldn't want to track up your carpet. I see you do have a carpet, Mr . . .

His eyes had lighted and then dimmed at the sight of the carpet. He shuddered. Then he took off his coat. He shook it out and hung it by the collar over the doorknob. That's a good place for it, he said. Damn weather, anyway. He bent over and unfastened his galoshes. He set his case inside the room. He stepped out of the galoshes and into the room in a pair of slippers.

I closed the door. He saw me staring at the slippers and said, W. H. Auden wore slippers all through China on his first visit there. Never took them off. Corns.

I shrugged. I took one more look down the street for the mailman and shut the door again.

Aubrey Bell stared at the carpet. He pulled his lips. Then he laughed. He laughed and shook his head.

What's so funny? I said.

Nothing. Lord, he said. He laughed again. I think I'm losing my mind. I think I have a fever. He reached a hand to his forehead. His hair was matted and there was a ring around his scalp where the hat had been.

Do I feel hot to you? he said. I don't know, I think I might have a fever. He was still staring at the carpet. You have any aspirin?

What's the matter with you? I said. I hope you're not getting sick on me. I got things I have to do.

He shook his head. He sat down on the sofa. He stirred at the carpet with his slippered foot.

I went to the kitchen, rinsed a cup, shook two aspirin out of a bottle.

Here, I said. Then I think you ought to leave.

Are you speaking for Mrs Slater? he hissed. No, no, forget I said that, forget I said that. He wiped his face. He swallowed the aspirin. His eyes skipped around the bare room. Then he leaned forward with some effort and unsnapped the buckles on his case. The case flopped open, revealing compartments filled with an array of hoses, brushes, shiny pipes, and some kind of heavy-looking blue thing mounted on little wheels. He stared at these things as if surprised. Quietly, in a churchly voice, he said, Do you know what this is?

I moved closer. I'd say it was a vacuum cleaner. I'm not in the market, I said. No way am I in the market for a vacuum cleaner.

I want to show you something, he said. He took a card out of his jacket pocket. Look at this, he said. He handed me the card. Nobody said you were in the market. But look at the signature. Is that Mrs Slater's signature or not?

I looked at the card. I held it up to the light. I turned it over, but the other side was blank. So what? I said.

Mrs Slater's card was pulled at random out of a basket of cards. Hundreds of cards just like this little card. She has won a free vacuuming and carpet shampoo. Mrs Slater is a winner. No strings. I am here even to do your mattress, Mr . . . You'll be surprised to see what can collect in a mattress over the months, over the years. Every day, every night of our lives, we're leaving little bits of ourselves, flakes of this and that, behind. Where do they go, these bits and pieces of ourselves? Right through the sheets and into the mattress, *that's* where! Pillows, too. It's all the same.

He had been removing lengths of the shiny pipe and joining the parts together. Now he inserted the fitted pipes into the hose. He was on his knees, grunting. He attached some sort of scoop to the hose and lifted out the blue thing with wheels.

He let me examine the filter he intended to use.

Do you have a car? he asked.

No car, I said. I don't have a car. If I had a car I would drive you someplace.

Too bad, he said. This little vacuum comes equipped with a sixty-foot extension cord. If you had a car, you could wheel this little vacuum right up to your car door and vacuum the plush carpeting and the luxurious reclining seats as well. You would be surprised how much of us gets lost, how much of us gathers, in those fine seats over the years.

Mr Bell, I said, I think you better pack up your things and go. I say this without any malice whatsoever.

But he was looking around the room for a plug-in. He found one at the end of the sofa. The machine rattled as if there were a marble inside, anyway something loose inside, then settled to a hum.

Rilke lived in one castle after another, all of his adult life. Benefactors, he said loudly over the hum of the vacuum. He seldom rode in motorcars; he preferred trains. Then look at Voltaire at Cirey with Madame Châtelet. His death mask. Such serenity. He raised his right hand as if I were about to disagree. No, no, it isn't right, is it? Don't say it. But who knows? With that he turned and began to pull the vacuum into the other room.

There was a bed, a window. The covers were heaped on the floor. One pillow, one sheet over the mattress. He slipped the case from the pillow and then quickly stripped the sheet from the mattress. He stared at the mattress and gave me a look out of the corner of his eye. I went to the kitchen and got the chair. I sat down in the doorway and watched. First he tested the suction by putting the scoop against the palm of his hand. He bent and turned a dial on the vacuum. You have to turn it up full strength for a job like this one, he said. He checked the suction again, then extended the hose to the head of the bed and began to move the scoop down the mattress. The scoop tugged at the mattress. The vacuum whirred louder. He made three passes over the mattress, then switched off the machine. He pressed a lever and the lid popped open. He took out the filter. This filter is just for demonstration purposes. In normal use, all of this, this *material*, would go into your bag, here, he said. He pinched some of the dusty stuff between his fingers. There must have been a cup of it.

He had this look to his face.

It's not my mattress, I said. I leaned forward in the chair and tried to show an interest.

Now the pillow, he said. He put the used filter on the sill and looked out the window for a minute. He turned. I want you to hold onto this end of the pillow, he said.

I got up and took hold of two corners of the pillow. I felt I was holding something by the ears.

Like this? I said.

He nodded. He went into the other room and came back with another filter.

How much do those things cost? I said.

Next to nothing, he said. They're only made out of paper and a little bit of plastic. Couldn't cost much.

He kicked on the vacuum and I held tight as the scoop sank into the pillow and moved down its length – once, twice, three times. He switched off the vacuum, removed the filter, and held it up without a word. He put it on the sill beside the other filter. Then he opened the closet door. He looked inside, but there was only a box of Mouse-Be-Gone.

I heard steps on the porch, the mail slot opened and clinked shut. We looked at each other.

He pulled on the vacuum and I followed him into the other room. We looked at the letter lying face down on the carpet near the front door.

I started toward the letter, turned and said, What else? It's getting late. This carpet's not worth fooling with. It's only a twelve-by-fifteen cotton carpet with no-skid backing from Rug City. It's not worth fooling with.

Do you have a full ashtray? he said. Or a potted plant or something like that? A handful of dirt would be fine.

I found the ashtray. He took it, dumped the contents onto the carpet, ground the ashes and cigarettes under his slipper. He got down on his knees again and inserted a new filter. He took off his jacket and threw it onto the sofa. He was sweating under the arms. Fat hung over his belt. He twisted off the scoop and attached another device to the hose. He adjusted his dial. He kicked on the machine and began to move back and forth, back and forth over the worn carpet. Twice I started for the letter. But he seemed to anticipate me, cut me off, so to speak, with his hose and his pipes and his sweeping and his sweeping. . . .

I took the chair back to the kitchen and sat there and watched him work. After a time he shut off the machine, opened the lid, and silently brought me the filter, alive with dust, hair, small grainy things. I looked at the filter, and then I got up and put it in the garbage.

He worked steadily now. No more explanations. He came out to the kitchen with a bottle that held a few ounces of green liquid. He put the bottle under the tap and filled it.

You know I can't pay anything, I said. I couldn't pay you a dollar if my life depended on it. You're going to have to write me off as a dead loss, that's all. You're wasting your time on me, I said.

I wanted it out in the open, no misunderstanding.

He went about his business. He put another attachment on the hose, in some complicated way hooked his bottle to the new attachment. He moved slowly over the carpet, now and then releasing little streams of emerald, moving the brush back and forth over the carpet, working up patches of foam.

I had said all that was on my mind. I sat on the chair in the kitchen, relaxed now, and watched him work. Once in a while I looked out the window at the rain. It had begun to get dark. He switched off the vacuum. He was in a corner near the front door.

You want coffee? I said.

He was breathing hard. He wiped his face.

I put on water and by the time it had boiled and I'd fixed up two cups he had everything dismantled and back in the case. Then he picked up the letter. He read the name on the letter and looked closely at the return address. He folded the letter in half and put it in his hip pocket. I kept watching him. That's all I did. The coffee began to cool.

It's for a Mr Slater, he said. I'll see to it. He said, Maybe I will skip the coffee. I better not walk across this carpet. I just shampooed it.

That's true, I said. Then I said, You're sure that's who the letter's for?

He reached to the sofa for his jacket, put it on, and opened the front door. It was still raining. He stepped into his galoshes, fastened them, and then pulled on the raincoat and looked back inside.

You want to see it? he said. You don't believe me?

It just seems strange, I said.

Well, I'd better be off, he said. But he kept standing there. You want the vacuum or not?

I looked at the big case, closed now and ready to move on.

No, I said, I guess not. I'm going to be leaving here soon. It would just be in the way.

All right, he said, and he shut the door.

Why, Honey?

Dear Sir,

I was so surprised to receive your letter asking about my son, how did you know I was here? I moved here years ago right after it started to happen. No one knows who I am here but I'm afraid all the same. Who I am afraid of is him. When I look at the paper I shake my head and wonder. I read what they write about him and I ask myself is that man really my son, is he really doing these things?

He was a good boy except for his outbursts and that he could not tell the truth. I can't give you any reasons. It started one summer over the Fourth of July, he would have been about fifteen. Our cat Trudy disappeared and was gone all night and the next day. Mrs Cooper who lives behind us came the next evening to tell me Trudy crawled into her backyard that afternoon to die. Trudy was cut up she said but she recognized Trudy. Mr Cooper buried the remains.

Cut up? I said. What do you mean cut up?

Mr Cooper saw two boys in the field putting firecrackers in Trudy's ears and in her you know what. He tried to stop them but they ran.

Who, who would do such a thing, did he see who it was?

He didn't know the other boy but one of them ran this way. Mr Cooper thought it was your son.

I shook my head. No, that's just not so, he wouldn't do a thing like that, he loved Trudy, Trudy has been in the family for years, no, it wasn't my son.

That evening I told him about Trudy and he acted surprised and shocked and said we should offer a reward. He typed something up and promised to post it at school. But

97

just as he was going to his room that night he said don't take it too hard, mom, she was old, in cat years she was 65 or 70, she lived a long time.

He went to work afternoons and Saturdays as a stockboy at Hartley's. A friend of mine who worked there, Betty Wilks, told me about the job and said she would put in a word for him. I mentioned it to him that evening and he said good, jobs for young people are hard to find.

The night he was to draw his first check I cooked his favorite supper and had everything on the table when he walked in. Here's the man of the house, I said, hugging him. I am so proud, how much did you draw, honey? Eighty dollars, he said. I was flabbergasted. That's wonderful, honey, I just cannot believe it. I'm starved, he said, let's eat.

I was happy, but I couldn't understand it, it was more than I was making.

When I did the laundry I found the stub from Hartley's in his pocket, it was for 28 dollars, he said 80. Why didn't he just tell the truth? I couldn't understand.

I would ask him where did you go last night, honey? To the show he would answer. Then I would find out he went to the school dance or spent the evening riding around with somebody in a car. I would think what difference could it make, why doesn't he just be truthful, there is no reason to lie to his mother.

I remember once he was supposed to have gone on a field trip, so I asked him what did you see on the field trip, honey? And he shrugged and said land formations, volcanic rock, ash, they showed us where there used to be a big lake a million years ago, now it's just a desert. He looked me in the eyes and went on talking. Then I got a note from the school the next day saying they wanted permission for a field trip, could he have permission to go.

Near the end of his senior year he bought a car and was always gone. I was concerned about his grades but he only laughed. You know he was an excellent student, you know

that about him if you know anything. After that he bought
a shotgun and a hunting knife.

I hated to see those things in the house and I told him so.
He laughed, he always had a laugh for you. He said he
would keep the gun and the knife in the trunk of his car,
he said they would be easier to get to there anyway.

One Saturday night he did not come home. I worried
myself into a terrible state. About ten o'clock the next morning he came in and asked me to cook him breakfast, he said
he had worked up an appetite out hunting, he said he was
sorry for being gone all night, he said they had driven a
long way to get to this place. It sounded strange. He was
nervous.

Where did you go?

Up to the Wenas. We got a few shots.

Who did you go with, honey?

Fred.

Fred?

He stared and I didn't say anything else.

On the Sunday right after I tiptoed into his room for his
car keys. He had promised to pick up some breakfast items
on his way home from work the night before and I thought
he might have left the things in his car. I saw his new shoes
sitting half under his bed and covered with mud and sand.
He opened his eyes.

Honey, what happened to your shoes? Look at your
shoes.

I ran out of gas, I had to walk for gas. He sat up. What
do you care?

I am your mother.

While he was in the shower I took the keys and went out
to his car. I opened the trunk. I didn't find the groceries. I
saw the shotgun lying on a quilt and the knife too and I
saw a shirt of his rolled in a ball and I shook it out and it
was full of blood. It was wet. I dropped it. I closed the
trunk and started back for the house and I saw him watching
at the window and he opened the door.

I forgot to tell you, he said, I had a bad bloody nose, I don't know if that shirt can be washed, throw it away. He smiled.

A few days later I asked how he was getting along at work. Fine, he said, he had gotten a raise. But I met Betty Wilks on the street and she said they were all sorry at Hartley's that he had quit, he was so well liked, she said, Betty Wilks.

Two nights after that I was in bed but I couldn't sleep, I stared at the ceiling. I heard his car pull up out front and I listened as he put the key in the lock and he came through the kitchen and down the hall to his room and he shut the door after him. I got up. I could see light under his door, I knocked and pushed on the door and said would you like a hot cup of tea, honey, I can't sleep. He was bent over by the dresser and slammed a drawer and turned on me, get out he screamed, get out of here, I'm sick of you spying he screamed. I went to my room and cried myself to sleep. He broke my heart that night.

The next morning he was up and out before I could see him, but that was all right with me. From then on I was going to treat him like a lodger unless he wanted to mend his ways, I was at my limit. He would have to apologize if he wanted us to be more than just strangers living together under the same roof.

When I came in that evening he had supper ready. How are you? he said, he took my coat. How was your day?

I said I didn't sleep last night, honey. I promised myself I wouldn't bring it up and I'm not trying to make you feel guilty but I'm not used to being talked to like that by my son.

I want to show you something, he said, and he showed me this essay he was writing for his civics class. I believe it was on relations between the congress and the supreme court. (It was the paper that won a prize for him at graduation!) I tried to read it and then I decided, this was the time. Honey, I'd like to have a talk with you, it's hard to raise a child with things the way they are these days, it's especially hard for us having no father in the house, no man to turn to when we need him. You are nearly grown now but I am still responsible and I feel I am entitled to some respect and consideration and have tried to be fair and honest with you. I want the truth, honey, that's all I've ever asked from you, the truth. Honey, I took a breath, suppose you had a child who when you asked him something, anything, where he's been or where he's going, what he's doing with his time, anything, never, he never once told you the truth? Who if you asked him is it raining outside, would answer no, it is nice and sunny, and I guess laugh to himself and think you were too old or too stupid to see his clothes are wet. Why should he lie, you ask yourself, what does he gain I don't understand. I keep asking myself why but I don't have the answer. Why, honey?

He didn't say anything, he kept staring, then he moved over alongside me and said I'll show you. Kneel is what I say, kneel down is what I say, he said, that's the first reason why.

I ran to my room and locked the door. He left that night, he took his things, what he wanted, and he left. Believe it or not I never saw him again. I saw him at his graduation but that was with a lot of people around. I sat in the audience and watched him get his diploma and a prize for his essay, then I heard him give the speech and then I clapped right along with the rest.

I went home after that.

I have never seen him again. Oh sure I have seen him on the TV and I have seen his pictures in the paper.

I found out he joined the marines and then I heard from someone he was out of the marines and going to college back east and then he married that girl and got himself in politics. I began to see his name in the paper. I found out his address and wrote to him, I wrote a letter every few months, there never was an answer. He ran for governor and was elected, and was famous now. That's when I began to worry.

I built up all these fears, I became afraid, I stopped writing him of course and then I hoped he would think I was dead. I moved here. I had them give me an unlisted number. And then I had to change my name. If you are a powerful man and want to find somebody, you can find them, it wouldn't be that hard.

I should be so proud but I am afraid. Last week I saw a car on the street with a man inside I know was watching me, I came straight back and locked the door. A few days ago the phone rang and rang, I was lying down. I picked up the receiver but there was nothing there.

I am old. I am his mother. I should be the proudest mother in all the land but I am only afraid.

Thank you for writing. I wanted someone to know. I am very ashamed.

I also wanted to ask how you got my name and knew where to write, I have been praying no one knew. But you did. Why did you? Please tell me why.

Yours truly,

Are these Actual Miles?

Fact is the car needs to be sold in a hurry, and Leo sends Toni
out to do it. Toni is smart and has personality. She used to sell
children's encyclopedias door to door. She signed him up, even
though he didn't have kids. Afterward, Leo asked her for a date,
and the date led to this. This deal has to be cash, and it has to be
done tonight. Tomorrow somebody they owe might slap a lien
on the car. Monday they'll be in court, home free – but word on
them went out yesterday, when their lawyer mailed the letters
of intention. The hearing on Monday is nothing to worry about,
the lawyer has said. They'll be asked some questions, and they'll
sign some papers, and that's it. But sell the convertible, he said
– today, *tonight*. They can hold onto the little car, Leo's car, no
problem. But they go into court with that big convertible, the
court will take it, and that's that.

Toni dresses up. It's four o'clock in the afternoon. Leo worries
the lots will close. But Toni takes her time dressing. She puts on
a new white blouse, wide lacy cuffs, the new two-piece suit, new
heels. She transfers the stuff from her straw purse into the new
patent-leather handbag. She studies the lizard makeup pouch and
puts that in too. Toni has been two hours on her hair and face.
Leo stands in the bedroom doorway and taps his lips with his
knuckles, watching.

"You're making me nervous," she says. "I wish you wouldn't
just stand," she says. "So tell me how I look."

"You look fine," he says. "You look great. I'd buy a car from
you anytime."

"But you don't have money," she says, peering into the
mirror. She pats her hair, frowns. "And your credit's lousy.
You're nothing," she says. "Teasing," she says and looks at him
in the mirror. "Don't be serious," she says. "It has to be done,

103

so I'll do it. You take it out, you'd be lucky to get three, four hundred and we both know it. Honey, you'd be lucky if you didn't have to pay *them*." She gives her hair a final pat, gums her lips, blots the lipstick with a tissue. She turns away from the mirror and picks up her purse. "I'll have to have dinner or something, I told you that already, that's the way they work, I know them. But don't worry, I'll get out of it," she says. "I can handle it."

"Jesus," Leo says, "did you have to say that?"

She looks at him steadily. "Wish me luck," she says.

"Luck," he says. "You have the pink slip?" he says.

She nods. He follows her through the house, a tall woman with a small high bust, broad hips and thighs. He scratches a pimple on his neck. "You're sure?" he says. "Make sure. You have to have the pink slip."

"I have the pink slip," she says.

"Make sure."

She starts to say something, instead looks at herself in the front window and then shakes her head.

"At least call," he says. "Let me know what's going on."

"I'll call," she says. "Kiss, kiss. Here," she says and points to the corner of her mouth. "Careful," she says.

He holds the door for her. "Where are you going to try first?" he says. She moves past him and onto the porch.

Ernest Williams looks from across the street. In his Bermuda shorts, stomach hanging, he looks at Leo and Toni as he directs a spray onto his begonias. Once, last winter, during the holidays, when Toni and the kids were visiting his mother's, Leo brought a woman home. Nine o'clock the next morning, a cold foggy Saturday, Leo walked the woman to the car, surprised Ernest Williams on the sidewalk with a newspaper in his hand. Fog drifted, Ernest Williams stared, then slapped the paper against his leg, hard.

Leo recalls that slap, hunches his shoulders, says, "You have someplace in mind first?"

"I'll just go down the line," she says. "The first lot, then I'll just go down the line."

"Open at nine hundred," he says. "Then come down. Nine hundred is low bluebook, even on a cash deal."

"I know where to start," she says.

Ernest Williams turns the hose in their direction. He stares at them through the spray of water. Leo has an urge to cry out a confession.

"Just making sure," he says.

"Okay, okay," she says. "I'm off."

It's her car, they call it her car, and that makes it all the worse. They bought it new that summer three years ago. She wanted something to do after the kids started school, so she went back selling. He was working six days a week in the fiber-glass plant. For a while they didn't know how to spend the money. Then they put a thousand on the convertible and doubled and tripled the payments until in a year they had it paid. Earlier, while she was dressing, he took the jack and spare from the trunk and emptied the glove compartment of pencils, matchbooks, Blue Chip stamps. Then he washed it and vacuumed inside. The red hood and fenders shine.

"Good luck," he says and touches her elbow.

She nods. He sees she is already gone, already negotiating.

"Things are going to be different!" he calls to her as she reaches the driveway. "We start over Monday. I mean it."

Ernest Williams looks at them and turns his head and spits. She gets into the car and lights a cigarette.

"This time next week!" Leo calls again. "Ancient history!"

He waves as she backs into the street. She changes gear and starts ahead. She accelerates and the tires give a little scream.

In the kitchen Leo pours Scotch and carries the drink to the backyard. The kids are at his mother's. There was a letter three days ago, his name penciled on the outside of the dirty envelope, the only letter all summer not demanding payment in full. We are having fun, the letter said. We like Grandma. We have a new dog called Mr Six. He is nice. We love him. Good-bye.

He goes for another drink. He adds ice and sees that his hand trembles. He holds the hand over the sink. He looks at the hand for a while, sets down the glass, and holds out the other hand. Then he picks up the glass and goes back outside to sit on the steps. He recalls when he was a kid his dad pointing at a fine house, a tall white house surrounded by apple trees and a high white rail fence. "That's Finch," his dad said admiringly. "He's been in bankruptcy at least twice. Look at that house." But bankruptcy is a company collapsing utterly, executives cutting their wrists and throwing themselves from windows, thousands of men on the street.

Leo and Toni still had furniture. Leo and Toni had furniture and Toni and the kids had clothes. Those things were exempt. What else? Bicycles for the kids, but these he had sent to his mother's for safekeeping. The portable air-conditioner and the appliances, new washer and dryer, trucks came for those things weeks ago. What else did they have? This and that, nothing mainly, stuff that wore out or fell to pieces long ago. But there were some big parties back there, some fine travel. To Reno and Tahoe, at eighty with the top down and the radio playing. Food, that was one of the big items. They gorged on food. He figures thousands on luxury items alone. Toni would go to the grocery and put in everything she saw. "I had to do without when I was a kid," she says. "These kids are not going to do without," as if he'd been insisting they should. She joins all the book clubs. "We never had books around when I was a kid," she says as she tears open the heavy packages. They enroll in the record clubs for something to play on the new stereo. They sign up for it all. Even a pedigreed terrier named Ginger. He paid two hundred and found her run over in the street a week later. They buy what they want. If they can't pay, they charge. They sign up.

His undershirt is wet; he can feel the sweat rolling from his underarms. He sits on the step with the empty glass in his hand and watches the shadows fill up the yard. He stretches, wipes his face. He listens to the traffic on the highway and considers whether he should go to the basement, stand on the utility sink, and hang himself with his belt. He understands he is willing to be dead.

Inside he makes a large drink and he turns the TV on and he

fixes something to eat. He sits at the table with chili and crackers and watches something about a blind detective. He clears the table. He washes the pan and the bowl, dries these things and puts them away, then allows himself a look at the clock.

It's after nine. She's been gone nearly five hours.

He pours Scotch, adds water, carries the drink to the living room. He sits on the couch but finds his shoulders so stiff they won't let him lean back. He stares at the screen and sips, and soon he goes for another drink. He sits again. A news program begins – it's ten o'clock – and he says, "God, what in God's name has gone wrong?" and goes to the kitchen to return with more Scotch. He sits, he closes his eyes, and opens them when he hears the telephone ringing.

"I wanted to call," she says.

"Where are you?" he says. He hears piano music, and his heart moves.

"I don't know," she says. "Someplace. We're having a drink, then we're going someplace else for dinner. I'm with the sales manager. He's crude, but he's all right. He bought the car. I have to go now. I was on my way to the ladies and saw the phone."

"Did somebody buy the car?" Leo says. He looks out the kitchen window to the place in the drive where she always parks.

"I told you," she says. "I have to go now."

"Wait, wait a minute, for Christ's sake," he says. "Did somebody buy the car or not?"

"He had his checkbook out when I left," she says. "I have to go now. I have to go to the bathroom."

"Wait!" he yells. The line goes dead. He listens to the dial tone. "Jesus Christ," he says as he stands with the receiver in his hand.

He circles the kitchen and goes back to the living room. He sits. He gets up. In the bathroom he brushes his teeth very carefully. Then he uses dental floss. He washes his face and goes back to the kitchen. He looks at the clock and takes a clean glass from a set that has a hand of playing cards painted on each glass. He fills the glass with ice. He stares for a while at the glass he left in the sink.

He sits against one end of the couch and puts his legs up at the other end. He looks at the screen, realizes he can't make out what the people are saying. He turns the empty glass in his hand and considers biting off the rim. He shivers for a time and thinks of going to bed, though he knows he will dream of a large woman with gray hair. In the dream he is always leaning over tying his shoelaces. When he straightens up, she looks at him, and he bends to tie again. He looks at his hand. It makes a fist as he watches. The telephone is ringing.

"Where are you, honey?" he says slowly, gently.

"We're at this restaurant," she says, her voice strong, bright.

"Honey, which restaurant?" he says. He puts the heel of his hand against his eye and pushes.

"Downtown someplace," she says. "I think it's New Jimmy's. Excuse me," she says to someone off the line, "is this place New Jimmy's? This is New Jimmy's, Leo," she says to him. "Everything is all right, we're almost finished, then he's going to bring me home."

"Honey?" he says. He holds the receiver against his ear and rocks back and forth, eyes closed. "Honey?"

"I have to go," she says. "I wanted to call. Anyway, guess how much?"

"Honey," he says.

"Six and a quarter," she says. "I have it in my purse. He said there's no market for convertibles. I guess we're born lucky," she says and laughs. "I told him everything. I think I had to."

"Honey," Leo says.

"What?" she says.

"Please, honey," Leo says.

"He said he sympathizes," she says. "But he would have said anything." She laughs again. "He said personally he'd rather be classified a robber or a rapist than a bankrupt. He's nice enough, though," she says.

"Come home," Leo says. "Take a cab and come home."

"I can't," she says. "I told you, we're halfway through dinner."

"I'll come for you," he says.

"No," she says. "I said we're just finishing. I told you, it's part of the deal. They're out for all they can get. But don't worry, we're about to leave. I'll be home in a little while." She hangs up.

In a few minutes he calls New Jimmy's. A man answers. "New Jimmy's has closed for the evening," the man says.

"I'd like to talk to my wife," Leo says.

"Does she work here?" the man asks. "Who is she?"

"She's a customer," Leo says. "She's with someone. A business person."

"Would I know her?" the man says. "What is her name?"

"I don't think you know her," Leo says.

"That's all right," Leo says. "That's all right. I see her now."

"Thank you for calling New Jimmy's," the man says.

Leo hurries to the window. A car he doesn't recognize slows in front of the house, then picks up speed. He waits. Two, three hours later, the telephone rings again. There is no one at the other end when he picks up the receiver. There is only a dial tone.

"I'm right here!" Leo screams into the receiver.

Near dawn he hears footsteps on the porch. He gets up from the couch. The set hums, the screen glows. He opens the door. She bumps the wall coming in. She grins. Her face is puffy, as if she's been sleeping under sedation. She works her lips, ducks heavily and sways as he cocks his fist.

"Go ahead," she says thickly. She stands there swaying. Then she makes a noise and lunges, catches his shirt, tears it down the front. "Bankrupt!" she screams. She twists loose, grabs and tears his undershirt at the neck. "You son of a bitch," she says, clawing.

He squeezes her wrists, then lets go, steps back, looking for something heavy. She stumbles as she heads for the bedroom. "Bankrupt," she mutters. He hears her fall on the bed and groan.

He waits awhile, then splashes water on his face and goes to the bedroom. He turns the lights on, looks at her, and begins to take her clothes off. He pulls and pushes her from side to side undressing her. She says something in her sleep and moves her hand. He takes off her underpants, looks at them closely under the light, and throws them into a corner. He turns back the covers and rolls her in, naked. Then he opens her purse. He is reading the check when he hears the car come into the drive.

He looks through the front curtain and sees the convertible in the drive, its motor running smoothly, the headlamps burning, and he closes and opens his eyes. He sees a tall man come around in front of the car and up to the front porch. The man lays something on the porch and starts back to the car. He wears a white linen suit.

Leo turns on the porch light and opens the door cautiously. Her makeup pouch lies on the top step. The man looks at Leo across the front of the car, and then gets back inside and releases the handbrake.

"Wait!" Leo calls and starts down the steps. The man brakes the car as Leo walks in front of the lights. The car creaks against the brake. Leo tries to pull the two pieces of his shirt together, tries to bunch it all into his trousers.

"What is it you want?" the man says. "Look," the man says, "I have to go. No offense. I buy and sell cars, right? The lady left her makeup. She's a fine lady, very refined. What is it?"

Leo leans against the door and looks at the man. The man takes his hands off the wheel and puts them back. He drops the gear into reverse and the car moves backward a little.

"I want to tell you," Leo says and wets his lips.

The light in Ernest Williams' bedroom goes on. The shade rolls up.

Leo shakes his head, tucks in his shirt again. He steps back from the car. "Monday," he says.

"Monday," the man says and watches for sudden movement. Leo nods slowly.

"Well, goodnight," the man says and coughs. "Take it easy, hear? Monday, that's right. Okay, then." He takes his foot off the brake, puts it on again after he has rolled back two or three feet. "Hey, one question. Between friends, are these actual miles?" The man waits, then clears his throat. "Okay, look, it doesn't matter either way," the man says. "I have to go. Take it easy." He backs into the street, pulls away quickly, and turns the corner without stopping.

Leo tucks at his shirt and goes back in the house. He locks the front door and checks it. Then he goes to the bedroom and locks that door and turns back the covers. He looks at her before he flicks the light. He takes off his clothes, folds them carefully on the floor, and gets in beside her. He lies on his back for a time and pulls the hair on his stomach, considering. He looks at the bedroom door, outlined now in the faint outside light. Presently he reaches out his hand and touches her hip. She does not move. He turns on his side and puts his hand on her hip. He runs his fingers over her hip and feels the stretch marks there. They are like roads, and he traces them in her flesh. He runs his fingers back and forth, first one, then another. They run everywhere in her flesh, dozens, perhaps hundreds of them. He remembers waking up the morning after they bought the car, seeing it, there in the drive, in the sun, gleaming.

Gazebo

That morning she pours Teacher's over my belly and licks it off. That afternoon she tries to jump out the window.

I go, "Holly, this can't continue. This has got to stop."

We are sitting on the sofa in one of the upstairs suites. There were any number of vacancies to choose from. But we needed a suite, a place to move around in and be able to talk. So we'd locked up the motel office that morning and gone upstairs to a suite.

She goes, "Duane, this is killing me."

We are drinking Teacher's with ice and water. We'd slept awhile between morning and afternoon. Then she was out of bed and threatening to climb out the window in her undergarments. had to get her in a hold. We were only two floors up. But even so.

"I've had it," she goes. "I can't take it anymore."

She puts her hand to her cheek and closes her eyes. She turns her head back and forth and makes this humming noise.

I could die seeing her like this.

"Take what?" I go, though of course I know.

"I don't have to spell it out for you again," she goes. "I've lost control. I've lost pride. I used to be a proud woman."

She's an attractive woman just past thirty. She is tall and has long black hair and green eyes, the only green-eyed woman I've ever known. In the old days I used to say things about her green eyes, and she'd tell me it was because of them she knew she was meant for something special.

And didn't I know it!

I feel so awful from one thing and the other.

I can hear the telephone ringing downstairs in the office. It has been ringing off and on all day. Even when I was dozing I could

hear it. I'd open my eyes and look at the ceiling and listen to it
ring and wonder at what was happening to us.

But maybe I should be looking at the floor.

"My heart is broken," she goes. "It's turned to a piece of stone.
I'm no good. That's what's as bad as anything, that I'm no good
anymore."

"Holly," I go.

When we'd first moved down here and taken over as managers,
we thought we were out of the woods. Free rent and free utilities
plus three hundred a month. You couldn't beat it with a stick.

Holly took care of the books. She was good with figures, and
she did most of the renting of the units. She liked people, and
people liked her back. I saw to the grounds, mowed the grass
and cut weeds, kept the swimming pool clean, did the small
repairs.

Everything was fine for the first year. I was holding down
another job nights, and we were getting ahead. We had plans.
Then one morning, I don't know. I'd just laid some bathroom
tile in one of the units when this little Mexican maid comes in
to clean. It was Holly had hired her. I can't really say I'd noticed
the little thing before, though we spoke when we saw each other.
She called me, I remember, Mister.

Anyway, one thing and the other.

So after that morning I started paying attention. She was a neat
little thing with fine white teeth. I used to watch her mouth.

She started calling me by my name.

One morning I was doing a washer for one of the bathroom
faucets, and she comes in and turns on the TV as maids are like
to do. While they clean, that is. I stopped what I was doing and
stepped outside the bathroom. She was surprised to see me. She
smiles and says my name.

It was right after she said it that we got down on the bed.

"Holly, you're still a proud woman," I go. "You're still number
one. Come on, Holly."

She shakes her head.

"Something's died in me," she goes. "It took a long time for it to do it, but it's dead. You've killed something, just like you'd taken an axe to it. Everything is dirt now."

She finishes her drink. Then she begins to cry. I make to hug her. But it's no good.

I freshen our drinks and look out the window.

Two cars with out-of-state plates are parked in front of the office, and the drivers are standing at the door, talking. One of them finishes saying something to the other, and looks around at the units and pulls his chin. There's a woman there too, and she has her face up to the glass, hand shielding her eyes, peering inside. She tries the door.

The phone downstairs begins to ring.

"Even a while ago when we were doing it, you were thinking of her," Holly goes. "Duane, this is hurtful."

She takes the drink I give her.

"Holly," I go.

"It's true, Duane," she goes. "Just don't argue with me," she goes.

She walks up and down the room in her underpants and her brassiere, her drink in her hand.

Holly goes, "You've gone outside the marriage. It's trust that you killed."

I get down on my knees and I start to beg. But I am thinking of Juanita. This is awful. I don't know what's going to happen to me or to anyone else in the world.

I go, "Holly, honey, I love you."

In the lot someone leans on a horn, stops, and then leans again.

Holly wipes her eyes. She goes, "Fix me a drink. This one's too watery. Let them blow their stinking horns. I don't care. I'm moving to Nevada."

"Don't move to Nevada," I go. "You're talking crazy," I go.

"I'm not talking crazy," she goes. "Nothing's crazy about Nevada. You can stay here with your cleaning woman. I'm moving to Nevada. Either there or kill myself."

"Holly!" I go.

"Holly *nothing!*" she goes.

She sits on the sofa and draws her knees up to under her chin.

"Fix me another pop, you son of a bitch," she goes. She goes, "Fuck those horn-blowers. Let them do their dirt in the Travelodge. Is that where your cleaning woman cleans now? Fix me another, you son of a bitch!"

She sets her lips and gives me this look.

Drinking's funny. When I look back on it, all of our important decisions have been figured out when we were drinking. Even when we talked about having to cut back on our drinking, we'd be sitting at the kitchen table or out at the picnic table with a six-pack or whiskey. When we made up our minds to move down here and take this job as managers, we sat up a couple of nights drinking while we weighed the pros and the cons.

I pour the last of the Teacher's into our glasses and add cubes and a spill of water.

Holly gets off the sofa and stretches on out across the bed.

She goes, "Did you do it to her in this bed?"

I don't have anything to say. I feel all out of words inside. I give her the glass and sit down in the chair. I drink my drink and think it's not ever going to be the same.

"Duane?" she goes.

"Holly?"

My heart has slowed. I wait.

Holly was my own true love.

The thing with Juanita was five days a week between the hours of ten and eleven. It was in whatever unit she was in when she was making her cleaning rounds. I'd just walk in where she was working and shut the door behind me.

But mostly it was in 11. It was 11 that was our lucky room.

We were sweet with each other, but swift. It was fine.

I think Holly could maybe have weathered it out. I think the thing she had to do was really give it a try.

Me, I held on to the night job. A monkey could do that work. But things here were going downhill fast. We just didn't have the heart for it anymore.

I stopped cleaning the pool. It filled up with green gick so that the guests wouldn't use it anymore. I didn't fix any more faucets or lay any more tile or do any of the touch-up painting. Well, the truth is we were both hitting it pretty hard. Booze takes a lot of time and effort if you're going to do a good job with it.

Holly wasn't registering the guests right, either. She was charging too much or else not collecting what she should. Sometimes she'd put three people to a room with only one bed in it, or else she'd put a single in where the bed was a king-size. I tell you, there were complaints, and sometimes there were words. Folks would load up and go somewhere else.

The next thing, there's a letter from the management people. Then there's another, certified.

There's telephone calls. There's someone coming down from the city.

But we had stopped caring, and that's a fact. We knew our days were numbered. We had fouled our lives and we were getting ready for a shake-up.

Holly's a smart woman. She knew it first.

Then that Saturday morning we woke up after a night of rehashing the situation. We opened our eyes and turned in bed to take a good look at each other. We both knew it then. We'd reached the end of something, and the thing was to find out where new to start.

We got up and got dressed, had coffee, and decided on this talk. Without nothing interrupting. No calls. No guests.

That's when I got the Teacher's. We locked up and came upstairs here with ice, glasses, bottles. First off, we watched the color TV and frolicked some and let the phone ring away downstairs. For food, we went out and got cheese crisps from the machine.

There was this funny thing of anything could happen now that we realized everything had.

*

"When we were just kids before we married?" Holly goes. "When we had big plans and hopes? You remember?" She was sitting on the bed, holding her knees and her drink.

"I remember, Holly."

"You weren't my first, you know. My first was Wyatt. Imagine. Wyatt. And your name's Duane. Wyatt and Duane. Who knows what I was missing all those years? You were my everything, just like the song."

I go, "You're a wonderful woman, Holly. I know you've had the opportunities."

"But I didn't take them up on it!" she goes. "I couldn't go outside the marriage."

"Holly, please," I go. "No more now, honey. Let's not torture ourselves. What is it we should do?"

"Listen," she goes. "You remember the time we drove out to that old farm place outside of Yakima, out past Terrace Heights? We were just driving around? We were on this little dirt road and it was hot and dusty? We kept going and came to that old house, and you asked if we could have a drink of water? Can you imagine us doing that now? Going up to a house and asking for a drink of water?

"Those old people must be dead now," she goes, "side by side out there in some cemetery. You remember they asked us in for cake? And later on they showed us around? And there was this gazebo there out back? It was out back under some trees? It had a little peaked roof and the paint was gone and there were these weeds growing up over the steps. And the woman said that years before, I mean a real long time ago, men used to come around and play music out there on a Sunday, and the people would sit and listen. I thought we'd be like that too when we got old enough. Dignified. And in a place. And people would come to our door."

I can't say anything just yet. Then I go, "Holly, these things, we'll look back on them too. We'll go, 'Remember the motel with all the crud in the pool?'" I go, "You see what I'm saying, Holly?"

But Holly just sits there on the bed with her glass.

I can see she doesn't know.

I move over to the window and look out from behind the curtain. Someone says something below and rattles the door to the office. I stay there. I pray for a sign from Holly. I pray for Holly to show me.

I hear a car start. Then another. They turn on their lights against the building and, one after the other, they pull away and go out into the traffic.

"Duane," Holly goes.

In this too, she was right.

One More Thing

L.D.'s wife, Maxine, told him to get out the night she came
home from work and found L.D. drunk again and being abusive
to Rae, their fifteen-year-old. L.D. and Rae were at the kitchen
table, arguing. Maxine didn't have time to put her purse away
or take off her coat.

Rae said, "Tell him, Mom. Tell him what we talked about."

L.D. turned the glass in his hand, but he didn't drink from it.
Maxine had him in a fierce and disquieting gaze.

"Keep your nose out of things you don't know anything
about," L.D. said. L.D. said, "I can't take anybody seriously
who sits around all day reading astrology magazines."

"This has nothing to do with astrology," Rae said. "You don't
have to insult me."

As for Rae, she hadn't been to school for weeks. She said no
one could make her go. Maxine said it was another tragedy in a
long line of low-rent tragedies.

"Why don't you both shut up!" Maxine said. "My God, I
already have a headache."

"Tell him, Mom," Rae said. "Tell him it's all in his head.
Anybody who knows anything about it will tell you that's where
it is!"

"How about sugar diabetes?" L.D. said. "What about epilepsy?
Can the brain control that?"

He raised the glass right under Maxine's eyes and finished his
drink.

"Diabetes, too," Rae said. "Epilepsy. Anything! The brain is
the most powerful organ in the body, for your information."

She picked up his cigarettes and lit one for herself.

"Cancer. What about cancer?" L.D. said.

He thought he might have her there. He looked at Maxine.

"I don't know how we got started on this," L.D. said to Maxine.

"Cancer," Rae said, and shook her head at his simplicity. "Cancer, too. Cancer *starts* in the brain."

"That's crazy!" L.D. said. He hit the table with the flat of his hand. The ashtray jumped. His glass fell on its side and rolled off. "You're crazy, Rae! Do you know that?"

"Shut up!" Maxine said.

She unbuttoned her coat and put her purse down on the counter. She looked at L.D. and said, " L.D., I've had it. So has Rae. So has everyone who knows you. I've been thinking it over. I want you out of here. Tonight. This minute. Now. Get the hell out of here right now."

L.D. had no intention of going anywhere. He looked from Maxine to the jar of pickles that had been on the table since lunch. He picked up the jar and pitched it through the kitchen window.

Rae jumped away from her chair. "God! He's crazy!"

She went to stand next to her mother. She took in little breaths through her mouth.

"Call the police," Maxine said. "He's violent. Get out of the kitchen before he hurts you. Call the police," Maxine said.

They started backing out of the kitchen.

"I'm going," L.D. said. "All right, I'm going right now," he said. "It suits me to a tee. You're nuts here, anyway. This is a nuthouse. There's another life out there. Believe me, this is no picnic, this nuthouse."

He could feel air from the hole in the window on his face.

"That's where I'm going," he said. "Out there," he said and pointed.

"Good," Maxine said.

"All right, I'm going," L.D. said.

He slammed down his hand on the table. He kicked back his chair. He stood up.

"You won't ever see me again," L.D. said.

"You've given me plenty to remember you by," Maxine said.

"Okay," L.D. said.

"Go on, get out," Maxine said. "I'm paying the rent here, and I'm saying go. Now."

"I'm going," he said. "Don't push me," he said. "I'm going."

"Just go," Maxine said.

"I'm leaving this nuthouse," L.D. said.

He made his way into the bedroom and took one of her suitcases from the closet. It was an old white Naugahyde suitcase with a broken clasp. She'd used to pack it full of sweater sets and carry it with her to college. He had gone to college too. He threw the suitcase onto the bed and began putting in his underwear, his trousers, his shirts, his sweaters, his old leather belt with the brass buckle, his socks, and everything else he had. From, the nightstand he took magazines for reading material. He took the ashtray. He put everything he could into the suitcase, everything it could hold. He fastened the one good side, secured the strap, and then he remembered his bathroom things. He found the vinyl shaving bag up on the closet shelf behind her hats. Into it went his razor and his shaving cream, his talcum powder and his stick deodorant and his toothbrush. He took the toothpaste, too. And then he got the dental floss.

He could hear them in the living room talking in their low voices.

He washed his face. He put the soap and towel into the shaving bag. Then he put in the soap dish and the glass from over the sink and the fingernail clippers and her eyelash curlers.

He couldn't get the shaving bag closed, but that was okay. He put on his coat and picked up the suitcase. He went into the living room.

When she saw him, Maxine put her arm around Rae's shoulders.

"This is it," L.D. said. "This is good-bye," he said. "I don't know what else to say except I guess I'll never see you again. You too," L.D. said to Rae. "You and your crackpot ideas."

"Go," Maxine said. She took Rae's hand. "Haven't you done enough damage in this house already? Go on, L.D. Get out of here and leave us in peace."

"Just remember," Rae said. "It's in your head."

"I'm going, that's all I can say," L.D. said. "Anyplace. Away from this nuthouse," he said. "That's the main thing."

He took a last look around the living room and then he moved the suitcase from one hand to the other and put the shaving bag under his arm. "I'll be in touch, Rae. Maxine, you're better off out of this nuthouse yourself."

"You made it into a nuthouse," Maxine said. "If it's a nuthouse, then that's what you made it."

He put the suitcase down and the shaving bag on top of the suitcase. He drew himself up and faced them.

They moved back.

"Watch it, Mom," Rae said.

"I'm not afraid of him," Maxine said.

L.D. put the shaving bag under his arm and picked up the suitcase.

He said, "I just want to say one more thing."

But then he could not think what it could possibly be.

Little Things

Early that day the weather turned and the snow was melting into dirty water. Streaks of it ran down from the little shoulder-high window that faced the backyard. Cars slushed by on the street outside, where it was getting dark. But it was getting dark on the inside too.

He was in the bedroom pushing clothes into a suitcase when she came to the door.

I'm glad you're leaving! I'm glad you're leaving! she said. Do you hear?

He kept on putting his things into the suitcase.

Son of a bitch! I'm so glad you're leaving! She began to cry. You can't even look me in the face, can you?

Then she noticed the baby's picture on the bed and picked it up.

He looked at her and she wiped her eyes and stared at him before turning and going back to the living room.

Bring that back, he said.

Just get your things and get out, she said.

He did not answer. He fastened the suitcase, put on his coat, looked around the bedroom before turning off the light. Then he went out to the living room.

She stood in the doorway of the little kitchen, holding the baby.

I want the baby, he said.

Are you crazy?

No, but I want the baby. I'll get someone to come by for his things.

You're not touching this baby, she said.

The baby had begun to cry and she uncovered the blanket from around his head.

Oh, oh, she said, looking at the baby.

He moved toward her.

For God's sake! she said. She took a step back into the kitchen.

I want the baby.

Get out of here!

She turned and tried to hold the baby over in a corner behind the stove.

But he came up. He reached across the stove and tightened his hands on the baby.

Let go of him, he said.

Get away, get away! she cried.

The baby was red-faced and screaming. In the scuffle they knocked down a flowerpot that hung behind the stove.

He crowded her into the wall then, trying to break her grip. He held on to the baby and pushed with all his weight.

Let go of him, he said.

Don't, she said. You're hurting the baby, she said.

I'm not hurting the baby, he said.

The kitchen window gave no light. In the near-dark he worked on her fisted fingers with one hand and with the other hand he gripped the screaming baby up under an arm near the shoulder.

She felt her fingers being forced open. She felt the baby going from her.

No! she screamed just as her hands came loose.

She would have it, this baby. She grabbed for the baby's other arm. She caught the baby around the wrist and leaned back.

But he would not let go. He felt the baby slipping out of his hands and he pulled back very hard.

In this manner, the issue was decided.

Why Don't You Dance?

In the kitchen, he poured another drink and looked at the bedroom suite in his front yard. The mattress was stripped and the candy-striped sheets lay beside two pillows on the chiffonier. Except for that, things looked much the way they had in the bedroom—nightstand and reading lamp on his side of the bed, nightstand and reading lamp on her side.

His side, her side.

He considered this as he sipped the whiskey.

The chiffonier stood a few feet from the foot of the bed. He had emptied the drawers into cartons that morning, and the cartons were in the living room. A portable heater was next to the chiffonier. A rattan chair with a decorator pillow stood at the foot of the bed. The buffed aluminum kitchen set took up a part of the driveway. A yellow muslin cloth, much too large, a gift, covered the table and hung down over the sides. A potted fern was on the table, along with a box of silverware and a record player, also gifts. A big console-model television set rested on a coffee table, and a few feet away from this stood a sofa and chair and a floor lamp. The desk was pushed against the garage door. A few utensils were on the desk, along with a wall clock and two framed prints. There was also in the driveway a carton with cups, glasses, and plates, each object wrapped in newspaper. That morning he had cleared out the closets, and except for the three cartons in the living room, all the stuff was out of the house. He had run an extension cord on out there and everything was connected. Things worked, no different from how it was when they were inside.

Now and then a car slowed and people stared. But no one stopped.

It occurred to him that he wouldn't, either.

*

125

"It must be a yard sale," the girl said to the boy.

This girl and this boy were furnishing a little apartment.

"Let's see what they want for the bed," the girl said.

"And for the TV," the boy said.

The boy pulled into the driveway and stopped in front of the kitchen table.

They got out of the car and began to examine things, the girl touching the muslin cloth, the boy plugging in the blender and turning the dial to MINCE, the girl picking up a chafing dish, the boy turning on the television set and making little adjustments.

He sat down on the sofa to watch. He lit a cigarette, looked around, flipped the match into the grass.

The girl sat on the bed. She pushed off her shoes and lay back. She thought she could see a star.

"Come here, Jack. Try this bed. Bring one of those pillows," she said.

"How is it?" he said.

"Try it," she said.

He looked around. The house was dark.

"I feel funny," he said. "Better see if anybody's home."

She bounced on the bed.

"Try it first," she said.

He lay down on the bed and put the pillow under his head.

"How does it feel?" she said.

"It feels firm," he said.

She turned on her side and put her hand to his face.

"Kiss me," she said.

"Let's get up," he said.

"Kiss me," she said.

She closed her eyes. She held him.

He said, "I'll see if anybody's home."

But he just sat up and stayed where he was, making believe he was watching the television.

Lights came on in houses up and down the street.

"Wouldn't it be funny if," the girl said and grinned and didn't finish.

The boy laughed, but for no good reason. For no good reason, he switched the reading lamp on.

The girl brushed away a mosquito, whereupon the boy stood up and tucked in his shirt.

"I'll see if anybody's home," he said. "I don't think anybody's home. But if anybody is, I'll see what things are going for."

"Whatever they ask, offer ten dollars less. It's always a good idea," she said. "And, besides, they must be desperate or something."

"It's a pretty good TV," the boy said.

"Ask them how much," the girl said.

The man came down the sidewalk with a sack from the market. He had sandwiches, beer, whiskey. He saw the car in the driveway and the girl on the bed. He saw the television set going and the boy on the porch.

"Hello," the man said to the girl. "You found the bed. That's good."

"Hello," the girl said, and got up. "I was just trying it out." She patted the bed. "It's a pretty good bed."

"It's a good bed," the man said, and put down the sack and took out the beer and the whiskey.

"We thought nobody was here," the boy said. "We're interested in the bed and maybe in the TV. Also maybe the desk. How much do you want for the bed?"

"I was thinking fifty dollars for the bed," the man said.

"Would you take forty?" the girl asked.

"I'll take forty," the man said.

He took a glass out of the carton. He took the newspaper off the glass. He broke the seal on the whiskey.

"How about the TV?" the boy said.

"Twenty-five."

"Would you take fifteen?" the girl said.

"Fifteen's okay. I could take fifteen," the man said.

The girl looked at the boy.

"You kids, you'll want a drink," the man said. "Glasses in

that box. I'm going to sit down. I'm going to sit down on the sofa."

The man sat on the sofa, leaned back, and stared at the boy and the girl.

The boy found two glasses and poured whiskey.

"That's enough," the girl said. "I think I want water in mine."

She pulled out a chair and sat at the kitchen table.

"There's water in that spigot over there," the man said. "Turn on that spigot."

The boy came back with the watered whiskey. He cleared his throat and sat down at the kitchen table. He grinned. But he didn't drink anything from his glass.

The man gazed at the television. He finished his drink and started another. He reached to turn on the floor lamp. It was then that his cigarette dropped from his fingers and fell between the cushions.

The girl got up to help him find it.

"So what do you want?" the boy said to the girl.

The boy took out the checkbook and held it to his lips as if thinking.

"I want the desk," the girl said. "How much money is the desk?"

The man waved his hand at this preposterous question.

"Name a figure," he said.

He looked at them as they sat at the table. In the lamplight, there was something about their faces. It was nice or it was nasty. There was no telling.

"I'm going to turn off this TV and put on a record," the man said. "This record-player is going, too. Cheap. Make me an offer."

He poured more whiskey and opened a beer.

"Everything goes," said the man.

The girl held out her glass and the man poured.

"Thank you," she said. "You're very nice," she said.

"It goes to your head," the boy said. "I'm getting it in the head." He held up his glass and jiggled it.

The man finished his drink and poured another, and then he found the box with the records.

"Pick something," the man said to the girl, and he held the records out to her.

The boy was writing the check.

"Here," the girl said, picking something, picking anything, for she did not know the names on these labels. She got up from the table and sat down again. She did not want to sit still.

"I'm making it out to cash," the boy said.

"Sure," the man said.

They drank. They listened to the record. And then the man put on another.

Why don't you kids dance? he decided to say, and then he said it. "Why don't you dance?"

"I don't think so," the boy said.

"Go ahead," the man said. "It's my yard. You can dance if you want to."

Arms about each other, their bodies pressed together, the boy and the girl moved up and down the driveway. They were dancing. And when the record was over, they did it again, and when that one ended, the boy said, "I'm drunk."

The girl said, "You're not drunk."

"Well, I'm drunk," the boy said.

The man turned the record over and the boy said, "I am."

"Dance with me," the girl said to the boy and then to the man, and when the man stood up, she came to him with her arms wide open.

"Those people over there, they're watching," she said.

"It's okay," the man said. "It's my place," he said.

"Let them watch," the girl said.

"That's right," the man said. "They thought they'd seen everything over here. But they haven't seen this, have they?" he said.

He felt her breath on his neck.

"I hope you like your bed," he said.

The girl closed and then opened her eyes. She pushed her face into the man's shoulder. She pulled the man closer.

"You must be desperate or something," she said.

Weeks later, she said: "The guy was about middle-aged. All his things right there in his yard. No lie. We got real pissed and danced. In the driveway. Oh, my God. Don't laugh. He played us these records. Look at this record-player. The old guy gave it to us. And all these crappy records. Will you look at this shit?"

She kept talking. She told everyone. There was more to it, and she was trying to get it talked out. After a time, she quit trying.

A Serious Talk

Vera's car was there, no others, and Burt gave thanks for that. He pulled into the drive and stopped beside the pie he'd dropped the night before. It was still there, the aluminum pan upside down, a halo of pumpkin filling on the pavement. It was the day after Christmas.

He'd come on Christmas day to visit his wife and children. Vera had warned him beforehand. She'd told him the score. She'd said he had to be out by six o'clock because her friend and his children were coming for dinner.

They had sat in the living room and solemnly opened the presents Burt had brought over. They had opened his packages while other packages wrapped in festive paper lay piled under the tree waiting for after six o'clock.

He had watched the children open their gifts, waited while Vera undid the ribbon on hers. He saw her slip off the paper, lift the lid, take out the cashmere sweater.

"It's nice," she said. "Thank you, Burt."

"Try it on," his daughter said.

"Put it on," his son said.

Burt looked at his son, grateful for his backing him up.

She did try it on. Vera went into the bedroom and came out with it on.

"It's nice," she said.

"It's nice on *you*," Burt said, and felt a welling in his chest.

He opened his gifts. From Vera, a gift certificate at Sondheim's men's store. From his daughter, a matching comb and brush. From his son, a ballpoint pen.

Vera served sodas, and they did a little talking. But mostly they looked at the tree. Then his daughter got up and began setting the dining-room table, and his son went off to his room.

131

But Burt liked it where he was. He liked it in front of the fireplace, a glass in his hand, his house, his home.

Then Vera went into the kitchen.

From time to time his daughter walked into the dining room with something for the table. Burt watched her. He watched her fold the linen napkins into the wine glasses. He watched her put a slender vase in the middle of the table. He watched her lower a flower into the vase, doing it ever so carefully.

A small wax and sawdust log burned on the grate. A carton of five more sat ready on the hearth. He got up from the sofa and put them all in the fireplace. He watched until they flamed. Then he finished his soda and made for the patio door. On the way, he saw the pies lined up on the sideboard. He stacked them in his arms, all six, one for every ten times she had ever betrayed him.

In the driveway in the dark, he'd let one fall as he fumbled with the door.

The front door was permanently locked since the night his key had broken off inside it. He went around to the back. There was a wreath on the patio door. He rapped on the glass. Vera was in her bathrobe. She looked out at him and frowned. She opened the door a little.

Burt said, "I want to apologize to you for last night. I want to apologize to the kids, too."

Vera said, "They're not here."

She stood in the doorway and he stood on the patio next to the philodendron plant. He pulled at some lint on his sleeve.

She said, "I can't take any more. You tried to burn the house down."

"I did not."

"You did. Everybody here was a witness."

He said, "Can I come in and talk about it?"

She drew the robe together at her throat and moved back inside.

She said, "I have to go somewhere in an hour."

He looked around. The tree blinked on and off. There was a

pile of colored tissue paper and shiny boxes at one end of the sofa. A turkey carcass sat on a platter in the center of the dining-room table, the leathery remains in a bed of parsley as if in a horrible nest. A cone of ash filled the fireplace. There were some empty Shasta cola cans in there too. A trail of smoke stains rose up to the bricks to the mantel, where the wood that stopped them was scorched black.

He turned around and went back to the kitchen.

He said, "What time did your friend leave last night?"

She said, "If you're going to start that, you can go right now."

He pulled a chair out and sat down at the kitchen table in front of the big ashtray. He closed his eyes and opened them. He moved the curtain aside and looked out at the backyard. He saw a bicycle without a front wheel standing upside down. He saw weeds growing along the redwood fence.

She ran water into a saucepan. "Do you remember Thanks-giving?" she said. "I said then that was the last holiday you were going to wreck for us. Eating bacon and eggs instead of turkey at ten o'clock at night."

"I know it," he said. "I said I'm sorry."

"Sorry isn't good enough."

The pilot light was out again. She was at the stove trying to get the gas going under the pan of water.

"Don't burn yourself," he said. "Don't catch yourself on fire."

He considered her robe catching fire, him jumping up from the table, throwing her down onto the floor and rolling her over and over into the living room, where he would cover her with his body. Or should he run to the bedroom for a blanket?

"Vera?"

She looked at him.

"Do you have anything to drink? I could use a drink this morning."

"There's some vodka in the freezer."

"When did you start keeping vodka in the freezer?"

"Don't ask."

"Okay," he said, "I won't ask."

He got out the vodka and poured some into a cup he found on the counter.

She said, "Are you just going to drink it like that, out of a cup?" She said, "Jesus, Burt. What'd you want to talk about, anyway? I told you I have someplace to go. I have a flute lesson at one o'clock."

"Are you still taking flute?"

"I just said so. What is it? Tell me what's on your mind, and then I have to get ready."

"I wanted to say I was sorry."

She said, "You said that."

He said, "If you have any juice, I'll mix it with this vodka."

She opened the refrigerator and moved things around.

"There's cranapple juice," she said.

"That's fine," he said.

"I'm going to the bathroom," she said.

He drank the cup of cranapple juice and vodka. He lit a cigarette and tossed the match into the big ashtray that always sat on the kitchen table. He studied the butts in it. Some of them were Vera's brand, and some of them weren't. Some even were lavender-colored. He got up and dumped it all under the sink.

The ashtray was not really an ashtray. It was a big dish of stoneware they'd bought from a bearded potter on the mall in Santa Clara. He rinsed it out and dried it. He put it back on the table. And then he ground out his cigarette in it.

The water on the stove began to bubble just as the phone began to ring.

He heard her open the bathroom door and call to him through the living room. "Answer that! I'm about to get into the shower."

The kitchen phone was on the counter in a corner behind the roasting pan. He moved the roasting pan and picked up the receiver.

"Is Charlie there?" the voice said.

"No," Burt said.

"Okay," the voice said.

While he was seeing to the coffee, the phone rang again.

"Charlie?"

"Not here," Burt said.

This time he left the receiver off the hook.

Vera came back into the kitchen wearing jeans and a sweater and brushing her hair.

He spooned the instant into the cups of hot water and then spilled some vodka into his. He carried the cups over to the table.

She picked up the receiver, listened. She said, "What's this? Who was on the phone?"

"Nobody," he said. "Who smokes colored cigarettes?"

"I do."

"I didn't know you did that."

"Well, I do."

She sat across from him and drank her coffee. They smoked and used the ashtray.

There were things he wanted to say, grieving things, consoling things, things like that.

"I'm smoking three packs a day," Vera said. "I mean, if you really want to know what goes on around here."

"God almighty," Burt said.

Vera nodded.

"I didn't come over here to hear that," he said.

"What did you come over here to hear, then? You want to hear the house burned down?"

"Vera," he said. "It's Christmas. That's why I came."

"It's the day after Christmas," she said. "Christmas has come and gone," she said. "I don't ever want to see another one."

"What about me?" he said. "You think I look forward to holidays?"

The phone rang again. Burt picked it up.

"It's someone wanting Charlie," he said.

"What?"

"Charlie," Burt said.

Vera took the phone. She kept her back to him as she talked. Then she turned to him and said, "I'll take this call in the bedroom. So would you please hang up after I've picked it up in there? I can tell, so hang it up when I say."

He took the receiver. She left the kitchen. He held the receiver to his ear and listened. He heard nothing. Then he heard a man clear his throat. Then he heard Vera pick up the other phone. She shouted, "Okay, Burt! I have it now, Burt!"

He put down the receiver and stood looking at it. He opened the silverware drawer and pushed things around inside. He opened another drawer. He looked in the sink. He went into the dining room and got the carving knife. He held it under hot water until the grease broke and ran off. He wiped the blade on his sleeve. He moved to the phone, doubled the cord, and sawed through without any trouble at all. He examined the ends of the cord. Then he shoved the phone back into its corner behind the roasting pan.

She came in. She said, "The phone went dead. Did you do anything to the telephone?" She looked at the phone and then picked it up from the counter.

"Son of a bitch!" she screamed. She screamed, "Out, out, where you belong!" She was shaking the phone at him. "That's it! I'm going to get a restraining order, that's what I'm going to get!"

The phone made a *ding* when she banged it down on the counter.

"I'm going next door to call the police if you don't get out of here now!"

He picked up the ashtray. He held it by its edge. He posed with it like a man preparing to hurl the discus.

"Please," she said. "That's our ashtray."

He left through the patio door. He was not certain, but he thought he had proved something. He hoped he had made something clear. The thing was, they had to have a serious talk soon. There were things that needed talking about, important things that had to be discussed. They'd talk again. Maybe after the holidays were over and things got back to normal. He'd tell her the goddamn ashtray was a goddamn dish, for example.

He stepped around the pie in the driveway and got back into his car. He started the car and put it into reverse. It was hard managing until he put the ashtray down.

What We Talk about When We Talk about Love

My friend Mel McGinnis was talking. Mel McGinnis is a cardiologist, and sometimes that gives him the right.

The four of us were sitting around his kitchen table drinking gin. Sunlight filled the kitchen from the big window behind the sink. There were Mel and me and his second wife, Teresa – Terri, we called her – and my wife, Laura. We lived in Albuquerque then. But we were all from somewhere else.

There was an ice bucket on the table. The gin and the tonic water kept going around, and we somehow got on the subject of love. Mel thought real love was nothing less than spiritual love. He said he'd spent five years in a seminary before quitting to go to medical school. He said he still looked back on those years in the seminary as the most important years in his life.

Terri said the man she lived with before she lived with Mel loved her so much he tried to kill her. Then Terri said, "He beat me up one night. He dragged me around the living room by my ankles. He kept saying, 'I love you, I love you, you bitch.' He went on dragging me around the living room. My head kept knocking on things." Terri looked around the table. "What do you do with love like that?"

She was a bone-thin woman with a pretty face, dark eyes, and brown hair that hung down her back. She liked necklaces made of turquoise, and long pendant earrings.

"My God, don't be silly. That's not love, and you know it," Mel said. "I don't know what you'd call it, but I sure know you wouldn't call it love."

"Say what you want to, but I know it was," Terri said. "It may sound crazy to you, but it's true just the same. People are different, Mel. Sure, sometimes he may have acted crazy. Okay.

But he loved me. In his own way maybe, but he loved me. There was love there, Mel. Don't say there wasn't."

Mel let out his breath. He held his glass and turned to Laura and me. "The man threatened to kill me," Mel said. He finished his drink and reached for the gin bottle. "Terri's a romantic. Terri's of the kick-me-so-I'll-know-you-love-me school. Terri, hon, don't look that way." Mel reached across the table and touched Terri's cheek with his fingers. He grinned at her.

"Now he wants to make up," Terri said.

"Make up what?" Mel said. "What is there to make up? I know what I know. That's all."

"How'd we get started on this subject, anyway?" Terri said. She raised her glass and drank from it. "Mel always has love on his mind," she said. "Don't you, honey?" She smiled, and I thought that was the last of it.

"I just wouldn't call Ed's behavior love. That's all I'm saying, honey," Mel said. "What about you guys?" Mel said to Laura and me. "Does that sound like love to you?"

"I'm the wrong person to ask," I said. "I didn't even know the man. I've only heard his name mentioned in passing. I wouldn't know. You'd have to know the particulars. But I think what you're saying is that love is an absolute."

Mel said, "The kind of love I'm talking about is. The kind of love I'm talking about, you don't try to kill people."

Laura said, "I don't know anything about Ed, or anything about the situation. But who can judge anyone else's situation?"

I touched the back of Laura's hand. She gave me a quick smile. I picked up Laura's hand. It was warm, the nails polished, perfectly manicured. I encircled the broad wrist with my fingers, and I held her.

"When I left, he drank rat poison," Terri said. She clasped her arms with her hands. "They took him to the hospital in Santa Fe. That's where we lived then, about ten miles out. They saved his life. But his gums went crazy from it. I mean they pulled away from his teeth. After that, his teeth stood out like fangs.

My God," Terri said. She waited a minute, then let go of her arms and picked up her glass.

"What people won't do!" Laura said.

"He's out of the action now," Mel said. "He's dead."

Mel handed me the saucer of limes. I took a section, squeezed it over my drink, and stirred the ice cubes with my finger.

"It gets worse," Terri said. "He shot himself in the mouth. But he bungled that too. Poor Ed," she said. Terri shook her head.

"Poor Ed nothing," Mel said. "He was dangerous."

Mel was forty-five years old. He was tall and rangy with curly soft hair. His face and arms were brown from the tennis he played. When he was sober, his gestures, all his movements, were precise, very careful.

"He did love me though, Mel. Grant me that," Terri said. "That's all I'm asking. He didn't love me the way you love me. I'm not saying that. But he loved me. You can grant me that, can't you?"

"What do you mean, he bungled it?" I said.

Laura leaned forward with her glass. She put her elbows on the table and held her glass in both hands. She glanced from Mel to Terri and waited with a look of bewilderment on her open face, as if amazed that such things happened to people you were friendly with.

"How'd he bungle it when he killed himself?" I said.

"I'll tell you what happened," Mel said. "He took this twenty-two pistol he'd bought to threaten Terri and me with. Oh, I'm serious, the man was always threatening. You should have seen the way we lived in those days. Like fugitives. I even bought a gun myself. Can you believe it? A guy like me? But I did. I bought one for self-defense and carried it in the glove compartment. Sometimes I'd have to leave the apartment in the middle of the night. To go to the hospital, you know? Terri and I weren't married then, and my first wife had the house and kids, the dog, everything, and Terri and I were living in this apartment here. Sometimes, as I say, I'd get a call in the middle of the night and have to go in to the hospital at two or three in the morning. It'd be dark out there in the parking lot, and I'd break into a sweat before I could even get to my car. I never knew if he was going to come up out of the shrubbery or from behind a car and start shooting. I mean, the man was crazy. He was capable of wiring a bomb, anything. He used to call my service at all hours and say he needed to talk to the doctor, and when I'd return the call, he'd say, 'Son of a bitch, your days are numbered.' Little things like that. It was scary, I'm telling you."

"I still feel sorry for him," Terri said.

"It sounds like a nightmare," Laura said. "But what exactly happened after he shot himself?"

Laura is a legal secretary. We'd met in a professional capacity. Before we knew it, it was a courtship. She's thirty-five, three years younger than I am. In addition to being in love, we like each other and enjoy one another's company. She's easy to be with.

"What happened?" Laura said.

Mel said, "He shot himself in the mouth in his room. Someone heard the shot and told the manager. They came in with a pass-key, saw what had happened, and called an ambulance. I happened to be there when they brought him in, alive but past recall. The man lived for three days. His head swelled up to twice the size of a normal head. I'd never seen anything like it, and I hope I never do again. Terri wanted to go in and sit with him when she found out about it. We had a fight over it. I didn't think she should see him like that. I didn't think she should see him, and I still don't."

"Who won the fight?" Laura said.

"I was in the room with him when he died," Terri said. "He never came up out of it. But I sat with him. He didn't have anyone else."

"He was dangerous," Mel said. "If you call that love, you can have it."

"It was love," Terri said. "Sure, it's abnormal in most people's eyes. But he was willing to die for it. He did die for it."

"I sure as hell wouldn't call it love," Mel said. "I mean, no one knows what he did it for. I've seen a lot of suicides, and I couldn't say anyone ever knew what they did it for."

Mel put his hands behind his neck and tilted his chair back. "I'm not interested in that kind of love," he said. "If that's love, you can have it."

Terri said, "We were afraid. Mel even made a will out and wrote to his brother in California who used to be a Green Beret. Mel told him who to look for if something happened to him."

Terri drank from her glass. She said, "But Mel's right – we lived like fugitives. We were afraid. Mel was, weren't you, honey? I even called the police at one point, but they were no help. They said they couldn't do anything until Ed actually did something. Isn't that a laugh?" Terri said.

She poured the last of the gin into her glass and waggled the bottle. Mel got up from the table and went to the cupboard. He took down another bottle.

"Well, Nick and I know what love is," Laura said. "For us, I mean," Laura said. She bumped my knee with her knee. "You're supposed to say something now," Laura said, and turned her smile on me.

For an answer, I took Laura's hand and raised it to my lips. I made a big production out of kissing her hand. Everyone was amused.

"We're lucky," I said.

"You guys," Terri said. "Stop that now. You're making me sick. You're still on the honeymoon, for God's sake. You're still gaga, for crying out loud. Just wait. How long have you been together now? How long has it been? A year? Longer than a year?"

"Going on a year and a half," Laura said, flushed and smiling.

"Oh, now," Terri said. "Wait awhile."

She held her drink and gazed at Laura.

"I'm only kidding," Terri said.

Mel opened the gin and went around the table with the bottle.

"Here, you guys," he said. "Let's have a toast. I want to propose a toast. A toast to love. To true love," Mel said.

We touched glasses.

"To love," we said.

Outside in the backyard, one of the dogs began to bark. The leaves of the aspen that leaned past the window ticked against the glass. The afternoon sun was like a presence in this room, the spacious light of ease and generosity. We could have been anywhere, somewhere enchanted. We raised our glasses again and grinned at each other like children who had agreed on something forbidden.

"I'll tell you what real love is," Mel said. "I mean, I'll give you a good example. And then you can draw your own conclusions." He poured more gin into his glass. He added an ice cube and a sliver of lime. We waited and sipped our drinks. Laura and I touched knees again. I put a hand on her warm thigh and left it there.

"What do any of us really know about love?" Mel said. "It seems to me we're just beginners at love. We say we love each other and we do, I don't doubt it. I love Terri and Terri loves me, and you guys love each other too. You know the kind of love I'm talking about now. Physical love, that impulse that drives you to someone special, as well as love of the other person's being, his or her essence, as it were. Carnal love and, well, call it sentimental love, the day-to-day caring about the other person. But sometimes I have a hard time accounting for the fact that I must have loved my first wife too. But I did, I know I did. So I suppose I am like Terri in that regard. Terri and Ed." He thought about it and then he went on. "There was a time when I thought I loved my first wife more than life itself. But now I hate her guts. I do. How do you explain that? What happened to that love? What happened to it, is what I'd like to know. I wish someone could tell me. Then there's Ed. Okay, we're back to Ed. He loves Terri so much he tries to kill her and he winds up killing himself." Mel stopped talking and swallowed from his glass. "You guys have been together eighteen months and you love each other. It shows all over you. You glow with it. But you both loved other people before you met each other. You've both been married before, just like us. And you probably loved other people before that too, even. Terri and I have been together five years, been married for four. And the terrible thing, the terrible thing is, but the good thing too, the saving grace, you might say, is that if something happened to one of us – excuse me for saying this – but if something happened to one of us tomorrow, I think the other one, the other person, would grieve for a while, you know, but then the surviving party would go out and love again, have someone else soon enough. All this, all of this love we're talking about, it would just be a memory. Maybe not even a memory. Am I wrong? Am I way off base? Because I want you to set me straight if you think I'm wrong. I want to know. I mean, I don't know anything, and I'm the first one to admit it."

"Mel, for God's sake," Terri said. She reached out and took hold of his wrist. "Are you getting drunk? Honey? Are you drunk?"

"Honey, I'm just talking," Mel said. "All right? I don't have to be drunk to say what I think. I mean, we're all just talking, right?" Mel said. He fixed his eyes on her.

"Sweetie, I'm not criticizing," Terri said.

She picked up her glass.

"I'm not on call today," Mel said. "Let me remind you of that. I am not on call," he said.

"Mel, we love you," Laura said.

Mel looked at Laura. He looked at her as if he could not place her, as if she was not the woman she was.

"Love you too, Laura," Mel said. "And you, Nick, love you too. You know something?" Mel said. "You guys are our pals," Mel said.

He picked up his glass.

Mel said, "I was going to tell you about something. I mean, I was going to prove a point. You see, this happened a few months ago, but it's still going on right now, and it ought to make us feel ashamed when we talk like we know what we're talking about when we talk about love."

144

"Come on now," Terri said. "Don't talk like you're drunk if you're not drunk."

"Just shut up for once in your life," Mel said very quietly. "Will you do me a favor and do that for a minute? So as I was saying, there's this old couple who had this car wreck out on the interstate. A kid hit them and they were all torn to shit and nobody was giving them much chance to pull through."

Terri looked at us and then back at Mel. She seemed anxious, or maybe that's too strong a word.

Mel was handing the bottle around the table.

"I was on call that night," Mel said. "It was May or maybe it was June. Terri and I had just sat down to dinner when the hospital called. There'd been this thing out on the interstate. Drunk kid, teenager, plowed his dad's pickup into this camper with this old couple in it. They were up in their mid-seventies, that couple. The kid – eighteen, nineteen, something – he was DOA. Taken the steering wheel through his sternum. The old couple, they were alive, you understand. I mean, just barely. But they had everything. Multiple fractures, internal injuries, hemorrhaging, contusions, lacerations, the works, and they each of them had themselves concussions. They were in a bad way, believe me. And, of course, their age was two strikes against them. I'd say she was worse off than he was. Ruptured spleen along with everything else. Both kneecaps broken. But they'd been wearing their seatbelts and, God knows, that's what saved them for the time being."

"Folks, this is an advertisement for the National Safety Council," Terri said. "This is your spokesman, Dr Melvin R. McGinnis, talking." Terri laughed. "Mel," she said, "sometimes you're just too much. But I love you, hon," she said.

"Honey, I love you," Mel said.

He leaned across the table. Terri met him halfway. They kissed.

"Terri's right," Mel said as he settled himself again. "Get those seatbelts on. But seriously, they were in some shape, those old-sters. By the time I got down there, the kid was dead, as I said. He was off in a corner, laid out on a gurney. I took one look at the old couple and told the ER nurse to get me a neurologist and an orthopedic man and a couple of surgeons down there right away."

He drank from his glass. "I'll try to keep this short," he said. "So we took the two of them up to the OR and worked like fuck on them most of the night. They had these incredible reserves, those two. You see that once in a while. So we did everything that could be done, and toward morning we're giving them a fifty-fifty chance, maybe less than that for her. So here they are, still alive the next morning. So, okay, we move them into the ICU, which is where they both kept plugging away at it for two weeks, hitting it better and better on all the scopes. So we transfer them out to their own room."

Mel stopped talking. "Here," he said, "let's drink this cheapo gin the hell up. Then we're going to dinner, right? Terri and I know a new place. That's where we'll go, to this new place we know about. But we're not going until we finish up this cut-rate, lousy gin."

Terri said, "We haven't actually eaten there yet. But it looks good. From the outside, you know."

"I like food," Mel said. "If I had it to do all over again, I'd be a chef, you know? Right, Terri?" Mel said.

He laughed. He fingered the ice in his glass.

"Terri knows," he said. "Terri can tell you. But let me say this. If I could come back again in a different life, a different time and all, you know what? I'd like to come back as a knight. You were pretty safe wearing all that armor. It was all right being a knight until gunpowder and muskets and pistols came along."

"Mel would like to ride a horse and carry a lance," Terri said.

"Carry a woman's scarf with you everywhere," Laura said.

"Or just a woman," Mel said.

"Shame on you," Laura said.

Terri said, "Suppose you came back as a serf. The serfs didn't have it so good in those days," Terri said.

"The serfs never had it good," Mel said. "But I guess even the knights were vessels to someone. Isn't that the way it worked? But then everyone is always a vessel to someone. Isn't that right, Terri? But what I liked about knights, besides their ladies, was

146

that they had that suit of armor, you know, and they couldn't get hurt very easy. No cars in those days, you know? No drunk teenagers to tear into your ass."

"Vassals," Terri said.

"What?" Mel said.

"Vassals," Terri said. "They were called vassals, not vessels."

"Vassals, vessels," Mel said, "what the fuck's the difference? You knew what I meant anyway. All right," Mel said. "So I'm not educated. I learned my stuff. I'm a heart surgeon, sure, but I'm just a mechanic. I go in and I fuck around and I fix things. Shit," Mel said.

"Modesty doesn't become you," Terri said.

"He's just a humble sawbones," I said. "But sometimes they suffocated in all that armor, Mel. They'd even have heart attacks if it got too hot and they were too tired and worn out. I read somewhere that they'd fall off their horses and not be able to get up because they were too tired to stand with all that armor on them. They got trampled by their own horses sometimes."

"That's terrible," Mel said. "That's a terrible thing, Nicky. I guess they'd just lay there and wait until somebody came along and made a shish kebab out of them."

"Some other vessel," Terri said.

"That's right," Mel said. "Some vassal would come along and spear the bastard in the name of love. Or whatever the fuck it was they fought over in those days."

"Same things we fight over these days," Terri said.

Laura said, "Nothing's changed."

The color was still high in Laura's cheeks. Her eyes were bright. She brought her glass to her lips.

Mel poured himself another drink. He looked at the label closely as if studying a long row of numbers. Then he slowly put the bottle down on the table and slowly reached for the tonic water.

"What about the old couple?" Laura said. "You didn't finish that story you started."

Laura was having a hard time lighting her cigarette. Her matches kept going out.

The sunshine inside the room was different now, changing, getting thinner. But the leaves outside the window were still shimmering, and I stared at the pattern they made on the panes and on the Formica counter. They weren't the same patterns, of course.

"What about the old couple?" I said.

"Older but wiser," Terri said.

Mel stared at her.

Terri said, "Go on with your story, hon. I was only kidding. Then what happened?"

"Terri, sometimes," Mel said.

"Please, Mel," Terri said. "Don't always be so serious, sweetie. Can't you take a joke?"

"Where's the joke?" Mel said.

He held his glass and gazed steadily at his wife.

"What happened?" Laura said.

Mel fastened his eyes on Laura. He said, "Laura, if I didn't have Terri and if I didn't love her so much, and if Nick wasn't my best friend, I'd fall in love with you. I'd carry you off, honey," he said.

"Tell your story," Terri said. "Then we'll go to that new place, okay?"

"Okay," Mel said. "Where was I?" he said. He stared at the table and then he began again.

"I dropped in to see each of them every day, sometimes twice a day if I was up doing other calls anyway. Casts and bandages, head to foot, the both of them. You know, you've seen it in the movies. That's just the way they looked, just like in the movies. Little eye-holes and nose-holes and mouth-holes. And she had to have her legs slung up on top of it. Well, the husband was very depressed for the longest while. Even after he found out that his wife was going to pull through, he was still very depressed. Not about the accident, though. I mean, the accident was one thing, but it wasn't everything. I'd get up to his mouth-hole, you know, and he'd say no, it wasn't the accident exactly but it was because

148

he couldn't see her through his eye-holes. He said that was what was making him feel so bad. Can you imagine? I'm telling you, the man's heart was breaking because he couldn't turn his god-damn head and *see* his goddamn wife.''

Mel looked around the table and shook his head at what he was going to say.

"I mean, it was killing the old fart just because he couldn't *look* at the fucking woman.''

We all looked at Mel.

"Do you see what I'm saying?'' he said.

Maybe we were a little drunk by then. I know it was hard keeping things in focus. The light was draining out of the room, going back through the window where it had come from. Yet nobody made a move to get up from the table to turn on the overhead light.

"Listen," Mel said. "Let's finish this fucking gin. There's about enough left here for one shooter all around. Then let's go eat. Let's go to the new place.''

"He's depressed," Terri said. "Mel, why don't you take a pill?''

Mel shook his head. "I've taken everything there is.''

"We all need a pill now and then," I said.

"Some people are born needing them," Terri said.

She was using her finger to rub at something on the table. Then she stopped rubbing.

"I think I want to call my kids," Mel said. "Is that all right with everybody? I'll call my kids," he said.

Terri said, "What if Marjorie answers the phone? You guys, you've heard us on the subject of Marjorie? Honey, you know you don't want to talk to Marjorie. It'll make you feel even worse.''

"I don't want to talk to Marjorie," Mel said. "But I want to talk to my kids.''

"There isn't a day goes by that Mel doesn't say he wishes she'd get married again. Or else die," Terri said. "For one thing," Terri said, "she's bankrupting us. Mel says it's just to spite him that she won't get married again. She has a boyfriend who lives with her and the kids, so Mel is supporting the boyfriend too."

"She's allergic to bees," Mel said. "If I'm not praying she'll get married again, I'm praying she'll get herself stung to death by a swarm of fucking bees."

"Shame on you," Laura said.

"Bzzzzzzz," Mel said, turning his fingers into bees and buzzing them at Terri's throat. Then he let his hands drop all the way to his sides.

"She's vicious," Mel said. "Sometimes I think I'll go up there dressed like a beekeeper. You know, that hat that's like a helmet with the plate that comes down over your face, the big gloves, and the padded coat? I'll knock on the door and let loose a hive of bees in the house. But first I'd make sure the kids were out, of course."

He crossed one leg over the other. It seemed to take him a lot of time to do it. Then he put both feet on the floor and leaned forward, elbows on the table, his chin cupped in his hands.

"Maybe I won't call the kids, after all. Maybe it isn't such a hot idea. Maybe we'll just go eat. How does that sound?"

"Sounds fine to me," I said. "Eat or not eat. Or keep drinking. I could head right on out into the sunset."

"What does that mean, honey?" Laura said.

"It just means what I said," I said. "It means I could just keep going. That's all it means."

"I could eat something myself," Laura said. "I don't think I've ever been so hungry in my life. Is there something to nibble on?"

"I'll put out some cheese and crackers," Terri said.

But Terri just sat there. She did not get up to get anything.

Mel turned his glass over. He spilled it out on the table.

"Gin's gone," Mel said.

Terri said, "Now what?"

I could hear my heart beating. I could hear everyone's heart. I could hear the human noise we sat there making, not one of us moving, not even when the room went dark.

Distance

She's in Milan for Christmas and wants to know what it was like when she was a kid. Always that on the rare occasions when he sees her.

Tell me, she says. Tell me what it was like then. She sips Strega, waits, eyes him closely.

She is a cool, slim, attractive girl, a survivor from top to bottom.

That was a long time ago. That was twenty years ago, he says. They're in his apartment on the Via Fabroni near the Cascina Gardens.

You can remember, she says. Go on, tell me.

What do you want to hear? he asks. What can I tell you? I could tell you about something that happened when you were a baby. It involves you, he says. But only in a minor way.

Tell me, she says. But first get us another drink, so you won't have to interrupt half way through.

He comes back from the kitchen with drinks, settles into his chair, begins.

They were kids themselves, but they were crazy in love, this eighteen-year-old boy and his seventeen-year-old girl friend when they married. Not all that long afterward they had a daughter.

The baby came along in late November during a severe cold spell that just happened to coincide with the peak of the waterfowl season in that part of the country. The boy loved to hunt, you see, that's part of it.

The boy and girl, husband and wife now, father and mother, lived in a three-room apartment under a dentist's office. Each night they cleaned the upstairs office in exchange for their rent and utilities. In the summer they were expected to maintain the lawn and the flowers, and in winter the boy shoveled snow from the walks and spread rock salt on the pavement. The two kids, I'm telling you, were very much in love. On top of this they had great ambitions and they were wild dreamers. They were always talking about the things they were going to do and the places they were going to go.

He gets up from his chair and looks out the window for a minute over the slate rooftops at the snow that falls steadily through the late afternoon light.

Tell the story, she says.

The boy and girl slept in the bedroom, and the baby slept in a crib in the living room. You see, the baby was about three weeks old at this time and had only just begun to sleep through the night.

One Saturday night, after finishing his work upstairs, the boy went into the dentist's private office, put his feet up on the desk, and called Carl Sutherland, an old hunting and fishing friend of his father's.

Carl, he said when the man picked up the receiver. I'm a father. We had a baby girl.

Congratulations, boy, Carl said. How is the wife?

She's fine, Carl. The baby's fine, too, the boy said. Everybody's fine.

That's good, Carl said. I'm glad to hear it. Well, you give my regards to the wife. If you called about going hunting, I'll tell you something. The geese are flying down there to beat the band. I don't think I've ever seen so many of them and I've been going for years. I shot five today. Two this morning and three this afternoon. I'm going back in the morning and you come along if you want to.

I want to, the boy said. That's why I called.

You be here at five-thirty sharp then and we'll go, Carl said. Bring lots of shells. We'll get some shooting in all right. I'll see you in the morning.

The boy liked Carl Sutherland. He'd been a friend of the boy's father, who was dead now. After the father's death, maybe trying to replace a loss they both felt, the boy and Sutherland had started hunting together. Sutherland was a lean, balding man who lived alone and was not given to casual talk. Once in a while, when they were together, the boy felt uncomfortable, wondered if he had said or done something wrong because he was not used to being around people who kept still for long periods of time. But when he did talk the older man was often opinionated, and frequently the boy didn't agree with the opinions. Yet the man had a toughness and woods-savvy about him that the boy liked and admired.

The boy hung up the telephone and went downstairs to tell the girl. She watched while he laid out his things. Hunting coat, shell bag, boots, socks, hunting cap, woolen underwear, pump gun.

What time will you be back? the girl asked.

Probably around noon, he said. But maybe not until after five or six o'clock. Is that too late?

It's fine, she said. We'll get along just fine. You go and have some fun. You deserve it. Maybe tomorrow evening we'll dress Catherine up and go visit Sally.

Sure, that sounds like a good idea, he said. Let's plan on that.

Sally was the girl's sister. She was ten years older. The boy was a little in love with her, just as he was a little in love with Betsy, who was another sister the girl had. He'd said to the girl, if we weren't married I could go for Sally.

What about Betsy? the girl had said. I hate to admit it but I truly feel she's better looking than Sally or me. What about her?

Betsy too, the boy said and laughed. But not in the same way I could go for Sally. There's something about Sally you could fall for. No, I believe I'd prefer Sally over Betsy, if I had to make a choice.

But who do you really love? the girl asked. Who do you love most in all the world? Who's your wife?

You're my wife, the boy said.

And will we always love each other? the girl asked, enormously enjoying this conversation he could tell.

Always, the boy said. And we'll always be together. We're

like the Canada geese, he said, taking the first comparison that came to mind, for they were often on his mind in those days. They only mate once. They choose a mate early in life, and they stay together always. If one of them dies or something, the other one will live by itself, or even continue to live with the flock, but it will stay single and alone amongst all the other geese.

That's sad, the girl said. It's sadder for it to live that way, I think, alone but with all the others, than just to live off by itself somewhere.

It is sad, the boy said. But it's Nature.

Have you ever killed one of those? she asked. You know what I mean.

He nodded. He said, Two or three times I've shot a goose, then a minute or two later I'd see another goose turn back from the rest and begin to circle and call over the goose that lay on the ground.

Did you shoot it too? she asked with concern.

If I could, he answered. Sometimes I missed.

And it didn't bother you? she said.

Never, he said. You can't think about it when you're doing it. You see, I love everything there is about geese. I love to just watch them even when I'm not hunting them. But there are all kinds of contradictions in life. You can't think about the contradictions.

After dinner he turned up the furnace and helped her bathe the baby. He marveled again at the infant who had half his features, the eyes and mouth, and half the girl's, the chin and the nose. He powdered the tiny body and then powdered in between the fingers and toes. He watched the girl put the baby into its diaper and pajamas.

He emptied the bath into the shower basin and then he went upstairs. It was cold and overcast outside. His breath streamed in the air. The grass, what there was of it, looked like canvas, stiff and gray under the street light. Snow lay in piles beside the walk. A car went by and he heard sand grinding under the tires. He let himself imagine what it might be like tomorrow, geese milling in the air over his head, the gun plunging against his shoulder.

Then he locked the door and went downstairs.

In bed they tried to read but both of them fell asleep, she first, letting the magazine sink to the quilt. His eyes closed, but he roused himself, checked the alarm, and turned off the lamp.

He woke to the baby's cries. The light was on out in the living room. He could see the girl standing beside the crib rocking the baby in her arms. In a minute she put the baby down, turned out the light and came back to bed.

It was two o'clock in the morning and the boy fell asleep once more.

The baby's cries woke him again. This time the girl continued to sleep. The baby cried fitfully for a few minutes and stopped. The boy listened, then began to doze.

He opened his eyes. The living room light was burning. He sat up and turned on the lamp.

I don't know what's wrong, the girl said, walking back and forth with the baby. I've changed her and given her something more to eat. But she keeps crying. She won't stop crying. I'm so tired I'm afraid I might drop her.

You come back to bed, the boy said. I'll hold her for a while.

He got up and took the baby while the girl went to lie down.

Just rock her for a few minutes, the girl said from the bedroom. Maybe she'll go back to sleep.

The boy sat on the sofa and held the baby. He jiggled it in his lap until its eyes closed. His own eyes were near closing. He rose carefully and put the baby back in the crib.

It was fifteen minutes to four and he still had forty-five minutes that he could sleep. He crawled into bed.

But a few minutes later the baby began to cry once more. This time they both got up, and the boy swore.

For God's sake what's the matter with you? the girl said to him. Maybe she's sick or something. Maybe we shouldn't have given her the bath.

The boy picked up the baby. The baby kicked its feet and was quiet. Look, the boy said, I really don't think there's anything wrong with her.

How do you know that? the girl said. Here, let me have her. I know that I ought to give her something, but I don't know what I should give her.

After a few minutes had passed and the baby had not cried, the girl put the baby down again. The boy and the girl looked at the baby, and then they looked at each other as the baby opened its eyes and began to cry.

The girl took the baby. Baby, baby, she said with tears in her eyes.

Probably it's something on her stomach, the boy said.

The girl didn't answer. She went on rocking the baby in her arms, paying no attention now to the boy.

The boy waited a minute longer then went to the kitchen and put on water for coffee. He drew on his woolen underwear and buttoned up. Then he got into his clothes.

What are you doing? the girl said to him.

Going hunting, he said.

I don't think you should, she said. Maybe you could go later on in the day if the baby is all right then. But I don't think you should go hunting this morning. I don't want to be left alone with the baby crying like this.

Carl's planning on me going, the boy said. We've planned it.

I don't give a damn about what you and Carl have planned, she said. And I don't give a damn about Carl, either. I don't even know the man. I don't want you to go is all. I don't think you should even consider wanting to go under the circumstances.

You've met Carl before, you know him, the boy said. What do you mean you don't know him?

That's not the point and you know it, the girl said. The point is I don't intend to be left alone with a sick baby.

Wait a minute, the boy said. You don't understand.

No, you don't understand, she said. I'm your wife. This is your baby. She's sick or something. Look at her. Why is she crying? You can't leave us to go hunting.

Don't get hysterical, he said.

I'm saying you can go hunting any time, she said. Something's wrong with this baby and you want to leave us to go hunting.

She began to cry. She put the baby back in the crib, but the baby started up again. The girl dried her eyes hastily on the sleeve of her nightgown and picked the baby up once more.

The boy laced his boots slowly, put on his shirt, sweater, and his coat. The kettle whistled on the stove in the kitchen.

You're going to have to choose, the girl said. Carl or us. I mean it, you've got to choose.

What do you mean? the boy said.

You heard what I said, the girl answered. If you want a family you're going to have to choose.

They stared at each other. Then the boy took his hunting gear and went upstairs. He started the car, went around to the windows, and, making a job of it, scraped away the ice.

The temperature had dropped during the night, but the weather had cleared so that stars had come out. The stars gleamed in the sky over his head. Driving, the boy looked out at the stars and was moved when he considered their distance.

Carl's porchlight was on, his station wagon parked in the drive with the motor idling. Carl came outside as the boy pulled to the curb. The boy had decided.

You might want to park off the street, Carl said as the boy came up the walk. I'm ready, just let me hit the lights. I feel like hell, I really do, he went on. I thought maybe you had overslept so I just this minute called your place. Your wife said you had left. I feel like hell.

It's okay, the boy said, trying to pick his words. He leaned his weight on one leg and turned up his collar. He put his hands in his coat pockets. She was already up, Carl. We've both been up for a while. I guess there's something wrong with the baby. I don't know. The baby keeps crying, I mean. The thing is, I guess I can't go this time, Carl.

You should have just stepped to the phone and called me, boy, Carl said. It's okay. You know you didn't have to come over here to tell me. What the hell, this hunting business you can take it or leave it. It's not important. You want a cup of coffee?

I'd better get back, the boy said.

Well, I expect I'll go ahead then, Carl said. He looked at the boy.

The boy kept standing on the porch, not saying anything.

It's cleared up, Carl said. I don't look for much action this morning. Probably you won't have missed anything anyway.

The boy nodded. I'll see you, Carl, he said.

So long, Carl said. Hey, don't let anybody ever tell you otherwise, Carl said. You're a lucky boy and I mean that.

The boy started his car and waited. He watched Carl go through the house and turn off all the lights. Then the boy put the car in gear and pulled away from the curb.

The living room light was on, but the girl was asleep on the bed and the baby was asleep beside her.

The boy took off his boots, pants, and shirt. He was quiet about it. In his socks and woolen underwear, he sat on the sofa and read the morning paper.

Soon it began to turn light outside. The girl and the baby slept on. After a while the boy went to the kitchen and began to fry bacon.

The girl came out in her robe a few minutes later and put her arms around him without saying anything.

Hey, don't catch your robe on fire, the boy said. She was leaning against him but touching the stove, too.

I'm sorry about earlier, she said. I don't know what got into me. I don't know why I said those things.

It's all right, he said. Here, let me get this bacon.

I didn't mean to snap like that, she said. It was awful.

It was my fault, he said. How's Catherine?

She's fine now. I don't know what was the matter with her earlier. I changed her again after you left, and then she was fine. She was just fine and she went right off to sleep. I don't know what it was. Don't be mad with us.

The boy laughed. I'm not mad with you. Don't be silly, he said. Here, let me do something with this pan.

You sit down, the girl said. I'll fix this breakfast. How does a waffle sound with this bacon?

Sounds great, he said. I'm starved.

She took the bacon out of the pan and then she made waffle batter. He sat at the table, relaxed now, and watched her move around the kitchen.

She left to close their bedroom door. In the living room she put on a record that they both liked.

We don't want to wake that one up again, the girl said.

That's for sure, the boy said and laughed.

She put a plate in front of him with bacon, a fried egg, and a waffle. She put another plate on the table for herself. It's ready, she said.

It looks swell, he said. He spread butter and poured syrup over the waffle. But as he started to cut into the waffle, he turned the plate into his lap.

I don't believe it, he said, jumping up from the table.

The girl looked at him and then at the expression on his face. She began to laugh.

If you could see yourself in the mirror, she said. She kept laughing.

He looked down at the syrup that covered the front of his woolen underwear, at the pieces of waffle, bacon, and egg that clung to the syrup. He began to laugh.

I was starved, he said, shaking his head.

You were starved, she said, laughing.

He peeled off the woolen underwear and threw it at the bathroom door. Then he opened his arms and she moved into them.

We won't fight any more, she said. It's not worth it, is it?

That's right, he said.

We won't fight any more, she said.

The boy said, We won't. Then he kissed her.

He gets up from his chair and refills their glasses.

That's it, he says. End of story. I admit it's not much of one.

I was interested, she says. It was very interesting if you want to know. But what happened? she says. I mean later.

He shrugs and carries his drink over to the window. It's dark now but still snowing.

Things change, he says. I don't know how they do. But they do without your realizing it or wanting them to.

Yes, that's true, only – but she does not finish what she started.

She drops the subject then. In the window's reflection he sees her study her nails. Then she raises her head. Speaking brightly, she asks if he is going to show her the city, after all.

He says, Put your boots on and let's go.

But he stays by the window, remembering that life. They had laughed. They had leaned on each other and laughed until the tears had come, while everything else – the cold and where he'd go in it – was outside, for a while anyway.

The Third Thing that Killed
My Father Off

I'll tell you what did my father in. The third thing was Dummy, that Dummy died. The first thing was Pearl Harbor. And the second thing was moving to my grandfather's farm near Wenatchee. That's where my father finished out his days, except they were probably finished before that.

My father blamed Dummy's death on Dummy's wife. Then he blamed it on the fish. And finally he blamed himself – because he was the one that showed Dummy the ad in the back of *Field and Stream* for live black bass shipped anywhere in the U.S.

It was after he got the fish that Dummy started acting peculiar. The fish changed Dummy's whole personality. That's what my father said.

I never knew Dummy's real name. If anyone did, I never heard it. Dummy it was then, and it's Dummy I remember him by now. He was a little wrinkled man, bald-headed, short but very powerful in the arms and legs. If he grinned, which was seldom, his lips folded back over brown, broken teeth. It gave him a crafty expression. His watery eyes stayed fastened on your mouth when you were talking – and if you weren't, they'd go to someplace queer on your body.

I don't think he was really deaf. At least not as deaf as he made out. But he sure couldn't talk. That was for certain.

Deaf or no, Dummy'd been on as a common laborer out at the sawmill since the 1920s. This was the Cascade Lumber Company in Yakima, Washington. The years I knew him, Dummy was working as a cleanup man. And all those years I never saw him with anything different on. Meaning a felt hat, a khaki workshirt, a denim jacket over a pair of coveralls. In his top pockets he carried rolls of toilet paper, as one of his jobs was to clean and supply the toilets. It kept him busy, seeing as how the men on nights used to walk off after their shifts with a roll or two in their lunchboxes.

Dummy carried a flashlight, even though he worked days. He also carried wrenches, pliers, screwdrivers, friction tape, all the same things the millwrights carried. Well, it made them kid Dummy, the way he was, always carrying everything. Carl Lowe, Ted Slade, Johnny Wait, they were the worst kidders of the ones that kidded Dummy. But Dummy took it all in stride. I think he'd gotten used to it.

My father never kidded Dummy. Not to my knowledge, anyway. Dad was a big, heavy-shouldered man with a crew-haircut, double chin, and a belly of real size. Dummy was always staring at that belly. He'd come to the filing room where my father worked, and he'd sit on a stool and watch my dad's belly while he used the big emery wheels on the saws.

Dummy had a house as good as anyone's.

It was a tarpaper-covered affair near the river, five or six miles from town. Half a mile behind the house, at the end of a pasture, there lay a big gravel pit that the state had dug when they were paving the roads around there. Three good-sized holes had been scooped out, and over the years they'd filled with water. By and by, the three ponds came together to make one.

It was deep. It had a darkish look to it.

Dummy had a wife as well as a house. She was a woman years younger and said to go around with Mexicans. Father said it was busybodies that said that, men like Lowe and Wait and Slade.

She was a small stout woman with glittery little eyes. The first time I saw her, I saw those eyes. It was when I was with Pete Jensen and we were on our bicycles and we stopped at Dummy's to get a glass of water.

When she opened the door, I told her I was Del Fraser's son. I said, "He works with –" And then I realized. "You know, your husband. We were on our bicycles and thought we could get a drink."

"Wait here," she said.

She came back with a little tin cup of water in each hand. I downed mine in a single gulp.

But she didn't offer us more. She watched us without saying anything. When we started to get on our bicycles, she came over to the edge of the porch.

"You little fellas had a car now, I might catch a ride with you."

She grinned. Her teeth looked too big for her mouth.

"Let's go," Pete said, and we went.

There weren't many places you could fish for bass in our part of the state. There was rainbow mostly, a few brook and Dolly Varden in some of the high mountain streams, and silvers in Blue Lake and Lake Rimrock. That was mostly it, except for the runs of steelhead and salmon in some of the freshwater rivers in late fall. But if you were a fisherman, it was enough to keep you busy. No one fished for bass. A lot of people I knew had never seen a bass except for pictures. But my father had seen plenty of them when he was growing up in Arkansas and Georgia, and he had high hopes to do with Dummy's bass, Dummy being a friend.

The day the fish arrived, I'd gone swimming at the city pool. I remember coming home and going out again to get them since Dad was going to give Dummy a hand – three tanks Parcel Post from Baton Rouge, Louisiana.

We went in Dummy's pickup, Dad and Dummy and me.

These tanks turned out to be barrels, really, the three of them crated in pine lath. They were standing in the shade out back of the train depot, and it took my dad and Dummy both to lift each crate into the truck.

Dummy drove very carefully through town and just as carefully all the way to his house. He went right through his yard without stopping. He went on down to within feet of the pond. By that time it was nearly dark, so he kept his headlights on and took out a hammer and a tire iron from under the seat, and then the two of them lugged the crates up close to the water and started tearing open the first one.

163

The barrel inside was wrapped in burlap, and there were these nickel-sized holes in the lid. They raised it off and Dummy aimed his flashlight in.

It looked like a million bass fingerlings were finning inside. It was the strangest sight, all those live things busy in there, like a little ocean that had come on the train.

Dummy scooted the barrel to the edge of the water and poured it out. He took his flashlight and shined it into the pond. But there was nothing to be seen anymore. You could hear the frogs going, but you could hear them going anytime it newly got dark.

"Let me get the other crates," my father said, and he reached over as if to take the hammer from Dummy's coveralls. But Dummy pulled back and shook his head.

He undid the other two crates himself, leaving dark drops of blood on the lath where he ripped his hand doing it.

From that night on, Dummy was different.

Dummy wouldn't let anyone come around now anymore. He put up fencing all around the pasture, and then he fenced off the pond with electrical barbed wire. They said it cost him all his savings for that fence.

Of course, my father wouldn't have anything to do with Dummy after that. Not since Dummy ran him off. Not from fishing, mind you, because the bass were just babies still. But even from trying to get a look.

One evening two years after, when Dad was working late and I took him his food and a jar of iced tea, I found him standing talking with Syd Glover, the millwright. Just as I came in, I heard Dad saying, "You'd reckon the fool was married to them fish, the way he acts."

"From what I hear," Syd said, "he'd do better to put that fence round his house."

My father saw me then, and I saw him signal Syd Glover with his eyes.

But a month later my dad finally made Dummy do it. What he did was, he told Dummy how you had to thin out the weak ones on account of keeping things fit for the rest of them.

Dummy stood there pulling at his ear and staring at the floor. Dad said, Yeah, he'd be down to do it tomorrow because it had to be done. Dummy never said yes, actually. He just never said no, is all. All he did was pull on his ear some more.

When Dad got home that day, I was ready and waiting. I had his old bass plugs out and was testing the treble hooks with my finger.

"You set?" he called to me, jumping out of the car. "I'll go to the toilet, you put the stuff in. You can drive us out there if you want."

I'd stowed everything in the back seat and was trying out the wheel when he came back out wearing his fishing hat and eating a wedge of cake with both hands.

Mother was standing in the door watching. She was a fair-skinned woman, her blonde hair pulled back in a tight bun and fastened down with a rhinestone clip. I wonder if she ever went around back in those happy days, or what she ever really did.

I let out the handbrake. Mother watched until I'd shifted gears, and then, still unsmiling, she went back inside.

It was a fine afternoon. We had all the windows down to let the air in. We crossed the Moxee Bridge and swung west onto Slater Road. Alfalfa fields stood off to either side, and farther on it was cornfields.

Dad had his hand out the window. He was letting the wind carry it back. He was restless, I could see.

It wasn't long before we pulled up at Dummy's. He came out of the house wearing his hat. His wife was looking out the window.

"You got your frying pan ready?" Dad hollered out to Dummy, but Dummy just stood there eyeing the car. "Hey, Dummy!" Dad yelled. "Hey, Dummy, where's your pole, Dummy?"

Dummy jerked his head back and forth. He moved his weight from one leg to the other and looked at the ground and then at us. His tongue rested on his lower lip, and he began working his foot into the dirt.

I shouldered the creel. I handed Dad his pole and picked up my own.

"We set to go?" Dad said. "Hey, Dummy, we set to go?"

Dummy took off his hat and, with the same hand, he wiped his wrist over his head. He turned abruptly, and we followed him across the spongy pasture. Every twenty feet or so a snipe sprang up from the clumps of grass at the edge of the old furrows.

At the end of the pasture, the ground sloped gently and became dry and rocky, nettle bushes and scrub oaks scattered here and there. We cut to the right, following an old set of car tracks, going through a field of milkweed that came up to our waists, the dry pods at the tops of the stalks rattling angrily as we pushed through. Presently, I saw the sheen of water over Dummy's shoulder, and I heard Dad shout, "Oh, Lord, look at that!"

But Dummy slowed down and kept bringing his hand up and moving his hat back and forth over his head, and then he just stopped flat.

Dad said, "Well, what do you think, Dummy? One place good as another? Where do you say we should come onto it?"

Dummy wet his lower lip.

"What's the matter with you, Dummy?" Dad said. "This your pond, ain't it?"

Dummy looked down and picked an ant off his coveralls.

"Well, hell," Dad said, letting out his breath. He took out his watch. "If it's still all right with you, we'll get to it before it gets too dark."

Dummy stuck his hands in his pockets and turned back to the pond. He started walking again. We trailed along behind. We could see the whole pond now, the water dimpled with rising fish. Every so often a bass would leap clear and come down in a splash.

"Great God," I heard my father say.

We came up to the pond at an open place, a gravel beach kind of.

Dad motioned to me and dropped into a crouch. I dropped

166

too. He was peering into the water in front of us, and when I looked, I saw what had taken him so.

"Honest to God," he whispered.

A school of bass was cruising, twenty, thirty, not one of them under two pounds. They veered off, and then they shifted and came back, so densely spaced they looked like they were bumping up against each other. I could see their big, heavy-lidded eyes watching us as they went by. They flashed away again, and again they came back.

They were asking for it. It didn't make any difference if we stayed squatted or stood up. The fish just didn't think a thing about us. I tell you, it was a sight to behold.

We sat there for quite a while, watching that school of bass go so innocently about their business, Dummy the whole time pulling at his fingers and looking around as if he expected someone to show up. All over the pond the bass were coming up to nuzzle the water, or jumping clear and falling back, or coming up to the surface to swim along with their dorsals sticking out.

Dad signaled, and we got up to cast. I tell you, I was shaky with excitement. I could hardly get the plug loose from the cork handle of my pole. It was while I was trying to get the hooks out that I felt Dummy seize my shoulder with his big fingers. I looked, and in answer Dummy worked his chin in Dad's direction. What he wanted was clear enough, no more than one pole.

Dad took off his hat and then put it back on and then he moved over to where I stood.

"You go on, Jack," he said. "That's all right, son – you do it now."

I looked at Dummy just before I laid out my cast. His face had gone rigid, and there was a thin line of drool on his chin.

"Come back stout on the sucker when he strikes," Dad said. "Sons of bitches got mouths hard as doorknobs."

I flipped off the drag lever and threw back my arm. I sent her out a good forty feet. The water was boiling even before I had time to take up the slack.

"Hit him!" Dad yelled. "Hit the son of a bitch! Hit him good!"

I came back hard, twice. I had him, all right. The rod bowed over and jerked back and forth. Dad kept yelling what to do.

"Let him go, let him go! Let him run! Give him more line! Now wind in! Wind in! No, let him run! Woo-ee! Will you look at that!"

The bass danced around the pond. Every time it came up out of the water, it shook its head so hard you could hear the plug rattle. And then he'd take off again. But by and by I wore him out and had him in up close. He looked enormous, six or seven pounds maybe. He lay on his side, whipped, mouth open, gills working. My knees felt so weak I could hardly stand. But I held the rod up, the line tight.

Dad waded out over his shoes. But when he reached for the fish, Dummy started sputtering, shaking his head, waving his arms.

"Now what the hell's the matter with you, Dummy? The boy's got hold of the biggest bass I ever seen, and he ain't going to throw him back, by God!"

Dummy kept carrying on and gesturing toward the pond.

"I ain't about to let this boy's fish go. You hear me, Dummy? You got another think coming if you think I'm going to do that."

Dummy reached for my line. Meanwhile, the bass had gained some strength back. He turned himself over and started swimming again. I yelled and then I lost my head and slammed down the brake on the reel and started winding. The bass made a last, furious run.

That was that. The line broke. I almost fell over on my back.

"Come on, Jack," Dad said, and I saw him grabbing up his pole. "Come on, goddamn the fool, before I knock the man down."

That February the river flooded.

It had snowed pretty heavy the first weeks of December, and turned real cold before Christmas. The ground froze. The snow stayed where it was. But toward the end of January, the Chinook wind struck. I woke up one morning to hear the house getting buffeted and the steady drizzle of water running off the roof.

It blew for five days, and on the third day the river began to rise.

"She's up to fifteen feet," my father said one evening, looking over his newspaper. "Which is three feet over what you need to flood. Old Dummy going to lose his darlings."

I wanted to go down to the Moxee Bridge to see how high the water was running. But my dad wouldn't let me. He said a flood was nothing to see.

Two days later the river crested, and after that the water began to subside.

Orin Marshall and Danny Owens and I bicycled out to Dummy's one morning a week after. We parked our bicycles and walked across the pasture that bordered Dummy's property.

It was a wet, blustery day, the clouds dark and broken, moving fast across the sky. The ground was soppy wet and we kept coming to puddles in the thick grass. Danny was just learning how to cuss, and he filled the air with the best he had every time he stepped in over his shoes. We could see the swollen river at the end of the pasture. The water was still high and out of its channel, surging around the trunks of trees and eating away at the edge of the land. Out toward the middle, the current moved heavy and swift, and now and then a bush floated by, or a tree with its branches sticking up.

We came to Dummy's fence and found a cow wedged in up against the wire. She was bloated and her skin was shiny-looking and gray. It was the first dead thing of any size I'd ever seen. I remember Orin took a stick and touched the open eyes.

We moved on down the fence, toward the river. We were afraid to go near the wire because we thought it might still have electricity in it. But at the edge of what looked like a deep canal, the fence came to an end. The ground had simply dropped into the water here, and the fence along with it.

We crossed over and followed the new channel that cut directly into Dummy's land and headed straight for his pond, going into it lengthwise and forcing an outlet for itself at the other end, then twisting off until it joined up with the river farther on.

You didn't doubt that most of Dummy's fish had been carried

off. But those that hadn't been were free to come and go.

Then I caught sight of Dummy. It scared me, seeing him. I motioned to the other fellows, and we all got down.

Dummy was standing at the far side of the pond near where the water was rushing out. He was just standing there, the saddest man I ever saw.

"I sure do feel sorry for old Dummy, though," my father said at supper a few weeks after. "Mind, the poor devil brought it on himself. But you can't help but be troubled for him."

Dad went on to say George Laycock saw Dummy's wife sitting in the Sportsman's Club with a big Mexican fellow.

"And that ain't the half of it – "

Mother looked up at him sharply and then at me. But I just went on eating like I hadn't heard a thing.

Dad said, "Damn it to hell, Bea, the boy's old enough!"

He'd changed a lot, Dummy had. He was never around any of the men anymore, not if he could help it. No one felt like joking with him either, not since he'd chased Carl Lowe with a two-by-four stud after Carl tipped Dummy's hat off. But the worst of it was that Dummy was missing from work a day or two a week on the average now, and there was some talk of his being laid off.

"The man's going off the deep end," Dad said. "Clear crazy if he don't watch out."

Then on a Sunday afternoon just before my birthday, Dad and I were cleaning the garage. It was a warm, drifty day. You could see the dust hanging in the air. Mother came to the back door and said, "Del, it's for you. I think it's Vern."

I followed Dad in to wash up. When he was through talking, he put the phone down and turned to us.

"It's Dummy," he said. "Did in his wife with a hammer and drowned himself. Vern just heard it in town."

When we got out there, cars were parked all around. The gate to the pasture stood open, and I could see tire marks that led on to the pond.

The screen door was propped ajar with a box, and there was this lean, pock-faced man in slacks and sports shirt and wearing a shoulder holster. He watched Dad and me get out of the car.

"I was his friend," Dad said to the man.

The man shook his head. "Don't care who you are. Clear off unless you got business here."

"Did they find him?" Dad said.

"They're dragging," the man said, and adjusted the fit of his gun.

"All right if we walk down? I knew him pretty well."

The man said, "Take your chances. They chase you off, don't say you wasn't warned."

We went on across the pasture, taking pretty much the same route we had the day we tried fishing. There were motorboats going on the pond, dirty fluffs of exhaust hanging over it. You could see where the high water had cut away the ground and carried off trees and rocks. The two boats had uniformed men in them, and they were going back and forth, one man steering and the other man handling the rope and hooks.

An ambulance waited on the gravel beach where we'd set ourselves to cast for Dummy's bass. Two men in white lounged against the back, smoking cigarettes.

One of the motorboats cut off. We all looked up. The man in back stood up and started heaving on his rope. After a time, an arm came out of the water. It looked like the hooks had gotten Dummy in the side. The arm went back down and then it came out again, along with a bundle of something.

It's not him, I thought. It's something else that has been in there for years.

The man in the front of the boat moved to the back, and together the two men hauled the dripping thing over the side.

I looked at Dad. His face was funny the way it was set.

"Women," he said. He said, "That's what the wrong kind of woman can do to you, Jack."

But I don't think Dad really believed it. I think he just didn't know who to blame or what to say.

It seemed to me everything took a bad turn for my father after that. Just like Dummy, he wasn't the same man anymore. That arm coming up and going back down in the water, it was like so long to good times and hello to bad. Because it was nothing but that all the years after Dummy drowned himself in that dark water.

Is that what happens when a friend dies? Bad luck for the pals he left behind?

But as I said, Pearl Harbor and having to move back to his dad's place didn't do my dad one bit of good, either.

So Much Water So Close to Home

My husband eats with good appetite but he seems tired, edgy. He chews slowly, arms on the table, and stares at something across the room. He looks at me and looks away again. He wipes his mouth on the napkin. He shrugs and goes on eating. Something has come between us though he would like me to believe otherwise.

"What are you staring at me for?" he asks. "What is it?" he says and puts his fork down.

"Was I staring?" I say and shake my head stupidly, stupidly.

The telephone rings. "Don't answer it," he says.

"It might be your mother," I say. "Dean – it might be something about Dean."

"Watch and see," he says.

I pick up the receiver and listen for a minute. He stops eating. I bite my lip and hang up.

"What did I tell you?" he says. He starts to eat again, then throws the napkin onto his plate. "Goddamn it, why can't people mind their own business? Tell me what I did wrong and I'll listen! It's not fair. She was dead, wasn't she? There were other men there besides me. We talked it over and we all decided. We'd only just got there. We'd walked for hours. We couldn't just turn around, we were five miles from the car. It was opening day. What the hell, I don't see anything wrong. No, I don't. And don't look at me that way, do you hear? I won't have you passing judgment on me. Not you."

"You know," I say and shake my head.

"What do I know, Claire? Tell me. Tell me what I know. I don't know anything except one thing: you hadn't better get worked up over this." He gives me what he thinks is a *meaningful* look. "She was dead, dead, dead, do you hear?" he says after a

173

minute. "It's a damn shame, I agree. She was a young girl and it's a shame, and I'm sorry, as sorry as anyone else, but she was dead, Claire, dead. Now let's leave it alone. Please, Claire. Let's leave it alone now."

"That's the point," I say. "She was dead. But don't you see? She needed help."

"I give up," he says and raises his hands. He pushes his chair away from the table, takes his cigarettes and goes out to the patio with a can of beer. He walks back and forth for a minute and then sits in a lawn chair and picks up the paper once more. His name is there on the first page along with the names of his friends, the other men who made the "grisly find".

I close my eyes for a minute and hold onto the drainboard. I must not dwell on this any longer. I must get over it, put it out of sight, out of mind, etc., and "go on". I open my eyes. Despite everything, knowing all that may be in store, I rake my arm across the drainboard and send the dishes and glasses smashing and scattering across the floor.

He doesn't move. I know he has heard, he raises his head as if listening, but he doesn't move otherwise, doesn't turn around to look. I hate him for that, for not moving. He waits a minute, then draws on his cigarette and leans back in the chair. I pity him for listening, detached, and then settling back and drawing on his cigarette. The wind takes the smoke out of his mouth in a thin stream. Why do I notice that? He can never know how much I pity him for that, for sitting still and listening, and letting the smoke stream out of his mouth. . . .

He planned his fishing trip into the mountains last Sunday, a week before the Memorial Day weekend. He and Gordon Johnson, Mel Dorn, Vern Williams. They play poker, bowl, and fish together. They fish together every spring and early summer, the first two or three months of the season, before family vacations, little league baseball, and visiting relatives can intrude. They are decent men, family men, responsible at their jobs. They have sons and daughters who go to school with our son, Dean. On Friday afternoon these four men left for a three-day fishing trip to the Naches River. They parked the car in the mountains and hiked several miles to where they wanted to fish. They carried their bedrolls, food and cooking utensils, their playing cards, their whiskey. The first evening at the river, even before they could set up camp, Mel Dorn found the girl floating face down in the river, nude, lodged near the shore in some branches. He called the other men and they all came to look at her. They talked about what to do. One of the men – Stuart didn't say which – perhaps it was Vern Williams, he is a heavy-set, easy man who laughs often – one of them thought they should start back to the car at once. The others stirred the sand with their shoes and said they felt inclined to stay. They pleaded fatigue, the late hour, the fact that the girl "wasn't going anywhere". In the end they all decided to stay. They went ahead and set up the camp and built a fire and drank their whiskey. They drank a lot of whiskey and when the moon came up they talked about the girl. Someone thought they should do something to prevent the body from floating away. Somehow they thought that this might create a problem for them if it floated away during the night. They took flashlights and stumbled down to the river. The wind was up, a cold wind, and waves from the river lapped the sandy bank. One of the men, I don't know who, it might have been Stuart, he could have done it, waded into the water and took the girl by the fingers and pulled her, still face down, closer to shore, into shallow water, and then took a piece of nylon cord and tied it around her wrist and then secured the cord to tree roots, all the while the flashlights of the other men played over the girl's body. Afterward, they went back to camp and drank more whiskey. Then they went to sleep. The next morning, Saturday, they cooked breakfast, drank lots of coffee, more whiskey, and then split up to fish, two men upriver, two men down.

That night, after they had cooked their fish and potatoes and had more coffee and whiskey, they took their dishes down to the river and rinsed them off a few yards from where the body lay in the water. They drank again and then they took out their cards and played and drank until they couldn't see the cards any longer. Vern Williams went to sleep, but the others told coarse stories and spoke of vulgar or dishonest escapades out of their past, and no one mentioned the girl until Gordon Johnson, who'd forgotten for a minute, commented on the firmness of the trout they'd caught, and the terrible coldness of the river water. They stopped talking then but continued to drink until one of them tripped and fell cursing against the lantern, and then they climbed into their sleeping bags.

The next morning they got up late, drank more whiskey, fished a little as they kept drinking whiskey. Then, at one o'clock in the afternoon, Sunday, a day earlier than they'd planned, they decided to leave. They took down their tents, rolled their sleeping bags, gathered their pans, pots, fish, and fishing gear, and hiked out. They didn't look at the girl again before they left. When they reached the car they drove the highway in silence until they came to a telephone. Stuart made the call to the sheriff's office while the others stood around in the hot sun and listened. He gave the man on the other end of the line all of their names – they had nothing to hide, they weren't ashamed of anything – and agreed to wait at the service station until someone could come for more detailed directions and individual statements.

He came home at eleven o'clock that night. I was asleep but woke when I heard him in the kitchen. I found him leaning against the refrigerator drinking a can of beer. He put his heavy arms around me and rubbed his hands up and down my back, the same hands he'd left with two days before, I thought.

In bed he put his hands on me again and then waited, as if thinking of something else. I turned slightly and then moved my legs. Afterward, I know he stayed awake for a long time, for he was awake when I fell asleep; and later, when I stirred for a minute, opening my eyes at a slight noise, a rustle of sheets, it was almost daylight outside, birds were singing, and he was on his back smoking and looking at the curtained window. Half-asleep I said his name, but he didn't answer. I fell asleep again.

He was up this morning before I could get out of bed – to see if there was anything about it in the paper, I suppose. The telephone began to ring shortly after eight o'clock.

"Go to hell," I heard him shout into the receiver. The telephone rang again a minute later, and I hurried into the kitchen. "I have nothing else to add to what I've already said to the sheriff. That's right!" He slammed down the receiver.

"What is going on?" I said, alarmed.

"Sit down," he said slowly. His fingers scraped, scraped against his stubble of whiskers. "I have to tell you something. Something happened while we were fishing." We sat across from each other at the table, and then he told me.

I drank coffee and stared at him as he spoke. Then I read the account in the newspaper that he shoved across the table: ". . . unidentified girl eighteen to twenty-four years of age . . . body three to five days in the water . . . rape a possible motive . . . preliminary results show death by strangulation . . . cuts and bruises on her breasts and pelvic area . . . autopsy . . . rape, pending further investigation."

"You've got to understand," he said. "Don't look at me like that. Be careful now, I mean it. Take it easy, Claire."

"Why didn't you tell me last night?" I asked.

"I just . . . didn't. What do you mean?" he said.

"You know what I mean," I said. I looked at his hands, the broad fingers, knuckles covered with hair, moving, lighting a cigarette now, fingers that had moved over me, into me last night.

He shrugged. "What difference does it make, last night, this morning? It was late. You were sleepy, I thought I'd wait until this morning to tell you." He looked out to the patio: a robin flew from the lawn to the picnic table and preened its feathers.

"It isn't true," I said. "You didn't leave her there like that?"

He turned quickly and said, "What'd I do? Listen to me carefully now, once and for all. Nothing happened. I have nothing to be sorry for or feel guilty about. Do you hear me?"

I got up from the table and went to Dean's room. He was awake and in his pajamas, putting together a puzzle. I helped him find his clothes and then went back to the kitchen and put his breakfast on the table. The telephone rang two or three more times and each time Stuart was abrupt while he talked and angry when he hung up. He called Mel Dorn and Gordon Johnson and spoke with them, slowly, seriously, and then he opened a beer and smoked a cigarette while Dean ate, asked him about school, his friends, etc., exactly as if nothing had happened.

Dean wanted to know what he'd done while he was gone, and Stuart took some fish out of the freezer to show him.

"I'm taking him to your mother's for the day," I said.

"Sure," Stuart said and looked at Dean who was holding one of the frozen trout. "If you want to and he wants to, that is. You don't have to, you know. There's nothing wrong."

"I'd like to anyway," I said.

"Can I go swimming there?" Dean asked and wiped his fingers on his pants.

"I believe so," I said. "It's a warm day so take your suit, and I'm sure your grandmother will say it's okay."

Stuart lighted a cigarette and looked at us.

Dean and I drove across town to Stuart's mother's. She lives in an apartment building with a pool and a sauna bath. Her name is Catherine Kane. Her name, Kane, is the same as mine, which seems impossible. Years ago, Stuart has told me, she used to be called Candy by her friends. She is a tall, cold woman with white-blonde hair. She gives me the feeling that she is always judging, judging. I explain briefly in a low voice what has happened (she hasn't yet read the newspaper) and promise to pick Dean up that evening. "He brought his swimming suit," I say. "Stuart and I have to talk about some things," I add vaguely. She looks at me steadily from over her glasses. Then she nods and turns to Dean, saying "How are you, my little man?" She stoops and puts her arms around him. She looks at me again as I open the door to leave. She has a way of looking at me without saying anything.

When I return home Stuart is eating something at the table and drinking beer. . . .

After a time I sweep up the broken dishes and glassware and go outside. Stuart is lying on his back on the grass now, the newspaper and can of beer within reach, staring at the sky. It's breezy but warm out and birds call.

"Stuart, could we go for a drive?" I say. "Anywhere."

He rolls over and looks at me and nods. "We'll pick up some

beer," he says. "I hope you're feeling better about this. Try to understand, that's all I ask." He gets to his feet and touches me on the hip as he goes past. "Give me a minute and I'll be ready."

We drive through town without speaking. Before we reach the country he stops at a roadside market for beer. I notice a great stack of papers just inside the door. On the top step a fat woman in a print dress holds out a licorice stick to a little girl. In a few minutes we cross Everson Creek and turn into a picnic area a few feet from the water. The creek flows under the bridge and into a large pond a few hundred yards away. There are a dozen or so men and boys scattered around the banks of the pond under the willows, fishing.

So much water so close to home, why did he have to go miles away to fish?

"Why did you have to go there of all places?" I say.

"The Naches? We always go there. Every year, at least once." We sit on a bench in the sun and he opens two cans of beer and gives one to me. "How the hell was I to know anything like that would happen?" He shakes his head and shrugs, as if it had all happened years ago, or to someone else. "Enjoy the afternoon, Claire. Look at this weather."

"They said they were innocent."

"Who? What are you talking about?"

"The Maddox brothers. They killed a girl named Arlene Hubly near the town where I grew up, and then cut off her head and threw her into the Cle Elum River. She and I went to the same high school. It happened when I was a girl."

"What a hell of a thing to be thinking about," he says. "Come on, get off it. You're going to get me riled in a minute. How about it now? Claire?"

I look at the creek. I float toward the pond, eyes open, face down, staring at the rocks and moss on the creek bottom until I am carried into the lake where I am pushed by the breeze. Nothing will be any different. We will go on and on and on and on. We will go on even now, as if nothing had happened. I look at him across the picnic table with such intensity that his face drains.

"I don't know what's wrong with you," he says. "I don't –"

I slap him before I realize. I raise my hand, wait a fraction of a second, and then slap his cheek hard. This is crazy, I think as I slap him. We need to lock our fingers together. We need to help one another. This is crazy.

He catches my wrist before I can strike again and raises his own hand. I crouch, waiting, and see something come into his eyes and then dart away. He drops his hand. I drift even faster around and around in the pond.

"Come on, get in the car," he says. "I'm taking you home."

"No, no," I say, pulling back from him.

"Come on," he says. "Goddamn it."

"You're not being fair to me," he says later in the car. Fields and trees and farmhouses fly by outside the window. "You're not being fair. To either one of us. Or to Dean, I might add. Think about Dean for a minute. Think about me. Think about someone else besides your goddamn self for a change."

There is nothing I can say to him now. He tries to concentrate on the road, but he keeps looking into the rearview mirror. Out of the corner of his eye, he looks across the seat to where I sit with my knees drawn up under my chin. The sun blazes against my arm and the side of my face. He opens another beer while he drives, drinks from it, then shoves the can between his legs and lets out breath. He knows. I could laugh in his face. I could weep.

Stuart believes he is letting me sleep this morning. But I was awake long before the alarm sounded, thinking, lying on the far side of the bed, away from his hairy legs and his thick, sleeping fingers. He gets Dean off for school, and then he shaves, dresses, and leaves for work. Twice he looks into the bedroom and clears his throat, but I keep my eyes closed.

In the kitchen I find a note from him signed "Love". I sit in the breakfast nook in the sunlight and drink coffee and make a coffee ring on the note. The telephone has stopped ringing, that's something. No more calls since last night. I look at the paper and turn it this way and that on the table. Then I pull it close and read what it says. The body is still unidentified, unclaimed, apparently unmissed. But for the last twenty-four hours men have been examining it, putting things into it, cutting, weighing, measuring, putting back again, sewing up, looking for the exact cause and moment of death. Looking for evidence of rape. I'm sure they hope for rape. Rape would make it easier to understand. The paper says the body will be taken to Keith & Keith Funeral Home pending arrangements. People are asked to come forward with information, etc.

Two things are certain: 1) people no longer care what happens to other people; and 2) nothing makes any real difference any longer. Look at what has happened. Yet nothing will change for Stuart and me. Really change, I mean. We will grow older, both of us, you can see it in our faces already, in the bathroom mirror, for instance, mornings when we use the bathroom at the same time. And certain things around us will change, become easier or harder, one thing or the other, but nothing will ever really be any different. I believe that. We have made our decisions, our lives have been set in motion, and they will go on and on until they stop. But if that is true, then what? I mean, what if you believe that, but you keep it covered up, until one day something happens that should change something, but then you see nothing is going to change after all. What then? Meanwhile, the people around you continue to talk and act as if you were the same person as yesterday, or last night, or five minutes before, but you are really undergoing a crisis, your heart feels damaged. . . .

The past is unclear. It's as if there is a film over those early years. I can't even be sure that the things I remember happening really happened to me. There was a girl who had a mother and father – the father ran a small café where the mother acted as waitress and cashier – who moved as if in a dream through grade school and high school and then, in a year or two, into secretarial school. Later, much later – what happened to the time in between? – she is in another town working as a receptionist for an electronics parts firm and becomes acquainted with one of the engineers who asks her for a date. Eventually, seeing that's his aim, she lets him seduce her. She had an intuition at the time, an insight about the seduction that later, try as she might, she couldn't recall. After a short while they decide to get married, but already the past, her past, is slipping away. The future is something she can't imagine. She smiles, as if she has a secret, when she thinks about the future. Once, during a particularly bad argument, over what she can't now remember, five years or so after they were married, he tells her that someday this affair (his words: "this affair") will end in violence. She remembers this. She files this away somewhere and begins repeating it aloud from time to time. Sometimes she spends the whole morning on her knees in the sandbox behind the garage playing with Dean and one or two of his friends. But every afternoon at four o'clock her head begins to hurt. She holds her forehead and feels dizzy with the pain. Stuart asks her to see a doctor and she does, secretly pleased at the doctor's solicitous attention. She goes away for a while to a place the doctor recommends. Stuart's mother comes out from Ohio in a hurry to care for the child. But she, Claire, spoils everything and returns home in a few weeks. His mother moves out of the house and takes an apartment across town and perches there, as if waiting. One night in bed when they are both near sleep, Claire tells him that she heard some women patients at the clinic discussing fellatio. She thinks this is something he might like to hear. Stuart is pleased at hearing this. He strokes her arm. Things are going to be okay, he says. From now on everything is going to be different and better for them. He has received a promotion and a substantial raise. They've even bought another car, a station wagon, her car. They're going to live in the here and now. He says he feels able to relax for the first time in years. In the dark, he goes on stroking her arm. . . . He continues to bowl and play cards regularly. He goes fishing with three friends of his.

That evening three things happen: Dean says that the children at school told him that his father found a dead body in the river. He wants to know about it.

Stuart explains quickly, leaving out most of the story, saying only that, yes, he and three other men did find a body while they were fishing.

"What kind of body?" Dean asks. "Was it a girl?"

"Yes, it was a girl. A woman. Then we called the sheriff."
Stuart looks at me.

"What'd he say?" Dean asks.

"He said he'd take care of it."

"What did it look like? Was it scary?"

"That's enough talk," I say. "Rinse your plate, Dean, and then
you're excused."

"But what'd it look like?" he persists. "I want to know."

"You heard me," I say. "Did you hear me, Dean? Dean!" I
want to shake him. I want to shake him until he cries.

"Do what your mother says," Stuart tells him quietly. "It was
just a body, and that's all there is to it."

I am clearing the table when Stuart comes up behind and
touches my arm. His fingers burn. I start, almost losing a plate.

"What's the matter with you?" he says, dropping his hand.
"Claire, what is it?"

"You scared me," I say.

"That's what I mean. I should be able to touch you without
you jumping out of your skin." He stands in front of me with a
little grin, trying to catch my eyes, and then he puts his arm
around my waist. With his other hand he takes my free hand and
puts it on the front of his pants.

"Please, Stuart." I pull away and he steps back and snaps his
fingers.

"Hell with it then," he says. "Be that way if you want. But
just remember."

"Remember what?" I say quickly. I look at him and hold my
breath.

He shrugs. "Nothing, nothing," he says.

The second thing that happens is that while we are watching
television that evening, he in his leather recliner chair, I on the
sofa with a blanket and magazine, the house quiet except for the
television, a voice cuts into the program to say that the murdered
girl has been identified. Full details will follow on the eleven
o'clock news.

We look at each other. In a few minutes he gets up and says
he is going to fix a nightcap. Do I want one?

"No," I say.

"I don't mind drinking alone," he says. "I thought I'd ask."

I can see he is obscurely hurt, and I look away, ashamed and yet angry at the same time.

He stays in the kitchen a long while, but comes back with his drink just when the news begins.

First the announcer repeats the story of the four local fishermen finding the body. Then the station shows a high school graduation photograph of the girl, a dark-haired girl with a round face and full, smiling lips. There's a film of the girl's parents entering the funeral home to make the identification. Bewildered, sad, they shuffle slowly up the sidewalk to the front steps to where a man in a dark suit stands waiting, holding the door. Then, it seems as if only seconds have passed, as if they have merely gone inside the door and turned around and come out again, the same couple is shown leaving the building, the woman in tears, covering her face with a handkerchief, the man stopping long enough to say to a reporter, "It's her, it's Susan. I can't say anything right now. I hope they get the person or persons who did it before it happens again. This violence. . . ." He motions feebly at the television camera. Then the man and woman get into an old car and drive away into the late afternoon traffic.

The announcer goes on to say that the girl, Susan Miller, had gotten off work as a cashier in a movie theater in Summit, a town 120 miles north of our town. A green, late-model car pulled up in front of the theater and the girl, who according to witnesses looked as if she'd been waiting, went over to the car and got in, leading the authorities to suspect that the driver of the car was a friend, or at least an acquaintance. The authorities would like to talk to the driver of the green car.

Stuart clears his throat, then leans back in the chair and sips his drink.

The third thing that happens is that after the news Stuart stretches, yawns, and looks at me. I get up and begin making a bed for myself on the sofa.

"What are you doing?" he says, puzzled.

"I'm not sleepy," I say, avoiding his eyes. "I think I'll stay up a while longer and then read something until I fall asleep."

He stares as I spread a sheet over the sofa. When I start to go for a pillow, he stands at the bedroom door, blocking the way.

"I'm going to ask you once more," he says. "What the hell do you think you're going to accomplish by this?"

"I need to be by myself tonight," I say. "I need to have time to think."

He lets out breath. "I'm thinking you're making a big mistake by doing this. I'm thinking you'd better think again about what you're doing. Claire?"

I can't answer. I don't know what I want to say. I turn and begin to tuck in the edges of the blanket. He stares at me a minute longer and then I see him raise his shoulders. "Suit yourself then. I could give a fuck less what you do," he says. He turns and walks down the hall scratching his neck.

This morning I read in the paper that services for Susan Miller are to be held in Chapel of the Pines, Summit, at two o'clock the next afternoon. Also, that police have taken statements from three people who saw her get into the green Chevrolet. But they still have no license number for the car. They are getting warmer, though, and the investigation is continuing. I sit for a long while holding the paper, thinking, then I call to make an appointment at the hairdresser's.

I sit under the dryer with a magazine on my lap and let Millie do my nails.

"I'm going to a funeral tomorrow," I say after we have talked a bit about a girl who no longer works there.

Millie looks up at me and then back at my fingers. "I'm sorry to hear that, Mrs Kane. I'm real sorry."

"It's a young girl's funeral," I say.

"That's the worst kind. My sister died when I was a girl, and I'm still not over it to this day. Who died?" she says after a minute.

"A girl. We weren't all that close, you know, but still."

"Too bad. I'm real sorry. But we'll get you fixed up for it, don't worry. How's that look?"

"That looks . . . fine. Millie, did you ever wish you were somebody else, or else just nobody, nothing, nothing at all?"

She looks at me. "I can't say I ever felt that, no. No, if I was somebody else I'd be afraid I might not like who I was." She holds my fingers and seems to think about something for a minute. "I don't know, I just don't know. . . . Let me have your other hand now, Mrs Kane."

At eleven o'clock that night I make another bed on the sofa and this time Stuart only looks at me, rolls his tongue behind his lips, and goes down the hall to the bedroom. In the night I wake and listen to the wind slamming the gate against the fence. I don't want to be awake, and I lie for a long while with my eyes closed. Finally I get up and go down the hall with my pillow. The light is burning in our bedroom and Stuart is on his back with his mouth open, breathing heavily. I go into Dean's room and get into bed with him. In his sleep he moves over to give me space. I lie there for a minute and then hold him, my face against his hair.

"What is it, Mama?" he says.

"Nothing, honey. Go back to sleep. It's nothing, it's all right."

I get up when I hear Stuart's alarm, put on coffee and prepare breakfast while he shaves.

He appears in the kitchen doorway, towel over his bare shoulder, appraising.

"Here's coffee," I say. "Eggs will be ready in a minute."

He nods.

I wake Dean and the three of us have breakfast. Once or twice Stuart looks at me as if he wants to say something, but each time I ask Dean if he wants more milk, more toast, etc.

"I'll call you today," Stuart says as he opens the door.

"I don't think I'll be home today," I say quickly. "I have a lot of things to do today. In fact, I may be late for dinner."

"All right. Sure." He moves his briefcase from one hand to the other. "Maybe we'll go out for dinner tonight? How would you like that?" He keeps looking at me. He's forgotten about the girl already. "Are you all right?"

I move to straighten his tie, then drop my hand. He wants to kiss me goodbye. I move back a step. "Have a nice day then," he says finally. He turns and goes down the walk to his car.

I dress carefully. I try on a hat that I haven't worn in several years and look at myself in the mirror. Then I remove the hat, apply a light makeup, and write a note for Dean.

Honey, Mommy has things to do this afternoon, but will be home later. You are to stay in the house or in the back/yard until one of us comes home.
Love

I look at the word "Love" and then I underline it. As I am writing the note I realize I don't know whether *back yard* is one word or two. I have never considered it before. I think about it and then I draw a line and make two words of it.

I stop for gas and ask directions to Summit. Barry, a forty-year-old mechanic with a moustache, comes out from the restroom and leans against the front fender while the other man, Lewis, puts the hose into the tank and begins to slowly wash the windshield.

"Summit," Barry says, looking at me and smoothing a finger down each side of his moustache. "There's no best way to get to Summit, Mrs Kane. It's about a two-, two-and-a-half-hour drive each way. Across the mountains. It's quite a drive for a woman. Summit? What's in Summit, Mrs Kane?"

"I have business," I say, vaguely uneasy. Lewis has gone to wait on another customer.

"Ah. Well, if I wasn't tied up there –" he gestures with his thumb toward the bay – "I'd offer to drive you to Summit and back again. Road's not all that good. I mean it's good enough, there's just a lot of curves and so on."

"I'll be all right. But thank you." He leans against the fender. I can feel his eyes as I open my purse.

Barry takes the credit card. "Don't drive it at night," he says. "It's not all that good a road, like I said. And while I'd be willing to bet you wouldn't have car trouble with this, I know this car, you can never be sure about blowouts and things like that. Just to be on the safe side I'd better check these tires." He taps one of the front tires with his shoe. "We'll run it onto the hoist. Won't take long."

"No, no, it's all right. Really, I can't take any more time. The tires look fine to me."

"Only takes a minute," he says. "Be on the safe side."

"I said no. No! They look fine to me. I have to go now. Barry. . . ."

"Mrs Kane?"

"I have to go now."

I sign something. He gives me the receipt, the card, some stamps. I put everything into my purse. "You take it easy," he says. "Be seeing you."

As I wait to pull into the traffic, I look back and see him watching. I close my eyes, then open them. He waves.

I turn at the first light, then turn again and drive until I come to the highway and read the sign: SUMMIT 117 Miles. It is ten-thirty and warm.

The highway skirts the edge of town, then passes through farm country, through fields of oats and sugar beets and apple orchards, with here and there a small herd of cattle grazing in open pastures. Then everything changes, the farms become fewer and fewer, more like shacks now than houses, and stands of timber replace the orchards. All at once I'm in the mountains and on the right, far below, I catch glimpses of the Naches River.

In a little while I see a green pickup truck behind me, and it stays behind me for miles. I keep slowing at the wrong times, hoping it will pass, and then increasing my speed, again at the wrong times. I grip the wheel until my fingers hurt. Then on a clear stretch he does pass, but he drives along beside for a minute, a crew-cut man in a blue workshirt in his early thirties, and we look at each other. Then he waves, toots the horn twice, and pulls ahead of me.

I slow down and find a place, a dirt road off of the shoulder. I pull over and turn off the ignition. I can hear the river some-where down below the trees. Ahead of me the dirt road goes into the trees. Then I hear the pickup returning.

I start the engine just as the truck pulls up behind me. I lock the doors and roll up the windows. Perspiration breaks on my face and arms as I put the car in gear, but there is no place to drive.

"You all right?" the man says as he comes up to the car. "Hello. Hello in there." He raps the glass. "You okay?" He leans his arms on the door and brings his face close to the window.

I stare at him and can't find any words.

"After I passed I slowed up some," he says. "But when I didn't see you in the mirror I pulled off and waited a couple of minutes. When you still didn't show I thought I'd better drive back and check. Is everything all right? How come you're locked up in there?"

I shake my head.

"Come on, roll down your window. Hey, are you sure you're okay? You know it's not good for a woman to be batting around the country by herself." He shakes his head and looks at the highway, then back at me. "Now come on, roll down the window, how about it? We can't talk this way."

"Please, I have to go."

"Open the door, all right?" he says, as if he isn't listening. "At least roll the window down. You're going to smother in there." He looks at my breasts and legs. The skirt has pulled up over my knees. His eyes linger on my legs, but I sit still, afraid to move.

"I want to smother," I say. "I am smothering, can't you see?"

"What in the hell?" he says and moves back from the door. He turns and walks back to his truck. Then, in the side mirror, I watch him returning, and I close my eyes.

"You don't want me to follow you toward Summit or anything? I don't mind. I got some extra time this morning," he says.

I shake my head.

He hesitates and then shrugs. "Okay, lady, have it your way then," he says. "Okay."

I wait until he has reached the highway, and then I back out. He shifts gears and pulls away slowly, looking back at me in his

rearview mirror. I stop the car on the shoulder and put my head
on the wheel.

The casket is closed and covered with floral sprays. The organ
begins soon after I take a seat near the back of the chapel. People
begin to file in and find chairs, some middle-aged and older
people, but most of them in their early twenties or even younger.
They are people who look uncomfortable in their suits and ties,
sport coats and slacks, their dark dresses and leather gloves. One
boy in flared pants and a yellow short-sleeved shirt takes the chair
next to mine and begins to bite his lips. A door opens at one side
of the chapel and I look up and for a minute the parking lot
reminds me of a meadow. But then the sun flashes on car
windows. The family enters in a group and moves into a curtained area off to the side. Chairs creak as they settle themselves.
In a few minutes a slim, blond man in a dark suit stands and asks
us to bow our heads. He speaks a brief prayer for us, the living,
and when he finishes he asks us to pray in silence for the soul of
Susan Miller, departed. I close my eyes and remember her picture
in the newspaper and on television. I see her leaving the theater
and getting into the green Chevrolet. Then I imagine her journey
down the river, the nude body hitting rocks, caught at by
branches, the body floating and turning, her hair streaming in
the water. Then the hands and hair catching in the overhanging
branches, holding, until four men come along to stare at her. I
can see a man who is drunk (Stuart?) take her by the wrist. Does
anyone here know about that? What if these people knew that?
I look around at the other faces. There is a connection to be made
of these things, these events, these faces, if I can find it. My head
aches with the effort to find it.

He talks about Susan Miller's gifts: cheerfulness and beauty,
grace and enthusiasm. From behind the closed curtain someone
clears his throat, someone else sobs. The organ music begins.
The service is over.

Along with the others I file slowly past the casket. Then I
move out onto the front steps and into the bright, hot afternoon
light. A middle-aged woman who limps as she goes down the

stairs ahead of me reaches the sidewalk and looks around, her eyes falling on me. "Well, they got him," she says. "If that's any consolation. They arrested him this morning. I heard it on the radio before I came. A guy right here in town. A longhair, you might have guessed." We move a few steps down the hot sidewalk. People are starting cars. I put out my hand and hold on to a parking meter. Sunlight glances off polished hoods and fenders. My head swims. "He's admitted having relations with her that night, but he says he didn't kill her." She snorts. "They'll put him on probation and then turn him loose."

"He might not have acted alone," I say. "They'll have to be sure. He might be covering up for someone, a brother, or some friends."

"I have known that child since she was a little girl," the woman goes on, and her lips tremble. "She used to come over and I'd bake cookies for her and let her eat them in front of the TV." She looks off and begins shaking her head as the tears roll down her cheeks.

Stuart sits at the table with a drink in front of him. His eyes are red and for a minute I think he has been crying. He looks at me and doesn't say anything. For a wild instant I feel something has happened to Dean, and my heart turns.

"Where is he?" I say. "Where is Dean?"

"Outside," he says.

"Stuart, I'm so afraid, so afraid," I say, leaning against the door.

"What are you afraid of, Claire? Tell me, honey, and maybe I can help. I'd like to help, just try me. That's what husbands are for."

"I can't explain," I say. "I'm just afraid. I feel like, I feel like, I feel like. . . ."

He drains his glass and stands up, not taking his eyes from me. "I think I know what you need, honey. Let me play doctor, okay? Just take it easy now." He reaches an arm around my waist and with his other hand begins to unbutton my jacket, then my blouse. "First things first," he says, trying to joke.

"Not now, please," I say.

"Not now, please," he says, teasing. "Please nothing." Then he steps behind me and locks an arm around my waist. One of his hands slips under my brassiere.

"Stop, stop, stop," I say. I stamp on his toes.

And then I am lifted up and then falling. I sit on the floor looking up at him and my neck hurts and my skirt is over my knees. He leans down and says, "You go to hell then, do you hear, bitch? I hope your cunt drops off before I touch it again." He sobs once and I realize he can't help it, he can't help himself either. I feel a rush of pity for him as he heads for the living room.

He didn't sleep at home last night.

This morning, flowers, red and yellow chrysanthemums. I am drinking coffee when the doorbell rings.

"Mrs Kane?" the young man says, holding his box of flowers.

I nod and pull the robe tighter at my throat.

"The man who called, he said you'd know." The boy looks at my robe, open at the throat, and touches his cap. He stands with his legs apart, feet firmly planted on the top step. "Have a nice day," he says.

A little later the telephone rings and Stuart says, "Honey, how are you? I'll be home early, I love you. Did you hear me? I love you, I'm sorry, I'll make it up to you. Goodbye, I have to run now."

I put the flowers into a vase in the center of the dining room table and then I move my things into the extra bedroom.

Last night, around midnight, Stuart breaks the lock on my door. He does it just to show me that he can, I suppose, for he doesn't do anything when the door springs open except stand there in his underwear looking surprised and foolish while the anger slips from his face. He shuts the door slowly, and a few minutes later I hear him in the kitchen prying open a tray of ice cubes.

I'm in bed when he calls today to tell me that he's asked his mother to come stay with us for a few days. I wait a minute, thinking about this, and then hang up while he is still talking.

But in a little while I dial his number at work. When he finally comes on the line I say, "It doesn't matter, Stuart. Really, I tell you it doesn't matter one way or the other."

"I love you," he says.

He says something else and I listen and nod slowly. I feel sleepy. Then I wake up and say, "For God's sake, Stuart, she was only a child."

The Calm

I was getting a haircut. I was in the chair and three men were sitting along the wall across from me. Two of the men waiting I'd never seen before. But one of them I recognized, though I couldn't exactly place him. I kept looking at him as the barber worked on my hair. The man was moving a toothpick around in his mouth, a heavyset man, short wavy hair. And then I saw him in a cap and uniform, little eyes watchful in the lobby of a bank.

Of the other two, one was considerably the older, with a full head of curly gray hair. He was smoking. The third, though not so old, was nearly bald on top, but the hair at the sides hung over his ears. He had on logging boots, pants shiny with machine oil.

The barber put a hand on top of my head to turn me for a better look. Then he said to the guard, "Did you get your deer, Charles?"

I liked this barber. We weren't acquainted well enough to call each other by name. But when I came in for a haircut, he knew me. He knew I used to fish. So we'd talk fishing. I don't think he hunted. But he could talk on any subject. In this regard, he was a good barber.

"Bill, it's a funny story. The damnedest thing," the guard said. He took out the toothpick and laid it in the ashtray. He shook his head. "I did and I didn't. So yes and no to your question."

I didn't like the man's voice. For a guard, the voice didn't fit. It wasn't the voice you'd expect.

The two other men looked up. The older man was turning the pages of a magazine, smoking, and the other fellow was holding a newspaper. They put down what they were looking at and turned to listen to the guard.

"Go on, Charles," the barber said. "Let's hear it."

The barber turned my head again, and went back to work with his clippers.

"We were up on Fikle Ridge. My old man and me and the kid. We were hunting those draws. My old man was stationed at the head of one, and me and the kid were at the head of another. The kid had a hangover, goddamn his hide. The kid, he was green around the gills and drank water all day, mine and his both. It was in the afternoon and we'd been out since daybreak. But we had our hopes. We figured the hunters down below would move a deer in our direction. So we were sitting behind a log and watching the draw when we heard this shooting down in the valley."

"There's orchards down there," said the fellow with the newspaper. He was fidgeting a lot and kept crossing a leg, swinging his boot for a time, and then crossing his legs the other way. "Those deer hang out around those orchards."

"That's right," said the guard. "They'll go in there at night, the bastards, and eat those little green apples. Well, we heard this shooting and we're just sitting there on our hands when this big old buck comes up out of the underbrush not a hundred feet away. The kid sees him the same time I do, of course, and he throws down and starts banging. The knothead. That old buck wasn't in any danger. Not from the kid, as it turns out. But he can't tell where the shots are coming from. He doesn't know which way to jump. Then I get off a shot. But in all the commotion, I just stun him."

"Stunned him?" the barber said.

"You know, stun him," the guard said. "It was a gut shot. It just like stuns him. So he drops his head and begins this trembling. He trembles all over. The kid's still shooting. Me, I felt like I was back in Korea. So I shot again but missed. Then old Mr Buck moves back into the brush. But now, by God, he doesn't have any oompf left in him. The kid has emptied his goddamn gun all to no purpose. But I hit solid. I'd rammed one right in his guts. That's what I meant by stunned him."

"Then what?" said the fellow with the newspaper, who had rolled it and was tapping it against his knee. "Then what? You must have trailed him. They find a hard place to die every time."

"But you trailed him?" the older man asked, though it wasn't really a question.

"I did. Me and the kid, we trailed him. But the kid wasn't good for much. He gets sick on the trail, slows us down. That chucklehead." The guard had to laugh now, thinking about that situation. "Drinking beer and chasing all night, then saying he can hunt deer. He knows better now, by God. But, sure, we trailed him. A good trail, too. Blood on the ground and blood on the leaves. Blood everywhere. Never seen a buck with so much blood. I don't know how the sucker kept going."

"Sometimes they'll go forever," the fellow with the newspaper said. "They find them a hard place to die every time."

"I chewed the kid out for missing his shot, and when he smarted off at me, I cuffed him a good one. Right here." The guard pointed to the side of his head and grinned. "I boxed his goddamn ears for him, that goddamn kid. He's not too old. He needed it. So the point is, it got too dark to trail, what with the kid laying back to vomit and all."

"Well, the coyotes will have that deer by now," the fellow with the newspaper said. "Them and the crows and the buzzards."

He unrolled the newspaper, smoothed it all the way out, and put it off to one side. He crossed a leg again. He looked around at the rest of us and shook his head.

The older man had turned in his chair and was looking out the window. He lit a cigarette.

"I figure so," the guard said. "Pity too. He was a big old son of a bitch. So in answer to your question, Bill, I both got my deer and I didn't. But we had venison on the table anyway. Because it turns out the old man has got himself a little spike in the meantime. Already has him back to camp, hanging up and gutted slick as a whistle, liver, heart, and kidneys wrapped in waxed paper and already setting in the cooler. A spike. Just a little bastard. But the old man, he was tickled."

The guard looked around the shop as if remembering. Then

196

he picked up his toothpick and stuck it back in his mouth.

The older man put his cigarette out and turned to the guard. He drew a breath and said, "You ought to be out there right now looking for that deer instead of in here getting a haircut."

"You can't talk like that," the guard said. "You old fart. I've seen you someplace."

"I've seen you too," the old fellow said.

"Boys, that's enough. This is my barbershop," the barber said.

"I ought to box *your* ears," the old fellow said.

"You ought to try it," the guard said.

"Charles," the barber said.

The barber put his comb and scissors on the counter and his hands on my shoulders, as if he thought I was thinking to spring from the chair into the middle of it. "Albert, I've been cutting Charles's head of hair, and his boy's too, for years now. I wish you wouldn't pursue this."

The barber looked from one man to the other and kept his hands on my shoulders.

"Take it outside," the fellow with the newspaper said, flushed and hoping for something.

"That'll be enough," the barber said. "Charles, I don't want to hear anything more on the subject. Albert, you're next in line. Now." The barber turned to the fellow with the newspaper. "I don't know you from Adam, mister, but I'd appreciate it if you wouldn't put your oar in."

The guard got up. He said, "I think I'll come back for my cut later. Right now the company leaves something to be desired."

The guard went out and pulled the door closed, hard.

The old fellow sat smoking his cigarette. He looked out the window. He examined something on the back of his hand. He got up and put on his hat.

"I'm sorry, Bill," the old fellow said. "I can go a few more days."

"That's all right, Albert," the barber said.

When the old fellow went out, the barber stepped over to the window to watch him go.

"Albert's about dead from emphysema," the barber said from the window. "We used to fish together. He taught me salmon inside out. The women. They used to crawl all over that old boy. He's picked up a temper, though. But in all honesty, there was provocation."

The man with the newspaper couldn't sit still. He was on his feet and moving around, stopping to examine everything, the hat rack, the photos of Bill and his friends, the calendar from the hardware showing scenes for each month of the year. He flipped every page. He even went so far as to stand and scrutinize Bill's barbering license, which was up on the wall in a frame. Then he turned and said, "I'm going too," and out he went just like he said.

"Well, do you want me to finish barbering this hair or not?" the barber said to me as if I was the cause of everything.

The barber turned me in the chair to face the mirror. He put a hand to either side of my head. He positioned me a last time, and then he brought his head down next to mine.

We looked into the mirror together, his hands still framing my head.

I was looking at myself, and he was looking at me too. But if the barber saw something, he didn't offer comment.

He ran his fingers through my hair. He did it slowly, as if thinking about something else. He ran his fingers through my hair. He did it tenderly, as a lover would.

That was in Crescent City, California, up near the Oregon border. I left soon after. But today I was thinking of that place, of Crescent City, and of how I was trying out a new life there with my wife, and how, in the barber's chair that morning, I had made up my mind to go. I was thinking today about the calm I felt when I closed my eyes and let the barber's fingers move through my hair, the sweetness of those fingers, the hair already starting to grow.

Vitamins

I had a job and Patti didn't. I worked a few hours a night for the hospital. It was a nothing job. I did some work, signed the card for eight hours, went drinking with the nurses. After a while, Patti wanted a job. She said she needed a job for her self-respect. So she started selling multiple vitamins door to door.

For a while, she was just another girl who went up and down blocks in strange neighborhoods, knocking on doors. But she learned the ropes. She was quick and had excelled at things in school. She had personality. Pretty soon the company gave her a promotion. Some of the girls who weren't doing so hot were put to work under her. Before long, she had herself a crew and a little office out in the mall. But the girls who worked for her were always changing. Some would quit after a couple of days – after a couple of hours, sometimes. But sometimes there were girls who were good at it. They could sell vitamins. These were the girls that stuck with Patti. They formed the core of the crew. But there were girls who couldn't give away vitamins.

The girls who couldn't cut it would just quit. Just not show up for work. If they had a phone, they'd take it off the hook. They wouldn't answer the door. Patti took these losses to heart, like the girls were new converts who had lost their way. She blamed herself. But she got over it. There were too many not to get over it.

Once in a while a girl would freeze and not be able to push the doorbell. Or maybe she'd get to the door and something would happen to her voice. Or she'd get the greeting mixed up with something she shouldn't be saying until she got inside. A girl like this, she'd decide to pack it in, take the sample case, head for the car, hang around until Patti and the others finished.

There'd be a conference. Then they'd all ride back to the office. They'd say things to buck themselves up. "When the going gets tough, the tough get going." And, "Do the right things and the right things will happen." Things like that.

Sometimes a girl just disappeared in the field, sample case and all. She'd hitch a ride into town, then beat it. But there were always girls to take her place. Girls were coming and going in those days. Patti had a list. Every few weeks she'd run a little ad in *The Pennysaver*. There'd be more girls and more training. There was no end of girls.

The core group was made up of Patti, Donna, and Sheila. Patti was a looker. Donna and Sheila were only medium-pretty. One night this Sheila said to Patti that she loved her more than anything on earth. Patti told me these were the words. Patti had driven Sheila home and they were sitting in front of Sheila's place. Patti said to Sheila she loved her, too. Patti said to Sheila she loved all her girls. But not in the way Sheila had in mind. Then Sheila touched Patti's breast. Patti said she took Sheila's hand and held it. She said she told her she didn't swing that way. She said Sheila didn't bat an eye, that she only nodded, held on to Patti's hand, kissed it, and got out of the car.

That was around Christmas. The vitamin business was pretty bad off back then, so we thought we'd have a party to cheer everybody up. It seemed like a good idea at the time. Sheila was the first to get drunk and pass out. She passed out on her feet, fell over, and didn't wake up for hours. One minute she was standing in the middle of the living room, then her eyes closed, the legs buckled, and she went down with a glass in her hand. The hand holding the drink smacked the coffee table when she fell. She didn't make a sound otherwise. The drink poured out onto the rug. Patti and I and somebody else lugged her out to the back porch and put her down on a cot and did what we could to forget about her.

Everybody got drunk and went home. Patti went to bed. I wanted to keep on, so I sat at the table with a drink until it began to get light out. Then Sheila came in from the porch and started up. She said she had this headache that was so bad it was like somebody was sticking wires in her brain. She said it was such a bad headache she was afraid it was going to leave her with a permanent squint. And she was sure her little finger was broken. She showed it to me. It looked purple. She bitched about us letting her sleep all night with her contacts in. She wanted to know didn't anybody give a shit. She brought the finger up close and looked at it. She shook her head. She held the finger as far away as she could and looked some more. It was like she couldn't believe the things that must have happened to her that night. Her face was puffy, and her hair was all over. She ran cold water on her finger. "God. Oh, God," she said and cried some over the sink. But she'd made a serious pass at Patti, a declaration of love, and I didn't have any sympathy.

I was drinking Scotch and milk with a sliver of ice. Sheila was leaning on the drainboard. She watched me from her little slits of eyes. I took some of my drink. I didn't say anything. She went back to telling me how bad she felt. She said she needed to see a doctor. She said she was going to wake Patti. She said she was quitting, leaving the state, going to Portland. That she had to say goodbye to Patti first. She kept on. She wanted Patti to drive her to the hospital for her finger and her eyes.

"I'll drive you," I said. I didn't want to do it, but I would.

"I want Patti to drive me," Sheila said.

She was holding the wrist of her bad hand with her good hand, the little finger as big as a pocket flashlight. "Besides, we need to talk. I need to tell her I'm going to Portland. I need to say goodbye."

I said, "I guess I'll have to tell her for you. She's asleep."

Sheila turned mean. "We're *friends*," she said. "I have to talk to her. I have to tell her myself."

I shook my head. "She's asleep. I just said so."

"We're friends and we love each other," Sheila said. "I have to say goodbye to her."

Sheila made to leave the kitchen.

I started to get up. I said, "I said I'll drive you."

"You're drunk! You haven't even been to bed yet." She looked at her finger again and said, "Goddamn, why'd this have to happen?"

"Not too drunk to drive you to the hospital," I said.

"I won't ride with you!" Sheila yelled.

"Suit yourself. But you're not going to wake Patti. Lesbo bitch," I said.

"Bastard," she said.

That's what she said, and then she went out of the kitchen and out the front door without using the bathroom or even washing her face. I got up and looked through the window. She was walking down the road toward Euclid. Nobody else was up. It was too early.

I finished my drink and thought about fixing another one.

I fixed it.

Nobody saw any more of Sheila after that. None of us vitamin-related people, anyway. She walked to Euclid Avenue and out of our lives.

Later on Patti said, "What happened to Sheila?" and I said, "She went to Portland."

I had the hots for Donna, the other member of the core group. We'd danced to some Duke Ellington records that night of the party. I'd held her pretty tight, smelled her hair, kept a hand low on her back as I moved her over the rug. It was great dancing with her. I was the only fellow at the party, and there were seven girls, six of them dancing with each other. It was great just looking around the living room.

I was in the kitchen when Donna came in with her empty glass. We were alone for a bit. I got her into a little embrace. She hugged me back. We stood there and hugged.

Then she said, "Don't. Not now."

When I heard that "Not now," I let go. I figured it was money in the bank.

I'd been at the table thinking about that hug when Sheila came in with her finger.

I thought some more about Donna. I finished the drink. I took the phone off the hook and headed for the bedroom. I took off my clothes and got in next to Patti. I lay for a while, winding down. Then I started in. But she didn't wake up. Afterward, I closed my eyes.

It was the afternoon when I opened them again. I was in bed alone. Rain was blowing against the window. A sugar doughnut was lying on Patti's pillow, and a glass of old water was on the nightstand. I was still drunk and couldn't figure anything out. I knew it was Sunday and close to Christmas. I ate the doughnut and drank the water. I went back to sleep until I heard Patti running the vacuum. She came into the bedroom and asked about Sheila. That's when I told her, said she'd gone to Portland.

A week or so into the new year, Patti and I were having a drink. She'd just come home from work. It wasn't so late, but it was dark and rainy. I was going to work in a couple of hours. But first we were having us some Scotch and talking. Patti was tired. She was down in the dumps and into her third drink. Nobody was buying vitamins. All she had was Donna and Pam, a semi-new girl who was a klepto. We were talking about things like negative weather and the number of parking tickets you could get away with. Then we got to talking about how we'd be better off if we moved to Arizona, someplace like that.

I fixed us another one. I looked out the window. Arizona wasn't a bad idea.

Patti said, "Vitamins." She picked up her glass and spun the ice. "For shit's sake!" she said. "I mean, when I was a girl, this is the last thing I ever saw myself doing. Jesus, I never thought I'd grow up to sell vitamins. Door-to-door vitamins. This beats all. This really blows my mind."

"I never thought so either, honey," I said.

"That's right," she said. "You said it in a nutshell."

"Honey."

"Don't honey me," she said. "This is hard, brother. This life is not easy, any way you cut it."

She seemed to think things over for a bit. She shook her head. Then she finished her drink. She said, "I even dream of vitamins when I'm asleep. I don't have any relief. There's no relief! At least you can walk away from your job and leave it behind. I'll bet you haven't had one dream about it. I'll bet you don't dream about waxing floors or whatever you do down there. After you've left the goddamn place, you don't come home and dream about it, do you?" she screamed.

I said, "I can't remember what I dream. Maybe I don't dream. I don't remember anything when I wake up." I shrugged. I didn't keep track of what went on in my head when I was asleep. I didn't care.

"You dream!" Patti said. "Even if you don't remember. Everybody dreams. If you didn't dream, you'd go crazy. I read about it. It's an outlet. People dream when they're asleep. Or else they'd go nuts. But when I dream, I dream of vitamins. Do you see what I'm saying?" She had her eyes fixed on me.

"Yes and no," I said.

It wasn't a simple question.

"I dream I'm pitching vitamins," she said. "I'm selling vitamins day and night. Jesus, what a life," she said.

She finished her drink.

"How's Pam doing?" I said. "She still stealing things?" I wanted to get us off this subject. But there wasn't anything else I could think of.

Patti said, "Shit," and shook her head like I didn't know anything. We listened to it rain.

"Nobody's selling vitamins," Patti said. She picked up her glass. But it was empty. "Nobody's buying vitamins. That's what I'm telling you. Didn't you hear me?"

I got up to fix us another. "Donna doing anything?" I said. I read the label on the bottle and waited.

Patti said, "She made a little sale two days ago. That's all. That's all that any of us has done this week. It wouldn't surprise me if she quit. I wouldn't blame her," Patti said. "If I was in her place, I'd quit. But if she quits, then what? Then I'm back at the start, that's what. Ground zero. Middle of winter, people sick all over the state, people dying, and nobody thinks they need vitamins. I'm sick as hell myself."

"What's wrong, honey?" I put the drinks on the table and sat down. She went on like I hadn't said anything. Maybe I hadn't.

"I'm my only customer," she said. "I think taking all these vitamins is doing something to my skin. Does my skin look okay to you? Can a person get overdosed on vitamins? I'm getting to where I can't even take a crap like a normal person."

"Honey," I said.

Patti said, "You don't care if I take vitamins. That's the point. You don't care about anything. The windshield wiper quit this afternoon in the rain. I almost had a wreck. I came this close."

We went on drinking and talking until it was time for me to go to work. Patti said she was going to soak in a tub if she didn't fall asleep first. "I'm asleep on my feet," she said. She said, "Vitamins. That's all there is anymore." She looked around the kitchen. She looked at her empty glass. She was drunk. But she let me kiss her. Then I left for work.

There was a place I went to after work. I'd started going for the music and because I could get a drink there after closing hours. It was a place called the Off-Broadway. It was a spade place in a spade neighborhood. It was run by a spade named Khaki. People would show up after the other places had stopped serving. They'd ask for house specials – RC Colas with a shooter of whiskey – or else they'd bring in their own stuff under their coats, order RC, and build their own. Musicians showed up to jam, and the drinkers who wanted to keep drinking came to drink and listen to the music. Sometimes people danced. But mainly they sat around and drank and listened.

Now and then a spade hit a spade in the head with a bottle. A story went around once that somebody had followed somebody into the Gents and cut the man's throat while he had his hands down pissing. But I never saw any trouble. Nothing that Khaki couldn't handle. Khaki was a big spade with a bald head that lit up weird under the fluorescents. He wore Hawaiian shirts that hung over his pants. I think he carried something inside his waistband. At least a sap, maybe. If somebody started to get out of line, Khaki would go over to where it was beginning. He'd rest his big hand on the party's shoulder and say a few words and that was that. I'd been going there off and on for months. I was pleased that he'd say things to me, things like, "How're you doing tonight, friend?" Or, "Friend, I haven't seen you for a spell."

The Off-Broadway is where I took Donna on our date. It was the one date we ever had.

I'd walked out of the hospital just after midnight. It'd cleared up and stars were out. I still had this buzz on from the Scotch I'd had with Patti. But I was thinking to hit Birney's for a quick one on the way home. Donna's car was parked in the space next to my car, and Donna was inside the car. I remembered that hug we'd had in the kitchen. "Not now," she'd said.

She rolled the window down and knocked ashes from her cigarette.

"I couldn't sleep," she said. "I have some things on my mind, and I couldn't sleep."

I said, "Donna. Hey, I'm glad to see you, Donna."

"I don't know what's wrong with me," she said.

"You want to go someplace for a drink?" I said.

"Patti's my friend," she said.

"She's my friend, too," I said. Then I said, "Let's go."

"Just so you know," she said.

"There's this place. It's a spade place," I said. "They have music. We can get a drink, listen to some music."

"You want to drive me?" Donna said.

I said, "Scoot over."

She started right in about vitamins. Vitamins were on the skids, vitamins had taken a nose dive. The bottom had fallen out of the vitamin market.

Donna said, "I hate to do this to Patti. She's my best friend, and she's trying to build things up for us. But I may have to quit. This is between us. Swear it! But I have to eat. I have to pay rent. I need new shoes and a new coat. Vitamins can't cut it," Donna said. "I don't think vitamins is where it's at anymore. I haven't said anything to Patti. Like I said, I'm still just thinking about it."

Donna laid her hand next to my leg. I reached down and squeezed her fingers. She squeezed back. Then she took her hand away and pushed in the lighter. After she had her cigarette going, she put the hand back. "Worse than anything, I hate to let Patti down. You know what I'm saying? We were a team." She reached me her cigarette. "I know it's a different brand," she said, "but try it, go ahead."

I pulled into the lot for the Off-Broadway. Three spades were up against an old Chrysler that had a cracked windshield. They were just lounging, passing a bottle in a sack. They looked us over. I got out and went around to open up for Donna. I checked the doors, took her arm, and we headed for the street. The spades just watched us.

I said, "You're not thinking about moving to Portland, are you?"

We were on the sidewalk. I put my arm around her waist.

"I don't know anything about Portland. Portland hasn't crossed my mind once."

The front half of the Off-Broadway was like a regular café and bar. A few spades sat at the counter and a few more worked over plates of food at tables with red oilcloth. We went through the café and into the big room in back. There was a long counter with booths against the wall and farther back a platform where musicians could set up. In front of the platform was what passed for a dance floor. The bars and nightclubs were still serving, so people hadn't turned up in any real numbers yet. I helped Donna take off her coat. We picked a booth and put our cigarettes on the table. The spade waitress named Hannah came over. Hannah and me nodded. She looked at Donna. I ordered us two RC specials and decided to feel good about things.

After the drinks came and I'd paid and we'd each had a sip, we started hugging. We carried on like this for a while, squeezing and patting, kissing each other's face. Every so often Donna would stop and draw back, push me away a little, then hold me by the wrists. She'd gaze into my eyes. Then her lids would close slowly and we'd fall to kissing again. Pretty soon the place began to fill up. We stopped kissing. But I kept my arm around her.

She put her fingers on my leg. A couple of spade horn-players and a white drummer began fooling around with something. I figured Donna and me would have another drink and listen to the set. Then we'd leave and go to her place to finish things.

I'd just ordered two more from Hannah when this spade named Benny came over with this other spade – this big, dressed-up spade. This big spade had little red eyes and was wearing a three-piece pinstripe. He had on a rose-colored shirt, a tie, a topcoat, a fedora – all of it.

"How's my man?" said Benny.

Benny stuck out his hand for a brother handshake. Benny and I had talked. He knew I liked the music, and he used to come over to talk whenever we were both in the place. He liked to talk about Johnny Hodges, how he'd played sax backup for Johnny. He'd say things like, "When Johnny and me had this gig in Mason City."

"Hi, Benny," I said.

"I want you to meet Nelson," Benny said. "He just back from Nam today. This morning. He here to listen to some of these good sounds. He got on his dancing shoes in case." Benny looked at Nelson and nodded. "This here is Nelson."

I was looking at Nelson's shiny shoes, and then I looked at Nelson. He seemed to want to place me from somewhere. He studied me. Then he let loose a rolling grin that showed his teeth.

"This is Donna," I said. "Donna, this is Benny, and this is Nelson. Nelson, this is Donna."

"Hello, girl," Nelson said, and Donna said right back, "Hello there, Nelson. Hello, Benny."

"Maybe we'll just slide in and join you folks?" Benny said. "Okay?"

I said, "Sure."

But I was sorry they hadn't found someplace else.

"We're not going to be here long," I said. "Just long enough to finish this drink, is all."

"I know, man, I know," Benny said. He sat across from me after Nelson had let himself down into the booth. "Things to do, places to go. Yes sir, Benny knows," Benny said, and winked.

Nelson looked across the booth to Donna. Then he took off the hat. He seemed to be looking for something on the brim as he turned the hat around in his big hands. He made room for the hat on the table. He looked up at Donna. He grinned and squared his shoulders. He had to square his shoulders every few minutes. It was like he was very tired of carrying them around.

"You real good friends with him, I bet," Nelson said to Donna.

"We're good friends," Donna said.

Hannah came over. Benny asked for RCs. Hannah went away, and Nelson worked a pint of whiskey from his topcoat.

"Good friends," Nelson said. "Real good friends." He unscrewed the cap on his whiskey.

"Watch it, Nelson," Benny said. "Keep that out of sight. Nelson just got off the plane from Nam," Benny said.

Nelson raised the bottle and drank some of his whiskey. He screwed the cap back on, laid the bottle on the table, and put his hat down on top of it. "Real good friends," he said.

Benny looked at me and rolled his eyes. But he was drunk, too. "I got to get into shape," he said to me. He drank RC from both of their glasses and then held the glasses under the table and poured whiskey. He put the bottle in his coat pocket. "Man, I ain't put my lips to a reed for a month now. I got to get with it."

We were bunched in the booth, glasses in front of us, Nelson's hat on the table. "You," Nelson said to me. "You with somebody else, ain't you? This beautiful woman, she ain't your wife. I know that. But you real good friends with this woman. Ain't I right?"

I had some of my drink. I couldn't taste the whiskey. I couldn't taste anything. I said, "Is all that shit about Vietnam true we see on the TV?"

Nelson had his red eyes fixed on me. He said, "What I want to say is, do you know where your wife is? I bet she out with some dude and she be seizing his nipples for him and pulling his pud for him while you setting here big as life with your good friend. I bet she have herself a good friend, too."

"Nelson," Benny said.

209

"Nelson nothing," Nelson said.

Benny said, "Nelson, let's leave these people be. There's somebody in that other booth. Somebody I told you about. Nelson just this morning got off a plane," Benny said.

"I bet I know what you thinking," Nelson said. "I bet you thinking, 'Now here a big drunk nigger and what am I going to do with him? Maybe I have to whip his ass for him!' That what you thinking?"

I looked around the room. I saw Khaki standing near the platform, the musicians working away behind him. Some dancers were on the floor. I thought Khaki looked right at me – but if he did, he looked away again.

"Ain't it your turn to talk?" Nelson said. "I just teasing you. I ain't done any teasing since I left Nam. I teased the gooks some." He grinned again, his big lips rolling back. Then he stopped grinning and just stared.

"Show them that ear," Benny said. He put his glass on the table. "Nelson got himself an ear off one of them little dudes," Benny said. "He carry it with him. Show them, Nelson."

Nelson sat there. Then he started feeling the pockets of his topcoat. He took things out of one pocket. He took out some keys and a box of cough drops.

Donna said, "I don't want to see an ear. Ugh. Double ugh. Jesus." She looked at me.

"We have to go," I said.

Nelson was still feeling in his pockets. He took a wallet from a pocket inside the suit coat and put it on the table. He patted the wallet. "Five big ones there. Listen here," he said to Donna. "I going to give you two bills. You with me? I give you two big ones, and then you French me. Just like his woman doing some other big fellow. You hear? You know she got her mouth on somebody's hammer right this minute while he here with his hand up your skirt. Fair's fair. Here." He pulled the corners of the bills from his wallet. "Hell, here another hundred for your good friend, so he won't feel left out. He don't have to do nothing. You don't have to do nothing," Nelson said to me. "You just sit there and drink your drink and listen to the music. Good music. Me and this woman walk out together like good friends. And she walk back in by herself. Won't be long, she be back."

"Nelson," Benny said, "this is no way to talk, Nelson."

Nelson grinned. "I finished talking," he said.

He found what he'd been feeling for. It was a silver cigarette case. He opened it up. I looked at the ear inside. It sat on a bed of cotton. It looked like a dried mushroom. But it was a real ear, and it was hooked up to a key chain.

"Jesus," said Donna. "Yuck."

"Ain't that something?" Nelson said. He was watching Donna.

"No way. Fuck off," Donna said.

"Girl," Nelson said.

"Nelson," I said. And then Nelson fixed his red eyes on me. He pushed the hat and wallet and cigarette case out of his way.

"What do you want?" Nelson said. "I give you what you want."

Khaki had a hand on my shoulder and the other one on Benny's shoulder. He leaned over the table, his head shining under the lights. "How you folks? You all having fun?"

"Everything all right, Khaki," Benny said. "Everything A-okay. These people here was just fixing to leave. Me and Nelson going to sit and listen to the music."

"That's good," Khaki said. "Folks be happy is my motto."

He looked around the booth. He looked at Nelson's wallet on the table and at the open cigarette case next to the wallet. He saw the ear.

"That a real ear?" Khaki said.

Benny said, "It is. Show him that ear, Nelson. Nelson just stepped off the plane from Nam with this ear. This ear has traveled halfway around the world to be on this table tonight. Nelson, show him," Benny said.

Nelson picked up the case and handed it to Khaki.

Khaki examined the ear. He took up the chain and dangled the ear in front of his face. He looked at it. He let it swing back and forth on the chain. "I heard about these dried-up ears and dicks and such."

"I took it off one of them gooks," Nelson said. "He couldn't hear nothing with it no more. I wanted me a keepsake."

Khaki turned the ear on its chain.

Donna and I began getting out of the booth.

"Girl, don't go," Nelson said.

"Nelson," Benny said.

Khaki was watching Nelson now. I stood beside the booth with Donna's coat. My legs were crazy.

Nelson raised his voice. He said, "You go with this mother here, you let him put his face in your sweets, you both going to have to deal with me."

We started to move away from the booth. People were looking.

"Nelson just got off the plane from Nam this morning," I heard Benny say. "We been drinking all day. This been the longest day on record. But me and him, we going to be fine, Khaki."

Nelson yelled something over the music. He yelled, "It ain't going to do no good! Whatever you do, it ain't going to help none!" I heard him say that, and then I couldn't hear anymore. The music stopped, and then it started again. We didn't look back. We kept going. We got out to the sidewalk.

I opened the door for her. I started us back to the hospital. Donna stayed over on her side. She'd used the lighter on a cigarette, but she wouldn't talk.

I tried to say something. I said, "Look, Donna, don't get on a downer because of this. I'm sorry it happened," I said.

"I could of used the money," Donna said. "That's what I was thinking."

I kept driving and didn't look at her.

"It's true," she said. "I could of used the money." She shook her head. "I don't know," she said. She put her chin down and cried.

"Don't cry," I said.

"I'm not going in to work tomorrow, today, whenever it is the alarm goes off," she said. "I'm not going in. I'm leaving town. I take what happened back there as a sign." She pushed in the lighter and waited for it to pop out.

I pulled in beside my car and killed the engine. I looked in the rearview, half thinking I'd see that old Chrysler drive into the lot behind me with Nelson in the seat. I kept my hands on the wheel for a minute, and then dropped them to my lap. I didn't want to touch Donna. The hug we'd given each other in my kitchen that night, the kissing we'd done at the Off-Broadway, that was all over.

I said, "What are you going to do?" But I didn't care. Right then she could have died of a heart attack and it wouldn't have meant anything.

"Maybe I could go up to Portland," she said. "There must be something in Portland. Portland's on everybody's mind these days. Portland's a drawing card. Portland this, Portland that. Portland's as good a place as any. It's all the same."

"Donna," I said, "I'd better go."

I started to let myself out. I cracked the door, and the overhead light came on.

"For Christ's sake, turn off that light!"

I got out in a hurry. "'Night, Donna," I said.

I left her staring at the dashboard. I started up my car and turned on the lights. I slipped it in gear and fed it the gas.

I poured Scotch, drank some of it, and took the glass into the bathroom. I brushed my teeth. Then I pulled open a drawer. Patti yelled something from the bedroom. She opened the bathroom door. She was still dressed. She'd been sleeping with her clothes on, I guess.

"What time is it?" she screamed. "I've overslept! Jesus, oh my God! You've let me oversleep, goddamn you!"

She was wild. She stood in the doorway with her clothes on. She could have been fixing to go to work. But there was no sample case, no vitamins. She was having a bad dream, is all. She began shaking her head from side to side.

I couldn't take any more tonight. "Go back to sleep, honey. I'm looking for something," I said. I knocked some stuff out of the medicine chest. Things rolled into the sink. "Where's the aspirin?" I said. I knocked down some more things. I didn't care. Things kept falling.

Careful

After a lot of talking – what his wife, Inez, called *assessment* – Lloyd moved out of the house and into his own place. He had two rooms and a bath on the top floor of a three-story house. Inside the rooms, the roof slanted down sharply. If he walked around, he had to duck his head. He had to stoop to look from his windows and be careful getting in and out of bed. There were two keys. One key let him into the house itself. Then he climbed some stairs that passed through the house to a landing. He went up another flight of stairs to the door of his room and used the other key on that lock.

Once, when he was coming back to his place in the afternoon, carrying a sack with three bottles of André champagne and some lunch meat, he stopped on the landing and looked into his landlady's living room. He saw the old woman lying on her back on the carpet. She seemed to be asleep. Then it occurred to him she might be dead. But the TV was going, so he chose to think she was asleep. He didn't know what to make of it. He moved the sack from one arm to the other. It was then that the woman gave a little cough, brought her hand to her side, and went back to being quiet and still again. Lloyd continued on up the stairs and unlocked his door. Later that day, toward evening, as he looked from his kitchen window, he saw the old woman down in the yard, wearing a straw hat and holding her hand against her side. She was using a little watering can on some pansies.

In his kitchen, he had a combination refrigerator and stove. The refrigerator and stove was a tiny affair wedged into a space between the sink and the wall. He had to bend over, almost get down on his knees, to get anything out of the refrigerator. But it was all right because he didn't keep much in there, anyway – except fruit juice, lunch meat, and champagne. The stove had two burners. Now and then he heated water in a saucepan and made instant coffee. But some days he didn't drink any coffee. He forgot, or else he just didn't feel like coffee. One morning he woke up and promptly fell to eating crumb doughnuts and drinking champagne. There'd been a time, some years back, when he would have laughed at having a breakfast like this. Now, there didn't seem to be anything very unusual about it. In fact, he hadn't thought anything about it until he was in bed and trying to recall the things he'd done that day, starting with when he'd gotten up that morning. At first, he couldn't remember anything noteworthy. Then he remembered eating those doughnuts and drinking champagne. Time was when he would have considered this a mildly crazy thing to do, something to tell friends about. Then, the more he thought about it, the more he could see it didn't matter much one way or the other. He'd had doughnuts and champagne for breakfast. So what?

In his furnished rooms, he also had a dinette set, a little sofa, an old easy chair, and a TV set that stood on a coffee table. He wasn't paying the electricity here, it wasn't even his TV, so sometimes he left the set on all day and all night. But he kept the volume down unless he saw there was something he wanted to watch. He did not have a telephone, which was fine with him. He didn't want a telephone. There was a bedroom with a double bed, a nightstand, a chest of drawers, a bathroom.

The one time Inez came to visit, it was eleven o'clock in the morning. He'd been in his new place for two weeks, and he'd been wondering if she were going to drop by. But he was trying to do something about his drinking, too, so he was glad to be alone. He'd made that much clear – being alone was the thing he needed most. The day she came, he was on the sofa, in his pajamas, hitting his fist against the right side of his head. Just before he could hit himself again, he heard voices downstairs on the landing. He could make out his wife's voice. The sound was like the murmur of voices from a faraway crowd, but he knew it was Inez and somehow knew the visit was an important one. He gave his head another jolt with his fist, then got to his feet.

He'd awakened that morning and found that his ear had

stopped up with wax. He couldn't hear anything clearly, and he seemed to have lost his sense of balance, his equilibrium, in the process. For the last hour, he'd been on the sofa, working frustratedly on his ear, now and again slamming his head with his fist. Once in a while he'd massage the gristly underpart of his ear, or else tug at his lobe. Then he'd dig furiously in his ear with his little finger and open his mouth, simulating yawns. But he'd tried everything he could think of, and he was nearing the end of his rope. He could hear the voices below break off their murmuring. He pounded his head a good one and finished the glass of champagne. He turned off the TV and carried the glass to the sink. He picked up the open bottle of champagne from the drainboard and took it into the bathroom, where he put it behind the stool. Then he went to answer the door.

"Hi, Lloyd," Inez said. She didn't smile. She stood in the doorway in a bright spring outfit. He hadn't seen these clothes before. She was holding a canvas handbag that had sunflowers stitched onto its sides. He hadn't seen the handbag before, either.

"I didn't think you heard me," she said. "I thought you might be gone or something. But the woman downstairs – what's her name? Mrs Matthews – she thought you were up here."

"I heard you," Lloyd said. "But just barely." He hitched his pajamas and ran a hand through his hair. "Actually, I'm in one hell of a shape. Come on in."

"It's eleven o'clock," she said. She came inside and shut the door behind her. She acted as if she hadn't heard him. Maybe she hadn't.

"I know what time it is," he said. "I've been up for a long time. I've been up since eight. I watched part of the *Today* show. But just now I'm about to go crazy with something. My ear's plugged up. You remember that other time it happened? We were living in that place near the Chinese takeout joint. Where the kids found that bulldog dragging its chain? I had to go to the doctor then and have my ears flushed out. I know you remember. You drove me and we had to wait a long time. Well, it's like that now. I mean it's that bad. Only I can't go to a doctor this morning. I don't have a doctor for one thing. I'm about to go

217

nuts, Inez. I feel like I want to cut my head off or something."

He sat down at one end of the sofa, and she sat down at the other end. But it was a small sofa, and they were still sitting close to each other. They were so close he could have put out his hand and touched her knee. But he didn't. She glanced around the room and then fixed her eyes on him again. He knew he hadn't shaved and that his hair stood up. But she was his wife, and she knew everything there was to know about him.

"What have you tried?" she said. She looked in her purse and brought up a cigarette. "I mean, what have you done for it so far?"

"What'd you say?" He turned the left side of his head to her. "Inez, I swear, I'm not exaggerating. This thing is driving me crazy. When I talk, I feel like I'm talking inside a barrel. My head rumbles. And I can't hear good, either. When *you* talk, it sounds like you're talking through a lead pipe."

"Do you have any Q-tips, or else Wesson oil?" Inez said.

"Honey, this is serious," he said. "I don't have any Q-tips or Wesson oil. Are you kidding?"

"If we had some Wesson oil, I could heat it and put some of that in your ear. My mother used to do that," she said. "It might soften things up in there."

He shook his head. His head felt full and like it was awash with fluid. It felt like it had when he used to swim near the bottom of the municipal pool and come up with his ears filled with water. But back then it'd been easy to clear the water out. All he had to do was fill his lungs with air, close his mouth, and clamp down on his nose. Then he'd blow out his cheeks and force air into his head. His ears would pop, and for a few seconds he'd have the pleasant sensation of water running out of his head and dripping onto his shoulders. Then he'd heave himself out of the pool.

Inez finished her cigarette and put it out. "Lloyd, we have things to talk about. But I guess we'll have to take things one at a time. Go sit in the chair. Not *that* chair, the chair in the kitchen! So we can have some light on the situation."

He whacked his head once more. Then he went over to sit on

a dinette chair. She moved over and stood behind him. She touched his hair with her fingers. Then she moved the hair away from his ears. He reached for her hand, but she drew it away.

"Which ear did you say it was?" she said.

"The right ear," he said. "The right one."

"First," she said, "you have to sit here and not move. I'll find a hairpin and some tissue paper. I'll try to get in there with that. Maybe it'll do the trick."

He was alarmed at the prospect of her putting a hairpin inside his ear. He said something to that effect.

"What?" she said. "Christ, I can't hear you, either. Maybe this is catching."

"When I was a kid, in school," Lloyd said, "we had this health teacher. She was like a nurse, too. She said we should never put anything smaller than an elbow into our ear." He vaguely remembered a wall chart showing a massive diagram of the ear, along with an intricate system of canals, passageways, and walls.

"Well, your nurse was never faced with this exact problem," Inez said. "Anyway, we need to try *something*. We'll try this first. If it doesn't work, we'll try something else. That's life, isn't it?"

"Does that have a hidden meaning or something?" Lloyd said.

"It means just what I said. But you're free to think as you please. I mean, it's a free country," she said. "Now, let me get fixed up with what I need. You just sit there."

She went through her purse, but she didn't find what she was looking for. Finally, she emptied the purse out onto the sofa. "No hairpins," she said. "Damn." But it was as if she were saying the words from another room. In a way, it was almost as if he'd imagined her saying them. There'd been a time, long ago, when they used to feel they had ESP when it came to what the other one was thinking. They could finish sentences that the other had started.

She picked up some nail clippers, worked for a minute, and then he saw the device separate in her fingers and part of it swing away from the other part. A nail file protruded from the clippers. It looked to him as if she were holding a small dagger.

"You're going to put that in my ear?" he said.

"Maybe you have a better idea," she said. "It's this, or else I don't know what. Maybe you have a pencil? You want me to use that? Or maybe you have a screwdriver around," she said and laughed. "Don't worry. Listen, Lloyd, I won't hurt you. I said I'd be careful. I'll wrap some tissue around the end of this. It'll be all right. I'll be careful, like I said. You just stay where you are, and I'll get some tissue for this. I'll make a swab."

She went into the bathroom. She was gone for a time. He stayed where he was on the dinette chair. He began thinking of things he ought to say to her. He wanted to tell her he was limiting himself to champagne and champagne only. He wanted to tell her he was tapering off the champagne, too. It was only a matter of time now. But when she came back into the room, he couldn't say anything. He didn't know where to start. But she didn't look at him, anyway. She fished a cigarette from the heap of things she'd emptied onto the sofa cushion. She lit the cigarette with her lighter and went to stand by the window that faced onto the street. She said something, but he couldn't make out the words. When she stopped talking, he didn't ask her what it was she'd said. Whatever it was, he knew he didn't want her to say it again. She put out the cigarette. But she went on standing at the window, leaning forward, the slope of the roof just inches from her head.

"Inez," he said.

She turned and came over to him. He could see tissue on the point of the nail file.

"Turn your head to the side and keep it that way," she said. "That's right. Sit still now and don't move. Don't move," she said again.

"Be careful," he said. "For Christ's sake."

She didn't answer him.

"Please, please," he said. Then he didn't say any more. He was afraid. He closed his eyes and held his breath as he felt the nail file turn past the inner part of his ear and begin its probe. He was sure his heart would stop beating. Then she went a little farther and began turning the blade back and forth, working at whatever it was in there. Inside his ear, he heard a squeaking sound.

"Ouch!" he said.

"Did I hurt you?" She took the nail file out of his ear and moved back a step. "Does anything feel different, Lloyd?"

He brought his hands up to his ears and lowered his head.

"It's just the same," he said.

She looked at him and bit her lips.

"Let me go to the bathroom," he said. "Before we go any farther, I have to go to the bathroom."

"Go ahead," Inez said. "I think I'll go downstairs and see if your landlady has any Wesson oil, or anything like that. She might even have some Q-tips. I don't know why I didn't think of that before. Of asking her."

"That's a good idea," he said. "I'll go to the bathroom."

She stopped at the door and looked at him, and then she opened the door and went out. He crossed the living room, went into his bedroom, and opened the bathroom door. He reached down behind the stool and brought up the bottle of champagne. He took a long drink. It was warm but it went right down. He took some more. In the beginning, he'd really thought he could continue drinking if he limited himself to champagne. But in no time he found he was drinking three or four bottles a day. He knew he'd have to deal with this pretty soon. But first, he'd have to get his hearing back. One thing at a time, just like she'd said. He finished off the rest of the champagne and put the empty bottle in its place behind the stool. Then he ran water and brushed his teeth. After he'd used the towel, he went back into the other room.

Inez had returned and was at the stove heating something in a little pan. She glanced in his direction, but didn't say anything at first. He looked past her shoulder and out the window. A bird flew from one tree to another and preened its feathers. But if it made any kind of bird noise, he didn't hear it.

She said something that he didn't catch.

"Say again," he said.

She shook her head and turned back to the stove. But then she turned again and said, loud enough and slow enough so he could hear it: "I found your stash in the bathroom."

"I'm trying to cut back," he said.

She said something else. "What?" he said. "What'd you say?" He really hadn't heard her.

"We'll talk later," she said. "We have things to discuss, Lloyd. Money is one thing. But there are other things, too. First we have to see about this ear." She put her finger into the pan and then took the pan off the stove. "I'll let it cool for a minute," she said. "It's too hot right now. Sit down. Put this towel around your shoulders."

He did as he was told. He sat on a chair and put the towel around his neck and shoulders. Then he hit the side of his head with his fist.

"Goddamn it," he said.

She didn't look up. She put her finger into the pan once more, testing. Then she poured the liquid from the pan into his plastic glass. She picked up the glass and came over to him.

"Don't be scared," she said. "It's just some of your landlady's baby oil, that's all it is. I told her what was wrong, and she thought this might help. No guarantees," Inez said. "But maybe this'll loosen things up in there. She said it used to happen to her husband. She said this one time she saw a piece of wax fall out of his ear, and it was like a big plug of something. It was ear wax, was what it was. She said try this. And she didn't have any Q-tips. I can't understand that, her not having any Q-tips. That part really surprises me."

"Okay," he said. "All right. I'm willing to try anything. Inez, if I had to go on like this, I think I'd rather be dead. You know? I mean it, Inez."

"Tilt your head all the way to the side now," she said. "Don't move. I'll pour this in until your ear fills up, then I'll stopper it with this dishrag. And you just sit there for ten minutes, say. Then we'll see. If this doesn't do it, well, I don't have any other suggestions. I just don't know what to do then."

"This'll work," he said. "If this doesn't work, I'll find a gun and shoot myself. I'm serious. That's what I feel like doing, anyway."

He turned his head to the side and let it hang down. He looked at the things in the room from this new perspective. But it wasn't any different from the old way of looking, except that everything was on its side.

"Farther," she said. He held on to the chair for balance and lowered his head even more. All of the objects in his vision, all of the objects in his life, it seemed, were at the far end of this room. He could feel the warm liquid pour into his ear. Then she brought the dishrag up and held it there. In a little while, she began to massage the area around his ear. She pressed into the soft part of the flesh between his jaw and skull. She moved her fingers to the area over his ear and began to work the tips of her fingers back and forth. After a while, he didn't know how long he'd been sitting there. It could have been ten minutes. It could have been longer. He was still holding on to the chair. Now and then, as her fingers pressed the side of his head, he could feel the warm oil she'd poured in there wash back and forth in the canals inside his ear. When she pressed a certain way, he imagined he could hear, inside his head, a soft, swishing sound.

"Sit up straight," Inez said. He sat up and pressed the heel of his hand against his head while the liquid poured out of his ear. She caught it in the towel. Then she wiped the outside of his ear.

Inez was breathing through her nose. Lloyd heard the sound her breath made as it came and went. He heard a car pass on the street outside the house and, at the back of the house, down below his kitchen window, the clear *snick-snick* of pruning shears.

"Well?" Inez said. She waited with her hands on her hips, frowning.

"I can hear you," he said. "I'm all right! I mean, I can *hear*. It doesn't sound like you're talking underwater anymore. It's fine now. It's okay. God, I thought for a while I was going to go crazy. But I feel fine now. I can hear everything. Listen, honey, I'll make coffee. There's some juice, too."

"I have to go," she said. "I'm late for something. But I'll come back. We'll go out for lunch sometime. We need to talk."

"I just can't sleep on this side of my head, is all," he went on. He followed her into the living room. She lit a cigarette. "That's what happened. I slept all night on this side of my head, and my ear plugged up. I think I'll be all right as long as I don't forget and sleep on this side of my head. If I'm careful. You know what I'm saying? If I can just sleep on my back, or else on my left side."

She didn't look at him.

"Not forever, of course not, I know that. I couldn't do that. I couldn't do it the rest of my life. But for a while, anyway. Just my left side, or else flat on my back."

But even as he said this, he began to feel afraid of the night that was coming. He began to fear the moment he would begin to make his preparations for bed and what might happen afterward. That time was hours away, but already he was afraid. What if, in the middle of the night, he accidentally turned onto his right side, and the weight of his head pressing into the pillow were to seal the wax again into the dark canals of his ear? What if he woke up then, unable to hear, the ceiling inches from his head?

"Good God," he said. "Jesus, this is awful. Inez, I just had something like a terrible nightmare. Inez, where do you have to go?"

"I told you," she said, as she put everything back into her purse and made ready to leave. She looked at her watch. "I'm late for something." She went to the door. But at the door she turned and said something else to him. He didn't listen. He didn't want to. He watched her lips move until she'd said what she had to say. When she'd finished, she said, "Goodbye." Then she opened the door and closed it behind her.

He went into the bedroom to dress. But in a minute he hurried out, wearing only his trousers, and went to the door. He opened it and stood there, listening. On the landing below, he heard Inez thank Mrs Matthews for the oil. He heard the old woman say, "You're welcome." And then he heard her draw a connection between her late husband and himself. He heard her say, "Leave me your number. I'll call if something happens. You never know."

"I hope you don't have to," Inez said. "But I'll give it to you, anyway. Do you have something to write it down with?"

Lloyd heard Mrs Matthews open a drawer and rummage through it. Then her old woman's voice said, "Okay."

Inez gave her their telephone number at home. "Thanks," she said.

"It was nice meeting you," Mrs Matthews said.

He listened as Inez went on down the stairs and opened the front door. Then he heard it close. He waited until he heard her start their car and drive away. Then he shut the door and went back into the bedroom to finish dressing.

After he'd put on his shoes and tied the laces, he lay down on the bed and pulled the covers up to his chin. He let his arms rest under the covers at his sides. He closed his eyes and pretended it was night and pretended he was going to fall asleep. Then he brought his arms up and crossed them over his chest to see how this position would suit him. He kept his eyes closed, trying it out. All right, he thought. Okay. If he didn't want that ear to plug up again, he'd have to sleep on his back, that was all. He knew he could do it. He just couldn't forget, even in his sleep, and turn onto the wrong side. Four or five hours' sleep a night was all he needed, anyway. He'd manage. Worse things could happen to a man. In a way, it was a challenge. But he was up to it. He knew he was. In a minute, he threw back the covers and got up.

He still had the better part of the day ahead of him. He went into the kitchen, bent down in front of the little refrigerator, and took out a fresh bottle of champagne. He worked the plastic cork out of the bottle as carefully as he could, but there was still the festive *pop* of champagne being opened. He rinsed the baby oil out of his glass, then poured it full of champagne. He took the glass over to the sofa and sat down. He put the glass on the coffee table. Up went his feet onto the coffee table, next to the champagne. He leaned back. But after a time he began to worry some more about the night that was coming on. What if, despite all his efforts, the wax decided to plug his other ear? He closed his eyes and shook his head. Pretty soon he got up and went into the bedroom. He undressed and put his pajamas back on. Then he moved back into the living room. He sat down on the sofa once more, and once more put his feet up. He reached over and turned the TV on. He adjusted the volume. He knew he couldn't keep from worrying about what might happen when he went to bed. It was just something he'd have to learn to live with. In a way, this whole business reminded him of the thing with the doughnuts and champagne. It was not that remarkable at all, if you thought about it. He took some champagne. But it didn't taste right. He ran his tongue over his lips, then wiped his mouth on his sleeve. He looked and saw a film of oil on the champagne.

He got up and carried the glass to the sink, where he poured it into the drain. He took the bottle of champagne into the living room and made himself comfortable on the sofa. He held the bottle by its neck as he drank. He wasn't in the habit of drinking from the bottle, but it didn't seem that much out of the ordinary. He decided that even if he were to fall asleep sitting up on the sofa in the middle of the afternoon, it wouldn't be any more strange than somebody having to lie on his back for hours at a time. He lowered his head to peer out the window. Judging from the angle of sunlight, and the shadows that had entered the room, he guessed it was about three o'clock.

Where I'm Calling from

J.P. and I are on the front porch at Frank Martin's drying-out facility. Like the rest of us at Frank Martin's, J.P. is first and foremost a drunk. But he's also a chimney sweep. It's his first time here, and he's scared. I've been here once before. What's to say? I'm back. J.P.'s real name is Joe Penny, but he says I should call him J.P. He's about thirty years old. Younger than I am. Not much younger, but a little. He's telling me how he decided to go into his line of work, and he wants to use his hands when he talks. But his hands tremble. I mean, they won't keep still. "This has never happened to me before," he says. He means the trembling. I tell him I sympathize. I tell him the shakes will idle down. And they will. But it takes time.

We've only been in here a couple of days. We're not out of the woods yet. J.P. has these shakes, and every so often a nerve – maybe it isn't a nerve, but it's something – begins to jerk in my shoulder. Sometimes it's at the side of my neck. When this happens, my mouth dries up. It's an effort just to swallow then. I know something's about to happen and I want to head it off. I want to hide from it, that's what I want to do. Just close my eyes and let it pass by, let it take the next man. J.P. can wait a minute.

I saw a seizure yesterday morning. A guy they call Tiny. A big fat guy, an electrician from Santa Rosa. They said he'd been in here for nearly two weeks and that he was over the hump. He was going home in a day or two and would spend New Year's Eve with his wife in front of the TV. On New Year's Eve, Tiny planned to drink hot chocolate and eat cookies. Yesterday morning he seemed just fine when he came down for breakfast. He was letting out with quacking noises, showing some guy how he called ducks right down onto his head. "Blam. Blam," said

227

Tiny, picking off a couple. Tiny's hair was damp and was slicked back along the sides of his head. He'd just come out of the shower. He'd also nicked himself on the chin with his razor. But so what? Just about everybody at Frank Martin's has nicks on his face. It's something that happens. Tiny edged in at the head of the table and began telling about something that had happened on one of his drinking bouts. People at the table laughed and shook their heads as they shoveled up their eggs. Tiny would say something, grin, then look around the table for a sign of recognition. We'd all done things just as bad and crazy, so, sure, that's why we laughed. Tiny had scrambled eggs on his plate, and some biscuits and honey. I was at the table, but I wasn't hungry. I had some coffee in front of me. Suddenly, Tiny wasn't there anymore. He'd gone over in his chair with a big clatter. He was on his back on the floor with his eyes closed, his heels drumming the linoleum. People hollered for Frank Martin. But he was right there. A couple of guys got down on the floor beside Tiny. One of the guys put his fingers inside Tiny's mouth and tried to hold his tongue. Frank Martin yelled, "Everybody stand back!" Then I noticed that the bunch of us were leaning over Tiny, just looking at him, not able to take our eyes off him. "Give him air!" Frank Martin said. Then he ran into the office and called the ambulance.

Tiny is on board again today. Talk about bouncing back. This morning Frank Martin drove the station wagon to the hospital to get him. Tiny got back too late for his eggs, but he took some coffee into the dining room and sat down at the table anyway. Somebody in the kitchen made toast for him, but Tiny didn't eat it. He just sat with his coffee and looked into his cup. Every now and then he moved his cup back and forth in front of him.

I'd like to ask him if he had any signal just before it happened. I'd like to know if he felt his ticker skip a beat, or else begin to race. Did his eyelid twitch? But I'm not about to say anything. He doesn't look like he's hot to talk about it, anyway. But what happened to Tiny is something I won't ever forget. Old Tiny flat on the floor, kicking his heels. So every time this little flitter starts up anywhere, I draw some breath and wait to find myself on my back, looking up, somebody's fingers in my mouth.

In his chair on the front porch, J.P. keeps his hands in his lap. I smoke cigarettes and use an old coal bucket for an ashtray. I listen to J.P. ramble on. It's eleven o'clock in the morning – an hour and a half until lunch. Neither one of us is hungry. But just the same we look forward to going inside and sitting down at the table. Maybe we'll get hungry.

What's J.P. talking about, anyway? He's saying how when he was twelve years old he fell into a well in the vicinity of the farm he grew up on. It was a dry well, lucky for him. "Or unlucky," he says, looking around him and shaking his head. He says how late that afternoon, after he'd been located, his dad hauled him out with a rope. J.P. had wet his pants down there. He'd suffered all kinds of terror in that well, hollering for help, waiting, and then hollering some more. He hollered himself hoarse before it was over. But he told me that being at the bottom of that well had made a lasting impression. He'd sat there and looked up at the well mouth. Way up at the top, he could see a circle of blue sky. Every once in a while a white cloud passed over. A flock of birds flew across, and it seemed to J.P. their wingbeats set up this odd commotion. He heard other things. He heard tiny rustlings above him in the well, which made him wonder if things might fall down into his hair. He was thinking of insects. He heard wind blow over the well mouth, and that sound made an impression on him, too. In short, everything about his life was different for him at the bottom of that well. But nothing fell on him and nothing closed off that little circle of blue. Then his dad came along with the rope, and it wasn't long before J.P. was back in the world he'd always lived in.

"Keep talking, J.P. Then what?" I say.

When he was eighteen or nineteen years old and out of high school and had nothing whatsoever he wanted to do with his life, he went across town one afternoon to visit a friend. This friend lived in a house with a fireplace. J.P. and his friend sat around drinking beer and batting the breeze. They played some records. Then the doorbell rings. The friend goes to the door. This young woman chimney sweep is there with her cleaning things. She's wearing a top hat, the sight of which knocked J.P. for a loop. She tells J.P.'s friend that she has an appointment to clean the fireplace. The friend lets her in and bows. The young woman doesn't pay him any mind. She spreads a blanket on the hearth and lays out her gear. She's wearing these black pants, black shirt, black shoes and socks. Of course, by now she's taken her hat off. J.P. says it nearly drove him nuts to look at her. She does the work, she cleans the chimney, while J.P. and his friend play records and drink beer. But they watch her and they watch what she does. Now and then J.P. and his friend look at each other and grin, or else they wink. They raise their eyebrows when the upper half of the young woman disappears into the chimney. She was all-right-looking, too, J.P. said.

When she'd finished her work, she rolled her things up in the blanket. From J.P.'s friend, she took a check that had been made out to her by his parents. And then she asks the friend if he wants to kiss her. "It's supposed to bring good luck," she says. That does it for J.P. The friend rolls his eyes. He clowns some more. Then, probably blushing, he kisses her on the cheek. At this minute, J.P. made his mind up about something. He put his beer down. He got up from the sofa. He went over to the young woman as she was starting to go out the door.

"Me, too?" J.P. said to her.

She swept her eyes over him. J.P. says he could feel his heart knocking. The young woman's name, it turns out, was Roxy.

"Sure," Roxy says. "Why not? I've got some extra kisses." And she kissed him a good one right on the lips and then turned to go.

Like that, quick as a wink, J.P. followed her onto the porch. He held the porch screen door for her. He went down the steps with her and out to the drive, where she'd parked her panel truck. It was something that was out of his hands. Nothing else in the world counted for anything. He knew he'd met somebody who could set his legs atremble. He could feel her kiss still burning on his lips, etc. J.P. couldn't begin to sort anything out. He was filled with sensations that were carrying him every which way.

He opened the rear door of the panel truck for her. He helped her store her things inside. "Thanks," she told him. Then he blurted it out – that he'd like to see her again. Would she go to a movie with him sometime? He'd realized, too, what he wanted to do with his life. He wanted to do what she did. He wanted to be a chimney sweep. But he didn't tell her that then.

J.P. says she put her hands on her hips and looked him over. Then she found a business card in the front seat of her truck. She gave it to him. She said, "Call this number after ten tonight. We can talk. I have to go now." She put the top hat on and then took it off. She looked at J.P. once more. She must have liked what she saw, because this time she grinned. He told her there was a smudge near her mouth. Then she got into her truck, tooted the horn, and drove away.

"Then what?" I say. "Don't stop now, J.P."

I was interested. But I would have listened if he'd been going on about how one day he'd decided to start pitching horseshoes.

It rained last night. The clouds are banked up against the hills across the valley. J.P. clears his throat and looks at the hills and the clouds. He pulls his chin. Then he goes on with what he was saying.

Roxy starts going out with him on dates. And little by little he talks her into letting him go along on jobs with her. But Roxy's in business with her father and brother and they've got just the right amount of work. They don't need anybody else. Besides, who was this guy J.P.? J.P. what? Watch out, they warned her.

So she and J.P. saw some movies together. They went to a few dances. But mainly the courtship revolved around their cleaning chimneys together. Before you know it, J.P. says, they're talking about tying the knot. And after a while they do it, they get married. J.P.'s new father-in-law takes him in as a full partner. In a year or so, Roxy has a kid. She's quit being a chimney sweep. At any rate, she's quit doing the work. Pretty soon she has another kid. J.P.'s in his mid-twenties by now. He's buying a house. He says he was happy with his life. "I was happy with the way things were going," he says. "I had everything I wanted. I had a wife and kids I loved, and I was doing what I wanted to do with my life." But for some reason – who knows why we do what we do? – his drinking picks up. For a long time he drinks beer and beer only. Any kind of beer – it didn't matter. He says he could drink beer twenty-four hours a day. He'd drink beer at night while he watched TV. Sure, once in a while he drank hard stuff. But that was only if they went out on the town, which was not often, or else when they had company over. Then a time comes, he doesn't know why, when he makes the switch from beer to gin-and-tonic. And he'd have more gin-and-tonic after dinner, sitting in front of the TV. There was always a glass of gin-and-tonic in his hand. He says he actually liked the taste of it. He began stopping off after work for drinks before he went home to have more drinks. Then he began missing some dinners. He just wouldn't show up. Or else he'd show up, but he wouldn't want anything to eat. He'd filled up on snacks at the bar. Sometimes he'd walk in the door and for no good reason throw his lunch pail across the living room. When Roxy yelled at him, he'd turn around and go out again. He moved his drinking time up to early afternoon, while he was still supposed to be working. He tells me that he was starting off the morning with a couple of drinks. He'd have a belt of the stuff before he brushed his teeth. Then he'd have his coffee. He'd go to work with a thermos bottle of vodka in his lunch pail.

J.P. quits talking. He just clams up. What's going on? I'm listening. It's helping me relax, for one thing. It's taking me away from my own situation. After a minute, I say, "What the hell? Go on, J.P." He's pulling his chin. But pretty soon he starts talking again.

J.P. and Roxy are having some real fights now. I mean *fights*. J.P. says that one time she hit him in the face with her fist and broke his nose. "Look at this," he says. "Right here." He shows me a line across the bridge of his nose. "That's a broken nose." He returned the favor. He dislocated her shoulder for her. Another time he split her lip. They beat on each other in front of the kids. Things got out of hand. But he kept on drinking. He couldn't stop. And nothing could make him stop. Not even with Roxy's dad and her brother threatening to beat the hell out of him. They told Roxy she should take the kids and clear out. But Roxy said it was her problem. She got herself into it, and she'd solve it.

Now J.P. gets real quiet again. He hunches his shoulders and pulls down in his chair. He watches a car driving down the road between this place and the hills.

I say, "I want to hear the rest of this, J.P. You better keep talking."

"I just don't know," he says. He shrugs.

"It's all right," I say. And I mean it's okay for him to tell it. "Go on, J.P."

One way she tried to fix things, J.P. says, was by finding a boyfriend. J.P. would like to know how she found the time with the house and kids.

I look at him and I'm surprised. He's a grown man. "If you want to do that," I say, "you find the time. You make the time."

J.P. shakes his head. "I guess so," he says.

Anyway, he found out about it – about Roxy's boyfriend – and he went wild. He manages to get Roxy's wedding ring off her finger. And when he does, he cuts it into several pieces with a pair of wire-cutters. Good, solid fun. They'd already gone a couple of rounds on this occasion. On his way to work the next morning, he gets arrested on a drunk charge. He loses his driver's license. He can't drive the truck to work anymore. Just as well, he says. He'd already fallen off a roof the week before and broken his thumb. It was just a matter of time until he broke his neck, he says.

He was here at Frank Martin's to dry out and to figure how to get his life back on track. But he wasn't here against his will, any more than I was. We weren't locked up. We could leave any time we wanted. But a minimum stay of a week was recommended, and two weeks or a month was, as they put it, "strongly advised".

As I said, this is my second time at Frank Martin's. When I was trying to sign a check to pay in advance for a week's stay, Frank Martin said, "The holidays are always bad. Maybe you should think of sticking around a little longer this time? Think in terms of a couple of weeks. Can you do a couple of weeks? Think about it, anyway. You don't have to decide anything right now," he said. He held his thumb on the check and I signed my name. Then I walked my girlfriend to the front door and said goodbye. "Goodbye," she said, and she lurched into the door-jamb and then onto the porch. It's late afternoon. It's raining. I go from the door to the window. I move the curtain and watch her drive away. She's in my car. She's drunk. But I'm drunk, too, and there's nothing I can do. I make it to a big chair that's close to the radiator, and I sit down. Some guys look up from their TV. Then they shift back to what they were watching. I just sit there. Now and then I look up at something that's happening on the screen.

Later that afternoon the front door banged open and J.P. was brought in between these two big guys – his father-in-law and brother-in-law, I find out afterward. They steered J.P. across the room. The old guy signed him in and gave Frank Martin a check. Then these two guys helped J.P. upstairs. I guess they put him to bed. Pretty soon the old guy and the other guy came down-stairs and headed for the front door. They couldn't seem to get out of this place fast enough. It was like they couldn't wait to wash their hands of all this. I didn't blame them. Hell, no. I don't know how I'd act if I was in their shoes.

A day and a half later J.P. and I meet up on the front porch. We shake hands and comment on the weather. J.P. has a case of the shakes. We sit down and prop our feet up on the railing. We lean back in our chairs like we're just out there taking our ease, like we might be getting ready to talk about our bird dogs. That's when J.P. gets going with his story.

It's cold out, but not too cold. It's a little overcast. Frank Martin comes outside to finish his cigar. He has on a sweater buttoned all the way up. Frank Martin is short and heavy. He has curly gray hair and a small head. His head is too small for the rest of his body. Frank Martin puts the cigar in his mouth and stands with his arms crossed over his chest. He works that cigar in his mouth and looks across the valley. He stands there like a prizefighter, like somebody who knows the score.

J.P. gets quiet again. I mean, he's hardly breathing. I toss my cigarette into the coal bucket and look hard at J.P., who scoots farther down in his chair. J.P. pulls up his collar. What the hell's going on? I wonder. Frank Martin uncrosses his arms and takes a puff on the cigar. He lets the smoke carry out of his mouth. Then he raises his chin toward the hills and says, "Jack London used to have a big place on the other side of this valley. Right over there behind that green hill you're looking at. But alcohol killed him. Let that be a lesson to you. He was a better man than any of us. But he couldn't handle the stuff, either." Frank Martin looks at what's left of his cigar. It's gone out. He tosses it into the bucket. "You guys want to read something while you're here, read that book of his, *The Call of the Wild*. You know the one I'm talking about? We have it inside if you want to read something. It's about this animal that's half dog and half wolf. End of sermon," he says, and then hitches his pants up and tugs his sweater down. "I'm going inside," he says. "See you at lunch."

"I feel like a bug when he's around," J.P. says. "He makes me feel like a bug." J.P. shakes his head. Then he says, "Jack London. What a name! I wish I had me a name like that. Instead of the name I got."

My wife brought me up here the first time. That's when we were still together, trying to make things work out. She brought me here and she stayed around for an hour or two, talking to Frank Martin in private. Then she left. The next morning Frank Martin got me aside and said, "We can help you. If you want help and want to listen to what we say." But I didn't know if they could help me or not. Part of me wanted help. But there was another part.

This time around, it was my girlfriend who drove me here.

She was driving my car. She drove us through a rainstorm. We drank champagne all the way. We were both drunk when she pulled up in the drive. She intended to drop me off, turn around, and drive home again. She had things to do. One thing she had to do was to go to work the next day. She was a secretary. She had an okay job with this electronic-parts firm. She also had this mouthy teenaged son. I wanted her to get a room in town, spend the night, and then drive home. I don't know if she got the room or not. I haven't heard from her since she led me up the front steps the other day and walked me into Frank Martin's office and said, "Guess who's here."

But I wasn't mad at her. In the first place, she didn't have any idea what she was letting herself in for when she said I could stay with her after my wife asked me to leave. I felt sorry for her. The reason I felt sorry for her was that on the day before Christmas her Pap smear came back, and the news was not cheery. She'd have to go back to the doctor, and real soon. That kind of news was reason enough for both of us to start drinking. So what we did was get ourselves good and drunk. And on Christmas Day we were still drunk. We had to go out to a restaurant to eat, because she didn't feel like cooking. The two of us and her mouthy teenaged son opened some presents, and then we went to this steakhouse near her apartment. I wasn't hungry. I had some soup and a hot roll. I drank a bottle of wine with the soup. She drank some wine, too. Then we started in on Bloody Marys. For the next couple of days, I didn't eat anything except salted nuts. But I drank a lot of bourbon. Then I said to her, "Sugar, I think I'd better pack up. I better go back to Frank Martin's."

She tried to explain to her son that she was going to be gone for a while and he'd have to get his own food. But right as we were going out the door, this mouthy kid screamed at us. He screamed, "The hell with you! I hope you never come back. I hope you kill yourselves!" Imagine this kid!

Before we left town, I had her stop at the package store, where I bought us the champagne. We stopped someplace else for plastic glasses. Then we picked up a bucket of fried chicken. We set out for Frank Martin's in this rainstorm, drinking and listening to music. She drove. I looked after the radio and poured. We tried to make a little party of it. But we were sad, too. There was that fried chicken, but we didn't eat any.

I guess she got home okay. I think I would have heard something if she didn't. But she hasn't called me, and I haven't called her. Maybe she's had some news about herself by now. Then again, maybe she hasn't heard anything. Maybe it was all a mistake. Maybe it was somebody else's smear. But she has my car, and I have things at her house. I know we'll be seeing each other again.

They clang an old farm bell here to call you for mealtime. J.P. and I get out of our chairs and we go inside. It's starting to get too cold on the porch, anyway. We can see our breath drifting out from us as we talk.

New Year's Eve morning I try to call my wife. There's no answer. It's okay. But even if it wasn't okay, what am I supposed to do? The last time we talked on the phone, a couple of weeks ago, we screamed at each other. I hung a few names on her. "Wet brain!" she said, and put the phone back where it belonged.

But I wanted to talk to her now. Something had to be done about my stuff. I still had things at her house, too.

One of the guys here is a guy who travels. He goes to Europe and places. That's what he says, anyway. Business, he says. He also says he has his drinking under control and he doesn't have any idea why he's here at Frank Martin's. But he doesn't remember getting here. He laughs about it, about his not remembering. "Anyone can have a blackout," he says. "That doesn't prove a thing." He's not a drunk – he tells us this and we listen. "That's a serious charge to make," he says. "That kind of talk can ruin a good man's prospects." He says that if he'd only stick to whiskey and water, no ice, he'd never have these blackouts. It's the ice they put into your drink that does it. "Who do you know in Egypt?" he asks me. "I can use a few names over there."

For New Year's Eve dinner Frank Martin serves steak and baked potato. My appetite's coming back. I clean up everything on my plate and I could eat more. I look over at Tiny's plate.

Hell, he's hardly touched a thing. His steak is just sitting there. Tiny is not the same old Tiny. The poor bastard had planned to be at home tonight. He'd planned to be in his robe and slippers in front of the TV, holding hands with his wife. Now he's afraid to leave. I can understand. One seizure means you're ready for another. Tiny hasn't told any more nutty stories on himself since it happened. He's stayed quiet and kept to himself. I ask him if I can have his steak, and he pushes his plate over to me.

Some of us are still up, sitting around the TV, watching Times Square, when Frank Martin comes in to show us his cake. He brings it around and shows it to each of us. I know he didn't make it. It's just a bakery cake. But it's still a cake. It's a big white cake. Across the top there's writing in pink letters. The writing says, HAPPY NEW YEAR – ONE DAY AT A TIME.

"I don't want any fucking cake," says the guy who goes to Europe and places. "Where's the champagne?" he says, and laughs.

We all go into the dining room. Frank Martin cuts the cake. I sit next to J.P. He eats two pieces and drinks a Coke. I eat a piece and wrap another piece in a napkin, thinking of later.

J.P. lights a cigarette – his hands are steady now – and he tells me his wife is coming in the morning, the first day of the new year.

"That's great," I say. I nod. I lick the frosting off my finger. "That's good news, J.P."

"I'll introduce you," he says.

"I look forward to it," I say.

We say goodnight. We say Happy New Year. I use a napkin on my fingers. We shake hands.

I go to the phone, put in a dime, and call my wife collect. But nobody answers this time, either. I think about calling my girlfriend, and I'm dialing her number when I realize I really don't want to talk to her. She's probably at home watching the same thing on TV that I've been watching. Anyway, I don't want to talk to her. I hope she's okay. But if she has something wrong with her, I don't want to know about it.

★

238

After breakfast, J.P. and I take coffee out to the porch. The sky is clear, but it's cold enough for sweaters and jackets.

"She asked me if she should bring the kids," J.P. says. "I told her she should keep the kids at home. Can you imagine? My God, I don't want my kids up here."

We use the coal bucket for an ashtray. We look across the valley to where Jack London used to live. We're drinking more coffee when this car turns off the road and comes down the drive.

"That's her!" J.P. says. He puts his cup next to his chair. He gets up and goes down the steps.

I see this woman stop the car and set the brake. I see J.P. open the door. I watch her get out, and I see them hug each other. I look away. Then I look back. J.P. takes her by the arm and they come up the stairs. This woman broke a man's nose once. She has had two kids, and much trouble, but she loves this man who has her by the arm. I get up from the chair.

"This is my friend," J.P. says to his wife. "Hey, this is Roxy."

Roxy takes my hand. She's a tall, good-looking woman in a knit cap. She has on a coat, a heavy sweater, and slacks. I recall what J.P. told me about the boyfriend and the wire-cutters. I don't see any wedding ring. That's in pieces somewhere, I guess. Her hands are broad and the fingers have these big knuckles. This is a woman who can make fists if she has to.

"I've heard about you," I say. "J.P. told me how you got acquainted. Something about a chimney, J.P. said."

"Yes, a chimney," she says. "There's probably a lot else he didn't tell you," she says. "I bet he didn't tell you everything," she says, and laughs. Then – she can't wait any longer – she slips her arm around J.P. and kisses him on the cheek. They start to move to the door. "Nice meeting you," she says. "Hey, did he tell you he's the best sweep in the business?"

"Come on now, Roxy," J.P. says. He has his hand on the doorknob.

"He told me he learned everything he knew from you," I say.

"Well, that much is sure true," she says. She laughs again. But it's like she's thinking about something else. J.P. turns the doorknob. Roxy lays her hand over his. "Joe, can't we go into town for lunch? Can't I take you someplace?"

J.P. clears his throat. He says, "It hasn't been a week yet." He takes his hand off the doorknob and brings his fingers to his chin. "I think they'd like it if I didn't leave the place for a little while yet. We can have some coffee here," he says.

"That's fine," she says. Her eyes work over to me again. "I'm glad Joe's made a friend. Nice to meet you," she says.

They start to go inside. I know it's a dumb thing to do, but I do it anyway. "Roxy," I say. And they stop in the doorway and look at me. "I need some luck," I say. "No kidding. I could do with a kiss myself."

J.P. looks down. He's still holding the knob, even though the door is open. He turns the knob back and forth. But I keep looking at her. Roxy grins. "I'm not a sweep anymore," she says. "Not for years. Didn't Joe tell you that? But, sure, I'll kiss you, sure."

She moves over. She takes me by the shoulders – I'm a big man – and she plants this kiss on my lips. "How's that?" she says.

"That's fine," I say.

"Nothing to it," she says. She's still holding me by the shoulders. She's looking me right in the eyes. "Good luck," she says, and then she lets go of me.

"See you later, pal," J.P. says. He opens the door all the way, and they go in.

I sit down on the front steps and light a cigarette. I watch what my hand does, then I blow out the match. I've got the shakes. I started out with them this morning. This morning I wanted something to drink. It's depressing, but I didn't say anything about it to J.P. I try to put my mind on something else.

I'm thinking about chimney sweeps – all that stuff I heard from J.P. – when for some reason I start to think about a house my wife and I once lived in. That house didn't have a chimney, so I don't know what makes me remember it now. But I remember the house and how we'd only been in there a few weeks when I heard a noise outside one morning. It was Sunday morning and it was still dark in the bedroom. But there was this pale light coming in from the bedroom window. I listened. I could hear something scrape against the side of the house. I jumped out of bed and went to look.

"My God!" my wife says, sitting up in bed and shaking the hair away from her face. Then she starts to laugh. "It's Mr Venturini," she says. "I forgot to tell you. He said he was coming to paint the house today. Early. Before it gets too hot. I forgot all about it," she says, and laughs. "Come on back to bed, honey. It's just him."

"In a minute," I say.

I push the curtain away from the window. Outside, this old guy in white coveralls is standing next to his ladder. The sun is just starting to break above the mountains. The old guy and I look each other over. It's the landlord, all right – this old guy in coveralls. But his coveralls are too big for him. He needs a shave, too. And he's wearing this baseball cap to cover his bald head. Goddamn it, I think, if he isn't a weird old fellow. And a wave of happiness comes over me that I'm not him – that I'm me and that I'm inside this bedroom with my wife.

He jerks his thumb toward the sun. He pretends to wipe his forehead. He's letting me know he doesn't have all that much time. He breaks into a grin. It's then I realize I'm naked. I look down at myself. I look at him again and shrug. What did he expect?

My wife laughs. "Come *on*," she says. "Get back in this bed. Right now. This minute. Come on back to bed."

I let go of the curtain. But I keep standing there at the window. I can see the old fellow nod to himself like he's saying, "Go on, sonny, go back to bed. I understand." He tugs on the bill of his cap. Then he sets about his business. He picks up his bucket. He starts climbing the ladder.

I lean back into the step behind me now and cross one leg over the other. Maybe later this afternoon I'll try calling my wife again. And then I'll call to see what's happening with my girlfriend. But I don't want to get her mouthy kid on the line. If I do call, I hope he'll be out somewhere doing whatever he does when he's not around the house. I try to remember if I ever read any Jack London books. I can't remember. But there was a story of his I read in high school. "To Build a Fire", it was called. This guy in the Yukon is freezing. Imagine it – he's actually going to freeze to death if he can't get a fire going. With a fire, he can dry his socks and things and warm himself.

He gets his fire going, but then something happens to it. A branchful of snow drops on it. It goes out. Meanwhile, it's getting colder. Night is coming on.

I bring some change out of my pocket. I'll try my wife first. If she answers, I'll wish her a Happy New Year. But that's it. I won't bring up business. I won't raise my voice. Not even if she starts something. She'll ask me where I'm calling from, and I'll have to tell her. I won't say anything about New Year's resolutions. There's no way to make a joke out of this. After I talk to her, I'll call my girlfriend. Maybe I'll call her first. I'll just have to hope I don't get her kid on the line. "Hello, sugar," I'll say when she answers. "It's me."

Chef's House

That summer Wes rented a furnished house north of Eureka from a recovered alcoholic named Chef. Then he called to ask me to forget what I had going and to move up there and live with him. He said he was on the wagon. I knew about that wagon. But he wouldn't take no for an answer. He called again and said, Edna, you can see the ocean from the front window. You can smell salt in the air. I listened to him talk. He didn't slur his words. I said, I'll think about it. And I did. A week later he called again and said, Are you coming? I said I was still thinking. He said, We'll start over. I said, If I come up there, I want you to do something for me. Name it, Wes said. I said, I want you to try and be the Wes I used to know. The old Wes. The Wes I married. Wes began to cry, but I took it as a sign of his good intentions. So I said, All right, I'll come up.

Wes had quit his girlfriend, or she'd quit him – I didn't know, didn't care. When I made up my mind to go with Wes, I had to say goodbye to my friend. My friend said, You're making a mistake. He said, Don't do this to me. What about us? he said. I said, I have to do it for Wes's sake. He's trying to stay sober. You remember what that's like. I remember, my friend said, but I don't want you to go. I said, I'll go for the summer. Then I'll see. I'll come back, I said. He said, What about me? What about *my* sake? Don't come back, he said.

We drank coffee, pop, and all kinds of fruit juice that summer. The whole summer, that's what we had to drink. I found myself wishing the summer wouldn't end. I knew better, but after a month of being with Wes in Chef's house, I put my wedding ring back on. I hadn't worn the ring in two years. Not since the night Wes was drunk and threw his ring into a peach orchard.

243

Wes had a little money, so I didn't have to work. And it turned out Chef was letting us have the house for almost nothing. We didn't have a telephone. We paid the gas and light and shopped for specials at the Safeway. One Sunday afternoon Wes went out to get a sprinkler and came back with something for me. He came back with a nice bunch of daisies and a straw hat. Tuesday evenings we'd go to a movie. Other nights Wes would go to what he called his Don't Drink meetings. Chef would pick him up in his car at the door and drive him home again afterward. Some days Wes and I would go fishing for trout in one of the freshwater lagoons nearby. We'd fish off the bank and take all day to catch a few little ones. They'll do fine, I'd say, and that night I'd fry them for supper. Sometimes I'd take off my hat and fall asleep on a blanket next to my fishing pole. The last thing I'd remember would be clouds passing overhead toward the central valley. At night, Wes would take me in his arms and ask me if I was still his girl.

Our kids kept their distance. Cheryl lived with some people on a farm in Oregon. She looked after a herd of goats and sold the milk. She kept bees and put up jars of honey. She had her own life, and I didn't blame her. She didn't care one way or the other about what her dad and I did so long as we didn't get her into it. Bobby was in Washington working in the hay. After the haying season, he planned to work in the apples. He had a girl and was saving his money. I wrote letters and signed them, "Love always."

One afternoon Wes was in the yard pulling weeds when Chef drove up in front of the house. I was working at the sink. I looked and saw Chef's big car pull in. I could see his car, the access road and the freeway, and, behind the freeway, the dunes and the ocean. Clouds hung over the water. Chef got out of his car and hitched his pants. I knew there was something. Wes stopped what he was doing and stood up. He was wearing his gloves and a canvas hat. He took off the hat and wiped his face with the back of his hand. Chef walked over and put his arm around Wes's shoulders. Wes took off one of his gloves. I went to the door. I heard Chef say to Wes God knows he was sorry but he was going to have to ask us to leave at the end of the month. Wes pulled off his other glove. Why's that, Chef? Chef said his daughter, Linda, the woman Wes used to call Fat Linda from the time of his drinking days, needed a place to live and this place was it. Chef told Wes that Linda's husband had taken his fishing boat out a few weeks back and nobody had heard from him since. She's my own blood, Chef said to Wes. She's lost her husband. She's lost her baby's father. I can help. I'm glad I'm in a position to help, Chef said. I'm sorry, Wes, but you'll have to look for another house. Then Chef hugged Wes again, hitched his pants, and got in his big car and drove away.

Wes came inside the house. He dropped his hat and gloves on the carpet and sat down in the big chair. Chef's chair, it occurred to me. Chef's carpet, even. Wes looked pale. I poured two cups of coffee and gave one to him.

It's all right, I said. Wes, don't worry about it, I said. I sat down on Chef's sofa with my coffee.

Fat Linda's going to live here now instead of us, Wes said. He held his cup, but he didn't drink from it.

Wes, don't get stirred up, I said.

Her man will turn up in Ketchikan, Wes said. Fat Linda's husband has simply pulled out on them. And who could blame him? Wes said. Wes said if it came to that, he'd go down with his ship, too, rather than live the rest of his days with Fat Linda and her kid. Then Wes put his cup down next to his gloves. This has been a happy house up to now, he said.

We'll get another house, I said.

Not like this one, Wes said. It wouldn't be the same, anyway. This house has been a good house for us. This house has good memories to it. Now Fat Linda and her kid will be in here, Wes said. He picked up his cup and tasted from it.

It's Chef's house, I said. He has to do what he has to do.

I know that, Wes said. But I don't have to like it.

Wes had this look about him. I knew that look. He kept touching his lips with his tongue. He kept thumbing his shirt under his waistband. He got up from the chair and went to the window.

He stood looking out at the ocean and at the clouds, which were building up. He patted his chin with his fingers like he was thinking about something. And he *was* thinking.

Go easy, Wes, I said.

She wants me to go easy, Wes said. He kept standing there.

But in a minute he came over and sat next to me on the sofa. He crossed one leg over the other and began fooling with the buttons on his shirt. I took his hand. I started to talk. I talked about the summer. But I caught myself talking like it was something that had happened in the past. Maybe years back. At any rate, like something that was over. Then I started talking about the kids. Wes said he wished he could do it over again and do it right this time.

They love you, I said.

No, they don't, he said.

I said, Someday, they'll understand things.

Maybe, Wes said. But it won't matter then.

You don't know, I said.

I know a few things, Wes said, and looked at me. I know I'm glad you came up here. I won't forget you did it, Wes said.

I'm glad, too, I said. I'm glad you found this house, I said.

Wes snorted. Then he laughed. We both laughed. That Chef, Wes said, and shook his head. He threw us a knuckleball, that son of a bitch. But I'm glad you wore your ring. I'm glad we had us this time together, Wes said.

Then I said something. I said, Suppose, just suppose, nothing had ever happened. Suppose this was for the first time. Just suppose. It doesn't hurt to suppose. Say none of the other had ever happened. You know what I mean? Then what? I said.

Wes fixed his eyes on me. He said, Then I suppose we'd have to be somebody else if that was the case. Somebody we're not. I don't have that kind of supposing left in me. We were born who we are. Don't you see what I'm saying?

I said I hadn't thrown away a good thing and come six hundred miles to hear him talk like this.

He said, I'm sorry, but I can't talk like somebody I'm not. I'm not somebody else. If I was somebody else, I sure as hell wouldn't be here. If I was somebody else, I wouldn't be me. But I'm who I am. Don't you see?

Wes, it's all right, I said. I brought his hand to my cheek. Then, I don't know, I remembered how he was when he was nineteen, the way he looked running across this field to where his dad sat on a tractor, hand over his eyes, watching Wes run toward him. We'd just driven up from California. I got out with Cheryl and Bobby and said, There's Grandpa. But they were just babies.

Wes sat next to me patting his chin, like he was trying to figure out the next thing. Wes's dad was gone and our kids were grown up. I looked at Wes and then I looked around Chef's living room at Chef's things, and I thought, We have to do something now and do it quick.

Hon, I said. Wes, listen to me.

What do you want? he said. But that's all he said. He seemed to have made up his mind. But, having made up his mind, he was in no hurry. He leaned back on the sofa, folded his hands in his lap, and closed his eyes. He didn't say anything else. He didn't have to.

I said his name to myself. It was an easy name to say, and I'd been used to saying it for a long time. Then I said it once more. This time I said it out loud. Wes, I said.

He opened his eyes. But he didn't look at me. He just sat where he was and looked toward the window. Fat Linda, he said. But I knew it wasn't her. She was nothing. Just a name. Wes got up and pulled the drapes and the ocean was gone just like that. I went in to start supper. We still had some fish in the icebox. There wasn't much else. We'll clean it up tonight, I thought, and that will be the end of it.

247

Fever

Carlyle was in a spot. He'd been in a spot all summer, since early June when his wife had left him. But up until a little while ago, just a few days before he had to start meeting his classes at the high school, Carlyle hadn't needed a sitter. He'd been the sitter. Every day and every night he'd attended to the children. Their mother, he told them, was away on a long trip.

Debbie, the first sitter he contacted, was a fat girl, nineteen years old, who told Carlyle she came from a big family. Kids loved her, she said. She offered a couple of names for reference. She penciled them on a piece of notebook paper. Carlyle took the names, folded the piece of paper, and put it in his shirt pocket. He told her he had meetings the next day. He said she could start to work for him the next morning. She said, "Okay."

He understood that his life was entering a new period. Eileen had left while Carlyle was still filling out his grade reports. She'd said she was going to Southern California to begin a new life for herself there. She'd gone with Richard Hoopes, one of Carlyle's colleagues at the high school. Hoopes was a drama teacher and glass-blowing instructor who'd apparently turned his grades in on time, taken his things, and left town in a hurry with Eileen. Now, the long and painful summer nearly behind him, and his classes about to resume, Carlyle had finally turned his attention to this matter of finding a baby-sitter. His first efforts had not been successful. In his desperation to find someone – anyone – he'd taken Debbie on.

In the beginning, he was grateful to have this girl turn up in response to his call. He'd yielded up the house and children to her as if she were a relative. So he had no one to blame but himself, his own carelessness, he was convinced, when he came home early from school one day that first week and pulled into the drive next to a car that had a big pair of flannel dice hanging from the rearview mirror. To his astonishment, he saw his children in the front yard, their clothes filthy, playing with a dog big enough to bite off their hands. His son, Keith, had the hiccups and had been crying. Sarah, his daughter, began to cry when she saw him get out of the car. They were sitting on the grass, and the dog was licking their hands and faces. The dog growled at him and then moved off a little as Carlyle made for his children. He picked up Keith and then he picked up Sarah. One child under each arm, he made for his front door. Inside the house, the phonograph was turned up so high the front windows vibrated.

In the living room, three teenaged boys jumped to their feet from where they'd been sitting around the coffee table. Beer bottles stood on the table and cigarettes burned in the ashtray. Rod Stewart screamed from the stereo. On the sofa, Debbie, the fat girl, sat with another teenaged boy. She stared at Carlyle with dumb disbelief as he entered the living room. The fat girl's blouse was unbuttoned. She had her legs drawn under her, and she was smoking a cigarette. The living room was filled with smoke and music. The fat girl and her friend got off the sofa in a hurry.

"Mr Carlyle, wait a minute," Debbie said. "I can explain."

"Don't explain," Carlyle said. "Get the hell out of here. All of you. Before I throw you out." He tightened his grip on the children.

"You owe me for four days," the fat girl said, as she tried to button her blouse. She still had the cigarette between her fingers. Ashes fell from the cigarette as she tried to button up. "Forget today. You don't owe me for today. Mr Carlyle, it's not what it looks like. They dropped by to listen to this record."

"I understand, Debbie," he said. He let the children down onto the carpet. But they stayed close to his legs and watched the people in the living room. Debbie looked at them and shook her head slowly, as if she'd never laid eyes on them before. "Goddamn it, get out!" Carlyle said. "Now. Get going. All of you."

He went over and opened the front door. The boys acted as if they were in no real hurry. They picked up their beer and started slowly for the door. The Rod Stewart record was still playing. One of them said, "That's my record."

"Get it," Carlyle said. He took a step toward the boy and then stopped.

"Don't touch me, okay? Just don't touch me," the boy said. He went over to the phonograph, picked up the arm, swung it back, and took his record off while the turntable was still spinning.

Carlyle's hands were shaking. "If that car's not out of the drive in one minute – one minute – I'm calling the police." He felt sick and dizzy with his anger. He saw, really saw, spots dance in front of his eyes.

"Hey, listen, we're on our way, all right? We're going," the boy said.

They filed out of the house. Outside, the fat girl stumbled a little. She weaved as she moved toward the car. Carlyle saw her stop and bring her hands up to her face. She stood like that in the drive for a minute. Then one of the boys pushed her from behind and said her name. She dropped her hands and got into the backseat of the car.

"Daddy will get you into some clean clothes," Carlyle told his children, trying to keep his voice steady. "I'll give you a bath, and put you into some clean clothes. Then we'll go out for some pizza. How does pizza sound to you?"

"Where's Debbie?" Sarah asked him.

"She's gone," Carlyle said.

That evening, after he'd put the children to bed, he called Carol, the woman from school he'd been seeing for the past month. He told her what had happened with his sitter.

"My kids were out in the yard with this big dog," he said. "The dog was as big as a wolf. The baby-sitter was in the house with a bunch of her hoodlum boyfriends. They had Rod Stewart going full blast, and they were tying one on while my kids were outside playing with this strange dog." He brought his fingers to his temples and held them there while he talked.

"My God," Carol said. "Poor sweetie, I'm so sorry." Her

voice sounded indistinct. He pictured her letting the receiver slide down to her chin, as she was in the habit of doing while talking on the phone. He'd seen her do it before. It was a habit of hers he found vaguely irritating. Did he want her to come over to his place? she asked. She would. She thought maybe she'd better do that. She'd call her sitter. Then she'd drive to his place. She wanted to. He shouldn't be afraid to say when he needed affection, she said. Carol was one of the secretaries in the principal's office at the high school where Carlyle taught art classes. She was divorced and had one child, a neurotic ten-year-old the father had named Dodge, after his automobile.

"No, that's all right," Carlyle said. "But thanks. *Thanks*, Carol. The kids are in bed, but I think I'd feel a little funny, you know, having company tonight."

She didn't offer again. "Sweetie, I'm sorry about what happened. But I understand your wanting to be alone tonight. I respect that. I'll see you at school tomorrow."

He could hear her waiting for him to say something else. "That's two baby-sitters in less than a week," he said. "I'm going out of my tree with this."

"Honey, don't let it get you down," she said. "Something will turn up. I'll help you find somebody this weekend. It'll be all right, you'll see."

"Thanks again for being there when I need you," he said. "You're one in a million, you know."

"'Night, Carlyle," she said.

After he'd hung up, he wished he could have thought of something else to say to her instead of what he'd just said. He'd never talked that way before in his life. They weren't having a love affair, he wouldn't call it that, but he liked her. She knew it was a hard time for him, and she didn't make demands.

After Eileen had left for California, Carlyle had spent every waking minute for the first month with his children. He supposed the shock of her going had caused this, but he didn't want to let the children out of his sight. He'd certainly not been interested in seeing other women, and for a time he didn't think he ever would be. He felt as if he were in mourning. His days and nights were passed in the company of his children. He cooked for them – he had no appetite himself – washed and ironed their clothes, drove them into the country, where they picked flowers and ate sandwiches wrapped up in waxed paper. He took them to the supermarket and let them pick out what they liked. And every few days they went to the park, or else to the library, or the zoo. They took old bread to the zoo so they could feed the ducks. At night, before tucking them in, Carlyle read to them – Aesop, Hans Christian Andersen, the Brothers Grimm.

"When is Mama coming back?" one of them might ask him in the middle of a fairy tale.

"Soon," he'd say. "One of these days. Now listen to this." Then he'd read the tale to its conclusion, kiss them, and turn off the light.

And while they'd slept, he had wandered the rooms of his house with a glass in his hand, telling himself that, yes, sooner or later, Eileen would come back. In the next breath, he would say, "I never want to see your face again. I'll never forgive you for this, you crazy bitch." Then, a minute later, "Come back, sweetheart, please. I love you and need you. The kids need you, too." Some nights that summer he fell asleep in front of the TV and woke up with the set still going and the screen filled with snow. This was the period when he didn't think he would be seeing any women for a long time, if ever. At night, sitting in front of the TV with an unopened book or magazine next to him on the sofa, he often thought of Eileen. When he did, he might remember her sweet laugh, or else her hand rubbing his neck if he complained of a soreness there. It was at these times that he thought he could weep. He thought, You hear about stuff like this happening to other people.

Just before the incident with Debbie, when some of the shock and grief had worn off, he'd phoned an employment service to tell them something of his predicament and his requirements. Someone took down the information and said they would get back to him. Not many people wanted to do housework *and* baby-sit, they said, but they'd find somebody. A few days before he had to be at the high school for meetings and registration, he called again and was told there'd be somebody at his house first thing the next morning.

That person was a thirty-five-year-old woman with hairy arms and run-over shoes. She shook hands with him and listened to him talk without asking a single question about the children – not even their names. When he took her into the back of the house where the children were playing, she simply stared at them for a minute without saying anything. When she finally smiled, Carlyle noticed for the first time that she had a tooth missing. Sarah left her crayons and got up to come over and stand next to him. She took Carlyle's hand and stared at the woman. Keith stared at her, too. Then he went back to his coloring. Carlyle thanked the woman for her time and said he would be in touch.

That afternoon he took down a number from an index card tacked to the bulletin board at the supermarket. Someone was offering baby-sitting services. References furnished on request. Carlyle called the number and got Debbie, the fat girl.

Over the summer, Eileen had sent a few cards, letters, and photographs of herself to the children, and some pen-and-ink drawings of her own that she'd done since she'd gone away. She also sent Carlyle long, rambling letters in which she asked for his understanding in this matter – *this matter* – but told him that she was happy. Happy. As if, Carlyle thought, happiness was all there was to life. She told him that if he really loved her, as he said he did, and as she really believed – she loved him, too, don't forget – then he would understand and accept things as they were. She wrote, "That which is truly bonded can never become unbonded." Carlyle didn't know if she was talking about their own relationship or her way of life out in California. He hated the word *bonded*. What did it have to do with the two of them? Did she think they were a corporation? He thought Eileen must be losing her mind to talk like that. He read that part again and then crumpled the letter.

But a few hours later he retrieved the letter from the trash can where he'd thrown it, and put it with her other cards and letters in a box on the shelf in his closet. In one of the envelopes, there was a photograph of her in a big, floppy hat, wearing a bathing suit. And there was a pencil drawing on heavy paper of a woman on a riverbank in a filmy gown, her hands covering her eyes, her shoulders slumped. It was, Carlyle assumed, Eileen showing her heartbreak over the situation. In college, she had majored in art, and even though she'd agreed to marry him, she said she intended to do something with her talent. Carlyle said he wouldn't have it any other way. She owed it to herself, he said. She owed it to both of them. They had loved each other in those days. He knew they had. He couldn't imagine ever loving anyone again the way he'd loved her. And he'd felt loved, too. Then, after eight years of being married to him, Eileen had pulled out. She was, she said in her letter, "going for it."

After talking to Carol, he looked in on the children, who were asleep. Then he went into the kitchen and made himself a drink. He thought of calling Eileen to talk to her about the baby-sitting crisis, but decided against it. He had her phone number and her address out there, of course. But he'd only called once and, so far, had not written a letter. This was partly out of a feeling of bewilderment with the situation, partly out of anger and humiliation. Once, earlier in the summer, after a few drinks, he'd chanced humiliation and called. Richard Hoopes answered the phone. Richard had said, "Hey, Carlyle," as if he were still Carlyle's friend. And then, as if remembering something, he said, "Just a minute, all right?"

Eileen had come on the line and said, "Carlyle, how are you? How are the kids? Tell me about yourself." He told her the kids were fine. But before he could say anything else, she interrupted him to say, "I know *they're* fine. What about *you*?" Then she went on to tell him that her head was in the right place for the first time in a long time. Next she wanted to talk about his head and his karma. She'd looked into his karma. It was going to improve any time now, she said. Carlyle listened, hardly able to believe his ears. Then he said, "I have to go now, Eileen." And he hung up. The phone rang a minute or so later, but he let it ring. When it stopped ringing, he took the phone off the hook and left it off until he was ready for bed.

He wanted to call her now, but he was afraid to call. He still missed her and wanted to confide in her. He longed to hear her voice – sweet, steady, not manic as it had been for months now – but if he dialed her number, Richard Hoopes might answer the telephone. Carlyle knew he didn't want to hear that man's voice again. Richard had been a colleague for three years and, Carlyle supposed, a kind of friend. At least he was someone Carlyle ate lunch with in the faculty dining room, someone who talked about Tennessee Williams and the photographs of Ansel Adams. But even if Eileen answered the telephone, she might launch into something about his karma.

While he was sitting there with the glass in his hand, trying to remember what it had felt like to be married and intimate with someone, the phone rang. He picked up the receiver, heard a trace of static on the line, and knew, even before she'd said his name, that it was Eileen.

"I was just thinking about you," Carlyle said, and at once regretted saying it.

"See! I knew I was on your mind, Carlyle. Well, I was thinking about you, too. That's why I called." He drew a breath. She *was* losing her mind. That much was clear to him. She kept talking. "Now listen," she said. "The big reason I called is that I know things are in kind of a mess out there right now. Don't ask me how, but I know. I'm sorry, Carlyle. But here's the thing. You're still in need of a good housekeeper and sitter combined, right? Well, she's practically right there in the neighborhood! Oh, you may have found someone already, and that's good, if that's the case. If so, it's supposed to be that way. But see, just in case you're having trouble in that area, there's this woman who used to work for Richard's mother. I told Richard about the potential problem, and he put himself to work on it. You want to know what he did? Are you listening? He called his mother, who used to have this woman who kept house for her. The woman's name is Mrs Webster. She looked after things for Richard's mother before his aunt and her daughter moved in there. Richard was able to get a number through his mother. He talked to Mrs Webster today. Richard did. Mrs Webster is going to call you tonight. Or else maybe she'll call you in the morning. One or the other. Anyway, she's going to volunteer her services, if you need her. You might, you never can tell. Even if your situation is okay right now, which I hope it is. But some time or another you might need her. You know what I'm saying? If not this minute, some other time. Okay? How are the kids? What are they up to?"

"The children are fine, Eileen. They're asleep now," he said. Maybe he should tell her they cried themselves to sleep every night. He wondered if he should tell her the truth – that they hadn't asked about her even once in the last couple of weeks. He decided not to say anything.

"I called earlier, but the line was busy. I told Richard you were probably talking to your girlfriend," Eileen said and laughed. "Think positive thoughts. You sound depressed," she said.

"I have to go, Eileen." He started to hang up, and he took the receiver from his ear. But she was still talking.

"Tell Keith and Sarah I love them. Tell them I'm sending some more pictures. Tell them that. I don't want them to forget their mother is an artist. Maybe not a great artist yet, that's not important. But, you know, an artist. It's important they shouldn't forget that."

Carlyle said, "I'll tell them."

"Richard says hello."

Carlyle didn't say anything. He said the word to himself – *hello*. What could the man possibly mean by this? Then he said, "Thanks for calling. Thanks for talking to that woman."

"Mrs Webster!"

"Yes. I'd better get off the phone now. I don't want to run up your nickel."

Eileen laughed. "It's only money. Money's not important except as a necessary medium of exchange. There are more important things than money. But then you already know that."

He held the receiver out in front of him. He looked at the instrument from which her voice was issuing.

"Carlyle, things are going to get better for you. I *know* they are. You may think I'm crazy or something," she said. "But just remember."

Remember what? Carlyle wondered in alarm, thinking he must have missed something she'd said. He brought the receiver in close. "Eileen, thanks for calling," he said.

"We have to stay in touch," Eileen said. "We have to keep all lines of communication open. I think the worst is over. For both of us. I've suffered, too. But we're going to get what we're supposed to get out of this life, both of us, and we're going to be made *stronger* for it in the long run."

"Good night," he said. He put the receiver back. Then he looked at the phone. He waited. It didn't ring again. But an hour later it did ring. He answered it.

"Mr Carlyle." It was an old woman's voice. "You don't know me, but my name is Mrs Jim Webster. I was supposed to get in touch."

"Mrs Webster. Yes," he said. Eileen's mention of the woman came back to him. "Mrs Webster, can you come to my house in the morning? Early. Say seven o'clock?"

"I can do that easily," the old woman said. "Seven o'clock. Give me your address."

"I'd like to be able to count on you," Carlyle said.

"You can count on me," she said.

"I can't tell you how important it is," Carlyle said.

"Don't you worry," the old woman said.

The next morning, when the alarm went off, he wanted to keep his eyes closed and keep on with the dream he was having. Something about a farmhouse. And there was a waterfall in there, too. Someone, he didn't know who, was walking along the road carrying something. Maybe it was a picnic hamper. He was not made uneasy by the dream. In the dream, there seemed to exist a sense of well-being.

Finally, he rolled over and pushed something to stop the buzzing. He lay in bed a while longer. Then he got up, put his feet into his slippers, and went out to the kitchen to start the coffee.

He shaved and dressed for the day. Then he sat down at the kitchen table with coffee and a cigarette. The children were still in bed. But in five minutes or so he planned to put boxes of cereal on the table and lay out bowls and spoons, then go in to wake them for breakfast. He really couldn't believe that the old woman who'd phoned him last night would show up this morning, as she'd said she would. He decided he'd wait until five minutes after seven o'clock, and then he'd call in, take the day off, and make every effort in the book to locate someone reliable. He brought the cup of coffee to his lips.

It was then that he heard a rumbling sound out in the street. He left his cup and got up from the table to look out the window. A pickup truck had pulled over to the curb in front of his house. The pickup cab shook as the engine idled. Carlyle went to the front door, opened it, and waved. An old woman waved back and then let herself out of the vehicle. Carlyle saw the driver lean over and disappear under the dash. The truck gasped, shook itself once more, and fell still.

"Mr Carlyle?" the old woman said, as she came slowly up his walk carrying a large purse.

"Mrs Webster," he said. "Come on inside. Is that your husband? Ask him in. I just made coffee."

"It's okay," she said. "He has his thermos."

Carlyle shrugged. He held the door for her. She stepped inside and they shook hands. Mrs Webster smiled. Carlyle nodded. They moved out to the kitchen. "Did you want me today, then?" she asked.

"Let me get the children up," he said. "I'd like them to meet you before I leave for school."

"That'd be good," she said. She looked around his kitchen. She put her purse on the drainboard.

"Why don't I get the children?" he said. "I'll just be a minute or two."

In a little while, he brought the children out and introduced them. They were still in their pajamas. Sarah was rubbing her eyes. Keith was wide awake. "This is Keith," Carlyle said. "And this one here, this is my Sarah." He held on to Sarah's hand and turned to Mrs Webster. "They need someone, you see. We need someone we can count on. I guess that's our problem."

Mrs Webster moved over to the children. She fastened the top button of Keith's pajamas. She moved the hair away from Sarah's face. They let her do it. "Don't you kids worry, now," she said to them. "Mr Carlyle, it'll be all right. We're going to be fine. Give us a day or two to get to know each other, that's all. But if I'm going to stay, why don't you give Mr Webster the all-clear sign? Just wave at him through the window," she said, and then she gave her attention back to the children.

Carlyle stepped to the bay window and drew the curtain. An old man was watching the house from the cab of the truck. He was just bringing a thermos cup to his lips. Carlyle waved to him, and with his free hand the man waved back. Carlyle watched him roll down the truck window and throw out what was left in his cup. Then he bent down under the dash again – Carlyle imagined him touching some wires together – and in a minute the truck started and began to shake. The old man put the truck in gear and pulled away from the curb.

Carlyle turned from the window. "Mrs Webster," he said, "I'm glad you're here."

"Likewise, Mr Carlyle," she said. "Now you go on about your business before you're late. Don't worry about anything. We're going to be fine. Aren't we, kids?"

The children nodded their heads. Keith held on to her dress with one hand. He put the thumb of his other hand into his mouth.

"Thank you," Carlyle said. "I feel, I really feel a hundred percent better." He shook his head and grinned. He felt a welling in his chest as he kissed each of his children good-bye. He told Mrs Webster what time she could expect him home, put on his coat, said good-bye once more, and went out of the house. For the first time in months, it seemed, he felt his burden had lifted a little. Driving to school, he listened to some music on the radio.

During first-period art-history class, he lingered over slides of Byzantine paintings. He patiently explained the nuances of detail and motif. He pointed out the emotional power and fitness of the work. But he took so long trying to place the anonymous artists in their social milieu that some of his students began to scrape their shoes on the floor, or else clear their throats. They covered only a third of the lesson plan that day. He was still talking when the bell rang.

In his next class, watercolor painting, he felt unusually calm and insightful. "Like this, like this," he said, guiding their hands. "Delicately. Like a breath of air on the paper. Just a touch. Like so. See?" he'd say and felt on the edge of discovery himself. "*Suggestion* is what it's all about," he said, holding lightly to Sue Colvin's fingers as he guided her brush. "You've got to work with your mistakes until they look intended. Understand?"

As he moved down the lunch line in the faculty dining room, he saw Carol a few places ahead of him. She paid for her food. He waited impatiently while his own bill was being rung up. Carol was halfway across the room by the time he caught up with her. He slipped his hand under her elbow and guided her to an empty table near the window.

"God, Carlyle," she said after they'd seated themselves. She picked up her glass of iced tea. Her face was flushed. "Did you see the look Mrs Storr gave us? What's wrong with you? Everybody will know." She sipped from her iced tea and put the glass down.

"The hell with Mrs Storr," Carlyle said. "Hey, let me tell you something. Honey, I feel light-years better than I did this time yesterday. Jesus," he said.

"What's happened?" Carol said. "Carlyle, tell me." She moved her fruit cup to one side of her tray and shook cheese over her spaghetti. But she didn't eat anything. She waited for him to go on. "Tell me what it is."

He told her about Mrs Webster. He even told her about Mr Webster. How the man'd had to hot-wire the truck in order to start it. Carlyle ate his tapioca while he talked. Then he ate the garlic bread. He drank Carol's iced tea down before he realized he was doing it.

"You're nuts, Carlyle," she said, nodding at the spaghetti in his plate that he hadn't touched.

He shook his head. "My *God*, Carol. God, I feel good, you know? I feel better than I have all summer." He lowered his voice. "Come over tonight, will you?"

He reached under the table and put his hand on her knee. She turned red again. She raised her eyes and looked around the dining room. But no one was paying any attention to them. She nodded quickly. Then she reached under the table and touched his hand.

That afternoon he arrived home to find his house neat and orderly and his children in clean clothes. In the kitchen, Keith and Sarah stood on chairs, helping Mrs Webster with gingerbread cookies. Sarah's hair was out of her face and held back with a barrette.

"Daddy!" his children cried, happy, when they saw him.

"Keith, Sarah," he said. "Mrs Webster, I –" But she didn't let him finish.

"We've had a fine day, Mr Carlyle," Mrs Webster said quickly. She wiped her fingers on the apron she was wearing. It was an old apron with blue windmills on it and it had belonged to Eileen. "Such beautiful children. They're a treasure. Just a treasure."

"I don't know what to say." Carlyle stood by the drainboard and watched Sarah press out some dough. He could smell the spice. He took off his coat and sat down at the kitchen table. He loosened his tie.

"Today was a get-acquainted day," Mrs Webster said. "Tomorrow we have some other plans. I thought we'd walk to the park. We ought to take advantage of this good weather."

"That's a fine idea," Carlyle said. "That's just fine. Good. Good for you, Mrs Webster."

"I'll finish putting these cookies in the oven, and by that time Mr Webster should be here. You said four o'clock? I told him to come at four."

Carlyle nodded, his heart full.

"You had a call today," she said as she went over to the sink with the mixing bowl. "Mrs Carlyle called."

"Mrs Carlyle," he said. He waited for whatever it was Mrs Webster might say next.

"Yes. I identified myself, but she didn't seem surprised to find me here. She said a few words to each of the children."

Carlyle glanced at Keith and Sarah, but they weren't paying any attention. They were lining up cookies on another baking sheet.

Mrs Webster continued. "She left a message. Let me see, I wrote it down, but I think I can remember it. She said, 'Tell him' – that is, tell you – 'what goes around, comes around.' I think that's right. She said you'd understand."

Carlyle stared at her. He heard Mr Webster's truck outside.

"That's Mr Webster," she said and took off the apron.

Carlyle nodded.

"Seven o'clock in the morning?" she asked.

"That will be fine," he said. "And thank you again."

That evening he bathed each of the children, got them into their pajamas, and then read to them. He listened to their prayers, tucked in their covers, and turned out the light. It was nearly nine o'clock. He made himself a drink and watched something on TV until he heard Carol's car pull into the drive.

Around ten, while they were in bed together, the phone rang. He swore, but he didn't get up to answer it. It kept ringing.

"It might be important," Carol said, sitting up. "It might be my sitter. She has this number."

"It's my wife," Carlyle said. "I know it's her. She's losing her mind. She's going crazy. I'm not going to answer it."

"I have to go pretty soon anyway," Carol said. "It was real sweet tonight, honey." She touched his face.

It was the middle of the fall term. Mrs Webster had been with him for nearly six weeks. During this time, Carlyle's life had undergone a number of changes. For one thing, he was becoming reconciled to the fact that Eileen was gone and, as far as he could understand it, had no intention of coming back. He had stopped imagining that this might change. It was only late at night, on the nights he was not with Carol, that he wished for an end to the love he still had for Eileen and felt tormented as to why all of this had happened. But for the most part he and the children were happy; they thrived under Mrs Webster's attentions. Lately, she'd gotten into the routine of making their dinner and keeping it in the oven, warming, until his arrival home from school. He'd walk in the door to the smell of something good coming from the kitchen and find Keith and Sarah helping to set the dining-room table. Now and again he asked Mrs Webster if she would care for overtime work on Saturdays. She agreed, as long as it wouldn't entail her being at his house before noon. Saturday mornings, she said, she had things to do for Mr Webster and herself. On these days, Carol would leave Dodge with Carlyle's children, all of them under Mrs Webster's care, and Carol and he would drive to a restaurant out in the country for dinner. He believed his life was beginning again. Though he hadn't heard from Eileen since that call six weeks ago, he found himself able to think about her now without either being angry or else feeling close to tears.

At school, they were just leaving the medieval period and about to enter the Gothic. The Renaissance was still some time off, at least not until after the Christmas recess. It was during this time that Carlyle got sick. Overnight, it seemed, his chest tightened and his head began to hurt. The joints of his body became stiff. He felt dizzy when he moved around. The headache got worse. He woke up with it on a Sunday and thought of calling Mrs Webster to ask her to come and take the children somewhere. They'd been sweet to him, bringing him glasses of juice and some soda pop. But he couldn't take care of them. On the second morning of his illness, he was just able to get to the phone to call in sick. He gave his name, his school, department, and the nature of his illness to the person who answered the number. Then he recommended Mel Fisher as his substitute. Fisher was a man who painted abstract oils three or four days a week, sixteen hours a day, but who didn't sell or even show his work. He was a friend of Carlyle's. "Get Mel Fisher," Carlyle told the woman on the other end of the line. "Fisher," he whispered.

He made it back to his bed, got under the covers, and went to sleep. In his sleep, he heard the pickup engine running outside, and then the backfire it made as the engine was turned off. Sometime later he heard Mrs Webster's voice outside the bedroom door.

"Mr Carlyle?"

"Yes, Mrs Webster." His voice sounded strange to him. He kept his eyes shut. "I'm sick today. I called the school. I'm going to stay in bed today."

"I see. Don't worry, then," she said. "I'll look after things at this end."

He shut his eyes. Directly, still in a state between sleeping and waking, he thought he heard his front door open and close. He listened. Out in the kitchen, he heard a man say something in a low voice, and a chair being pulled away from the table. Pretty soon he heard the voices of the children. Sometime later – he wasn't sure how much time had passed – he heard Mrs Webster outside his door.

"Mr Carlyle, should I call the doctor?"

"No, that's all right," he said. "I think it's just a bad cold. But I feel hot all over. I think I have too many covers. And it's too warm in the house. Maybe you'll turn down the furnace." Then he felt himself drift back into sleep.

In a little while, he heard the children talking to Mrs Webster in the living room. Were they coming inside or going out? Carlyle wondered. Could it be the next day already?

He went back to sleep. But then he was aware of his door opening. Mrs Webster appeared beside his bed. She put her hand on his forehead.

"You're burning up," she said. "You have a fever."

"I'll be all right," Carlyle said. "I just need to sleep a little longer. And maybe you could turn the furnace down. Please, I'd appreciate it if you could get me some aspirin. I have an awful headache."

Mrs Webster left the room. But his door stood open. Carlyle could hear the TV going out there. "Keep it down, Jim," he heard her say, and the volume was lowered at once. Carlyle fell asleep again.

But he couldn't have slept more than a minute, because Mrs

Webster was suddenly back in his room with a tray. She sat down on the side of his bed. He roused himself and tried to sit up. She put a pillow behind his back.

"Take these," she said and gave him some tablets. "Drink this." She held a glass of juice for him. "I also brought you some Cream of Wheat. I want you to eat it. It'll be good for you."

He took the aspirin and drank the juice. He nodded. But he shut his eyes once more. He was going back to sleep.

"Mr Carlyle," she said.

He opened his eyes. "I'm awake," he said. "I'm sorry." He sat up a little. "I'm too warm, that's all. What time is it? Is it eight-thirty yet?"

"It's a little after nine-thirty," she said.

"Nine-thirty," he said.

"Now I'm going to feed this cereal to you. And you're going to open up and eat it. Six bites, that's all. Here, here's the first bite. Open," she said. "You're going to feel better after you eat this. Then I'll let you go back to sleep. You eat this, and then you can sleep all you want."

He ate the cereal she spooned to him and asked for more juice. He drank the juice, and then he pulled down in the bed again. Just as he was going off to sleep, he felt her covering him with another blanket.

The next time he awoke, it was afternoon. He could tell it was afternoon by the pale light that came through his window. He reached up and pulled the curtain back. He could see that it was overcast outside; the wintry sun was behind the clouds. He got out of bed slowly, found his slippers, and put on his robe. He went into the bathroom and looked at himself in the mirror. Then he washed his face and took some more aspirin. He used the towel and then went out to the living room.

On the dining-room table, Mrs Webster had spread some newspaper, and she and the children were pinching clay figures together. They had already made some things that had long necks and bulging eyes, things that resembled giraffes, or else dinosaurs. Mrs Webster looked up as he walked by the table.

"How are you feeling?" Mrs Webster asked him as he settled

265

onto the sofa. He could see into the dining-room area, where Mrs Webster and the children sat at the table.

"Better, thanks. A little better," he said. "I still have a head-ache, and I feel a little warm." He brought the back of his hand up to his forehead. "But I'm better. Yes, I'm better. Thanks for your help this morning."

"Can I get you anything now?" Mrs Webster said. "Some more juice or some tea? I don't think coffee would hurt, but I think tea would be better. Some juice would be best of all."

"No, no thanks," he said. "I'll just sit here for a while. It's good to be out of bed. I feel a little weak is all. Mrs Webster?"

She looked at him and waited.

"Did I hear Mr Webster in the house this morning? It's fine, of course. I'm just sorry I didn't get a chance to meet him and say hello."

"It was him," she said. "He wanted to meet you, too. I asked him to come in. He just picked the wrong morning, what with you being sick and all. I'd wanted to tell you something about our plans, Mr Webster's and mine, but this morning wasn't a good time for it."

"Tell me what?" he said, alert, fear plucking at his heart.

She shook her head. "It's all right," she said. "It can wait."

"Tell him what?" Sarah said. "Tell him what?"

"What, what?" Keith picked it up. The children stopped what they were doing.

"Just a minute, you two," Mrs Webster said as she got to her feet.

"Mrs Webster, Mrs Webster!" Keith cried.

"Now see here, little man," Mrs Webster said. "I need to talk to your father. Your father is sick today. You just take it easy. You go on and play with your clay. If you don't watch it, your sister is going to get ahead of you with these creatures."

Just as she began to move toward the living room, the phone rang. Carlyle reached over to the end table and picked up the receiver.

As before, he heard faint singing in the wire and knew that it was Eileen. "Yes," he said. "What is it?"

"Carlyle," his wife said, "I know, don't ask me how, that things are not going so well right now. You're sick, aren't you? Richard's been sick, too. It's something going around. He can't keep anything on his stomach. He's already missed a week of rehearsal for this play he's doing. I've had to go down myself and help block out scenes with his assistant. But I didn't call to tell you that. Tell me how things are out there."

"Nothing to tell," Carlyle said. "I'm sick, that's all. A touch of the flu. But I'm getting better."

"Are you still writing in your journal?" she asked. It caught him by surprise. Several years before, he'd told her that he was keeping a journal. Not a diary, he'd said, a journal — as if that explained something. But he'd never shown it to her, and he hadn't written in it for over a year. He'd forgotten about it.

"Because," she said, "you ought to write something in the journal during this period. How you feel and what you're think-ing. You know, where your head is at during this period of sickness. Remember, sickness is a message about your health and your well-being. It's telling you things. Keep a record. You know what I mean? When you're well, you can look back and see what the message was. You can read it later, after the fact. Colette did that," Eileen said. "When she had a fever this one time."

"Who?" Carlyle said. "What did you say?"

"Colette," Eileen answered. "The French writer. You know who I'm talking about. We had a book of hers around the house. *Gigi* or something. I didn't read *that* book, but I've been reading her since I've been out here. Richard turned me on to her. She wrote a little book about what it was like, about what she was thinking and feeling the whole time she had this fever. Sometimes her temperature was a hundred and two. Sometimes it was lower. Maybe it went higher than a hundred and two. But a hundred and two was the highest she ever took her temperature and wrote, too, when she had the fever. Anyway, she wrote about it. That's what I'm saying. Try writing about what it's like. Something might come of it," Eileen said and, inexplicably, it seemed to Carlyle, she laughed. "At least later on you'd have an hour-by-hour account of your sickness. To look back at. At least you'd have that to show for it. Right now you've just got this discomfort. You've got to translate that into something usable."

He pressed his fingertips against his temple and shut his eyes. But she was still on the line, waiting for him to say something. What could he say? It was clear to him that she was insane.

"Jesus," he said. "Jesus, Eileen. I don't know what to say to that. I really don't. I have to go now. Thanks for calling," he said.

"It's all right," she said. "We have to be able to communicate. Kiss the kids for me. Tell them I love them. And Richard sends his hellos to you. Even though he's flat on his back."

"Good-bye," Carlyle said and hung up. Then he brought his hands to his face. He remembered, for some reason, seeing the fat girl make the same gesture that time as she moved toward the car. He lowered his hands and looked at Mrs Webster, who was watching him.

"Not bad news, I hope," she said. The old woman had moved a chair near to where he sat on the sofa.

Carlyle shook his head.

"Good," Mrs Webster said. "That's good. Now, Mr Carlyle, this may not be the best time in the world to talk about this." She glanced out to the dining room. At the table, the children had their heads bent over the clay. "But since it has to be talked about sometime soon, and since it concerns you and the children, and you're up now, I have something to tell you. Jim and I, we're getting on. The thing is, we need something more than we have at the present. Do you know what I'm saying? This is hard for me," she said and shook her head. Carlyle nodded slowly. He knew that she was going to tell him she had to leave. He wiped his face on his sleeve. "Jim's son by a former marriage, Bob – the man is forty years old – called yesterday to invite us to go out to Oregon and help him with his mink ranch. Jim would be doing whatever they do with minks, and I'd cook, buy the groceries, clean house, and do anything else that needed doing. It's a chance for both of us. And it's board and room and then some. Jim and I won't have to worry anymore about what's going to happen to us. You know what I'm saying. Right now,

Jim doesn't have anything," she said. "He was sixty-two last
week. He hasn't had anything for some time. He came in this
morning to tell you about it himself, because I was going to have
to give notice, you see. We thought – I thought – it would help
if Jim was here when I told you." She waited for Carlyle to say
something. When he didn't, she went on. "I'll finish out the
week, and I could stay on a couple of days next week, if need
be. But then, you know, for sure, we really have to leave, and
you'll have to wish us luck. I mean, can you imagine – all the
way out there to Oregon in that old rattletrap of ours? But I'm
going to miss these little kids. They're so precious."

After a time, when he still hadn't moved to answer her, she
got up from her chair and went to sit on the cushion next to his.
She touched the sleeve of his robe. "Mr Carlyle?"

"I understand," he said. "I want you to know your being here
has made a big difference to me and the children." His head ached
so much that he had to squint his eyes. "This headache," he said.
"This headache is killing me."

Mrs Webster reached over and laid the back of her hand against
his forehead. "You still have some fever," she told him. "I'll get
more aspirin. That'll help bring it down. I'm still on the case
here," she said. "I'm still the doctor."

"My wife thinks I should write down what this feels like,"
Carlyle said. "She thinks it might be a good idea to describe what
the fever is like. So I can look back later and get the message."
He laughed. Some tears came to his eyes. He wiped them away
with the heel of his hand.

"I think I'll get your aspirin and juice and then go out there
with the kids," Mrs Webster said. "Looks to me like they've
about worn out their interest with that clay."

Carlyle was afraid she'd move into the other room and leave
him alone. He wanted to talk to her. He cleared his throat. "Mrs
Webster, there's something I want you to know. For a long time,
my wife and I loved each other more than anything or anybody
in the world. And that includes those children. We thought, well,
we *knew* that we'd grow old together. And we knew we'd do all
the things in the world that we wanted to do, and do them

together." He shook his head. That seemed the saddest thing of all to him now – that whatever they did from now on, each would do it without the other.

"There, it's all right," Mrs Webster said. She patted his hand. He sat forward and began to talk again. After a time, the children came out to the living room. Mrs Webster caught their attention and held a finger to her lips. Carlyle looked at them and went on talking. Let them listen, he thought. It concerns them, too. The children seemed to understand they had to remain quiet, even pretend some interest, so they sat down next to Mrs Webster's legs. Then they got down on their stomachs on the carpet and started to giggle. But Mrs Webster looked sternly in their direction, and that stopped it.

Carlyle went on talking. At first, his head still ached, and he felt awkward to be in his pajamas on the sofa with this old woman beside him, waiting patiently for him to go on to the next thing. But then his headache went away. And soon he stopped feeling awkward and forgot how he was supposed to feel. He had begun his story somewhere in the middle, after the children were born. But then he backed up and started at the beginning, back when Eileen was eighteen and he was nineteen, a boy and girl in love, burning with it.

He stopped to wipe his forehead. He moistened his lips.

"Go on," Mrs Webster said. "I know what you're saying. You just keep talking, Mr Carlyle. Sometimes it's good to talk about it. Sometimes it has to be talked about. Besides, I want to hear it. And you're going to feel better afterward. Something just like it happened to me once, something like what you're describing. Love. That's what it is."

The children fell asleep on the carpet. Keith had his thumb in his mouth. Carlyle was still talking when Mr Webster came to the door, knocked, and then stepped inside to collect Mrs Webster.

"Sit down, Jim," Mrs Webster said. "There's no hurry. Go on with what you were saying, Mr Carlyle."

Carlyle nodded at the old man, and the old man nodded back, then got himself one of the dining-room chairs and carried it into the living room. He brought the chair close to the sofa and sat

270

down on it with a sigh. Then he took off his cap and wearily lifted one leg over the other. When Carlyle began talking again, the old man put both feet on the floor. The children woke up. They sat up on the carpet and rolled their heads back and forth. But by then Carlyle had said all he knew to say, so he stopped talking.

"Good. Good for you," Mrs Webster said when she saw he had finished. "You're made out of good stuff. And so is she – so is Mrs Carlyle. And don't you forget it. You're both going to be okay after this is over." She got up and took off the apron she'd been wearing. Mr Webster got up, too, and put his cap back on.

At the door, Carlyle shook hands with both of the Websters.

"So long," Jim Webster said. He touched the bill of his cap.

"Good luck to you," Carlyle said.

Mrs Webster said she'd see him in the morning then, bright and early as always.

As if something important had been settled, Carlyle said, "Right!"

The old couple went carefully along the walk and got into their truck. Jim Webster bent down under the dashboard. Mrs Webster looked at Carlyle and waved. It was then, as he stood at the window, that he felt something come to an end. It had to do with Eileen and the life before this. Had he ever waved at her? He must have, of course, he knew he had, yet he could not remember just now. But he understood it was over, and he felt able to let her go. He was sure their life together had happened in the way he said it had. But it was something that had passed. And that passing – though it had seemed impossible and he'd fought against it – would become a part of him now, too, as surely as anything else he'd left behind.

As the pickup lurched forward, he lifted his arm once more. He saw the old couple lean toward him briefly as they drove away. Then he brought his arm down and turned to his children.

Feathers

This friend of mine from work, Bud, he asked Fran and me to supper. I didn't know his wife and he didn't know Fran. That made us even. But Bud and I were friends. And I knew there was a little baby at Bud's house. That baby must have been eight months old when Bud asked us to supper. Where'd those eight months go? Hell, where's the time gone since? I remember the day Bud came to work with a box of cigars. He handed them out in the lunchroom. They were drugstore cigars. Dutch Masters. But each cigar had a red sticker on it and a wrapper that said IT'S A BOY! I didn't smoke cigars, but I took one anyway. "Take a couple," Bud said. He shook the box. "I don't like cigars either. This is her idea." He was talking about his wife. Olla.

I'd never met Bud's wife, but once I'd heard her voice over the telephone. It was a Saturday afternoon, and I didn't have anything I wanted to do. So I called Bud to see if he wanted to do anything. This woman picked up the phone and said, "Hello". I blanked and couldn't remember her name. Bud's wife. Bud had said her name to me any number of times. But it went in one ear and out the other. "Hello!" the woman said again. I could hear a TV going. Then the woman said, "Who is this?" I heard a baby start up. "Bud!" the woman called. "What?" I heard Bud say. I still couldn't remember her name. So I hung up. The next time I saw Bud at work I sure as hell didn't tell him I'd called. But I made a point of getting him to mention his wife's name. "Olla," he said. Olla, I said to myself. *Olla.*

"No big deal," Bud said. We were in the lunchroom drinking coffee. "Just the four of us. You and your missus, and me and Olla. Nothing fancy. Come around seven. She feeds the baby at six. She'll put him down after that, and then we'll eat. Our place isn't hard to find. But here's a map." He gave me a sheet of paper with all kinds of lines indicating major and minor roads, lanes and such, with arrows pointing to the four poles of the compass. A large X marked the location of his house. I said, "We're looking forward to it." But Fran wasn't too thrilled.

That evening, watching TV, I asked her if we should take anything to Bud's.

"Like what?" Fran said. "Did he say to bring something? How should I know? I don't have any idea." She shrugged and gave me this look. She'd heard me before on the subject of Bud. But she didn't know him and she wasn't interested in knowing him. "We could take a bottle of wine," she said. "But I don't care. Why don't you take some wine?" She shook her head. Her long hair swung back and forth over her shoulders. Why do we need other people? she seemed to be saying. We have each other. "Come here," I said. She moved a little closer so I could hug her. Fran's a big tall drink of water. She has this blond hair that hangs down her back. I picked up some of her hair and sniffed it. I wound my hand in her hair. She let me hug her. I put my face right up in her hair and hugged her some more.

Sometimes when her hair gets in her way she has to pick it up and push it over her shoulder. She gets mad at it. "This hair," she says. "Nothing but trouble." Fran works in a creamery and has to wear her hair up when she goes to work. She has to wash it every night and take a brush to it when we're sitting in front of the TV. Now and then she threatens to cut it off. But I don't think she'd do that. She knows I like it too much. She knows I'm crazy about it. I tell her I fell in love with her because of her hair. I tell her I might stop loving her if she cut it. Sometimes I call her "Swede". She could pass for a Swede. Those times together in the evening she'd brush her hair and we'd wish out loud for things we didn't have. We wished for a new car, that's one of the things we wished for. And we wished we could spend a couple of weeks in Canada. But one thing we didn't wish for was kids. The reason we didn't have kids was that we didn't want kids. Maybe sometime, we said to each other. But right then, we were waiting. We thought we might keep on waiting. Some nights we went to a movie. Other nights we just stayed in and watched TV. Sometimes Fran baked things for me and we'd eat whatever it was all in a sitting.

"Maybe they don't drink wine," I said.

"Take some wine anyway," Fran said. "If they don't drink it, we'll drink it."

"White or red?" I said.

"We'll take something sweet," she said, not paying me any attention. "But I don't care if we take anything. This is your show. Let's not make a production out of it, or else I don't want to go. I can make a raspberry coffee ring. Or else some cupcakes."

"They'll have dessert," I said. "You don't invite people to supper without fixing a dessert."

"They might have rice pudding. Or Jell-O! Something we don't like," she said. "I don't know anything about the woman. How do we know what she'll have? What if she gives us Jell-O?" Fran shook her head. I shrugged. But she was right. "Those old cigars he gave you," she said. "Take them. Then you and him can go off to the parlor after supper and smoke cigars and drink port wine, or whatever those people in movies drink."

"Okay, we'll just take ourselves," I said.

Fran said, "We'll take a loaf of my bread."

Bud and Olla lived twenty miles or so from town. We'd lived in that town for three years, but, damn it, Fran and I hadn't so much as taken a spin in the country. It felt good driving those winding little roads. It was early evening, nice and warm, and we saw pastures, rail fences, milk cows moving slowly toward old barns. We saw red-winged blackbirds on the fences, and pigeons circling around haylofts. There were gardens and such, wildflowers in bloom, and little houses set back from the road. I said, "I wish we had us a place out here." It was just an idle thought, another wish that wouldn't amount to anything. Fran didn't answer. She was busy looking at Bud's map. We came to the four-way stop he'd marked. We turned right like the map said and drove exactly three and three-tenths miles. On the left side of the road, I saw a field of corn, a mailbox, and a long, graveled driveway. At the end of the driveway, back in some trees, stood a house with a front porch. There was a chimney on the house. But it was summer, so, of course, no smoke rose from the chimney. But I thought it was a pretty picture, and I said so to Fran.

"It's the sticks out here," she said.

I turned into the drive. Corn rose up on both sides of the drive. Corn stood higher than the car. I could hear gravel crunching under the tires. As we got up close to the house, we could see a garden with green things the size of baseballs hanging from the vines.

"What's that?" I said.

"How should I know?" she said. "Squash, maybe. I don't have a clue."

"Hey, Fran," I said. "Take it easy."

She didn't say anything. She drew in her lower lip and let it go. She turned off the radio as we got close to the house.

A baby's swing-set stood in the front yard and some toys lay on the porch. I pulled up in front and stopped the car. It was then that we heard this awful squall. There was a baby in the house, right, but this cry was too loud for a baby.

"What's that sound?" Fran said.

Then something as big as a vulture flapped heavily down from one of the trees and landed just in front of the car. It shook itself. It turned its long neck toward the car, raised its head, and regarded us.

"Goddamn it," I said. I sat there with my hands on the wheel and stared at the thing.

"Can you believe it?" Fran said. "I never saw a real one before."

We both knew it was a peacock, sure, but we didn't say the word out loud. We just watched it. The bird turned its head up in the air and made this harsh cry again. It had fluffed itself out and looked about twice the size it'd been when it landed.

"Goddamn," I said again. We stayed where we were in the front seat.

The bird moved forward a little. Then it turned its head to the side and braced itself. It kept its bright, wild eye right on us. Its tail was raised, and it was like a big fan folding in and out. There was every color in the rainbow shining from that tail.

"My God," Fran said quietly. She moved her hand over to my knee.

"Goddamn," I said. There was nothing else to say.

The bird made this strange wailing sound once more. "*May-awe, may-awe!*" it went. If it'd been something I was hearing late at night and for the first time, I'd have thought it was somebody dying, or else something wild and dangerous.

The front door opened and Bud came out on the porch. He was buttoning his shirt. His hair was wet. It looked like he'd just come from the shower.

"Shut yourself up, Joey!" he said to the peacock. He clapped his hands at the bird, and the thing moved back a little. "That's enough now. That's right, shut up! You shut up, you old devil!" Bud came down the steps. He tucked in his shirt as he came over to the car. He was wearing what he always wore to work – blue jeans and a denim shirt. I had on my slacks and a short-sleeved sport shirt. My good loafers. When I saw what Bud was wearing, I didn't like it that I was dressed up.

"Glad you could make it," Bud said as he came over beside the car. "Come on inside."

"Hey, Bud," I said.

Fran and I got out of the car. The peacock stood off a little to one side, dodging its mean-looking head this way and that. We were careful to keep some distance between it and us.

"Any trouble finding the place?" Bud said to me. He hadn't looked at Fran. He was waiting to be introduced.

"Good directions," I said. "Hey, Bud, this is Fran. Fran, Bud. She's got the word on you, Bud."

He laughed and they shook hands. Fran was taller than Bud. Bud had to look up.

"He talks about you," Fran said. She took her hand back. "Bud this, Bud that. You're about the only person down there he talks about. I feel like I know you." She was keeping an eye on the peacock. It had moved over near the porch.

"This here's my friend," Bud said. "He *ought* to talk about me." Bud said this and then he grinned and gave me a little punch on the arm.

Fran went on holding her loaf of bread. She didn't know what to do with it. She gave it to Bud. "We brought you something."

Bud took the loaf. He turned it over and looked at it as if it was the first loaf of bread he'd ever seen. "This is real nice of you." He brought the loaf up to his face and sniffed it.

"Fran baked that bread," I told Bud.

Bud nodded. Then he said, "Let's go inside and meet the wife and mother."

He was talking about Olla, sure. Olla was the only mother around. Bud had told me his own mother was dead and that his dad had pulled out when Bud was a kid.

The peacock scuttled ahead of us, then hopped onto the porch when Bud opened the door. It was trying to get inside the house.

"Oh," said Fran as the peacock pressed itself against her leg.

"Joey, goddamn it," Bud said. He thumped the bird on the top of its head. The peacock backed up on the porch and shook itself. The quills in its train rattled as it shook. Bud made as if to kick it, and the peacock backed up some more. Then Bud held the door for us. "She lets the goddamn thing in the house. Before long, it'll be wanting to eat at the goddamn table and sleep in the goddamn bed."

Fran stopped just inside the door. She looked back at the corn-field. "You have a nice place," she said. Bud was still holding the door. "Don't they, Jack?"

"You bet," I said. I was surprised to hear her say it.

"A place like this is not all it's cracked up to be," Bud said, still holding the door. He made a threatening move toward the peacock. "Keeps you going. Never a dull moment." Then he said, "Step on inside, folks."

I said, "Hey, Bud, what's that growing there?"

"Them's tomatoes," Bud said.

"Some farmer I got," Fran said, and shook her head.

Bud laughed. We went inside. This plump little woman with her hair done up in a bun was waiting for us in the living room.

She had her hands rolled up in her apron. The cheeks of her face were bright red. I thought at first she might be out of breath, or else mad at something. She gave me the once-over, and then her eyes went to Fran. Not unfriendly, just looking. She stared at Fran and continued to blush.

Bud said, "Olla, this is Fran. And this is my friend Jack. You know all about Jack. Folks, this is Olla." He handed Olla the bread.

"What's this?" she said. "Oh, it's homemade bread. Well, thanks. Sit down anywhere. Make yourselves at home. Bud, why don't you ask them what they'd like to drink. I've got something on the stove." Olla said that and went back into the kitchen with the bread.

"Have a seat," Bud said. Fran and I plunked ourselves down on the sofa. I reached for my cigarettes. Bud said, "Here's an ashtray." He picked up something heavy from the top of the TV. "Use this," he said, and he put the thing down on the coffee table in front of me. It was one of those glass ashtrays made to look like a swan. I lit up and dropped the match into the opening in the swan's back. I watched a little wisp of smoke drift out of the swan.

The color TV was going, so we looked at that for a minute. On the screen, stock cars were tearing around a track. The announcer talked in a grave voice. But it was like he was holding back some excitement, too. "We're still waiting to have official confirmation," the announcer said.

"You want to watch this?" Bud said. He was still standing.

I said I didn't care. And I didn't. Fran shrugged. What difference could it make to her? she seemed to say. The day was shot anyway.

"There's only about twenty laps left," Bud said. "It's close now. There was a big pile-up earlier. Knocked out half-a-dozen cars. Some drivers got hurt. They haven't said yet how bad."

"Leave it on," I said. "Let's watch it."

"Maybe one of those damn cars will explode right in front of us," Fran said. "Or else maybe one'll run up into the grandstand and smash the guy selling the crummy hot dogs." She took a strand of hair between her fingers and kept her eyes fixed on the TV.

Bud looked at Fran to see if she was kidding. "That other business, that pile-up, was something. One thing led to another. Cars, parts of cars, people all over the place. Well, what can I get you? We have ale, and there's a bottle of Old Crow."

"What are you drinking?" I said to Bud.

"Ale," Bud said. "It's good and cold."

"I'll have ale," I said.

"I'll have some of that Old Crow and a little water," Fran said. "In a tall glass, please. With some ice. Thank you, Bud."

"Can do," Bud said. He threw another look at the TV and moved off to the kitchen.

Fran nudged me and nodded in the direction of the TV. "Look up on top," she whispered. "Do you see what I see?" I looked at where she was looking. There was a slender red vase into which somebody had stuck a few garden daisies. Next to the vase, on the doily, sat an old plaster-of-Paris cast of the most crooked, jaggedy teeth in the world. There were no lips to the awful-looking thing, and no jaw either, just these old plaster teeth packed into something that resembled thick yellow gums.

Just then Olla came back with a can of mixed nuts and a bottle of root beer. She had her apron off now. She put the can of nuts onto the coffee table next to the swan. She said, "Help yourselves. Bud's getting your drinks." Olla's face came on red again as she said this. She sat down in an old cane rocking chair and set it in motion. She drank from her root beer and looked at the TV. Bud came back carrying a little wooden tray with Fran's glass of whiskey and water and my bottle of ale. He had a bottle of ale on the tray for himself.

"You want a glass?" he asked me.

I shook my head. He tapped me on the knee and turned to Fran.

She took her glass from Bud and said, "Thanks." Her eyes went to the teeth again. Bud saw where she was looking. The cars screamed around the track. I took the ale and gave my attention to the screen. The teeth were none of my business. "Them's what Olla's teeth looked like before she had her braces put on," Bud said to Fran. "I've got used to them. But I guess they look funny up there. For the life of me, I don't know why she keeps them around." He looked over at Olla. Then he looked at me and winked. He sat down in his La-Z-Boy and crossed one leg over the other. He drank from his ale and gazed at Olla.

Olla turned red once more. She was holding her bottle of root beer. She took a drink of it. Then she said, "They're to remind me how much I owe Bud."

"What was that?" Fran said. She was picking through the can of nuts, helping herself to the cashews. Fran stopped what she was doing and looked at Olla. "Sorry, but I missed that." Fran stared at the woman and waited for whatever thing it was she'd say next.

Olla's face turned red again. "I've got lots of things to be thankful for," she said. "That's one of the things I'm thankful for. I keep them around to remind me how much I owe Bud." She drank from her root beer. Then she lowered the bottle and said, "You've got pretty teeth, Fran. I noticed right away. But these teeth of mine, they came in crooked when I was a kid." With her fingernail, she tapped a couple of her front teeth. She said, "My folks couldn't afford to fix teeth. These teeth of mine came in just any which way. My first husband didn't care what I looked like. No, he didn't! He didn't care about anything except where his next drink was coming from. He had one friend only in this world, and that was his bottle." She shook her head. "Then Bud come along and got me out of that mess. After we were together, the first thing Bud said was, 'We're going to have them teeth fixed.' That mold was made right after Bud and I met, on the occasion of my second visit to the orthodontist. Right before the braces went on."

Olla's face stayed red. She looked at the picture on the screen. She drank from her root beer and didn't seem to have any more to say.

"That orthodontist must have been a whiz," Fran said. She looked back at the horror-show teeth on top of the TV.

"He was great," Olla said. She turned in her chair and said, "See?" She opened her mouth and showed us her teeth once more, not a bit shy now.

Bud had gone to the TV and picked up the teeth. He walked over to Olla and held them up against Olla's cheek. "Before and after," Bud said.

Olla reached up and took the mold from Bud. "You know something? That orthodontist wanted to keep this." She was holding it in her lap while she talked. "I said nothing doing. I pointed out to him they were *my* teeth. So he took pictures of the mold instead. He told me he was going to put the pictures in a magazine."

Bud said, "Imagine what kind of magazine that'd be. Not much call for that kind of publication, I don't think," he said, and we all laughed.

"After I got the braces off, I kept putting my hand up to my mouth when I laughed. Like this," she said. "Sometimes I still do it. Habit. One day Bud said, 'You can stop doing that anytime, Olla. You don't have to hide teeth as pretty as that. You have nice teeth now.'" Olla looked over at Bud. Bud winked at her. She grinned and lowered her eyes.

Fran drank from her glass. I took some of my ale. I didn't know what to say to this. Neither did Fran. But I knew Fran would have plenty to say about it later.

I said, "Olla, I called here once. You answered the phone. But I hung up. I don't know why I hung up." I said that and then sipped my ale. I didn't know why I'd brought it up now.

"I don't remember," Olla said. "When was that?"

"A while back."

"I don't remember," she said and shook her head. She fingered the plaster teeth in her lap. She looked at the race and went back to rocking.

Fran turned her eyes to me. She drew her lip under. But she didn't say anything.

Bud said, "Well, what else is new?"

"Have some more nuts," Olla said. "Supper'll be ready in a little while."

There was a cry from a room in the back of the house.

"Not him," Olla said to Bud, and made a face.

"Old Junior boy," Bud said. He leaned back in his chair, and we watched the rest of the race, three or four laps, no sound.

Once or twice we heard the baby again, little fretful cries coming from the room in the back of the house.

"I don't know," Olla said. She got up from her chair. "Everything's about ready for us to sit down. I just have to take up the gravy. But I'd better look in on him first. Why don't you folks go out and sit down at the table? I'll just be a minute."

"I'd like to see the baby," Fran said.

Olla was still holding the teeth. She went over and put them back on top of the TV. "It might upset him just now," she said. "He's not used to strangers. Wait and see if I can get him back to sleep. Then you can peek in. While he's asleep." She said this and then she went down the hall to a room, where she opened a door. She eased in and shut the door behind her. The baby stopped crying.

Bud killed the picture and we went in to sit at the table. Bud and I talked about things at work. Fran listened. Now and then she even asked a question. But I could tell she was bored, and maybe feeling put out with Olla for not letting her see the baby. She looked around Olla's kitchen. She wrapped a strand of hair around her fingers and checked out Olla's things.

Olla came back into the kitchen and said, "I changed him and gave him his rubber duck. Maybe he'll let us eat now. But don't bet on it." She raised a lid and took a pan off the stove. She poured red gravy into a bowl and put the bowl on the table. She took lids off some other pots and looked to see that everything was ready. On the table were baked ham, sweet potatoes, mashed potatoes, lima beans, corn on the cob, salad greens. Fran's loaf of bread was in a prominent place next to the ham.

"I forgot the napkins," Olla said. "You all get started. Who wants what to drink? Bud drinks milk with all of his meals."

"Milk's fine," I said.

"Water for me," Fran said. "But I can get it. I don't want you waiting on me. You have enough to do." She made as if to get up from her chair.

Olla said, "Please. You're company. Sit still. Let me get it." She was blushing again.

We sat with our hands in our laps and waited. I thought about those plaster teeth. Olla came back with napkins, big glasses of milk for Bud and me, and a glass of ice water for Fran. Fran said, "Thanks."

"You're welcome," Olla said. Then she seated herself. Bud cleared his throat. He bowed his head and said a few words of grace. He talked in a voice so low I could hardly make out the words. But I got the drift of things – he was thanking the Higher Power for the food we were about to put away.

"Amen," Olla said when he'd finished.

Bud passed me the platter of ham and helped himself to some mashed potatoes. We got down to it then. We didn't say much except now and then Bud or I would say, "This is real good ham." Or, "This sweet corn is the best sweet corn I ever ate."

"This bread is what's special," Olla said.

"I'll have some more salad, please, Olla," Fran said, softening up maybe a little.

"Have more of this," Bud would say as he passed me the platter of ham, or else the bowl of red gravy.

From time to time, we heard the baby make its noise. Olla would turn her head to listen, then, satisfied it was just fussing, she would give her attention back to her food.

"The baby's out of sorts tonight," Olla said to Bud.

"I'd still like to see him," Fran said. "My sister has a little baby. But she and the baby live in Denver. When will I ever get to Denver? I have a niece I haven't even seen." Fran thought about this for a minute, and then she went back to eating.

Olla forked some ham into her mouth. "Let's hope he'll drop off to sleep," she said.

Bud said, "There's a lot more of everything. Have some more ham and sweet potatoes, everybody."

"I can't eat another bite," Fran said. She laid her fork on her plate. "It's great, but I can't eat any more."

"Save room," Bud said. "Olla's made rhubarb pie."

Fran said, "I guess I could eat a little piece of that. When everybody else is ready."

"Me, too," I said. But I said it to be polite. I'd hated rhubarb pie since I was thirteen years old and had got sick on it, eating it with strawberry ice cream.

We finished what was on our plates. Then we heard that damn peacock again. The thing was on the roof this time. We could hear it over our heads. It made a ticking sound as it walked back and forth on the shingles.

Bud shook his head. "Joey will knock it off in a minute. He'll get tired and turn in pretty soon," Bud said. "He sleeps in one of them trees."

The bird let go with its cry once more. "*May-awe!*" it went. Nobody said anything. What was there to say?

Then Olla said, "He wants in, Bud."

"Well, he can't come in," Bud said. "We got company, in case you hadn't noticed. These people don't want a goddamn old bird in the house. That dirty bird and your old pair of teeth! What're people going to think?" He shook his head. He laughed. We all laughed. Fran laughed along with the rest of us.

"He's not *dirty*, Bud," Olla said. "What's gotten into you? You like Joey. Since when did you start calling him dirty?"

"Since he shit on the rug that time," Bud said. "Pardon the French," he said to Fran. "But, I'll tell you, sometimes I could wring that old bird's neck for him. He's not even worth killing, is he, Olla? Sometimes, in the middle of the night, he'll bring me up out of bed with that cry of his. He's not worth a nickel – right, Olla?"

Olla shook her head at Bud's nonsense. She moved a few lima beans around on her plate.

"How'd you get a peacock in the first place?" Fran wanted to know.

Olla looked up from her plate. She said, "I always dreamed of having me a peacock. Since I was a girl and found a picture of one in a magazine. I thought it was the most beautiful thing I ever saw. I cut the picture out and put it over my bed. I kept that picture for the longest time. Then when Bud and I got this place, I saw my chance. I said, 'Bud, I want a peacock.' Bud laughed at the idea."

"I finally asked around," Bud said. "I heard tell of an old boy who raised them over in the next county. Birds of paradise, he called them. We paid a hundred bucks for that bird of paradise," he said. He smacked his forehead. "God Almighty, I got me a woman with expensive tastes." He grinned at Olla.

"Bud," Olla said, "you know that isn't true. Besides everything else, Joey's a good watchdog," she said to Fran. "We don't need a watchdog with Joey. He can hear just about anything."

"If times get tough, as they might, I'll put Joey in a pot," Bud said. "Feathers and all."

"Bud! That's not funny," Olla said. But she laughed and we got a good look at her teeth again.

The baby started up once more. It was serious crying this time. Olla put down her napkin and got up from the table.

Bud said, "If it's not one thing, it's another. Bring him on out here, Olla."

"I'm going to," Olla said, and went to get the baby.

The peacock wailed again, and I could feel the hair on the back of my neck. I looked at Fran. She picked up her napkin and then put it down. I looked toward the kitchen window. It was dark outside. The window was raised, and there was a screen in the frame. I thought I heard the bird on the front porch.

Fran turned her eyes to look down the hall. She was watching for Olla and the baby.

After a time, Olla came back with it. I looked at the baby and drew a breath. Olla sat down at the table with the baby. She held it up under its arms so it could stand on her lap and face us. She looked at Fran and then at me. She wasn't blushing now. She waited for one of us to comment.

"Ah!" said Fran.

"What is it?" Olla said quickly.

"Nothing," Fran said. "I thought I saw something at the window. I thought I saw a bat."

"We don't have any bats around here," Olla said.

"Maybe it was a moth," Fran said. "It was something. Well," she said, "isn't that some baby."

Bud was looking at the baby. Then he looked over at Fran. He tipped his chair onto its back legs and nodded. He nodded again, and said, "That's all right, don't worry any. We know he wouldn't win no beauty contests right now. He's no Clark Gable. But give him time. With any luck, you know, he'll grow up to look like his old man."

The baby stood in Olla's lap, looking around the table at us. Olla had moved her hands down to its middle so that the baby could rock back and forth on its fat legs. Bar none, it was the ugliest baby I'd ever seen. It was so ugly I couldn't say anything. No words would come out of my mouth. I don't mean it was diseased or disfigured. Nothing like that. It was just ugly. It had a big red face, pop eyes, a broad forehead, and these big fat lips. It had no neck to speak of, and it had three or four fat chins. Its chins rolled right up under its ears, and its ears stuck out from its bald head. Fat hung over its wrists. Its arms and fingers were fat. Even calling it ugly does it credit.

The ugly baby made its noise and jumped up and down on its mother's lap. Then it stopped jumping. It leaned forward and tried to reach its fat hand into Olla's plate.

I've seen babies. When I was growing up, my two sisters had a total of six babies. I was around babies a lot when I was a kid. I've seen babies in stores and so on. But this baby beat anything. Fran stared at it, too. I guess she didn't know what to say either.

"He's a big fellow, isn't he?" I said.

Bud said, "He'll by God be turning out for football before long. He sure as hell won't go without meals around this house."

As if to make sure of this, Olla plunged her fork into some sweet potatoes and brought the fork up to the baby's mouth. "He's my baby, isn't he?" she said to the fat thing, ignoring us.

The baby leaned forward and opened up for the sweet potatoes. It reached for Olla's fork as she guided the sweet potatoes into its mouth, then clamped down. The baby chewed the stuff and rocked some more on Olla's lap. It was so pop-eyed, it was like it was plugged into something.

Fran said, "He's some baby, Olla."

The baby's face screwed up. It began to fuss all over again.

"Let Joey in," Olla said to Bud.

Bud let the legs of his chair come down on the floor. "I think we should at least ask these people if they mind," Bud said.

Olla looked at Fran and then she looked at me. Her face had gone red again. The baby kept prancing in her lap, squirming to get down.

"We're friends here," I said. "Do whatever you want."

Bud said, "Maybe they don't want a big old bird like Joey in the house. Did you ever think of that, Olla?"

"Do you folks mind?" Olla said to us. "If Joey comes inside? Things got headed in the wrong direction with that bird tonight. The baby, too, I think. He's used to having Joey come in and fool around with him a little before his bedtime. Neither of them can settle down tonight."

"Don't ask us," Fran said. "I don't mind if he comes in. I've never been up close to one before. But I don't mind." She looked at me. I suppose I could tell she wanted me to say something.

"Hell, no," I said. "Let him in." I picked up my glass and finished the milk.

Bud got up from his chair. He went to the front door and opened it. He flicked on the yard lights.

"What's your baby's name?" Fran wanted to know.

"Harold," Olla said. She gave Harold some more sweet potatoes from her plate. "He's real smart. Sharp as a tack. Always knows what you're saying to him. Don't you, Harold? You wait until you get your own baby, Fran. You'll see."

Fran just looked at her. I heard the front door open and then close.

"He's smart, all right," Bud said as he came back into the kitchen. "He takes after Olla's dad. Now there was one smart old boy for you."

*

I looked around behind Bud and could see that peacock hanging back in the living room, turning its head this way and that, like you'd turn a hand mirror. It shook itself, and the sound was like a deck of cards being shuffled in the other room.

It moved forward a step. Then another step.

"Can I hold the baby?" Fran said. She said it like it would be a favor if Olla would let her.

Olla handed the baby across the table to her.

Fran tried to get the baby settled in her lap. But the baby began to squirm and make its noises.

"Harold," Fran said.

Olla watched Fran with the baby. She said, "When Harold's grandpa was sixteen years old, he set out to read the encyclopedia from A to Z. He did it, too. He finished when he was twenty. Just before he met my mama."

"Where's he now?" I asked. "What's he do?" I wanted to know what had become of a man who'd set himself a goal like that.

"He's dead," Olla said. She was watching Fran, who by now had the baby down on its back and across her knees. Fran chucked the baby under one of its chins. She started to talk baby talk to it.

"He worked in the woods," Bud said. "Loggers dropped a tree on him."

"Mama got some insurance money," Olla said. "But she spent that. Bud sends her something every month."

"Not much," Bud said. "Don't have much ourselves. But she's Olla's mother."

By this time, the peacock had gathered its courage and was beginning to move slowly, with little swaying and jerking motions, into the kitchen. Its head was erect but at an angle, its red eyes fixed on us. Its crest, a little sprig of feathers, stood a few inches over its head. Plumes rose from its tail. The bird stopped a few feet away from the table and looked us over.

"They don't call them birds of paradise for nothing," Bud said.

Fran didn't look up. She was giving all her attention to the baby. She'd begun to patty-cake with it, which pleased the baby somewhat. I mean, at least the thing had stopped fussing. She brought it up to her neck and whispered something into its ear.

"Now," she said, "don't tell anyone what I said."

The baby stared at her with its pop eyes. Then it reached and got itself a baby handful of Fran's blond hair. The peacock stepped closer to the table. None of us said anything. We just sat still. Baby Harold saw the bird. It let go of Fran's hair and stood up on her lap. It pointed its fat fingers at the bird. It jumped up and down and made noises.

The peacock walked quickly around the table and went for the baby. It ran its long neck across the baby's legs. It pushed its beak in under the baby's pajama top and shook its stiff head back and forth. The baby laughed and kicked its feet. Scooting onto its back, the baby worked its way over Fran's knees and down onto the floor. The peacock kept pushing against the baby, as if it was a game they were playing. Fran held the baby against her legs while the baby strained forward.

"I just don't believe this," she said.

"That peacock is crazy, that's what," Bud said. "Damn bird doesn't know it's a bird, that's its major trouble."

Olla grinned and showed her teeth again. She looked over at Bud. Bud pushed his chair away from the table and nodded.

It *was* an ugly baby. But, for all I know, I guess it didn't matter that much to Bud and Olla. Or if it did, maybe they simply thought, So okay if it's ugly. It's our baby. And this is just a stage. Pretty soon there'll be another stage. There is this stage and then there is the next stage. Things will be okay in the long run, once all the stages have been gone through. They might have thought something like that.

Bud picked up the baby and swung him over his head until Harold shrieked. The peacock ruffled its feathers and watched.

Fran shook her head again. She smoothed out her dress where the baby had been. Olla picked up her fork and was working at some lima beans on her plate.

Bud shifted the baby onto his hip and said, "There's pie and coffee yet."

That evening at Bud and Olla's was special. I knew it was special. That evening I felt good about almost everything in my life. I couldn't wait to be alone with Fran to talk to her about what I was feeling. I made a wish that evening. Sitting there at the table, I closed my eyes for a minute and thought hard. What I wished for was that I'd never forget or otherwise let go of that evening. That's one wish of mine that came true. And it was bad luck for me that it did. But, of course, I couldn't know that then.

"What are you thinking about, Jack?" Bud said to me.

"I'm just thinking," I said. I grinned at him.

"A penny," Olla said.

I just grinned some more and shook my head.

After we got home from Bud and Olla's that night, and we were under the covers, Fran said, "Honey, fill me up with your seed!" When she said that, I heard her all the way down to my toes, and I hollered and let go.

Later, after things had changed for us, and the kid had come along, all of that, Fran would look back on that evening at Bud's place as the beginning of the change. But she's wrong. The change came later – and when it came, it was like something that happened to other people, not something that could have happened to us.

"Goddamn those people and their ugly baby," Fran will say, for no apparent reason, while we're watching TV late at night. "And that smelly bird," she'll say. "Christ, who needs it!" Fran will say. She says this kind of stuff a lot, even though she hasn't seen Bud and Olla since that one time.

Fran doesn't work at the creamery anymore, and she cut her hair a long time ago. She's gotten fat on me, too. We don't talk about it. What's to say?

I still see Bud at the plant. We work together and we open our lunch pails together. If I ask, he tells me about Olla and Harold. Joey's out of the picture. He flew into his tree one night and that was it for him. He didn't come down. Old age, maybe, Bud says. Then the owls took over. Bud shrugs. He eats his sandwich and says Harold's going to be a linebacker someday. "You ought to see that kid," Bud says. I nod. We're still friends. That hasn't changed any. But I've gotten careful with what I say to him.

And I know he feels that and wishes it could be different. I wish it could be, too.

Once in a blue moon, he asks about my family. When he does, I tell him everybody's fine. "Everybody's fine," I say. I close the lunch pail and take out my cigarettes. Bud nods and sips his coffee. The truth is, my kid has a conniving streak in him. But I don't talk about it. Not even with his mother. Especially her. She and I talk less and less as it is. Mostly it's just the TV. But I remember that night. I recall the way the peacock picked up its gray feet and inched around the table. And then my friend and his wife saying good night to us on the porch. Olla giving Fran some peacock feathers to take home. I remember all of us shaking hands, hugging each other, saying things. In the car, Fran sat close to me as we drove away. She kept her hand on my leg. We drove home like that from my friend's house.

Cathedral

This blind man, an old friend of my wife's, he was on his way to spend the night. His wife had died. So he was visiting the dead wife's relatives in Connecticut. He called my wife from his in-laws'. Arrangements were made. He would come by train, a five-hour trip, and my wife would meet him at the station. She hadn't seen him since she worked for him one summer in Seattle ten years ago. But she and the blind man had kept in touch. They made tapes and mailed them back and forth. I wasn't enthusiastic about his visit. He was no one I knew. And his being blind bothered me. My idea of blindness came from the movies. In the movies, the blind moved slowly and never laughed. Sometimes they were led by seeing-eye dogs. A blind man in my house was not something I looked forward to.

That summer in Seattle she had needed a job. She didn't have any money. The man she was going to marry at the end of the summer was in officers' training school. He didn't have any money, either. But she was in love with the guy, and he was in love with her, etc. She'd seen something in the paper: HELP WANTED – *Reading to Blind Man*, and a telephone number. She phoned and went over, was hired on the spot. She'd worked with this blind man all summer. She read stuff to him, case studies, reports, that sort of thing. She helped him organize his little office in the county social-service department. They'd become good friends, my wife and the blind man. How do I know these things? She told me. And she told me something else. On her last day in the office, the blind man asked if he could touch her face. She agreed to this. She told me he touched his fingers to every part of her face, her nose – even her neck! She never forgot it. She even tried to write a poem about it. She was always trying to write a poem. She wrote a poem or two every year, usually after something really important had happened to her.

When we first started going out together, she showed me the poem. In the poem, she recalled his fingers and the way they had moved around over her face. In the poem, she talked about what she had felt at the time, about what went through her mind when the blind man touched her nose and lips. I can remember I didn't think much of the poem. Of course, I didn't tell her that. Maybe I just don't understand poetry. I admit it's not the first thing I reach for when I pick up something to read.

Anyway, this man who'd first enjoyed her favors, the officer-to-be, he'd been her childhood sweetheart. So okay. I'm saying that at the end of the summer she let the blind man run his hands over her face, said good-bye to him, married her childhood etc., who was now a commissioned officer, and she moved away from Seattle. But they'd kept in touch, she and the blind man. She made the first contact after a year or so. She called him up one night from an Air Force base in Alabama. She wanted to talk. They talked. He asked her to send him a tape and tell him about her life. She did this. She sent the tape. On the tape, she told the blind man about her husband and about their life together in the military. She told the blind man she loved her husband but she didn't like it where they lived and she didn't like it that he was a part of the military-industrial thing. She told the blind man she'd written a poem and he was in it. She told him that she was writing a poem about what it was like to be an Air Force officer's wife. The poem wasn't finished yet. She was still writing it. The blind man made a tape. He sent her the tape. She made a tape. This went on for years. My wife's officer was posted to one base and then another. She sent tapes from Moody AFB, McGuire, McConnell, and finally Travis, near Sacramento, where one night she got to feeling lonely and cut off from people she kept losing in that moving-around life. She got to feeling she couldn't go it another step. She went in and swallowed all the pills and capsules in the medicine chest and washed them down with a bottle of gin. Then she got into a hot bath and passed out.

But instead of dying, she got sick. She threw up. Her officer

– why should he have a name? he was the childhood sweetheart, and what more does he want? – came home from somewhere, found her, and called the ambulance. In time, she put it all on a tape and sent the tape to the blind man. Over the years, she put all kinds of stuff on tapes and sent the tapes off lickety-split. Next to writing a poem every year, I think it was her chief means of recreation. On one tape, she told the blind man she'd decided to live away from her officer for a time. On another tape, she told him about her divorce. She and I began going out, and of course she told her blind man about it. She told him everything, or so it seemed to me. Once she asked me if I'd like to hear the latest tape from the blind man. This was a year ago. I was on the tape, she said. So I said okay, I'd listen to it. I got us drinks and we settled down in the living room. We made ready to listen. First she inserted the tape into the player and adjusted a couple of dials. Then she pushed a lever. The tape squeaked and someone began to talk in this loud voice. She lowered the volume. After a few minutes of harmless chitchat, I heard my own name in the mouth of this stranger, this blind man I didn't even know! And then this: "From all you've said about him, I can only conclude –" But we were interrupted, a knock at the door, something, and we didn't ever get back to the tape. Maybe it was just as well. I'd heard all I wanted to.

Now this same blind man was coming to sleep in my house.

"Maybe I could take him bowling," I said to my wife. She was at the draining board doing scalloped potatoes. She put down the knife she was using and turned around.

"If you love me," she said, "you can do this for me. If you don't love me, okay. But if you had a friend, any friend, and the friend came to visit, I'd make him feel comfortable." She wiped her hands with the dish towel.

"I don't have any blind friends," I said.

"You don't have *any* friends," she said. "Period. Besides," she said, "goddamn it, his wife's just died! Don't you understand that? The man's lost his wife!"

I didn't answer. She'd told me a little about the blind man's wife. Her name was Beulah. Beulah! That's a name for a colored woman.

"Was his wife a Negro?" I asked.

"Are you crazy?" my wife said. "Have you just flipped or something?" She picked up a potato. I saw it hit the floor, then roll under the stove. "What's wrong with you?" she said. "Are you drunk?"

"I'm just asking," I said.

Right then my wife filled me in with more detail than I cared to know. I made a drink and sat at the kitchen table to listen. Pieces of the story began to fall into place.

Beulah had gone to work for the blind man the summer after my wife had stopped working for him. Pretty soon Beulah and the blind man had themselves a church wedding. It was a little wedding – who'd want to go to such a wedding in the first place? – just the two of them, plus the minister and the minister's wife. But it was a church wedding just the same. It was what Beulah had wanted, he'd said. But even then Beulah must have been carrying the cancer in her glands. After they had been inseparable for eight years – my wife's word, *inseparable* – Beulah's health went into a rapid decline. She died in a Seattle hospital room, the blind man sitting beside the bed and holding on to her hand. They'd married, lived and worked together, slept together – had sex, sure – and then the blind man had to bury her. All this without his having ever seen what the goddamned woman looked like. It was beyond my understanding. Hearing this, I felt sorry for the blind man for a little bit. And then I found myself thinking what a pitiful life this woman must have led. Imagine a woman who could never see herself as she was seen in the eyes of her loved one. A woman who could go on day after day and never receive the smallest compliment from her beloved. A woman whose husband could never read the expression on her face, be it misery or something better. Someone who could wear makeup or not – what difference to him? She could, if she wanted, wear green eye-shadow around one eye, a straight pin in her nostril, yellow slacks, and purple shoes, no matter. And then to slip off into death, the blind man's hand on her hand, his blind eyes streaming tears – I'm imagining now – her last thought maybe this: that he never even knew what she looked like, and she on an express to the grave. Robert was left with a small insurance policy and half of a twenty-peso Mexican coin. The other half of the coin went into the box with her. Pathetic.

So when the time rolled around, my wife went to the depot to pick him up. With nothing to do but wait – sure, I blamed him for that – I was having a drink and watching the TV when I heard the car pull into the drive. I got up from the sofa with my drink and went to the window to have a look.

I saw my wife laughing as she parked the car. I saw her get out of the car and shut the door. She was still wearing a smile. Just amazing. She went around to the other side of the car to where the blind man was already starting to get out. This blind man, feature this, he was wearing a full beard! A beard on a blind man! Too much, I say. The blind man reached into the backseat and dragged out a suitcase. My wife took his arm, shut the car door, and, talking all the way, moved him down the drive and then up the steps to the front porch. I turned off the TV. I finished my drink, rinsed the glass, dried my hands. Then I went to the door.

My wife said, "I want you to meet Robert. Robert, this is my husband. I've told you all about him." She was beaming. She had this blind man by his coat sleeve.

The blind man let go of his suitcase and up came his hand.

I took it. He squeezed hard, held my hand, and then he let it go.

"I feel like we've already met," he boomed.

"Likewise," I said. I didn't know what else to say. Then I said, "Welcome. I've heard a lot about you." We began to move then, a little group, from the porch into the living room, my wife guiding him by the arm. The blind man was carrying his suitcase in his other hand. My wife said things like, "To your left here, Robert. That's right. Now watch it, there's a chair. That's it. Sit down right here. This is the sofa. We just bought this sofa two weeks ago."

I started to say something about the old sofa. I'd liked that old sofa. But I didn't say anything. Then I wanted to say something else, small-talk, about the scenic ride along the Hudson. How going *to* New York, you should sit on the right-hand side of the train, and coming *from* New York, the left-hand side.

"Did you have a good train ride?" I said. "Which side of the train did you sit on, by the way?"

"What a question, which side!" my wife said. "What's it matter which side?" she said.

"I just asked," I said.

"Right side," the blind man said. "I hadn't been on a train in nearly forty years. Not since I was a kid. With my folks. That's been a long time. I'd nearly forgotten the sensation. I have winter in my beard now," he said. "So I've been told, anyway. Do I look distinguished, my dear?" the blind man said to my wife.

"You look distinguished, Robert," she said. "Robert," she said. "Robert, it's just so good to see you."

My wife finally took her eyes off the blind man and looked at me. I had the feeling she didn't like what she saw. I shrugged.

I've never met, or personally known, anyone who was blind. This blind man was late forties, a heavy-set, balding man with stooped shoulders, as if he carried a great weight there. He wore brown slacks, brown shoes, a light-brown shirt, a tie, a sports coat. Spiffy. He also had this full beard. But he didn't use a cane and he didn't wear dark glasses. I'd always thought dark glasses were a must for the blind. Fact was, I wished he had a pair. At first glance, his eyes looked like anyone else's eyes. But if you looked close, there was something different about them. Too much white in the iris, for one thing, and the pupils seemed to move around in the sockets without his knowing it or being able to stop it. Creepy. As I stared at his face, I saw the left pupil turn in toward his nose while the other made an effort to keep in one place. But it was only an effort, for that eye was on the roam without his knowing it or wanting it to be.

I said, "Let me get you a drink. What's your pleasure? We have a little of everything. It's one of our pastimes."

"Bub, I'm a Scotch man myself," he said fast enough in this big voice.

"Right," I said. Bub! "Sure you are. I knew it."

He let his fingers touch his suitcase, which was sitting alongside the sofa. He was taking his bearings. I didn't blame him for that.

"I'll move that up to your room," my wife said.

"No, that's fine," the blind man said loudly. "It can go up when I go up."

"A little water with the Scotch?" I said.

"Very little," he said.

"I knew it," I said.

He said, "Just a tad. The Irish actor, Barry Fitzgerald? I'm like that fellow. When I drink water, Fitzgerald said, I drink water. When I drink whiskey, I drink whiskey." My wife laughed. The blind man brought his hand up under his beard. He lifted his beard slowly and let it drop.

I did the drinks, three big glasses of Scotch with a splash of water in each. Then we made ourselves comfortable and talked about Robert's travels. First the long flight from the West Coast to Connecticut, we covered that. Then from Connecticut up here by train. We had another drink concerning that leg of the trip.

I remembered having read somewhere that the blind didn't smoke because, as speculation had it, they couldn't see the smoke they exhaled. I thought I knew that much and that much only about blind people. But this blind man smoked his cigarette down to the nubbin and then lit another one. This blind man filled his ashtray and my wife emptied it.

When we sat down at the table for dinner, we had another drink. My wife heaped Robert's plate with cube steak, scalloped potatoes, green beans. I buttered him up two slices of bread. I said, "Here's bread and butter for you." I swallowed some of my drink. "Now let us pray," I said, and the blind man lowered his head. My wife looked at me, her mouth agape. "Pray the phone won't ring and the food doesn't get cold," I said.

We dug in. We ate everything there was to eat on the table. We ate like there was no tomorrow. We didn't talk. We ate. We scarfed. We grazed that table. We were into serious eating. The blind man had right away located his foods, he knew just where everything was on his plate. I watched with admiration as he used his knife and fork on the meat. He'd cut two pieces of meat, fork the meat into his mouth, and then go all out for the scalloped potatoes, the beans next, and then he'd tear off a hunk of buttered bread and eat that. He'd follow this up with a big drink of milk. It didn't seem to bother him to use his fingers once in a while, either.

We finished everything, including half a strawberry pie. For a few moments, we sat as if stunned. Sweat beaded on our faces. Finally, we got up from the table and left the dirty plates. We didn't look back. We took ourselves into the living room and sank into our places again. Robert and my wife sat on the sofa. I took the big chair. We had us two or three more drinks while they talked about the major things that had come to pass for them in the past ten years. For the most part, I just listened. Now and then I joined in. I didn't want him to think I'd left the room, and I didn't want her to think I was feeling left out. They talked of things that had happened to them – to them! – these past ten years. I waited in vain to hear my name on my wife's sweet lips: "And then my dear husband came into my life" – something like that. But I heard nothing of the sort. More talk of Robert. Robert had done a little of everything, it seemed, a regular blind jack-of-all-trades. But most recently he and his wife had had an Amway distributorship, from which, I gathered, they'd earned their living, such as it was. The blind man was also a ham radio operator. He talked in his loud voice about conversations he'd had with fellow operators in Guam, in the Philippines, in Alaska, and even in Tahiti. He said he'd have a lot of friends there if he ever wanted to go visit those places. From time to time, he'd turn his blind face toward me, put his hand under his beard, ask me something. How long had I been in my present position? (Three years.) Did I like my work? (I didn't.) Was I going to stay with it? (What were the options?) Finally, when I thought he was beginning to run down, I got up and turned on the TV.

My wife looked at me with irritation. She was heading toward a boil. Then she looked at the blind man and said, "Robert, do you have a TV?"

The blind man said, "My dear, I have two TVs. I have a color set and a black-and-white thing, an old relic. It's funny, but if I turn the TV on, and I'm always turning it on, I turn on the color set. It's funny, don't you think?"

I didn't know what to say to that. I had absolutely nothing to say to that. No opinion. So I watched the news program and tried to listen to what the announcer was saying.

"This is a color TV," the blind man said. "Don't ask me how, but I can tell."

"We traded up a while ago," I said.

The blind man had another taste of his drink. He lifted his beard, sniffed it, and let it fall. He leaned forward on the sofa. He positioned his ashtray on the coffee table, then put the lighter to his cigarette. He leaned back on the sofa and crossed his legs at the ankles.

My wife covered her mouth, and then she yawned. She stretched. She said, "I think I'll go upstairs and put on my robe. I think I'll change into something else. Robert, you make yourself comfortable," she said.

"I'm comfortable," the blind man said.

"I want you to feel comfortable in this house," she said.

"I am comfortable," the blind man said.

After she'd left the room, he and I listened to the weather report and then to the sports roundup. By that time, she'd been gone so long I didn't know if she was going to come back. I thought she might have gone to bed. I wished she'd come back downstairs. I didn't want to be left alone with a blind man. I asked him if he wanted another drink, and he said sure. Then I asked if he wanted to smoke some dope with me. I said I'd just rolled a number. I hadn't, but I planned to do so in about two shakes.

"I'll try some with you," he said.

"Damn right," I said. "That's the stuff."

I got our drinks and sat down on the sofa with him. Then I rolled us two fat numbers. I lit one and passed it. I brought it to his fingers. He took it and inhaled.

"Hold it as long as you can," I said. I could tell he didn't know the first thing.

My wife came back downstairs wearing her pink robe and her pink slippers.

"What do I smell?" she said.

"We thought we'd have us some cannabis," I said.

My wife gave me a savage look. Then she looked at the blind man and said, "Robert, I didn't know you smoked."

He said, "I do now, my dear. There's a first time for everything. But I don't feel anything yet."

"This stuff is pretty mellow," I said. "This stuff is mild. It's dope you can reason with," I said. "It doesn't mess you up."

"Not much it doesn't, bub," he said, and laughed.

My wife sat on the sofa between the blind man and me. I passed her the number. She took it and toked and then passed it back to me. "Which way is this going?" she said. Then she said, "I shouldn't be smoking this. I can hardly keep my eyes open as it is. That dinner did me in. I shouldn't have eaten so much."

"It was the strawberry pie," the blind man said. "That's what did it," he said, and he laughed his big laugh. Then he shook his head.

"There's more strawberry pie," I said.

"Do you want some more, Robert?" my wife said.

"Maybe in a little while," he said.

We gave our attention to the TV. My wife yawned again. She said, "Your bed is made up when you feel like going to bed, Robert. I know you must have had a long day. When you're ready to go to bed, say so." She pulled his arm. "Robert?"

He came to and said, "I've had a real nice time. This beats tapes, doesn't it?"

I said, "Coming at you," and I put the number between his fingers. He inhaled, held the smoke, and then let it go. It was like he'd been doing it since he was nine years old.

"Thanks, bub," he said. "But I think this is all for me. I think I'm beginning to feel it," he said. He held the burning roach out for my wife.

"Same here," she said. "Ditto. Me, too." She took the roach and passed it to me. "I may just sit here for a while between you two guys with my eyes closed. But don't let me bother you, okay? Either one of you. If it bothers you, say so. Otherwise, I may just sit here with my eyes closed until you're ready to go to bed," she said. "Your bed's made up, Robert, when you're ready. It's right next to our room at the top of the stairs. We'll show you up when you're ready. You wake me up now, you guys, if I fall asleep." She said that and then she closed her eyes and went to sleep.

The news program ended. I got up and changed the channel. I sat back down on the sofa. I wished my wife hadn't pooped out. Her head lay across the back of the sofa, her mouth open. She'd turned so that her robe had slipped away from her legs, exposing a juicy thigh. I reached to draw her robe back over her, and it was then that I glanced at the blind man. What the hell! I flipped the robe open again.

"You say when you want some strawberry pie," I said.

"I will," he said.

I said, "Are you tired? Do you want me to take you up to your bed? Are you ready to hit the hay?"

"Not yet," he said. "No, I'll stay up with you, bub. If that's all right. I'll stay up until you're ready to turn in. We haven't had a chance to talk. Know what I mean? I feel like me and her monopolized the evening." He lifted his beard and he let it fall. He picked up his cigarettes and his lighter.

"That's all right," I said. Then I said, "I'm glad for the company."

And I guess I was. Every night I smoked dope and stayed up as long as I could before I fell asleep. My wife and I hardly ever went to bed at the same time. When I did go to sleep, I had these dreams. Sometimes I'd wake up from one of them, my heart going crazy.

Something about the church and the Middle Ages was on the TV. Not your run-of-the-mill TV fare. I wanted to watch something else. I turned to the other channels. But there was nothing on them, either. So I turned back to the first channel and apologized.

"Bub, it's all right," the blind man said. "It's fine with me. Whatever you want to watch is okay. I'm always learning something. Learning never ends. It won't hurt me to learn something tonight. I got ears," he said.

He didn't say anything for a time. He was leaning forward with his head turned at me, his right ear aimed in the direction of the set. Very disconcerting. Now and then his eyelids drooped and then they snapped open again. Now and then he put his fingers into his beard and tugged, like he was thinking about something he was hearing on the television.

On the screen, a group of men wearing cowls was being set upon and tormented by men dressed in skeleton costumes and men dressed as devils. The men dressed as devils wore devil masks, horns, and long tails. This pageant was part of a procession. The Englishman who was narrating the thing said it took place in Spain once a year. I tried to explain to the blind man what was happening.

"Skeletons," he said. "I know about skeletons," he said, and he nodded.

The TV showed this one cathedral. Then there was a long, slow look at another one. Finally, the picture switched to the famous one in Paris, with its flying buttresses and its spires reaching up to the clouds. The camera pulled away to show the whole of the cathedral rising above the skyline.

There were times when the Englishman who was telling the thing would shut up, would simply let the camera move around over the cathedrals. Or else the camera would tour the countryside, men in fields walking behind oxen. I waited as long as I could. Then I felt I had to say something. I said, "They're showing the outside of this cathedral now. Gargoyles. Little statues carved to look like monsters. Now I guess they're in Italy. Yeah, they're in Italy. There's paintings on the walls of this one church."

"Are those fresco paintings, bub?" he asked, and he sipped from his drink.

I reached for my glass. But it was empty. I tried to remember what I could remember. "You're asking me are those frescoes?" I said. "That's a good question. I don't know."

The camera moved to a cathedral outside Lisbon. The differences in the Portuguese cathedral compared with the French and Italian were not that great. But they were there. Mostly the interior stuff. Then something occurred to me, and I said, "Something has occurred to me. Do you have any idea what a cathedral is? What they look like, that is? Do you follow me? If somebody says cathedral to you, do you have any notion what they're talking about? Do you know the difference between that and a Baptist church, say?"

He let the smoke dribble from his mouth. "I know they took hundreds of workers fifty or a hundred years to build," he said. "I just heard the man say that, of course. I know generations of the same families worked on a cathedral. I heard him say that, too. The men who began their life's work on them, they never lived to see the completion of their work. In that wise, bub, they're no different from the rest of us, right?" He laughed. Then his eyelids drooped again. His head nodded. He seemed to be snoozing. Maybe he was imagining himself in Portugal. The TV was showing another cathedral now. This one was in Germany. The Englishman's voice droned on. "Cathedrals," the blind man said. He sat up and rolled his head back and forth. "If you want the truth, bub, that's about all I know. What I just said. What I heard him say. But maybe you could describe one to me? I wish you'd do it. I'd like that. If you want to know, I really don't have a good idea."

I stared hard at the shot of the cathedral on the TV. How could I even begin to describe it? But say my life depended on it. Say my life was being threatened by an insane guy who said I had to do it or else.

I stared some more at the cathedral before the picture flipped off into the countryside. There was no use. I turned to the blind man and said, "To begin with, they're very tall." I was looking around the room for clues. "They reach way up. Up and up. Toward the sky. They're so big, some of them, they have to have these supports. To help hold them up, so to speak. These supports are called buttresses. They remind me of viaducts, for some reason. But maybe you don't know viaducts, either? Some-

304

times the cathedrals have devils and such carved into the front. Sometimes lords and ladies. Don't ask me why this is," I said.

He was nodding. The whole upper part of his body seemed to be moving back and forth.

"I'm not doing so good, am I?" I said.

He stopped nodding and leaned forward on the edge of the sofa. As he listened to me, he was running his fingers through his beard. I wasn't getting through to him, I could see that. But he waited for me to go on just the same. He nodded, like he was trying to encourage me. I tried to think what else to say. "They're really big," I said. "They're massive. They're built of stone. Marble, too, sometimes. In those olden days, when they built cathedrals, men wanted to be close to God. In those olden days, God was an important part of everyone's life. You could tell this from their cathedral-building. I'm sorry," I said, "but it looks like that's the best I can do for you. I'm just no good at it."

"That's all right, bub," the blind man said. "Hey, listen. I hope you don't mind my asking you. Can I ask you something? Let me ask you a simple question, yes or no. I'm just curious and there's no offense. You're my host. But let me ask if you are in any way religious? You don't mind my asking?"

I shook my head. He couldn't see that, though. A wink is the same as a nod to a blind man. "I guess I don't believe in it. In anything. Sometimes it's hard. You know what I'm saying?"

"Sure, I do," he said.

"Right," I said.

The Englishman was still holding forth. My wife sighed in her sleep. She drew a long breath and went on with her sleeping.

"You'll have to forgive me," I said. "But I can't tell you what a cathedral looks like. It just isn't in me to do it. I can't do any more than I've done."

The blind man sat very still, his head down, as he listened to me.

I said, "The truth is, cathedrals don't mean anything special to me. Nothing. Cathedrals. They're something to look at on late-night TV. That's all they are."

It was then that the blind man cleared his throat. He brought something up. He took a handkerchief from his back pocket. Then he said, "I get it, bub. It's okay. It happens. Don't worry about it," he said. "Hey, listen to me. Will you do me a favor? I got an idea. Why don't you find us some heavy paper? And a pen. We'll do something. We'll draw one together. Get us a pen and some heavy paper. Go on, bub, get the stuff," he said.

So I went upstairs. My legs felt like they didn't have any strength in them. They felt like they did after I'd done some running. In my wife's room, I looked around. I found some ballpoints in a little basket on her table. And then I tried to think where to look for the kind of paper he was talking about.

Downstairs, in the kitchen, I found a shopping bag with onion skins in the bottom of the bag. I emptied the bag and shook it. I brought it into the living room and sat down with it near his legs. I moved some things, smoothed the wrinkles from the bag, spread it out on the coffee table.

The blind man got down from the sofa and sat next to me on the carpet.

He ran his fingers over the paper. He went up and down the sides of the paper. The edges, even the edges. He fingered the corners.

"All right," he said. "All right, let's do her."

He found my hand, the hand with the pen. He closed his hand over my hand. "Go ahead, bub, draw," he said. "Draw. You'll see. I'll follow along with you. It'll be okay. Just begin now like I'm telling you. You'll see. Draw," the blind man said.

So I began. First I drew a box that looked like a house. It could have been the house I lived in. Then I put a roof on it. At either end of the roof, I drew spires. Crazy.

"Swell," he said. "Terrific. You're doing fine," he said. "Never thought anything like this could happen in your lifetime, did you, bub? Well, it's a strange life, we all know that. Go on now. Keep it up."

I put in windows with arches. I drew flying buttresses. I hung great doors. I couldn't stop. The TV station went off the air. I put down the pen and closed and opened my fingers. The blind man felt around over the paper. He moved the tips of his fingers over the paper, all over what I had drawn, and he nodded.

"Doing fine," the blind man said.

I took up the pen again, and he found my hand. I kept at it. I'm no artist. But I kept drawing just the same.

My wife opened up her eyes and gazed at us. She sat up on the sofa, her robe hanging open. She said, "What are you doing? Tell me, I want to know."

I didn't answer her.

The blind man said, "We're drawing a cathedral. Me and him are working on it. Press hard," he said to me. "That's right. That's good," he said. "Sure. You got it, bub. I can tell. You didn't think you could. But you can, can't you? You're cooking with gas now. You know what I'm saying? We're going to really have us something here in a minute. How's the old arm?" he said. "Put some people in there now. What's a cathedral without people?"

My wife said, "What's going on? Robert, what are you doing? What's going on?"

"It's all right," he said to her. "Close your eyes now," the blind man said to me.

I did it. I closed them just like he said.

"Are they closed?" he said. "Don't fudge."

"They're closed," I said.

"Keep them that way," he said. He said, "Don't stop now. Draw."

So we kept on with it. His fingers rode my fingers as my hand went over the paper. It was like nothing else in my life up to now.

Then he said, "I think that's it. I think you got it," he said. "Take a look. What do you think?"

But I had my eyes closed. I thought I'd keep them that way for a little longer. I thought it was something I ought to do.

"Well?" he said. "Are you looking?"

My eyes were still closed. I was in my house. I knew that. But I didn't feel like I was inside anything.

"It's really something," I said.

A Small, Good Thing

Saturday afternoon she drove to the bakery in the shopping center. After looking through a loose-leaf binder with photographs of cakes taped onto the pages, she ordered chocolate, the child's favorite. The cake she chose was decorated with a spaceship and launching pad under a sprinkling of white stars, and a planet made of red frosting at the other end. His name, SCOTTY, would be in green letters beneath the planet. The baker, who was an older man with a thick neck, listened without saying anything when she told him the child would be eight years old next Monday. The baker wore a white apron that looked like a smock. Straps cut under his arms, went around in back and then to the front again, where they were secured under his heavy waist. He wiped his hands on his apron as he listened to her. He kept his eyes down on the photographs and let her talk. He let her take her time. He'd just come to work and he'd be there all night, baking, and he was in no real hurry.

She gave the baker her name, Ann Weiss, and her telephone number. The cake would be ready on Monday morning, just out of the oven, in plenty of time for the child's party that afternoon. The baker was not jolly. There were no pleasantries between them, just the minimum exchange of words, the necessary information. He made her feel uncomfortable, and she didn't like that. While he was bent over the counter with the pencil in his hand, she studied his coarse features and wondered if he'd ever done anything else with his life besides be a baker. She was a mother and thirty-three years old, and it seemed to her that everyone, especially someone the baker's age – a man old enough to be her father – must have children who'd gone through this special time of cakes and birthday parties. There must be that between them, she thought. But he was abrupt with her – not rude, just abrupt.

She gave up trying to make friends with him. She looked into the back of the bakery and could see a long, heavy wooden table with aluminum pie pans stacked at one end; and beside the table a metal container filled with empty racks. There was an enormous oven. A radio was playing country-western music.

The baker finished printing the information on the special order card and closed up the binder. He looked at her and said, "Monday morning." She thanked him and drove home.

On Monday morning, the birthday boy was walking to school with another boy. They were passing a bag of potato chips back and forth and the birthday boy was trying to find out what his friend intended to give him for his birthday that afternoon. Without looking, the birthday boy stepped off the curb at an intersection and was immediately knocked down by a car. He fell on his side with his head in the gutter and his legs out in the road. His eyes were closed, but his legs moved back and forth as if he were trying to climb over something. His friend dropped the potato chips and started to cry. The car had gone a hundred feet or so and stopped in the middle of the road. The man in the driver's seat looked back over his shoulder. He waited until the boy got unsteadily to his feet. The boy wobbled a little. He looked dazed, but okay. The driver put the car into gear and drove away.

The birthday boy didn't cry, but he didn't have anything to say about anything either. He wouldn't answer when his friend asked him what it felt like to be hit by a car. He walked home, and his friend went on to school. But after the birthday boy was inside his house and was telling his mother about it – she sitting beside him on the sofa, holding his hands in her lap, saying, "Scotty, honey, are you sure you feel all right, baby?" thinking she would call the doctor anyway – he suddenly lay back on the sofa, closed his eyes, and went limp. When she couldn't wake him up, she hurried to the telephone and called her husband at work. Howard told her to remain calm, remain calm, and then he called an ambulance for the child and left for the hospital himself.

Of course, the birthday party was canceled. The child was in the hospital with a mild concussion and suffering from shock. There'd been vomiting, and his lungs had taken in fluid which needed pumping out that afternoon. Now he simply seemed to be in a very deep sleep – but no coma, Dr Francis had emphasized, no coma, when he saw the alarm in the parents' eyes. At eleven o'clock that night, when the boy seemed to be resting comfortably enough after the many X-rays and the lab work, and it was just a matter of his waking up and coming around, Howard left the hospital. He and Ann had been at the hospital with the child since that afternoon, and he was going home for a short while to bathe and change clothes. "I'll be back in an hour," he said. She nodded. "It's fine," she said. "I'll be right here." He kissed her on the forehead, and they touched hands. She sat in the chair beside the bed and looked at the child. She was waiting for him to wake up and be all right. Then she could begin to relax.

Howard drove home from the hospital. He took the wet, dark streets very fast, then caught himself and slowed down. Until now, his life had gone smoothly and to his satisfaction – college, marriage, another year of college for the advanced degree in business, a junior partnership in an investment firm. Fatherhood. He was happy and, so far, lucky – he knew that. His parents were still living, his brothers and his sister were established, his friends from college had gone out to take their places in the world. So far, he had kept away from any real harm, from those forces he knew existed and that could cripple or bring down a man if the luck went bad, if things suddenly turned. He pulled into the driveway and parked. His left leg began to tremble. He sat in the car for a minute and tried to deal with the present situation in a rational manner. Scotty had been hit by a car and was in the hospital, but he was going to be all right. Howard closed his eyes and ran his hand over his face. He got out of the car and went up to the front door. The dog was barking inside the house. The telephone rang and rang while he unlocked the door and fumbled for the light switch. He shouldn't have left the hospital, he shouldn't have. "Goddamn it!" he said. He picked up the receiver and said, "I just walked in the door!"

"There's a cake here that wasn't picked up," the voice on the other end of the line said.

"What are you saying?" Howard asked.

"A cake," the voice said. "A sixteen-dollar cake."

Howard held the receiver against his ear, trying to understand. "I don't know anything about a cake," he said. "Jesus, what are you talking about?"

"Don't hand me that," the voice said.

Howard hung up the telephone. He went into the kitchen and poured himself some whiskey. He called the hospital. But the child's condition remained the same; he was still sleeping and nothing had changed there. While water poured into the tub, Howard lathered his face and shaved. He'd just stretched out in the tub and closed his eyes when the telephone rang again. He hauled himself out, grabbed a towel, and hurried through the house, saying, "Stupid, stupid," for having left the hospital. But when he picked up the receiver and shouted, "Hello!" there was no sound at the other end of the line. Then the caller hung up.

He arrived back at the hospital a little after midnight. Ann still sat in the chair beside the bed. She looked up at Howard, and then she looked back at the child. The child's eyes stayed closed, the head was still wrapped in bandages. His breathing was quiet and regular. From an apparatus over the bed hung a bottle of glucose with a tube running from the bottle to the boy's arm.

"How is he?" Howard said. "What's all this?" waving at the glucose and the tube.

"Dr Francis's orders," she said. "He needs nourishment. He needs to keep up his strength. Why doesn't he wake up, Howard? I don't understand, if he's all right."

Howard put his hand against the back of her head. He ran his fingers through her hair. "He's going to be all right. He'll wake up in a little while. Dr Francis knows what's what."

After a time, he said, "Maybe you should go home and get some rest. I'll stay here. Just don't put up with this creep who keeps calling. Hang up right away."

"Who's calling?" she asked.

311

"I don't know who, just somebody with nothing better to do than call up people. You go on now."

She shook her head. "No," she said, "I'm fine."

"Really," he said. "Go home for a while, and then come back and spell me in the morning. It'll be all right. What did Dr Francis say? He said Scotty's going to be all right. We don't have to worry. He's just sleeping now, that's all."

A nurse pushed the door open. She nodded at them as she went to the bedside. She took the left arm out from under the covers and put her fingers on the wrist, found the pulse, then consulted her watch. In a little while, she put the arm back under the covers and moved to the foot of the bed, where she wrote something on a clipboard attached to the bed.

"How is he?" Ann said. Howard's hand was a weight on her shoulder. She was aware of the pressure from his fingers.

"He's stable," the nurse said. Then she said, "Doctor will be in again shortly. Doctor's back in the hospital. He's making rounds right now."

"I was saying maybe she'd want to go home and get a little rest," Howard said. "After the doctor comes," he said.

"She could do that," the nurse said. "I think you should both feel free to do that, if you wish." The nurse was a big Scandinavian woman with blond hair. There was the trace of an accent in her speech.

"We'll see what the doctor says," Ann said. "I want to talk to the doctor. I don't think he should keep sleeping like this. I don't think that's a good sign." She brought her hand up to her eyes and let her head come forward a little. Howard's grip tightened on her shoulder, and then his hand moved up to her neck, where his fingers began to knead the muscles there.

"Dr Francis will be here in a few minutes," the nurse said. Then she left the room.

Howard gazed at his son for a time, the small chest quietly rising and falling under the covers. For the first time since the terrible minutes after Ann's telephone call to him at his office, he felt a genuine fear starting in his limbs. He began shaking his head. Scotty was fine, but instead of sleeping at home in his own bed, he was in a hospital bed with bandages around his head and a tube in his arm. But this help was what he needed right now.

Dr Francis came in and shook hands with Howard, though they'd just seen each other a few hours before. Ann got up from the chair. "Doctor?"

"Ann," he said and nodded. "Let's just first see how he's doing," the doctor said. He moved to the side of the bed and took the boy's pulse. He peeled back one eyelid and then the other. Howard and Ann stood beside the doctor and watched. Then the doctor turned back the covers and listened to the boy's heart and lungs with his stethoscope. He pressed his fingers here and there on the abdomen. When he was finished, he went to the end of the bed and studied the chart. He noted the time, scribbled something on the chart, and then looked at Howard and Ann.

"Doctor, how is he?" Howard said. "What's the matter with him exactly?"

"Why doesn't he wake up?" Ann said.

The doctor was a handsome, big-shouldered man with a tanned face. He wore a three-piece blue suit, a striped tie, and ivory cuff links. His gray hair was combed along the sides of his head, and he looked as if he had just come from a concert. "He's all right," the doctor said. "Nothing to shout about, he could be better, I think. But he's all right. Still, I wish he'd wake up. He should wake up pretty soon." The doctor looked at the boy again. "We'll know some more in a couple of hours, after the results of a few more tests are in. But he's all right, believe me, except for the hairline fracture of the skull. He does have that."

"Oh, no," Ann said.

"And a bit of a concussion, as I said before. Of course, you know he's in shock," the doctor said. "Sometimes you see this in shock cases. This sleeping."

"But he's out of any real danger?" Howard said. "You said before he's not in a coma. You wouldn't call this a coma, then – would you, doctor?" Howard waited. He looked at the doctor.

"No, I don't want to call it a coma," the doctor said and glanced over at the boy once more. "He's just in a very deep sleep. It's a restorative measure the body is taking on its own. He's out of any real danger, I'd say that for certain, yes. But we'll know more when he wakes up and the other tests are in," the doctor said.

"It's a coma," Ann said. "Of sorts."

"It's not a coma yet, not exactly," the doctor said. "I wouldn't want to call it coma. Not yet, anyway. He's suffered shock. In shock cases, this kind of reaction is common enough; it's a temporary reaction to bodily trauma. Coma. Well, coma is a deep, prolonged unconsciousness, something that could go on for days, or weeks even. Scotty's not in that area, not as far as we can tell. I'm certain his condition will show improvement by morning. I'm betting that it will. We'll know more when he wakes up, which shouldn't be long now. Of course, you may do as you like, stay here or go home for a time. But by all means feel free to leave the hospital for a while if you want. This is not easy, I know." The doctor gazed at the boy again, watching him, and then he turned to Ann and said, "You try not to worry, little mother. Believe me, we're doing all that can be done. It's just a question of a little more time now." He nodded at her, shook hands with Howard again, and then he left the room.

Ann put her hand over the child's forehead. "At least he doesn't have a fever," she said. Then she said, "My God, he feels so cold, though. Howard? Is he supposed to feel like this? Feel his head."

Howard touched the child's temples. His own breathing had slowed. "I think he's supposed to feel this way right now," he said. "He's in shock, remember? That's what the doctor said. The doctor was just in here. He would have said something if Scotty wasn't okay."

Ann stood there a while longer, working her lip with her teeth. Then she moved over to her chair and sat down.

Howard sat in the chair next to her chair. They looked at each other. He wanted to say something else and reassure her, but he was afraid, too. He took her hand and put it in his lap, and this made him feel better, her hand being there. He picked up her hand and squeezed it. Then he just held her hand. They sat like that for a while, watching the boy and not talking. From time to time, he squeezed her hand. Finally, she took her hand away.

"I've been praying," she said.

He nodded.

She said, "I almost thought I'd forgotten how, but it came back to me. All I had to do was close my eyes and say, 'Please God, help us – help Scotty,' and then the rest was easy. The words were right there. Maybe if you prayed, too," she said to him.

"I've already prayed," he said. "I prayed this afternoon – yesterday afternoon, I mean – after you called, while I was driving to the hospital. I've been praying," he said.

"That's good," she said. For the first time, she felt they were together in it, this trouble. She realized with a start that, until now, it had only been happening to her and to Scotty. She hadn't let Howard into it, though he was there and needed all along. She felt glad to be his wife.

The same nurse came in and took the boy's pulse again and checked the flow from the bottle hanging above the bed.

In an hour, another doctor came in. He said his name was Parsons, from Radiology. He had a bushy moustache. He was wearing loafers, a western shirt, and a pair of jeans.

"We're going to take him downstairs for more pictures," he told them. "We need to do some more pictures, and we want to do a scan."

"What's that?" Ann said. "A scan?" She stood between this new doctor and the bed. "I thought you'd already taken all your X-rays."

"I'm afraid we need some more," he said. "Nothing to be alarmed about. We just need some more pictures, and we want to do a brain scan on him."

"My God," Ann said.

"It's perfectly normal procedure in cases like this," this new doctor said. "We just need to find out for sure why he isn't back awake yet. It's normal medical procedure, and nothing to be alarmed about. We'll be taking him down in a few minutes," this doctor said.

In a little while, two orderlies came into the room with a gurney. They were black-haired, dark-complexioned men in white uniforms, and they said a few words to each other in a foreign tongue as they unhooked the boy from the tube and moved him from his bed to the gurney. Then they wheeled him from the room. Howard and Ann got on the same elevator. Ann gazed at the child. She closed her eyes as the elevator began its descent. The orderlies stood at either end of the gurney without saying anything, though once one of the men made a comment to the other in their own language, and the other man nodded slowly in response.

Later that morning, just as the sun was beginning to lighten the windows in the waiting room outside the X-ray department, they brought the boy out and moved him back up to his room. Howard and Ann rode up on the elevator with him once more, and once more they took up their places beside the bed.

They waited all day, but still the boy did not wake up. Occasionally, one of them would leave the room to go downstairs to the cafeteria to drink coffee and then, as if suddenly remembering and feeling guilty, get up from the table and hurry back to the room. Dr Francis came again that afternoon and examined the boy once more and then left after telling them he was coming along and could wake up at any minute now. Nurses, different nurses from the night before, came in from time to time. Then a young woman from the lab knocked and entered the room. She wore white slacks and a white blouse and carried a little tray of things which she put on the stand beside the bed. Without a word to them, she took blood from the boy's arm. Howard closed his eyes as the woman found the right place on the boy's arm and pushed the needle in.

"I don't understand this," Ann said to the woman.

"Doctor's orders," the young woman said. "I do what I'm told. They say draw that one, I draw. What's wrong with him, anyway?" she said. "He's a sweetie."

"He was hit by a car," Howard said. "A hit-and-run."

The young woman shook her head and looked again at the boy. Then she took her tray and left the room.

"Why won't he wake up?" Ann said. "Howard? I want some answers from these people."

Howard didn't say anything. He sat down again in the chair and crossed one leg over the other. He rubbed his face. He looked at his son and then he settled back in the chair, closed his eyes, and went to sleep.

Ann walked to the window and looked out at the parking lot. It was night, and cars were driving into and out of the parking lot with their lights on. She stood at the window with her hands gripping the sill, and knew in her heart that they were into something now, something hard. She was afraid, and her teeth began to chatter until she tightened her jaws. She saw a big car stop in front of the hospital and someone, a woman in a long coat, get into the car. She wished she were that woman and somebody, anybody, was driving her away from here to somewhere else, a place where she would find Scotty waiting for her when she stepped out of the car, ready to say *Mom* and let her gather him in her arms.

In a little while, Howard woke up. He looked at the boy again. Then he got up from the chair, stretched, and went over to stand beside her at the window. They both stared out at the parking lot. They didn't say anything. But they seemed to feel each other's insides now, as though the worry had made them transparent in a perfectly natural way.

The door opened and Dr Francis came in. He was wearing a different suit and tie this time. His gray hair was combed along the sides of his head, and he looked as if he had just shaved. He went straight to the bed and examined the boy. "He ought to have come around by now. There's just no good reason for this," he said. "But I can tell you we're all convinced he's out of any danger. We'll just feel better when he wakes up. There's no reason, absolutely none, why he shouldn't come around. Very soon. Oh, he'll have himself a dilly of a headache when he does, you can count on that. But all of his signs are fine. They're as normal as can be."

"It is a coma, then?" Ann said.

The doctor rubbed his smooth cheek. "We'll call it that for the time being, until he wakes up. But you must be worn out. This is hard. I know this is hard. Feel free to go out for a bite," he said. "It would do you good. I'll put a nurse in here while you're gone if you'll feel better about going. Go and have yourselves something to eat."

"I couldn't eat anything," Ann said.

"Do what you need to do, of course," the doctor said. "Anyway, I wanted to tell you that all the signs are good, the tests are negative, nothing showed up at all, and just as soon as he wakes up he'll be over the hill."

"Thank you, doctor," Howard said. He shook hands with the doctor again. The doctor patted Howard's shoulder and went out.

"I suppose one of us should go home and check on things," Howard said. "Slug needs to be fed, for one thing."

"Call one of the neighbors," Ann said. "Call the Morgans. Anyone will feed a dog if you ask them to."

"All right," Howard said. After a while, he said, "Honey, why don't *you* do it? Why don't you go home and check on things, and then come back? It'll do you good. I'll be right here with him. Seriously," he said. "We need to keep up our strength on this. We'll want to be here for a while even after he wakes up."

"Why don't *you* go?" she said. "Feed Slug. Feed yourself."

"I already went," he said. "I was gone for exactly an hour and fifteen minutes. You go home for an hour and freshen up. Then come back."

She tried to think about it, but she was too tired. She closed her eyes and tried to think about it again. After a time, she said, "Maybe I *will* go home for a few minutes. Maybe if I'm not just sitting right here watching him every second, he'll wake up and be all right. You know? Maybe he'll wake up if I'm not here. I'll go home and take a bath and put on clean clothes. I'll feed Slug. Then I'll come back."

"I'll be right here," he said. "You go on home, honey. I'll

keep an eye on things here." His eyes were bloodshot and small, as if he'd been drinking for a long time. His clothes were rumpled. His beard had come out again. She touched his face, and then she took her hand back. She understood he wanted to be by himself for a while, not have to talk or share his worry for a time. She picked her purse up from the nightstand, and he helped her into her coat.

"I won't be gone long," she said.

"Just sit and rest for a little while when you get home," he said. "Eat something. Take a bath. After you get out of the bath, just sit for a while and rest. It'll do you a world of good, you'll see. Then come back," he said. "Let's try not to worry. You heard what Dr Francis said."

She stood in her coat for a minute trying to recall the doctor's exact words, looking for any nuances, any hint of something behind his words other than what he had said. She tried to remember if his expression had changed any when he bent over to examine the child. She remembered the way his features had composed themselves as he rolled back the child's eyelids and then listened to his breathing.

She went to the door, where she turned and looked back. She looked at the child, and then she looked at the father. Howard nodded. She stepped out of the room and pulled the door closed behind her.

She went past the nurses' station and down to the end of the corridor, looking for the elevator. At the end of the corridor, she turned to her right and entered a little waiting room where a Negro family sat in wicker chairs. There was a middle-aged man in a khaki shirt and pants, a baseball cap pushed back on his head. A large woman wearing a housedress and slippers was slumped in one of the chairs. A teenaged girl in jeans, hair done in dozens of little braids, lay stretched out in one of the chairs smoking a cigarette, her legs crossed at the ankles. The family swung their eyes to Ann as she entered the room. The little table was littered with hamburger wrappers and Styrofoam cups.

"Franklin," the large woman said as she roused herself. "Is it about Franklin?" Her eyes widened. "Tell me now, lady," the woman said. "Is it about Franklin?" She was trying to rise from her chair, but the man had closed his hand over her arm.

"Here, here," he said. "Evelyn."

"I'm sorry," Ann said. "I'm looking for the elevator. My son is in the hospital, and now I can't find the elevator."

"Elevator is down that way, turn left," the man said as he aimed a finger.

The girl drew on her cigarette and stared at Ann. Her eyes were narrowed to slits, and her broad lips parted slowly as she let the smoke escape. The Negro woman let her head fall on her shoulder and looked away from Ann, no longer interested.

"My son was hit by a car," Ann said to the man. She seemed to need to explain herself. "He has a concussion and a little skull fracture, but he's going to be all right. He's in shock now, but it might be some kind of coma, too. That's what really worries us, the coma part. I'm going out for a little while, but my husband is with him. Maybe he'll wake up while I'm gone."

"That's too bad," the man said and shifted in the chair. He shook his head. He looked down at the table, and then he looked back at Ann. She was still standing there. He said, "Our Franklin, he's on the operating table. Somebody cut him. Tried to kill him. There was a fight where he was at. At this party. They say he was just standing and watching. Not bothering nobody. But that don't mean nothing these days. Now he's on the operating table. We're just hoping and praying, that's all we can do now." He gazed at her steadily.

Ann looked at the girl again, who was still watching her, and at the older woman, who kept her head down, but whose eyes were now closed. Ann saw the lips moving silently, making words. She had an urge to ask what those words were. She wanted to talk more with these people who were in the same kind of waiting she was in. She was afraid, and they were afraid. They had that in common. She would have liked to have said something else about the accident, told them more about Scotty, that it had happened on the day of his birthday, Monday, and that he was still unconscious. Yet she didn't know how to begin. She stood looking at them without saying anything more.

She went down the corridor the man had indicated and found the elevator. She waited a minute in front of the closed doors, still wondering if she was doing the right thing. Then she put out her finger and touched the button.

She pulled into the driveway and cut the engine. She closed her eyes and leaned her head against the wheel for a minute. She listened to the ticking sounds the engine made as it began to cool. Then she got out of the car. She could hear the dog barking inside the house. She went to the front door, which was unlocked. She went inside and turned on lights and put on a kettle of water for tea. She opened some dog food and fed Slug on the back porch. The dog ate in hungry little smacks. It kept running into the kitchen to see that she was going to stay. As she sat down on the sofa with her tea, the telephone rang.

"Yes!" she said as she answered. "Hello!"

"Mrs Weiss," a man's voice said. It was five o'clock in the morning, and she thought she could hear machinery or equipment of some kind in the background.

"Yes, yes! What is it?" she said. "This is Mrs Weiss. This is she. What is it, please?" She listened to whatever it was in the background. "Is it Scotty, for Christ's sake?"

"Scotty," the man's voice said. "It's about Scotty, yes. It has to do with Scotty, that problem. Have you forgotten about Scotty?" the man said. Then he hung up.

She dialed the hospital's number and asked for the third floor. She demanded information about her son from the nurse who answered the telephone. Then she asked to speak to her husband. It was, she said, an emergency.

She waited, turning the telephone cord in her fingers. She closed her eyes and felt sick at her stomach. She would have to make herself eat. Slug came in from the back porch and lay down near her feet. He wagged his tail. She pulled at his ear while he licked her fingers. Howard was on the line.

"Somebody just called here," she said. She twisted the telephone cord. "He said it was about Scotty," she cried.

"Scotty's fine," Howard told her. "I mean, he's still sleeping.

There's been no change. The nurse has been in twice since you've been gone. A nurse or else a doctor. He's all right."

"This man called. He said it was about Scotty," she told him.

"Honey, you rest for a little while, you need the rest. It must be that same caller I had. Just forget it. Come back down here after you've rested. Then we'll have breakfast or something."

"Breakfast," she said. "I don't want any breakfast."

"You know what I mean," he said. "Juice, something. I don't know. I don't know anything, Ann. Jesus, I'm not hungry, either. Ann, it's hard to talk now. I'm standing here at the desk. Dr Francis is coming again at eight o'clock this morning. He's going to have something to tell us then, something more definite. That's what one of the nurses said. She didn't know any more than that. Ann? Honey, maybe we'll know something more then. At eight o'clock. Come back here before eight. Meanwhile, I'm right here and Scotty's all right. He's still the same," he added.

"I was drinking a cup of tea," she said, "when the telephone rang. They said it was about Scotty. There was a noise in the background. Was there a noise in the background on that call you had, Howard?"

"I don't remember," he said. "Maybe the driver of the car, maybe he's a psychopath and found out about Scotty somehow. But I'm here with him. Just rest like you were going to do. Take a bath and come back by seven or so, and we'll talk to the doctor together when he gets here. It's going to be all right, honey. I'm here, and there are doctors and nurses around. They say his condition is stable."

"I'm scared to death," she said.

She ran water, undressed, and got into the tub. She washed and dried quickly, not taking the time to wash her hair. She put on clean underwear, wool slacks, and a sweater. She went into the living room, where the dog looked up at her and let its tail thump once against the floor. It was just starting to get light outside when she went out to the car.

She drove into the parking lot of the hospital and found a space close to the front door. She felt she was in some obscure way responsible for what had happened to the child. She let her thoughts move to the Negro family. She remembered the name Franklin and the table that was covered with hamburger papers, and the teenaged girl staring at her as she drew on her cigarette. "Don't have children," she told the girl's image as she entered the front door of the hospital. "For God's sake, don't."

She took the elevator up to the third floor with two nurses who were just going on duty. It was Wednesday morning, a few minutes before seven. There was a page for a Dr Madison as the elevator doors slid open on the third floor. She got off behind the nurses, who turned in the other direction and continued the conversation she had interrupted when she'd gotten into the elevator. She walked down the corridor to the little alcove where the Negro family had been waiting. They were gone now, but the chairs were scattered in such a way that it looked as if people had just jumped up from them the minute before. The tabletop was cluttered with the same cups and papers, the ashtray was filled with cigarette butts.

She stopped at the nurses' station. A nurse was standing behind the counter, brushing her hair and yawning.

"There was a Negro boy in surgery last night," Ann said. "Franklin was his name. His family was in the waiting room. I'd like to inquire about his condition."

A nurse who was sitting at a desk behind the counter looked up from a chart in front of her. The telephone buzzed and she picked up the receiver, but she kept her eyes on Ann.

"He passed away," said the nurse at the counter. The nurse held the hairbrush and kept looking at her. "Are you a friend of the family or what?"

"I met the family last night," Ann said. "My own son is in the hospital. I guess he's in shock. We don't know for sure what's wrong. I just wondered about Franklin, that's all. Thank you." She moved down the corridor. Elevator doors the same color as the walls slid open and a gaunt, bald man in white pants and white canvas shoes pulled a heavy cart off the elevator. She hadn't noticed these doors last night. The man wheeled the cart out into the corridor and stopped in front of the room nearest the elevator

and consulted a clipboard. Then he reached down and slid a tray
out of the cart. He rapped lightly on the door and entered the
room. She could smell the unpleasant odors of warm food as she
passed the cart. She hurried on without looking at any of the
nurses and pushed open the door to the child's room.

Howard was standing at the window with his hands behind
his back. He turned around as she came in.

"How is he?" she said. She went over to the bed. She dropped
her purse on the floor beside the nightstand. It seemed to her
she had been gone a long time. She touched the child's face.
"Howard?"

"Dr Francis was here a little while ago," Howard said. She
looked at him closely and thought his shoulders were bunched a
little.

"I thought he wasn't coming until eight o'clock this morning,"
she said quickly.

"There was another doctor with him. A neurologist."

"A neurologist," she said.

Howard nodded. His shoulders were bunching, she could see
that. "What'd they say, Howard? For Christ's sake, what'd they
say? What is it?"

"They said they're going to take him down and run more tests
on him, Ann. They think they're going to operate, honey.
Honey, they *are* going to operate. They can't figure out why he
won't wake up. It's more than just shock or concussion, they
know that much now. It's in his skull, the fracture, it has something, something to do with that, they think. So they're going
to operate. I tried to call you, but I guess you'd already left the
house."

"Oh, God," she said. "Oh, please, Howard, please," she said,
taking his arms.

"Look!" Howard said. "Scotty! Look, Ann!" He turned her
toward the bed.

The boy had opened his eyes, then closed them. He opened
them again now. The eyes stared straight ahead for a minute,
then moved slowly in his head until they rested on Howard and
Ann, then traveled away again.

324

"Scotty," his mother said, moving to the bed.

"Hey, Scott," his father said. "Hey, son."

They leaned over the bed. Howard took the child's hand in his hands and began to pat and squeeze the hand. Ann bent over the boy and kissed his forehead again and again. She put her hands on either side of his face. "Scotty, honey, it's Mommy and Daddy," she said. "Scotty?"

The boy looked at them, but without any sign of recognition. Then his mouth opened, his eyes scrunched closed, and he howled until he had no more air in his lungs. His face seemed to relax and soften then. His lips parted as his last breath was puffed through his throat and exhaled gently through the clenched teeth.

The doctors called it a hidden occlusion and said it was a one-in-a-million circumstance. Maybe if it could have been detected somehow and surgery undertaken immediately, they could have saved him. But more than likely not. In any case, what would they have been looking for? Nothing had shown up in the tests or in the X-rays.

Dr Francis was shaken. "I can't tell you how badly I feel. I'm so very sorry, I can't tell you," he said as he led them into the doctors' lounge. There was a doctor sitting in a chair with his legs hooked over the back of another chair, watching an early-morning TV show. He was wearing a green delivery-room out-fit, loose green pants and green blouse, and a green cap that covered his hair. He looked at Howard and Ann and then looked at Dr Francis. He got to his feet and turned off the set and went out of the room. Dr Francis guided Ann to the sofa, sat down beside her, and began to talk in a low, consoling voice. At one point, he leaned over and embraced her. She could feel his chest rising and falling evenly against her shoulder. She kept her eyes open and let him hold her. Howard went into the bathroom, but he left the door open. After a violent fit of weeping, he ran water and washed his face. Then he came out and sat down at the little table that held a telephone. He looked at the telephone as though deciding what to do first. He made some calls. After a time, Dr Francis used the telephone.

"Is there anything else I can do for the moment?" he asked them.

Howard shook his head. Ann stared at Dr Francis as if unable to comprehend his words.

The doctor walked them to the hospital's front door. People were entering and leaving the hospital. It was eleven o'clock in the morning. Ann was aware of how slowly, almost reluctantly, she moved her feet. It seemed to her that Dr Francis was making them leave when she felt they should stay, when it would be more the right thing to do to stay. She gazed out into the parking lot and then turned around and looked back at the front of the hospital. She began shaking her head. "No, no," she said. "I can't leave him here, no." She heard herself say that and thought how unfair it was that the only words that came out were the sort of words used on TV shows where people were stunned by violent or sudden deaths. She wanted her words to be her own. "No," she said, and for some reason the memory of the Negro woman's head lolling on the woman's shoulder came to her. "No," she said again.

"I'll be talking to you later in the day," the doctor was saying to Howard. "There are still some things that have to be done, things that have to be cleared up to our satisfaction. Some things that need explaining."

"An autopsy," Howard said.

Dr Francis nodded.

"I understand," Howard said. Then he said, "Oh, Jesus. No, I don't understand, doctor. I can't, I can't. I just can't."

Dr Francis put his arm around Howard's shoulders. "I'm sorry. God, how I'm sorry." He let go of Howard's shoulders and held out his hand. Howard looked at the hand, and then he took it. Dr Francis put his arms around Ann once more. He seemed full of some goodness she didn't understand. She let her head rest on his shoulder, but her eyes stayed open. She kept looking at the hospital. As they drove out of the parking lot, she looked back at the hospital.

*

326

At home, she sat on the sofa with her hands in her coat pockets. Howard closed the door to the child's room. He got the coffee-maker going and then he found an empty box. He had thought to pick up some of the child's things that were scattered around the living room. But instead he sat down beside her on the sofa, pushed the box to one side, and leaned forward, arms between his knees. He began to weep. She pulled his head over into her lap and patted his shoulder. "He's gone," she said. She kept patting his shoulder. Over his sobs, she could hear the coffee-maker hissing in the kitchen. "There, there," she said tenderly. "Howard, he's gone. He's gone and now we'll have to get used to that. To being alone."

In a little while, Howard got up and began moving aimlessly around the room with the box, not putting anything into it, but collecting some things together on the floor at one end of the sofa. She continued to sit with her hands in her coat pockets. Howard put the box down and brought coffee into the living room. Later, Ann made calls to relatives. After each call had been placed and the party had answered, Ann would blurt out a few words and cry for a minute. Then she would quietly explain, in a measured voice, what had happened and tell them about arrangements. Howard took the box out to the garage, where he saw the child's bicycle. He dropped the box and sat down on the pavement beside the bicycle. He took hold of the bicycle awkwardly so that it leaned against his chest. He held it, the rubber pedal sticking into his chest. He gave the wheel a turn.

Ann hung up the telephone after talking to her sister. She was looking up another number when the telephone rang. She picked it up on the first ring.

"Hello," she said, and she heard something in the background, a humming noise. "Hello!" she said. "For God's sake," she said. "Who is this? What is it you want?"

"Your Scotty, I got him ready for you," the man's voice said. "Did you forget him?"

"You evil bastard!" she shouted into the receiver. "How can you do this, you evil son of a bitch?"

"Scotty," the man said. "Have you forgotten about Scotty?" Then the man hung up on her.

Howard heard the shouting and came in to find her with her head on her arms over the table, weeping. He picked up the receiver and listened to the dial tone.

Much later, just before midnight, after they had dealt with many things, the telephone rang again.

"You answer it," she said. "Howard, it's him, I know." They were sitting at the kitchen table with coffee in front of them. Howard had a small glass of whiskey beside his cup. He answered on the third ring.

"Hello," he said. "Who is this? Hello! Hello!" The line went dead. "He hung up," Howard said. "Whoever it was."

"It was him," she said. "That bastard. I'd like to kill him," she said. "I'd like to shoot him and watch him kick," she said.

"Ann, my God," he said.

"Could you hear anything?" she said. "In the background? A noise, machinery, something humming?"

"Nothing, really. Nothing like that," he said. "There wasn't much time. I think there was some radio music. Yes, there was a radio going, that's all I could tell. I don't know what in God's name is going on," he said.

She shook her head. "If I could, could get my hands on him." It came to her then. She knew who it was. Scotty, the cake, the telephone number. She pushed the chair away from the table and got up. "Drive me down to the shopping center," she said. "Howard."

"What are you saying?"

"The shopping center. I know who it is who's calling. I know who it is. It's the baker, the son-of-a-bitching baker, Howard. I had him bake a cake for Scotty's birthday. That's who's calling. That's who has the number and keeps calling us. To harass us about that cake. The baker, that bastard."

They drove down to the shopping center. The sky was clear and stars were out. It was cold, and they ran the heater in the car.

They parked in front of the bakery. All of the shops and stores were closed, but there were cars at the far end of the lot in front of the movie theater. The bakery windows were dark, but when they looked through the glass they could see a light in the back room and, now and then, a big man in an apron moving in and out of the white, even light. Through the glass, she could see the display cases and some little tables with chairs. She tried the door. She rapped on the glass. But if the baker heard them, he gave no sign. He didn't look in their direction.

They drove around behind the bakery and parked. They got out of the car. There was a lighted window too high up for them to see inside. A sign near the back door said THE PANTRY BAKERY, SPECIAL ORDERS. She could hear faintly a radio playing inside and something creak – an oven door as it was pulled down? She knocked on the door and waited. Then she knocked again, louder. The radio was turned down and there was a scraping sound now, the distinct sound of something, a drawer, being pulled open and then closed.

Someone unlocked the door and opened it. The baker stood in the light and peered out at them. "I'm closed for business," he said. "What do you want at this hour? It's midnight. Are you drunk or something?"

She stepped into the light that fell through the open door. He blinked his heavy eyelids as he recognized her. "It's you," he said.

"It's me," she said. "Scotty's mother. This is Scotty's father. We'd like to come in."

The baker said, "I'm busy now. I have work to do."

She had stepped inside the doorway anyway. Howard came in behind her. The baker moved back. "It smells like a bakery in here. Doesn't it smell like a bakery in here, Howard?"

"What do you want?" the baker said. "Maybe you want your cake? That's it, you decided you want your cake. You ordered a cake, didn't you?"

"You're pretty smart for a baker," she said. "Howard, this is the man who's been calling us." She clenched her fists. She stared at him fiercely. There was a deep burning inside her, an anger that made her feel larger than herself, larger than either of these men.

"Just a minute here," the baker said. "You want to pick up your three-day-old cake? That it? I don't want to argue with you, lady. There it sits over there, getting stale. I'll give it to you for half of what I quoted you. No. You want it? You can have it. It's no good to me, no good to anyone now. It cost me time and money to make that cake. If you want it, okay, if you don't, that's okay, too. I have to get back to work." He looked at them and rolled his tongue behind his teeth.

"More cakes," she said. She knew she was in control of it, of what was increasing in her. She was calm.

"Lady, I work sixteen hours a day in this place to earn a living," the baker said. He wiped his hands on his apron. "I work night and day in here, trying to make ends meet." A look crossed Ann's face that made the baker move back and say, "No trouble, now." He reached to the counter and picked up a rolling pin with his right hand and began to tap it against the palm of his other hand. "You want the cake or not? I have to get back to work. Bakers work at night," he said again. His eyes were small, mean-looking, she thought, nearly lost in the bristly flesh around his cheeks. His neck was thick with fat.

"I know bakers work at night," Ann said. "They make phone calls at night, too. You bastard," she said.

The baker continued to tap the rolling pin against his hand. He glanced at Howard. "Careful, careful," he said to Howard.

"My son's dead," she said with a cold, even finality. "He was hit by a car Monday morning. We've been waiting with him until he died. But, of course, you couldn't be expected to know that, could you? Bakers can't know everything – can they, Mr Baker? But he's dead. He's dead, you bastard!" Just as suddenly as it had welled in her, the anger dwindled, gave way to something else, a dizzy feeling of nausea. She leaned against the wooden table that was sprinkled with flour, put her hands over her face, and began to cry, her shoulders rocking back and forth. "It isn't fair," she said. "It isn't, isn't fair."

Howard put his hand at the small of her back and looked at

the baker. "Shame on you," Howard said to him. "Shame."

The baker put the rolling pin back on the counter. He undid his apron and threw it on the counter. He looked at them, and then he shook his head slowly. He pulled a chair out from under the card table that held papers and receipts, an adding machine, and a telephone directory. "Please sit down," he said. "Let me get you a chair," he said to Howard. "Sit down now, please." The baker went into the front of the shop and returned with two little wrought-iron chairs. "Please sit down, you people."

Ann wiped her eyes and looked at the baker. "I wanted to kill you," she said. "I wanted you dead."

The baker had cleared a space for them at the table. He shoved the adding machine to one side, along with the stacks of notepaper and receipts. He pushed the telephone directory onto the floor, where it landed with a thud. Howard and Ann sat down and pulled their chairs up to the table. The baker sat down, too.

"Let me say how sorry I am," the baker said, putting his elbows on the table. "God alone knows how sorry. Listen to me. I'm just a baker. I don't claim to be anything else. Maybe once, maybe years ago, I was a different kind of human being. I've forgotten, I don't know for sure. But I'm not any longer, if I ever was. Now I'm just a baker. That don't excuse my doing what I did, I know. But I'm deeply sorry. I'm sorry for your son, and sorry for my part in this," the baker said. He spread his hands out on the table and turned them over to reveal his palms. "I don't have any children myself, so I can only imagine what you must be feeling. All I can say to you now is that I'm sorry. Forgive me, if you can," the baker said. "I'm not an evil man, I don't think. Not evil, like you said on the phone. You got to understand what it comes down to is I don't know how to act anymore, it would seem. Please," the man said, "let me ask you if you can find it in your hearts to forgive me?"

It was warm inside the bakery. Howard stood up from the table and took off his coat. He helped Ann from her coat. The baker looked at them for a minute and then nodded and got up from the table. He went to the oven and turned off some switches. He found cups and poured coffee from an electric coffee-maker.

He put a carton of cream on the table, and a bowl of sugar.

"You probably need to eat something," the baker said. "I hope you'll eat some of my hot rolls. You have to eat and keep going. Eating is a small, good thing in a time like this," he said.

He served them warm cinnamon rolls just out of the oven, the icing still runny. He put butter on the table and knives to spread the butter. Then the baker sat down at the table with them. He waited. He waited until they each took a roll from the platter and began to eat. "It's good to eat something," he said, watching them. "There's more. Eat up. Eat all you want. There's all the rolls in the world in here."

They ate rolls and drank coffee. Ann was suddenly hungry, and the rolls were warm and sweet. She ate three of them, which pleased the baker. Then he began to talk. They listened carefully. Although they were tired and in anguish, they listened to what the baker had to say. They nodded when the baker began to speak of loneliness, and of the sense of doubt and limitation that had come to him in his middle years. He told them what it was like to be childless all these years. To repeat the days with the ovens endlessly full and endlessly empty. The party food, the celebrations he'd worked over. Icing knuckle-deep. The tiny wedding couples stuck into cakes. Hundreds of them, no, thousands by now. Birthdays. Just imagine all those candles burning. He had a necessary trade. He was a baker. He was glad he wasn't a florist. It was better to be feeding people. This was a better smell anytime than flowers.

"Smell this," the baker said, breaking open a dark loaf. "It's a heavy bread, but rich." They smelled it, then he had them taste it. It had the taste of molasses and coarse grains. They listened to him. They ate what they could. They swallowed the dark bread. It was like daylight under the fluorescent trays of light. They talked on into the early morning, the high, pale cast of light in the windows, and they did not think of leaving.

Boxes

My mother is packed and ready to move. But Sunday afternoon, at the last minute, she calls and says for us to come eat with her. "My icebox is defrosting," she tells me. "I have to fry up this chicken before it rots." She says we should bring our own plates and some knives and forks. She's packed most of her dishes and kitchen things. "Come on and eat with me one last time," she says. "You and Jill."

I hang up the phone and stand at the window for a minute longer, wishing I could figure this thing out. But I can't. So finally I turn to Jill and say, "Let's go to my mother's for a good-bye meal."

Jill is at the table with a Sears catalogue in front of her, trying to find us some curtains. But she's been listening. She makes a face. "Do we have to?" she says. She bends down the corner of a page and closes the catalogue. She sighs. "God, we been over there to eat two or three times in this last month alone. Is she ever actually going to leave?"

Jill always says what's on her mind. She's thirty-five years old, wears her hair short, and grooms dogs for a living. Before she became a groomer, something she likes, she used to be a house-wife and mother. Then all hell broke loose. Her two children were kidnapped by her first husband and taken to live in Aus-tralia. Her second husband, who drank, left her with a broken eardrum before he drove their car through a bridge into the Elwha River. He didn't have life insurance, not to mention property-damage insurance. Jill had to borrow money to bury him, and then – can you beat it? – she was presented with a bill for the bridge repair. Plus, she had her own medical bills. She can tell this story now. She's bounced back. But she has run out of patience with my mother. I've run out of patience, too. But I don't see my options.

"She's leaving day after tomorrow," I say. "Hey, Jill, don't do any favors. Do you want to come with me or not?" I tell her it doesn't matter to me one way or the other. I'll say she has a migraine. It's not like I've never told a lie before.

"I'm coming," she says. And like that she gets up and goes into the bathroom, where she likes to pout.

We've been together since last August, about the time my mother picked to move up here to Longview from California. Jill tried to make the best of it. But my mother pulling into town just when we were trying to get our act together was nothing either of us had bargained for. Jill said it reminded her of the situation with her first husband's mother. "She was a clinger," Jill said. "You know what I mean? I thought I was going to suffocate."

It's fair to say that my mother sees Jill as an intruder. As far as she's concerned, Jill is just another girl in a series of girls who have appeared in my life since my wife left me. Someone, to her mind, likely to take away affection, attention, maybe even some money that might otherwise come to her. But someone deserving of respect? No way. I remember – how can I forget it? – she called my wife a whore before we were married, and then called her a whore fifteen years later, after she left me for someone else.

Jill and my mother act friendly enough when they find themselves together. They hug each other when they say hello or good-bye. They talk about shopping specials. But Jill dreads the time she has to spend in my mother's company. She claims my mother bums her out. She says my mother is negative about everything and everybody and ought to find an outlet, like other people in her age bracket. Crocheting, maybe, or card games at the Senior Citizens Center, or else going to church. Something, anyway, so that she'll leave us in peace. But my mother had her own way of solving things. She announced she was moving back to California. The hell with everything and everybody in this town. What a place to live! She wouldn't continue to live in this town if they gave her the place and six more like it.

334

Within a day or two of deciding to move, she'd packed her
things into boxes. That was last January. Or maybe it was February. Anyway, last winter sometime. Now it's the end of June.
Boxes have been sitting around inside her house for months. You
have to walk around them or step over them to get from one
room to another. This is no way for anyone's mother to live.

After a while, ten minutes or so, Jill comes out of the bathroom. I've found a roach and am trying to smoke that and drink
a bottle of ginger ale while I watch one of the neighbors change
the oil in his car. Jill doesn't look at me. Instead, she goes into
the kitchen and puts some plates and utensils into a paper sack.
But when she comes back through the living room I stand up,
and we hug each other. Jill says, "It's okay." What's okay, I
wonder. As far as I can see, nothing's okay. But she holds me
and keeps patting my shoulder. I can smell the pet shampoo on
her. She comes home from work wearing the stuff. It's everywhere. Even when we're in bed together. She gives me a final
pat. Then we go out to the car and drive across town to my
mother's.

I like where I live. I didn't when I first moved here. There was
nothing to do at night, and I was lonely. Then I met Jill. Pretty
soon, after a few weeks, she brought her things over and started
living with me. We didn't set any long-term goals. We were
happy and we had a life together. We told each other we'd finally
got lucky. But my mother didn't have anything going in her life.
So she wrote me and said she'd decided on moving here. I wrote
her back and said I didn't think it was such a good idea. The
weather's terrible in the winter, I said. They're building a prison a
few miles from town, I told her. The place is bumper-to-bumper
tourists all summer, I said. But she acted as if she never got my
letters, and came anyway. Then, after she'd been in town a little
less than a month, she told me she hated the place. She acted as
if it were my fault she'd moved here and my fault she found
everything so disagreeable. She started calling me up and telling
me how crummy the place was. "Laying guilt trips," Jill called
it. She told me the bus service was terrible and the drivers

unfriendly. As for the people at the Senior Citizens – well, she didn't want to play casino. "They can go to hell," she said, "and take their card games with them." The clerks at the supermarket were surly, the guys in the service station didn't give a damn about her or her car. And she'd made up her mind about the man she rented from, Larry Hadlock. King Larry, she called him. "He thinks he's *superior* to everyone because he has some shacks for rent and a few dollars. I wish to God I'd never laid eyes on him."

It was too hot for her when she arrived, in August, and in September it started to rain. It rained almost every day for weeks. In October it turned cold. There was snow in November and December. But long before that she began to put the bad mouth on the place and the people to the extent that I didn't want to hear about it anymore, and I told her so finally. She cried, and I hugged her and thought that was the end of it. But a few days later she started in again, same stuff. Just before Christmas she called to see when I was coming by with her presents. She hadn't put up a tree and didn't intend to, she said. Then she said something else. She said if this weather didn't improve she was going to kill herself.

"Don't talk crazy," I said.

She said, "I mean it, honey. I don't want to see this place again except from my coffin. I hate this g.d. place. I don't know why I moved here. I wish I could just die and get it over with."

I remember hanging on to the phone and watching a man high up on a pole doing something to a power line. Snow whirled around his head. As I watched, he leaned out from the pole, supported only by his safety belt. Suppose he falls, I thought. I didn't have any idea what I was going to say next. I had to say something. But I was filled with unworthy feelings, thoughts no son should admit to. "You're my mother," I said finally. "What can I do to help?"

"Honey, you can't do anything," she said. "The time for doing anything has come and gone. It's too late to do anything. I wanted to like it here. I thought we'd go on picnics and take drives together. But none of that happened. You're always busy. You're off working, you and Jill. You're never at home. Or else if you are at home you have the phone off the hook all day. Anyway, I never see you," she said.

"That's not true," I said. And it wasn't. But she went on as if she hadn't heard me. Maybe she hadn't.

"Besides," she said, "this weather's killing me. It's too damned cold here. Why didn't you tell me this was the North Pole? If you had, I'd never have come. I want to go back to California, honey. I can get out and go places there. I don't know anywhere to go here. There are people back in California. I've got friends there who care what happens to me. Nobody gives a damn here. Well, I just pray I can get through to June. If I can make it that long, if I can last to June, I'm leaving this place forever. This is the worst place I've ever lived in."

What could I say? I didn't know what to say. I couldn't even say anything about the weather. Weather was a real sore point. We said good-bye and hung up.

Other people take vacations in the summer, but my mother moves. She started moving years ago, after my dad lost his job. When that happened, when he was laid off, they sold their home, as if this were what they should do, and went to where they thought things would be better. But things weren't any better there, either. They moved again. They kept on moving. They lived in rented houses, apartments, mobile homes, and motel units even. They kept moving, lightening their load with each move they made. A couple of times they landed in a town where I lived. They'd move in with my wife and me for a while and then they'd move on again. They were like migrating animals in this regard, except there was no pattern to their movement. They moved around for years, sometimes even leaving the state for what they thought would be greener pastures. But mostly they stayed in Northern California and did their moving there. Then my dad died, and I thought my mother would stop moving and stay in one place for a while. But she didn't. She kept moving. I suggested once that she go to a psychiatrist. I even said I'd pay for it. But she wouldn't hear of it. She packed and moved out of town instead. I was desperate about things or I wouldn't have said that about the psychiatrist.

She was always in the process of packing or else unpacking. Sometimes she'd move two or three times in the same year. She talked bitterly about the place she was leaving and optimistically about the place she was going to. Her mail got fouled up, her benefit checks went off somewhere else, and she spent hours writing letters, trying to get it all straightened out. Sometimes she'd move out of an apartment house, move to another one a few blocks away, and then, a month later, move back to the place she'd left, only to a different floor or a different side of the building. That's why when she moved here I rented a house for her and saw to it that it was furnished to her liking. "Moving around keeps her alive," Jill said. "It gives her something to do. She must get some kind of weird enjoyment out of it, I guess." But enjoyment or not, Jill thinks my mother must be losing her mind. I think so, too. But how do you tell your mother this? How do you deal with her if this is the case? Crazy doesn't stop her from planning and getting on with her next move.

She is waiting at the back door for us when we pull in. She's seventy years old, has gray hair, wears glasses with rhinestone frames, and has never been sick a day in her life. She hugs Jill, and then she hugs me. Her eyes are bright, as if she's been drinking. But she doesn't drink. She quit years ago, after my dad went on the wagon. We finish hugging and go inside. It's around five in the afternoon. I smell whatever it is drifting out of her kitchen and remember I haven't eaten since breakfast. My buzz has worn off.

"I'm starved," I say.

"Something smells good," Jill says.

"I hope it tastes good," my mother says. "I hope this chicken's done." She raises the lid on a fry pan and pushes a fork into a chicken breast. "If there's anything I can't stand, it's raw chicken. I think it's done. Why don't you sit down? Sit anyplace. I still can't regulate my stove. The burners heat up too fast. I don't like electric stoves and never have. Move that junk off the chair, Jill. I'm living here like a damned gypsy. But not for much

338

longer, I hope." She sees me looking around for the ashtray. "Behind you," she says. "On the windowsill, honey. Before you sit down, why don't you pour us some of that Pepsi? You'll have to use these paper cups. I should have told you to bring some glasses. Is the Pepsi cold? I don't have any ice. This icebox won't keep anything cold. It isn't worth a damn. My ice cream turns to soup. It's the worst icebox I've ever had."

She forks the chicken onto a plate and puts the plate on the table along with beans and coleslaw and white bread. Then she looks to see if there is anything she's forgetting. Salt and pepper! "Sit down," she says.

We draw our chairs up to the table, and Jill takes the plates out of the sack and hands them around the table to us. "Where are you going to live when you go back?" she says. "Do you have a place lined up?"

My mother passes the chicken to Jill and says, "I wrote that lady I rented from before. She wrote back and said she had a nice first-floor place I could have. It's close to the bus stop and there's lots of stores in the area. There's a bank and a Safeway. It's the nicest place. I don't know why I left there." She says that and helps herself to some coleslaw.

"Why'd you leave then?" Jill says. "If it was so nice and all." She picks up her drumstick, looks at it, and takes a bite of the meat.

"I'll tell you why. There was an old alcoholic woman who lived next door to me. She drank from morning to night. The walls were so thin I could hear her munching ice cubes all day. She had to use a walker to get around, but that still didn't stop her. I'd hear that walker *scrape, scrape* against the floor from morning to night. That and her icebox door closing." She shakes her head at all she had to put up with. "I had to get out of there. *Scrape, scrape* all day. I couldn't stand it. I just couldn't live like that. This time I told the manager I didn't want to be next to any alcoholics. And I didn't want anything on the second floor. The second floor looks out on the parking lot. Nothing to see from there." She waits for Jill to say something more. But Jill doesn't comment. My mother looks over at me.

339

I'm eating like a wolf and don't say anything, either. In any case, there's nothing more to say on the subject. I keep chewing and look over at the boxes stacked against the fridge. Then I help myself to more coleslaw.

Pretty soon I finish and push my chair back. Larry Hadlock pulls up in back of the house, next to my car, and takes a lawn mower out of his pickup. I watch him through the window behind the table. He doesn't look in our direction.

"What's he want?" my mother says and stops eating.

"He's going to cut your grass, it looks like," I say.

"It doesn't need cutting," she says. "He cut it last week. What's there for him to cut?"

"It's for the new tenant," Jill says. "Whoever that turns out to be."

My mother takes this in and then goes back to eating.

Larry Hadlock starts his mower and begins to cut the grass. I know him a little. He lowered the rent twenty-five a month when I told him it was my mother. He is a widower – a big fellow, mid-sixties. An unhappy man with a good sense of humor. His arms are covered with white hair, and white hair stands out from under his cap. He looks like a magazine illustration of a farmer. But he isn't a farmer. He is a retired construction worker who's saved a little money. For a while, in the beginning, I let myself imagine that he and my mother might take some meals together and become friends.

"There's the king," my mother says. "King Larry. Not everyone has as much money as he does and can live in a big house and charge other people high rents. Well, I hope I never see his cheap old face again once I leave here. Eat the rest of this chicken," she says to me. But I shake my head and light a cigarette. Larry pushes his mower past the window.

"You won't have to look at it much longer," Jill says.

"I'm sure glad of that, Jill. But I know he won't give me my deposit back."

"How do you know that?" I say.

"I just know," she says. "I've had dealings with his kind before. They're out for all they can get."

340

Jill says, "It won't be long now and you won't have to have anything more to do with him."

"I'll be so glad."

"But it'll be somebody just like him," Jill says.

"I don't want to think that, Jill," my mother says.

She makes coffee while Jill clears the table. I rinse the cups. Then I pour coffee, and we step around a box marked "Knick-knacks" and take our cups into the living room.

Larry Hadlock is at the side of the house. Traffic moves slowly on the street out in front, and the sun has started down over the trees. I can hear the commotion the mower makes. Some crows leave the phone line and settle onto the newly cut grass in the front yard.

"I'm going to miss you, honey," my mother says. Then she says, "I'll miss you, too, Jill. I'm going to miss both of you."

Jill sips from her coffee and nods. Then she says, "I hope you have a safe trip back and find the place you're looking for at the end of the road."

"When I get settled – and this is my last move, so help me – I hope you'll come and visit," my mother says. She looks at me and waits to be reassured.

"We will," I say. But even as I say it I know it isn't true. My life caved in on me down there, and I won't be going back.

"I wish you could have been happier here," Jill says. "I wish you'd been able to stick it out or something. You know what? Your son is worried sick about you."

"Jill," I say.

But she gives her head a little shake and goes on. "Sometimes he can't sleep over it. He wakes up sometimes in the night and says, 'I can't sleep. I'm thinking about my mother.' There," she says and looks at me. "I've said it. But it was on my mind."

"How do you think I must feel?" my mother says. Then she says, "Other women my age can be happy. Why can't I be like other women? All I want is a house and a town to live in that will make me happy. That isn't a crime, is it? I hope not. I hope I'm not asking too much out of life." She puts her cup on the floor next to her chair and waits for Jill to tell her she isn't asking

for too much. But Jill doesn't say anything, and in a minute my
mother begins to outline her plans to be happy.

After a time Jill lowers her eyes to her cup and has some more
coffee. I can tell she's stopped listening. But my mother keeps
talking anyway. The crows work their way through the grass in
the front yard. I hear the mower howl and then thud as it picks
up a clump of grass in the blade and comes to a stop. In a minute,
after several tries, Larry gets it going again. The crows fly off,
back to their wire. Jill picks at a fingernail. My mother is saying
that the secondhand-furniture dealer is coming around the next
morning to collect the things she isn't going to send on the bus
or carry with her in the car. The table and chairs, TV, sofa, and
bed are going with the dealer. But he's told her he doesn't have
any use for the card table, so my mother is going to throw it out
unless we want it.

"We'll take it," I say. Jill looks over. She starts to say something but changes her mind.

I will drive the boxes to the Greyhound station the next afternoon and start them on the way to California. My mother will
spend the last night with us, as arranged. And then, early the
next morning, two days from now, she'll be on her way.

She continues to talk. She talks on and on as she describes the
trip she is about to make. She'll drive until four o'clock in the
afternoon and then take a motel room for the night. She figures
to make Eugene by dark. Eugene is a nice town – she stayed
there once before, on the way up here. When she leaves the motel,
she'll leave at sunrise and should, if God is looking out for her,
be in California that afternoon. And God *is* looking out for her,
she knows he is. How else explain her being kept around on the
face of the earth? He has a plan for her. She's been praying a lot
lately. She's been praying for me, too.

"Why are you praying for him?" Jill wants to know.

"Because I feel like it. Because he's my son," my mother says.
"Is there anything the matter with that? Don't we all need praying
for sometimes? Maybe some people don't. I don't know. What
do I know anymore?" She brings a hand to her forehead and
rearranges some hair that's come loose from a pin.

342

The mower sputters off, and pretty soon we see Larry go around the house pulling the hose. He sets the hose out and then goes slowly back around the house to turn the water on. The sprinkler begins to turn.

My mother starts listing the ways she imagines Larry has wronged her since she's been in the house. But now I'm not listening, either. I am thinking how she is about to go down the highway again, and nobody can reason with her or do anything to stop her. What can I do? I can't tie her up, or commit her, though it may come to that eventually. I worry for her, and she is a heartache to me. She is all the family I have left. I'm sorry she didn't like it here and wants to leave. But I'm never going back to California. And when that's clear to me I understand something else, too. I understand that after she leaves I'm probably never going to see her again.

I look over at my mother. She stops talking. Jill raises her eyes. Both of them look at me.

"What is it, honey?" my mother says.

"What's wrong?" Jill says.

I lean forward in the chair and cover my face with my hands. I sit like that for a minute, feeling bad and stupid for doing it. But I can't help it. And the woman who brought me into this life, and this other woman I picked up with less than a year ago, they exclaim together and rise and come over to where I sit with my head in my hands like a fool. I don't open my eyes. I listen to the sprinkler whipping the grass.

"What's wrong? What's the matter?" they say.

"It's okay," I say. And in a minute it is. I open my eyes and bring my head up. I reach for a cigarette.

"See what I mean?" Jill says. "You're driving him crazy. He's going crazy with worry over you." She is on one side of my chair, and my mother is on the other side. They could tear me apart in no time at all.

"I wish I could die and get out of everyone's way," my mother says quietly. "So help me Hannah, I can't take much more of this."

"How about some more coffee?" I say. "Maybe we ought to

343

catch the news," I say. "Then I guess Jill and I better head for home."

Two days later, early in the morning, I say good-bye to my mother for what may be the last time. I've let Jill sleep. It won't hurt if she's late to work for a change. The dogs can wait for their baths and trimmings and such. My mother holds my arm as I walk her down the steps to the driveway and open the car door for her. She is wearing white slacks and a white blouse and white sandals. Her hair is pulled back and tied with a scarf. That's white, too. It's going to be a nice day, and the sky is clear and already blue.

On the front seat of the car I see maps and a thermos of coffee. My mother looks at these things as if she can't recall having come outside with them just a few minutes ago. She turns to me then and says, "Let me hug you once more. Let me love your neck. I know I won't see you for a long time." She puts an arm around my neck, draws me to her, and then begins to cry. But she stops almost at once and steps back, pushing the heel of her hand against her eyes. "I said I wouldn't do that, and I won't. But let me get a last look at you anyway. I'll miss you, honey," she says. "I'm just going to have to live through this. I've already lived through things I didn't think were possible. But I'll live through this, too, I guess." She gets into the car, starts it, and runs the engine for a minute. She rolls her window down.

"I'm going to miss you," I say. And I *am* going to miss her. She's my mother, after all, and why shouldn't I miss her? But, God forgive me, I'm glad, too, that it's finally time and that she is leaving.

"Good-bye," she says. "Tell Jill thanks for supper last night. Tell her I said good-bye."

"I will," I say. I stand there wanting to say something else. But I don't know what. We keep looking at each other, trying to smile and reassure each other. Then something comes into her eyes, and I believe she is thinking about the highway and how far she is going to have to drive that day. She takes her eyes off me and looks down the road. Then she rolls her window up,

344

puts the car into gear, and drives to the intersection, where she has to wait for the light to change. When I see she's made it into traffic and headed toward the highway, I go back in the house and drink some coffee. I feel sad for a while, and then the sadness goes away and I start thinking about other things.

A few nights later my mother calls to say she is in her new place. She is busy fixing it up, the way she does when she has a new place. She tells me I'll be happy to know she likes it just fine to be back in sunny California. But she says there's something in the air where she is living, maybe it's pollen, that is causing her to sneeze a lot. And the traffic is heavier than she remembers from before. She doesn't recall there being so much traffic in her neighborhood. Naturally, everyone still drives like crazy down there. "California drivers," she says. "What else can you expect?" She says it's hot for this time of the year. She doesn't think the air-conditioning unit in her apartment is working right. I tell her she should talk to the manager. "She's never around when you need her," my mother says. She hopes she hasn't made a mistake in moving back to California. She waits before she says anything else.

I'm standing at the window with the phone pressed to my ear, looking out at the lights from town and at the lighted houses closer by. Jill is at the table with the catalogue, listening.

"Are you still there?" my mother asks. "I wish you'd say something."

I don't know why, but it's then I recall the affectionate name my dad used sometimes when he was talking nice to my mother – those times, that is, when he wasn't drunk. It was a long time ago, and I was a kid, but always, hearing it, I felt better, less afraid, more hopeful about the future. *"Dear,"* he'd say. He called her "dear" sometimes – a sweet name. "Dear," he'd say, "if you're going to the store, will you bring me some cigarettes?" Or "Dear, is your cold any better?" "Dear, where is my coffee cup?"

The word issues from my lips before I can think what else I want to say to go along with it. "Dear." I say it again. I call her "dear." "Dear, try not to be afraid," I say. I tell my mother I love her and I'll write to her, yes. Then I say good-bye, and I hang up.

For a while I don't move from the window. I keep standing there, looking out at the lighted houses in our neighborhood. As I watch, a car turns off the road and pulls into a driveway. The porch light goes on. The door to the house opens and someone comes out on the porch and stands there waiting.

Jill turns the pages of her catalogue, and then she stops turning them. "This is what we want," she says. "This is more like what I had in mind. Look at this, will you." But I don't look. I don't care five cents for curtains. "What is it you see out there, honey?" Jill says. "Tell me."

What's there to tell? The people over there embrace for a minute, and then they go inside the house together. They leave the light burning. Then they remember, and it goes out.

Whoever Was Using This Bed

The call comes in the middle of the night, three in the morning, and it nearly scares us to death.

"Answer it, answer it!" my wife cries. "My God, who is it? Answer it!"

I can't find the light, but I get to the other room, where the phone is, and pick it up after the fourth ring.

"Is Bud there?" this woman says, very drunk.

"Jesus, you have the wrong number," I say, and hang up.

I turn the light on, and go into the bathroom, and that's when I hear the phone start again.

"Answer that!" my wife screams from the bedroom. "What in God's name do they want, Jack? I can't take any more."

I hurry out of the bathroom and pick up the phone.

"Bud?" the woman says. "What are you doing, Bud?"

I say, "Look here. You have a wrong number. Don't ever call this number again."

"I have to talk to Bud," she says.

I hang up, wait until it rings again, and then I take the receiver and lay on the table beside the phone. But I hear the woman's voice say, "Bud, talk to me, please." I leave the receiver on its side on the table, turn off the light, and close the door to the room.

In the bedroom I find the lamp on and my wife, Iris, sitting against the headboard with her knees drawn up under the covers. She has a pillow behind her back, and she's more on my side than her own side. The covers are up around her shoulders. The blankets and the sheet have been pulled out from the foot of the bed. If we want to go back to sleep – I want to go back to sleep, anyway – we may have to start from scratch and do this bed over again.

"What the hell was that all about?" Iris says. "We should have unplugged the phone. I guess we forgot. Try forgetting one night to unplug the phone and see what happens. I don't believe it."

After Iris and I started living together, my former wife, or else one of my kids, used to call up when we were asleep and want to harangue us. They kept doing it even after Iris and I were married. So we started unplugging our phone before we went to bed. We unplugged the phone every night of the year, just about. It was a habit. This time I slipped up, that's all.

"Some woman wanting *Bud*," I say. I'm standing there in my pajamas, wanting to get into bed, but I can't. "She was drunk. Move over, honey. I took the phone off the hook."

"She can't call again?"

"No," I say. "Why don't you move over a little and give me some of those covers?"

She takes her pillow and puts it on the far side of the bed, against the headboard, scoots over, and then she leans back once more. She doesn't look sleepy. She looks fully awake. I get into bed and take some covers. But the covers don't feel right. I don't have any sheet; all I have is blanket. I look down and see my feet sticking out. I turn onto my side, facing her, and bring my legs up so that my feet are under the blanket. We should make up the bed again. I ought to suggest that. But I'm thinking, too, that if we kill the light now, this minute, we might be able to go right back to sleep.

"How about you turning off your light, honey?" I say, as nice as I can.

"Let's have a cigarette first," she says. "Then we'll go to sleep. Get us the cigarettes and the ashtray, why don't you? We'll have a cigarette."

"Let's go to sleep," I say. "Look at what time it is." The clock radio is right there beside the bed. Anyone can see it says three-thirty.

"Come on," Iris says. "I need a cigarette after all that."

I get out of bed for the cigarettes and ashtray. I have to go into the room where the phone is, but I don't touch the phone. I don't even want to look at the phone, but I do, of course. The receiver is still on its side on the table.

I crawl back in bed and put the ashtray on the quilt between us. I light a cigarette, give it to her, and then light one for myself.

She tries to remember the dream she was having when the phone rang. "I can just about remember it, but I can't remember exactly. Something about, about – no, I don't know what it was about now. I can't be sure. I can't remember it," she says finally. "God damn that woman and her phone call. '*Bud,*'" she says. "I'd like to punch her." She puts out her cigarette and immediately lights another, blows smoke, and lets her eyes take in the chest of drawers and the window curtains. Her hair is undone and around her shoulders. She uses the ashtray and then stares over the foot of the bed, trying to remember.

But, really, I don't care what she's dreamed. I want to go back to sleep is all. I finish my cigarette and put it out and wait for her to finish. I lie still and don't say anything.

Iris is like my former wife in that when she sleeps she sometimes has violent dreams. She thrashes around in bed during the night and wakes in the morning drenched with sweat, the nightgown sticking to her body. And, like my former wife, she wants to tell me her dreams in great detail and speculate as to what this stands for or that portends. My former wife used to kick the covers off in the night and cry out in her sleep, as if someone were laying hands on her. Once, in a particularly violent dream, she hit me on the ear with her fist. I was in a dreamless sleep, but I struck out in the dark and hit her on the forehead. Then we began yelling. We both yelled and yelled. We'd hurt each other, but we were mainly scared. We had no idea what had happened until I turned the lamp on; then we sorted it out. Afterward, we joked about it – fistfighting in our sleep. But then so much else began to happen that was far more serious we tended to forget about that night. We never mentioned it again, even when we teased each other.

Once I woke up in the night to hear Iris grinding her teeth in her sleep. It was such a peculiar thing to have going on right next to my ear that it woke me up. I gave her a little shake, and she stopped. The next morning she told me she'd had a very bad dream, but that's all she'd tell me about it. I didn't press her for details. I guess I really didn't want to know what could have been so bad that she didn't want to say. When I told her she'd been grinding her teeth in her sleep, she frowned and said she was going to have to do something about that. The next night she brought home something called a Niteguard – something she was supposed to wear in her mouth while she slept. She had to do something, she said. She couldn't afford to keep grinding her teeth; pretty soon she wouldn't have any. So she wore this protective device in her mouth for a week or so, and then she stopped wearing it. She said it was uncomfortable and, anyway, it was not very cosmetic. Who'd want to kiss a woman wearing a thing like that in her mouth, she said. She had something there, of course.

Another time I woke up because she was stroking my face and calling me Earl. I took her hand and squeezed her fingers. "What is it?" I said. "What is it, sweetheart?" But instead of answering she simply squeezed back, sighed, and then lay still again. The next morning, when I asked her what she'd dreamed the night before, she claimed not to have had any dreams.

"So who's Earl?" I said. "Who is this Earl you were talking about in your sleep?" She blushed and said she didn't know anybody named Earl and never had.

The lamp is still on and, because I don't know what else to think about, I think about that phone being off the hook. I ought to hang it up and unplug the cord. Then we have to think about sleep.

"I'll go take care of that phone," I say. "Then let's go to sleep."

Iris uses the ashtray and says, "Make sure it's unplugged this time."

I get up again and go to the other room, open the door, and turn on the light. The receiver is still on its side on the table. I bring it to my ear, expecting to hear the dial tone. But I don't hear anything, not even the tone.

On an impulse, I say something. "Hello," I say.

"Oh, Bud, it's you," the woman says.

I hang up the phone and bend over and unplug it from the wall before it can ring again. This is a new one on me. This deal is a mystery, this woman and her Bud person. I don't know how to tell Iris about this new development, because it'll just lead to more discussion and further speculation. I decide not to say anything for now. Maybe I'll say something over breakfast.

Back in the bedroom I see she is smoking another cigarette. I see, too, that it's nearly four in the morning. I'm starting to worry. When it's four o'clock it'll soon be five o'clock, and then it will be six, then six-thirty, then time to get up for work. I lie back down, close my eyes, and decide I'll count to sixty, slowly, before I say anything else about the light.

"I'm starting to remember," Iris says. "It's coming back to me. You want to hear it, Jack?"

I stop counting, open my eyes, sit up. The bedroom is filled with smoke. I light one up, too. Why not? The hell with it.

She says, "There was a party going on in my dream."

"Where was I when this was going on?" Usually, for whatever reason, I don't figure in her dreams. It irritates me a little, but I don't let on. My feet are uncovered again. I pull them under the covers, raise myself up on my elbow, and use the ashtray. "Is this another dream that I'm not in? It's okay, if that's the case." I pull on the cigarette, hold the smoke, let it out.

"Honey, you weren't in the dream," Iris says. "I'm sorry, but you weren't. You weren't anywhere around. I *missed* you, though. I did miss you, I'm sure of it. It was like I knew you were somewhere nearby, but you weren't there where I needed you. You know how I get into those anxiety states sometimes? If we go someplace together where there's a group of people and we get separated and I can't find you? It was a little like that. You were there, I think, but I couldn't find you."

"Go ahead and tell me about the dream," I say.

She rearranges the covers around her waist and legs and reaches for a cigarette. I hold the lighter for her. Then she goes on to describe this party where all that was being served was beer. "I don't even like beer," she says. But she drank a large quantity anyway, and just when she went to leave – to go home, she says

– this little dog took hold of the hem of her dress and made her stay.

She laughs, and I laugh right along with her, even though, when I look at the clock, I see the hands are close to saying four-thirty.

There was some kind of music being played in her dream – a piano, maybe, or else it was an accordion, who knows? Dreams are that way sometimes, she says. Anyway, she vaguely remembers her former husband putting in an appearance. He might have been the one serving the beer. People were drinking beer from a keg, using plastic cups. She thought she might even have danced with him.

"Why are you telling me this?"

She says, "It was a dream, honey."

"I don't think I like it, knowing you're supposed to be here beside me all night but instead you're dreaming about strange dogs, parties, and ex-husbands. I don't like you dancing with him. What the hell is this? What if I told you I dreamed I danced the night away with Carol? Would you like it?"

"It's just a dream, right?" she says. "Don't get weird on me. I won't say any more. I see I can't. I can see it isn't a good idea." She brings her fingers to her lips slowly, the way she does sometimes when she's thinking. Her face shows how hard she's concentrating; little lines appear on her forehead. "I'm sorry that you weren't in the dream. But if I told you otherwise I'd be lying to you, right?"

I nod. I touch her arm to show her it's okay. I don't really mind. And I don't, I guess. "What happened then, honey? Finish telling the dream," I say. "And maybe we can go to sleep then." I guess I wanted to know the next thing. The last I'd heard, she'd been dancing with Jerry. If there was more, I needed to hear it.

She plumps up the pillow behind her back and says, "That's all I can remember. I can't remember any more about it. That was when the goddamn phone rang."

"Bud," I say. I can see smoke drifting in the light under the lamp, and smoke hangs in the air in the room. "Maybe we should open a window," I say.

"That's a good idea," she says. "Let some of this smoke out. It can't be any good for us."

"Hell no, it isn't," I say.

I get up again and go to the window and raise it a few inches. I can feel the cool air that comes in and from a distance I hear a truck gearing down as it starts up the grade that will take it to the pass and on over into the next state.

"I guess pretty soon we're going to be the last smokers left in America," she says. "Seriously, we should think about quitting." She says this as she puts her cigarette out and reaches for the pack next to the ashtray.

"It's open season on smokers," I say.

I get back in the bed. The covers are turned every which way, and it's five o'clock in the morning. I don't think we're going to sleep any more tonight. But so what if we don't? Is there a law on the books? Is something bad going to happen to us if we don't?

She takes some of her hair between her fingers. Then she pushes it behind her ear, looks at me, and says, "Lately I've been feeling this vein in my forehead. It *pulses* sometimes. It throbs. Do you know what I'm talking about? I don't know if you've ever had anything like that. I hate to think about it, but probably one of these days I'll have a stroke or something. Isn't that how they happen? A vein in your head bursts? That's probably what'll happen to me, eventually. My mother, my grandmother, and one of my aunts died of stroke. There's a history of stroke in my family. It can run in the family, you know. It's hereditary, just like heart disease, or being too fat, or whatever. Anyway," she says, "something's going to happen to me someday, right? So maybe that's what it'll be – a stroke. Maybe that's how I'll go. That's what it feels like it could be the beginning of. First it pulses a little, like it wants my attention, and then it starts to throb. Throb, throb, throb. It scares me silly," she says. "I want us to give up these goddamn cigarettes before it's too late." She looks at what's left of her cigarette, mashes it into the ashtray, and tries to fan the smoke away.

I'm on my back, studying the ceiling, thinking that this is the kind of talk that could only take place at five in the morning. I feel I ought to say something. "I get winded easy," I say. "I found myself out of breath when I ran in there to answer the phone."

"That could have been because of anxiety," Iris says. "Who needs it, anyway! The *idea* of somebody calling at this hour! I could tear that woman limb from limb."

I pull myself up in the bed and lean back against the headboard. I put the pillow behind my back and try to get comfortable, same as Iris. "I'll tell you something I haven't told you," I say. "Once in a while my heart palpitates. It's like it goes crazy." She's watching me closely, listening for whatever it is I'm going to say next. "Sometimes it feels like it's going to jump out of my chest. I don't know what the hell causes it."

"Why didn't you tell me?" she says. She takes my hand and holds it. She squeezes my hand. "You never said anything, honey. Listen, I don't know what I'd *do* if something ever happened to you. I'd fold up. How often does it happen? That's scary, you know." She's still holding my hand. But her fingers slide to my wrist, where my pulse is. She goes on holding my wrist like this.

"I never told you because I didn't want to scare you," I say. "But it happens sometimes. It happened as recently as a week ago. I don't have to be doing anything in particular when it happens, either. I can be sitting in a chair with the paper. Or else driving the car, or pushing a grocery basket. It doesn't matter if I'm exerting myself or not. It just starts – boom, boom, boom. Like that. I'm surprised people can't hear it. It's that loud, I think. *I* can hear it, anyway, and I don't mind telling you it scares me," I say. "So if emphysema doesn't get me, or lung cancer, or maybe a stroke like what you're talking about, then it's going to be a heart attack probably."

I reach for the cigarettes. I give her one. We're through with sleep for the night. Did we sleep? For a minute, I can't remember.

"Who knows what we'll die of?" Iris says. "It could be anything. If we live long enough, maybe it'll be kidney failure, or something like that. A friend of mine at work, her father just died of kidney failure. That's what can happen to you sometimes if you're lucky enough to get really old. When your kidneys fail, the body starts filling up with uric acid then. You finally turn a whole different color before you die."

"Great. That sounds wonderful," I say. "Maybe we should get off this subject. How'd we get onto this stuff, anyway?"

She doesn't answer. She leans forward, away from her pillow, arms clasping her legs. She closes her eyes and lays her head on her knees. Then she begins to rock back and forth, slowly. It's as if she were listening to music. But there isn't any music. None that I can hear, anyway.

"You know what I'd like?" she says. She stops moving, opens her eyes, and tilts her head at me. Then she grins, so I'll know she's all right.

"What would you like, honey?" I've got my leg hooked over her leg, at the ankle.

She says, "I'd like some coffee, that's what. I could go for a nice strong cup of black coffee. We're awake, aren't we? Who's going back to sleep? Let's have some coffee."

"We drink too much coffee," I say. "All that coffee isn't good for us, either. I'm not saying we shouldn't have any, I'm just saying we drink too much of it. It's just an observation," I add. "Actually, I could drink some coffee myself."

"Good," she says.

But neither of us makes a move.

She shakes out her hair and then lights another cigarette. Smoke drifts slowly in the room. Some of it drifts toward the open window. A little rain begins to fall on the patio outside the window. The alarm comes on, and I reach over and shut it off. Then I take the pillow and put it under my head again. I lie back and stare at the ceiling some more. "What happened to that bright idea we had about a girl who could bring us our coffee in bed?" I say.

"I wish *somebody* would bring us coffee," she says. "A girl or a boy, one or the other. I could really go for some coffee right now."

She moves the ashtray to the nightstand, and I think she's going to get up. Somebody has to get up and start the coffee and put a can of frozen juice in the blender. One of us has to make a move. But what she does instead is slide down in the bed until she's sitting somewhere in the middle. The covers are all over the place. She picks at something on the quilt, and then rubs her palm across whatever it is before she looks up. "Did you see in the paper where that guy took a shotgun into an intensive-care unit and made the nurses take his father off the life-support machine? Did you read about that?" Iris says.

"I saw something about it on the news," I say. "But mostly they were talking about this nurse who unplugged six or eight people from their machines. At this point they don't know exactly how many she unplugged. She started off by unplugging her mother, and then she went on from there. It was like a spree, I guess. She said she thought she was doing everybody a favor. She said she hoped somebody'd do it for *her*, if they cared about her."

Iris decides to move on down to the foot of the bed. She positions herself so that she is facing me. Her legs are still under the covers. She puts her legs between my legs and says, "What about that quadriplegic woman on the news who says she wants to die, wants to starve herself to death? Now she's suing her doctor and the hospital because they insist on force-feeding her to keep her alive. Can you believe it? It's insane. They strap her down three times a day so they can run this tube into her throat. They feed her breakfast, lunch, and dinner that way. And they keep her plugged into this machine, too, because her lungs don't want to work on their own. It said in the paper that she's *begging* them to unplug her, or else to just let her starve to death. She's having to plead with them to let her die, but they won't listen. She said she started out wanting to die with some dignity. Now she's just mad and looking to sue everybody. Isn't that amazing? Isn't that one for the books?" she says. "I have these headaches sometimes," she says. "Maybe it has something to do with the vein. Maybe not. Maybe they're not related. But I don't tell you when my head hurts, because I don't want to worry you."

"What are you talking about?" I say. "Look at me. Iris? I have a right to know. I'm your husband, in case you've forgotten. If something's wrong with you, I should know about it."

"But what could you *do*? You'd just worry." She bumps my leg with her leg, then bumps it again. "Right? You'd tell me to take some aspirin. I know you."

I look toward the window, where it's beginning to get light. I can feel a damp breeze from the window. It's stopped raining now, but it's one of those mornings where it could begin to pour. I look at her again. "To tell you the truth, Iris, I get sharp pains in my side from time to time." But the moment I say the words I'm sorry. She'll be concerned, and want to talk about it. We ought to be thinking of showers; we should be sitting down to breakfast.

"Which side?" she says.

"Right side."

"It could be your appendix," she says. "Something fairly simple like that."

I shrug. "Who knows? I don't know. All I know is it happens. Every so often, for just a minute or two, I feel something sharp down there. Very sharp. At first I thought it might be a pulled muscle. Which side's your gallbladder on, by the way? Is it the left or right side? Maybe it's my gallbladder. Or else maybe a gall*stone*, whatever the hell that is."

"It's not really a stone," she says. "A gallstone is like a little granule, or something like that. It's about as big as the tip of a pencil. No, wait, that might be a *kidney* stone I'm talking about. I guess I don't know anything about it." She shakes her head.

"What's the difference between kidney stone and gallstone?" I say. "Christ, we don't even know which side of the body they're on. You don't know, and I don't know. That's how much we know together. A total of nothing. But I read somewhere that you can pass a kidney stone, if that's what this is, and usually it won't kill you. Painful, yes. I don't know what they say about a gallstone."

"I like that 'usually,'" she says.

357

"I know," I say. "Listen, we'd better get up. It's getting really late. It's seven o'clock."

"I know," she says. "Okay." But she continues to sit there. Then she says, "My grandma had arthritis so bad toward the end she couldn't get around by herself, or even move her fingers. She had to sit in a chair and wear these mittens all day. Finally, she couldn't even hold a cup of cocoa. That's how bad her arthritis was. Then she had her stroke. And my *grandpa*," she says. "He went into a nursing home not long after Grandma died. It was either that or else somebody had to come in and be with him around the clock, and nobody could do that. Nobody had the money for twenty-four-hour-a-day care, either. So he goes into the nursing home. But he began to deteriorate fast in there. One time, after he'd been in that place for a while, my mom went to visit him and then she came home and said something. I'll never forget what she said." She looks at me as if I'm never going to forget it, either. And I'm not. "She said, 'My dad doesn't recognize me anymore. He doesn't even know who I am. My dad has become a vegetable.' That was my mom who said that."

She leans over and covers her face with her hands and begins to cry. I move down there to the foot of the bed and sit beside her. I take her hand and hold it in my lap. I put my arm around her. We're sitting together looking at the headboard and at the nightstand. The clock's there, too, and beside the clock a few magazines and a paperback. We're sitting on the part of the bed where we keep our feet when we sleep. It looks like whoever was using this bed left in a hurry. I know I won't ever look at this bed again without remembering it like this. We're into something now, but I don't know what, exactly.

"I don't want anything like that to ever happen to me," she says. "Or to you, either." She wipes her face with a corner of the blanket and takes a deep breath, which comes out as a sob. "I'm sorry. I just can't help it," she says.

"It won't happen to us. It won't," I say. "Don't worry about any of it, okay? We're fine, Iris, and we're going to stay fine. In any case, that time's a long time off. Hey, I love you. We love each other, don't we? That's the important thing. That's what counts. Don't worry, honey."

"I want you to promise me something," she says. She takes her hand back. She moves my arm away from her shoulder. "I want you to promise me you'll pull the plug on me, if and when it's ever necessary. If it ever comes to that, I mean. Do you hear what I'm saying? I'm serious about this, Jack. I want you to pull the plug on me if you ever have to. Will you promise?"

I don't say anything right away. What am I supposed to say? They haven't written the book on this one yet. I need a minute to think. I know it won't cost me anything to tell her I'll do whatever she wants. It's just words, right? Words are easy. But there's more to it than this; she wants an honest response from me. And I don't know what I feel about it yet. I shouldn't be hasty. I can't say something without thinking about what I'm saying, about consequences, about what she's going to feel when I say it – whatever it is I say.

I'm still thinking about it when she says, "What about you?"

"What about me what?"

"Do you want to be unplugged if it comes to that? God forbid it ever does, of course," she says. "But I should have some kind of idea, you know – some word from you now – about what you want me to do if worst comes to worst." She's looking at me closely, waiting for me to say. She wants something she can file away to use later, if and when she ever has to. Sure. Okay. Easy enough for me to say, *Unplug me, honey, if you think it's for the best.* But I need to consider this a little more. I haven't even said yet what I will or won't do for *her*. Now I have to think about me and *my* situation. I don't feel I should jump into this. This is nuts. *We're* nuts. But I realize that whatever I say now might come back to me sometime. It's important. This is a life-and-death thing we're talking about here.

She hasn't moved. She's still waiting for her answer. And I can see we're not going anywhere this morning until she has an answer. I think about it some more, and then I say what I mean. "No. Don't unplug me. I don't want to be unplugged. Leave me hooked up just as long as possible. Who's going to object? Are you going to object? Will I be offending anybody? As long as people can stand the sight of me, just so long as they don't start howling, don't unplug anything. Let me keep going, okay? Right to the bitter end. Invite my friends in to say good-bye. Don't do anything rash."

"Be serious," she says. "This is a very serious matter we're discussing."

"I am serious. Don't unplug me. It's as simple as that."

She nods. "Okay, then. I promise you I won't." She hugs me. She holds me tight for a minute. Then she lets me go. She looks at the clock radio and says, "Jesus, we better get moving."

So we get out of bed and start getting dressed. In some ways it's just like any other morning, except we do things faster. We drink coffee and juice and we eat English muffins. We remark on the weather, which is overcast and blustery. We don't talk anymore about plugs, or about sickness and hospitals and stuff like that. I kiss her and leave her on the front porch with her umbrella open, waiting for her ride to work. Then I hurry to my car and get in. In a minute, after I've run the motor, I wave and drive off.

But during the day, at work, I think about some of those things we talked about this morning. I can't help it. For one thing, I'm bone-tired from lack of sleep. I feel vulnerable and prey to any random, gruesome thought. Once, when nobody is around, I put my head on my desk and think I might catch a few minutes' sleep. But when I close my eyes I find myself thinking about it again. In my mind I can see a hospital bed. That's all – just a hospital bed. The bed's in a room, I guess. Then I see an oxygen tent over the bed, and beside the bed some of those screens and some big monitors – the kind they have in movies. I open my eyes and sit up in my chair and light a cigarette. I drink some coffee while I smoke the cigarette. Then I look at the time and get back to work.

At five o'clock, I'm so tired it's all I can do to drive home. It's raining, and I have to be careful driving. Very careful. There's been an accident, too. Someone has rear-ended someone else at a traffic light, but I don't think anyone has been hurt. The cars are still out in the road, and people are standing around in the rain, talking. Still, traffic moves slowly; the police have set out flares.

When I see my wife, I say, "God, what a day. I'm whipped. How are you doing?" We kiss each other. I take off my coat and hang it up. I take the drink Iris gives me. Then, because it's been on my mind, and because I want to clear the deck, so to speak, I say, "All right, if it's what you want to hear, I'll pull the plug for you. If that's what you want me to do, I'll do it. If it will make you happy, here and now, to hear me say so, I'll say it. I'll do it for you. I'll pull the plug, or have it pulled, if I ever think it's necessary. But what I said about my plug still stands. Now I don't want to have to think about this stuff ever again. I don't even want to have to *talk* about it again. I think we've said all there is to say on the subject. We've exhausted every angle. *I'm* exhausted."

Iris grins. "Okay," she says. "At least I know now, anyway. I didn't before. Maybe I'm crazy, but I feel better somehow, if you want to know. I don't want to think about it anymore, either. But I'm glad we talked it over. I'll never bring it up again, either, and that's a promise."

She takes my drink and puts it on the table, next to the phone. She puts her arms around me and holds me and lets her head rest on my shoulder. But here's the thing. What I've just said to her, what I've been thinking about off and on all day, well, I feel as if I've crossed some kind of invisible line. I feel as if I've come to a place I never thought I'd have to come to. And I don't know how I got here. It's a strange place. It's a place where a little harmless dreaming and then some sleepy, early-morning talk has led me into considerations of death and annihilation.

The phone rings. We let go of each other, and I reach to answer it. "Hello," I say.

"Hello, there," the woman says back.

It's the same woman who called this morning, but she isn't drunk now. At least, I don't think she is; she doesn't sound drunk.

She is speaking quietly, reasonably, and she is asking me if I can put her in touch with Bud Roberts. She apologizes. She hates to trouble me, she says, but this is an urgent matter. She's sorry for any trouble she might be giving.

While she talks, I fumble with my cigarettes. I put one in my mouth and use the lighter. Then it's my turn to talk. This is what I say to her: "Bud Roberts doesn't live here. He is not at this number, and I don't expect he ever will be. I will never, never lay eyes on this man you're talking about. Please don't ever call here again. Just don't, okay? Do you hear me? If you're not careful, I'll wring your neck for you."

"The *gall* of that woman," Iris says.

My hands are shaking. I think my voice is doing things. But while I'm trying to tell all this to the woman, while I'm trying to make myself understood, my wife moves quickly and bends over, and that's it. The line goes dead, and I can't hear anything.

Intimacy

I have some business out west anyway, so I stop off in this little town where my former wife lives. We haven't seen each other in four years. But from time to time, when something of mine appeared, or was written about me in the magazines or papers – a profile or an interview – I sent her these things. I don't know what I had in mind except I thought she might be interested. In any case, she never responded.

It is nine in the morning, I haven't called, and it's true I don't know what I am going to find.

But she lets me in. She doesn't seem surprised. We don't shake hands, much less kiss each other. She takes me into the living room. As soon as I sit down she brings me some coffee. Then she comes out with what's on her mind. She says I've caused her anguish, made her feel exposed and humiliated.

Make no mistake, I feel I'm home.

She says, But then you were into betrayal early. You always felt comfortable with betrayal. No, she says, that's not true. Not in the beginning, at any rate. You were different then. But I guess I was different too. Everything was different, she says. No, it was after you turned thirty-five, or thirty-six, whenever it was, around in there anyway, your mid-thirties somewhere, then you started in. You really started in. You turned on me. You did it up pretty then. You must be proud of yourself.

She says, Sometimes I could scream.

She says she wishes I'd forget about the hard times, the bad times, when I talk about back then. Spend some time on the good times, she says. Weren't there some good times? She wishes I'd get off that other subject. She's bored with it. Sick of hearing about it. Your private hobby horse, she says. What's done is done and water under the bridge, she says. A tragedy, yes. God knows it was a tragedy and then some. But why keep it going? Don't you ever get tired of dredging up that old business?

She says, Let go of the past, for Christ's sake. Those old hurts. You must have some other arrows in your quiver, she says.

She says, You know something? I think you're sick. I think you're crazy as a bedbug. Hey, you don't believe the things they're saying about you, do you? Don't believe them for a minute, she says. Listen, I could tell them a thing or two. Let them talk to me about it, if they want to hear a story.

She says, Are you listening to me?

I'm listening, I say. I'm all ears, I say.

She says, I've really had a bellyful of it, buster! Who asked you here today anyway? I sure as hell didn't. You just show up and walk in. What the hell do you want from me? Blood? You want more blood? I thought you had your fill by now.

She says, Think of me as dead. I want to be left in peace now. That's all I want anymore is to be left in peace and forgotten about. Hey, I'm forty-five years old, she says. Forty-five going on fifty-five, or sixty-five. Lay off, will you.

She says, Why don't you wipe the blackboard clean and see what you have left after that? Why don't you start with a clean slate? See how far that gets you, she says.

She has to laugh at this. I laugh too, but it's nerves.

She says, You know something? I had my chance once, but I let it go. I just let it go. I don't guess I ever told you. But now look at me. Look! Take a good look while you're at it. You threw me away, you son of a bitch.

She says, I was younger then and a better person. Maybe you were too, she says. A better person, I mean. You had to be. You were better then or I wouldn't have had anything to do with you.

She says, I loved you so much once. I loved you to the point of distraction. I did. More than anything in the whole wide world. Imagine that. What a laugh that is now. Can you imagine it? We were so *intimate* once upon a time I can't believe it now. I think that's the strangest thing of all now. The memory of being that intimate with somebody. We were so intimate I could puke. I can't imagine ever being that intimate with somebody else. I haven't been.

She says, Frankly, and I mean this, I want to be kept out of it from here on out. Who do you think you are anyway? You think you're God or somebody? You're not fit to lick God's boots, or anybody else's for that matter. Mister, you've been hanging out with the wrong people. But what do I know? I don't even know what I know any longer. I know I don't like what you've been dishing out. I know that much. You know what I'm talking about, don't you? Am I right?

Right, I say. Right as rain.

She says, You'll agree to anything, won't you? You give in too easy. You always did. You don't have any principles, not one. Anything to avoid a fuss. But that's neither here nor there.

She says, You remember that time I pulled the knife on you?

She says this as if in passing, as if it's not important.

Vaguely, I say. I must have deserved it, but I don't remember much about it. Go ahead, why don't you, and tell me about it.

She says, I'm beginning to understand something now. I think I know why you're here. Yes. I know why you're here, even if you don't. But you're a slyboots. You know why you're here. You're on a fishing expedition. You're hunting for *material*. Am I getting warm? Am I right?

Tell me about the knife, I say.

She says, If you want to know, I'm real sorry I didn't use that knife. I am. I really and truly am. I've thought and thought about it, and I'm sorry I didn't use it. I had the chance. But I hesitated. I hesitated and was lost, as somebody or other said. But I should have used it, the hell with everything and everybody. I should have nicked your arm with it at least. At least that.

Well, you didn't, I say. I thought you were going to cut me with it, but you didn't. I took it away from you.

She says, You were always lucky. You took it away and then you slapped me. Still, I regret I didn't use that knife just a little bit. Even a little would have been something to remember me by.

I remember a lot, I say. I say that, then wish I hadn't.

She says, Amen, brother. That's the bone of contention here, if you hadn't noticed. That's the whole problem. But like I said, in my opinion you remember the wrong things. You remember the low, shameful things. That's why you got interested when I brought up the knife.

She says, I wonder if you ever have any regret. For whatever that's worth on the market these days. Not much, I guess. But you ought to be a specialist in it by now.

Regret, I say. It doesn't interest me much, to tell the truth. Regret is not a word I use very often. I guess I mainly don't have it. I admit I hold to the dark view of things. Sometimes, anyway. But regret? I don't think so.

She says, You're a real son of a bitch, did you know that? A ruthless, coldhearted son of a bitch. Did anybody ever tell you that?

You did, I say. Plenty of times.

She says, I always speak the truth. Even when it hurts. You'll never catch me in a lie.

She says, My eyes were opened a long time ago, but by then it was too late. I had my chance but I let it slide through my fingers. I even thought for a while you'd come back. Why'd I think that anyway? I must have been out of my mind. I could cry my eyes out now, but I wouldn't give you that satisfaction.

She says, You know what? I think if you were on fire right now, if you suddenly burst into flame this minute, I wouldn't throw a bucket of water on you.

She laughs at this. Then her face closes down again.

She says, Why in hell *are* you here? You want to hear some more? I could go on for days. I think I know why you turned up, but I want to hear it from you.

When I don't answer, when I just keep sitting there, she goes on.

She says, After that time, when you went away, nothing much mattered after that. Not the kids, not God, not anything. It was like I didn't know what hit me. It was like I had *stopped living*. My life had been going along, going along, and then it just stopped. It didn't just come to a stop, it screeched to a stop. I

366

thought, If I'm not worth anything to him, well, I'm not worth anything to myself or anybody else either. That was the worst thing I felt. I thought my heart would break. What am I saying? It did break. Of course it broke. It broke, just like that. It's still broke, if you want to know. And so there you have it in a nutshell. My eggs in one basket, she says. A tisket, a tasket. All my rotten eggs in one basket.

She says, You found somebody else for yourself, didn't you? It didn't take long. And you're happy now. That's what they say about you anyway: "He's happy now." Hey, I read everything you send! You think I don't? Listen, I know your heart, mister. I always did. I knew it back then, and I know it now. I know your heart inside and out, and don't you ever forget it. Your heart is a jungle, a dark forest, it's a garbage pail, if you want to know. Let them talk to me if they want to ask somebody something. I know how you operate. Just let them come around here, and I'll give them an earful. I was there. I served, buddy boy. Then you held me up for display and ridicule in your so-called work. For any Tom or Harry to pity or pass judgment on. Ask me if I cared. Ask me if it embarrassed me. Go ahead, ask.

No, I say, I won't ask that. I don't want to get into that, I say.

Damn straight you don't! she says. And you know *why*, too!

She says, Honey, no offense, but sometimes I think I could shoot you and watch you kick.

She says, You can't look me in the eyes, can you?

She says, and this is exactly what she says, You can't even look me in the eyes when I'm talking to you.

So, okay, I look her in the eyes.

She says, Right. Okay, she says. Now we're getting someplace, maybe. That's better. You can tell a lot about the person you're talking to from his eyes. Everybody knows that. But you know something else? There's nobody in this whole world who would tell you this, but I can tell you. I have the right. I *earned* that right, sonny. You have yourself confused with somebody else. And that's the pure truth of it. But what do I know? they'll say in a hundred years. They'll say, Who was she anyway?

She says, In any case, you sure as hell have *me* confused with somebody else. Hey, I don't even have the same name anymore! Not the name I was born with, not the name I lived with you with, not even the name I had two years ago. What is this? What is this in hell all about anyway? Let me say something. I want to be left alone now. Please. That's not a crime.

She says, Don't you have someplace else you should be? Some plane to catch? Shouldn't you be somewhere far from here at this very minute?

No, I say. I say it again: No. No place, I say. I don't have anyplace I have to be.

And then I do something. I reach over and take the sleeve of her blouse between my thumb and forefinger. That's all. I just touch it that way, and then I just bring my hand back. She doesn't draw away. She doesn't move.

Then here's the thing I do next. I get down on my knees, a big guy like me, and I take the hem of her dress. What am I doing on the floor? I wish I could say. But I know it's where I ought to be, and I'm there on my knees holding on to the hem of her dress.

She is still for a minute. But in a minute she says, Hey, it's all right, stupid. You're so dumb, sometimes. Get up now. I'm telling you to get up. Listen, it's okay. I'm over it now. It took me a while to get over it. What do you think? Did you think it wouldn't? Then you walk in here and suddenly the whole cruddy business is back. I felt a need to ventilate. But you know, and I know, it's over and done with now.

She says, For the longest while, honey, I was inconsolable. *Inconsolable*, she says. Put that word in your little notebook. I can tell you from experience that's the saddest word in the English language. Anyway, I got over it finally. Time is a gentleman, a wise man said. Or else maybe a worn-out old woman, one or the other anyway.

She says, I have a life now. It's a different kind of life than yours, but I guess we don't need to compare. It's my life, and that's the important thing I have to realize as I get older. Don't feel *too* bad, anyway, she says. I mean, it's all right to feel a *little* bad, maybe. That won't hurt you, that's only to be expected after all. Even if you can't move yourself to regret.

She says, Now you have to get up and get out of here. My husband will be along pretty soon for his lunch. How would I explain this kind of thing?

It's crazy, but I'm still on my knees holding the hem of her dress. I won't let it go. I'm like a terrier, and it's like I'm stuck to the floor. It's like I can't move.

She says, Get up now. What is it? You still want something from me. What do you want? Want me to forgive you? Is that why you're doing this? That's it, isn't it? That's the reason you came all this way. The knife thing kind of perked you up, too. I think you'd forgotten about that. But you needed me to remind you. Okay, I'll say something if you'll just go.

She says, I forgive you.

She says, Are you satisfied now? Is that better? Are you happy? He's happy now, she says.

But I'm still there, knees to the floor.

She says, Did you hear what I said? You have to go now. Hey, stupid. Honey, I said I forgive you. And I even reminded you about the knife thing. I can't think what else I can do now. You got it made in the shade, baby. Come *on* now, you have to get out of here. Get up. That's right. You're still a big guy, aren't you. Here's your hat, don't forget your hat. You never used to wear a hat. I never in my life saw you in a hat before.

She says, Listen to me now. Look at me. Listen carefully to what I'm going to tell you.

She moves closer. She's about three inches from my face. We haven't been this close in a long time. I take these little breaths that she can't hear, and I wait. I think my heart slows way down, I think.

She says, You just tell it like you have to, I guess, and forget the rest. Like always. You been doing that for so long now anyway it shouldn't be hard for you.

She says, There, I've done it. You're free, aren't you? At least you think you are anyway. Free at last. That's a joke, but don't laugh. Anyway, you feel better, don't you?

She walks with me down the hall.

She says, I can't imagine how I'd explain this if my husband was to walk in this very minute. But who really cares anymore, right? In the final analysis, nobody gives a damn anymore. Besides which, I think everything that can happen that way has already happened. His name is Fred, by the way. He's a decent guy and works hard for his living. He cares for me.

So she walks me to the front door, which has been standing open all this while. The door that was letting in light and fresh air this morning, and sounds off the street, all of which we had ignored. I look outside and, Jesus, there's this white moon hanging in the morning sky. I can't think when I've ever seen anything so remarkable. But I'm afraid to comment on it. I am. I don't know what might happen. I might break into tears even. I might not understand a word I'd say.

She says, Maybe you'll be back sometime, and maybe you won't. This'll wear off, you know. Pretty soon you'll start feeling bad again. Maybe it'll make a good story, she says. But I don't want to know about it if it does.

I say good-bye. She doesn't say anything more. She looks at her hands, and then she puts them into the pockets of her dress. She shakes her head. She goes back inside, and this time she closes the door.

I move off down the sidewalk. Some kids are tossing a football at the end of the street. But they aren't my kids, and they aren't her kids either. There are these leaves everywhere, even in the gutters. Piles of leaves wherever I look. They're falling off the limbs as I walk. I can't take a step without putting my shoe into leaves. Somebody ought to make an effort here. Somebody ought to get a rake and take care of this.

Menudo

I can't sleep, but when I'm sure my wife Vicky is asleep, I get up and look through our bedroom window, across the street, at Oliver and Amanda's house. Oliver has been gone for three days, but his wife Amanda is awake. She can't sleep either. It's four in the morning, and there's not a sound outside – no wind, no cars, no moon even – just Oliver and Amanda's place with the lights on, leaves heaped up under the front windows.

A couple of days ago, when I couldn't sit still, I raked our yard – Vicky's and mine. I gathered all the leaves into bags, tied off the tops, and put the bags alongside the curb. I had an urge then to cross the street and rake over there, but I didn't follow through. It's my fault things are the way they are across the street.

I've only slept a few hours since Oliver left. Vicky saw me moping around the house, looking anxious, and decided to put two and two together. She's on her side of the bed now, scrunched on to about ten inches of mattress. She got into bed and tried to position herself so she wouldn't accidentally roll into me while she slept. She hasn't moved since she lay down, sobbed, and then dropped into sleep. She's exhausted. I'm exhausted too.

I've taken nearly all of Vicky's pills, but I still can't sleep. I'm keyed up. But maybe if I keep looking I'll catch a glimpse of Amanda moving around inside her house, or else find her peering from behind a curtain, trying to see what she can see over here.

What if I do see her? So what? What then?

Vicky says I'm crazy. She said worse things too last night. But who could blame her? I told her – I had to – but I didn't tell her it was Amanda. When Amanda's name came up, I insisted it wasn't her. Vicky suspects, but I wouldn't name names. I wouldn't say who, even though she kept pressing and then hit me a few times in the head.

"What's it matter *who*?" I said. "You've never met the woman," I lied. "You don't know her." That's when she started hitting me.

I feel *wired*. That's what my painter friend Alfredo used to call it when he talked about friends of his coming down off something. *Wired*. I'm wired.

This thing is nuts. I know it is, but I can't stop thinking about Amanda. Things are so bad just now I even find myself thinking about my first wife, Molly. I loved Molly, I thought, more than my own life.

I keep picturing Amanda in her pink nightgown, the one I like on her so much, along with her pink slippers. And I feel certain she's in the big leather chair right now, under the brass reading lamp. She's smoking cigarettes, one after the other. There are two ashtrays close at hand, and they're both full. To the left of her chair, next to the lamp, there's an end table stacked with magazines – the usual magazines that nice people read. We're nice people, all of us, to a point. Right this minute, Amanda is, I imagine, paging through a magazine, stopping every so often to look at an illustration or a cartoon.

Two days ago, in the afternoon, Amanda said to me, "I can't read books anymore. Who has the time?" It was the day after Oliver had left, and we were in this little café in the industrial part of the city. "Who can concentrate anymore?" she said, stirring her coffee. "Who reads? Do you read?" (I shook my head.) "Somebody must read, I guess. You see all these books around in store windows, and there are those clubs. Somebody's reading," she said. "Who? I don't know anybody who reads."

That's what she said, apropos of nothing – that is, we weren't talking about books, we were talking about our *lives*. Books had nothing to do with it.

"What did Oliver say when you told him?"

Then it struck me that what we were saying – the tense, watchful expressions we wore – belonged to the people on afternoon TV programs that I'd never done more than switch on and then off.

Amanda looked down and shook her head, as if she couldn't bear to remember.

"You didn't admit who it was you were involved with, did you?"

She shook her head again.

"You're sure of that?" I waited until she looked up from her coffee.

"I didn't mention any names, if that's what you mean."

"Did he say where he was going, or how long he'd be away?" I said, wishing I didn't have to hear myself. This was my neighbor I was talking about. Oliver Porter. A man I'd helped drive out of his home.

"He didn't say where. A hotel. He said I should make my arrangements and be gone – *be gone*, he said. It was like biblical the way he said it – out of his house, out of his *life*, in a week's time. I guess he's coming back then. So we have to decide something real important, real soon, honey. You and I have to make up our minds pretty damn quick."

It was her turn to look at me now, and I know she was looking for a sign of lifelong commitment. "A week," I said. I looked at my coffee, which had gotten cold. A lot had happened in a little while, and we were trying to take it in. I don't know what long-term things, if any, we'd thought about those months as we moved from flirtation to love, and then afternoon assignations. In any case, we were in a serious fix now. Very serious. We'd never expected – not in a hundred years – to be hiding out in a café, in the middle of the afternoon, trying to decide matters like this.

I raised my eyes, and Amanda began stirring her coffee. She kept stirring it. I touched her hand, and the spoon dropped out of her fingers. She picked it up and began stirring again. We could have been anybody drinking coffee at a table under fluorescent lights in a run-down café. Anybody, just about. I took Amanda's hand and held it, and it seemed to make a difference.

Vicky's still sleeping on her side when I go downstairs. I plan to heat some milk and drink that. I used to drink whiskey when I couldn't sleep, but I gave it up. Now it's strictly hot milk. In the whiskey days I'd wake up with this tremendous thirst in the middle of the night. But, back then, I was always looking ahead: I kept a bottle of water in the fridge, for instance. I'd be dehydrated, sweating from head to toe when I woke, but I'd wander out to the kitchen and could count on finding that bottle of cold water in the fridge. I'd drink it, all of it, down the hatch, an entire quart of water. Once in a while I'd use a glass, but not often. Suddenly I'd be drunk all over again and weaving around the kitchen. I can't begin to account for it – sober one minute, drunk the next.

The drinking was part of my destiny – according to Molly, anyway. She put a lot of stock in destiny.

I feel wild from lack of sleep. I'd give anything, just about, to be able to go to sleep, and sleep the sleep of an honest man.

Why do we have to sleep anyway? And why do we tend to sleep less during some crises and more during others? For instance, that time my dad had his stroke. He woke up after a coma – seven days and nights in a hospital bed – and calmly said "Hello" to the people in his room. Then his eyes picked me out. "Hello, son," he said. Five minutes later, he died. Just like that – he died. But, during that whole crisis, I never took my clothes off and didn't go to bed. I may have catnapped in a waiting-room chair from time to time, but I never went to bed and *slept*.

And then a year or so ago I found out Vicky was seeing somebody else. Instead of confronting *her*, I went to bed when I heard about it, and stayed there. I didn't get up for days, a week maybe – I don't know. I mean, I got up to go to the bathroom, or else to the kitchen to make a sandwich. I even went out to the living room in my pajamas, in the afternoon, and tried to read the papers. But I'd fall asleep sitting up. Then I'd stir, open my eyes and go back to bed and sleep some more. I couldn't get enough sleep.

It passed. We weathered it. Vicky quit her boyfriend, or he quit her, I never found out. I just know she went away from me for a while, and then she came back. But I have the feeling we're not going to weather this business. This thing is different. Oliver has given Amanda that ultimatum.

374

Still, isn't it possible that Oliver himself is awake at this moment and writing a letter to Amanda, urging reconciliation? Even now he might be scribbling away, trying to persuade her that what she's doing to him and their daughter Beth is foolish, disastrous, and finally a tragic thing for the three of them.

No, that's insane. I know Oliver. He's relentless, unforgiving. He could slam a croquet ball into the next block – and has. He isn't going to write any such letter. He gave her an ultimatum, right? – and that's that. A week. Four days now. Or is it three? Oliver may be awake, but if he is, he's sitting in a chair in his hotel room with a glass of iced vodka in his hand, his feet on the bed, TV turned on low. He's dressed, except for his shoes. He's not wearing shoes – that's the only concession he makes. That and the fact he's loosened his tie.

Oliver is relentless.

I heat the milk, spoon the skin from the surface and pour it up. Then I turn off the kitchen light and take the cup into the living room and sit on the sofa, where I can look across the street at the lighted windows. But I can hardly sit still. I keep fidgeting, crossing one leg and then the other. I feel like I could throw off sparks, or break a window – maybe rearrange all the furniture.

The things that go through your mind when you can't sleep! Earlier, thinking about Molly, for a moment I couldn't even remember what she *looked* like, for Christ's sake, yet we were together for years, more or less continuously, since we were kids. Molly, who said she'd love me forever. The only thing left was the memory of her sitting and weeping at the kitchen table, her shoulders bent forward, and her hands covering her face. *Forever*, she said. But it hadn't worked out that way. Finally, she said, it didn't matter, it was of no real concern to her, if she and I lived together the rest of our lives or not. Our love existed on a "higher plane". That's what she said to Vicky over the phone that time, after Vicky and I had set up housekeeping together. Molly called, got hold of Vicky, and said, "You have your relationship with him, but I'll always have mine. His destiny and mine are linked."

My first wife, Molly, she talked like that. "Our destinies are linked." She didn't talk like that in the beginning. It was only later, after so much had happened, that she started using words like "cosmic" and "empowerment" and so forth. But our destinies are *not* linked – not now, anyway, if they ever were. I don't even know where she is now, not for certain.

I think I could put my finger on the exact time, the real turning point, when it came undone for Molly. It was after I started seeing Vicky, and Molly found out. They called me up one day from the high school where Molly taught and said, "Please. Your wife is doing handsprings in front of the school. You'd better get down here." It was after I took her home that I began hearing about "higher power" and "going with the flow" – stuff of that sort. Our destiny had been "revised". And if I'd been hesitating before, well, I left her then as fast as I could – this woman I'd known all my life, the one who'd been my best friend for years, my intimate, my confidante. I bailed out on her. For one thing, I was scared. *Scared.*

This girl I'd started out with in life, this sweet thing, this gentle soul, she wound up going to fortune-tellers, palm readers, *crystal ball gazers*, looking for answers, trying to figure out what she should do with her life. She quit her job, drew out her teacher's retirement money, and thereafter never made a decision without consulting the *I Ching*. She began wearing strange clothes – clothes with permanent wrinkles and a lot of burgundy and orange. She even got involved with a group that sat around, I'm not kidding, trying to levitate.

When Molly and I were growing up together, she was a part of me and, sure, I was a part of her, too. We loved each other. It *was* our destiny. I believed in it then myself. But now I don't know what to believe in. I'm not complaining, simply stating a fact. I'm down to nothing. And I have to go on like this. No destiny. Just the next thing meaning whatever you think it does. Compulsion and error, just like everybody else.

Amanda? I'd like to believe in her, bless her heart. But she was looking for somebody when she met me. That's the way with people when they get restless: they start up something, knowing that's going to change things for good.

I'd like to go out in the front yard and shout something. "None of this is worth it!" That's what I'd like people to hear.

"Destiny," Molly said. For all I know she's still talking about it.

All the lights are off over there now, except for that light in the kitchen. I could try calling Amanda on the phone. I could do that and see how far it gets me! What if Vicky heard me dialing or talking on the phone and came downstairs? What if she lifted the receiver upstairs and listened? Besides, there's always the chance Beth might pick up the phone. I don't want to talk to any kids this morning. I don't want to talk to anybody. Actually, I'd talk to Molly, if I could, but I can't any longer – she's somebody else now. She isn't *Molly* anymore. But – what can I say? – I'm somebody else, too.

I wish I could be like everybody else in this neighborhood – your basic, normal, unaccomplished person – and go up to my bedroom, and lie down, and sleep. It's going to be a big day today, and I'd like to be ready for it. I wish I could sleep and wake up and find everything in my life different – not necessarily just the big things, like this thing with Amanda or the past with Molly. But things clearly within my power.

Take the situation with my mother: I used to send money every month. But then I started sending her the same amount in twice-yearly sums. I gave her money on her birthday, and I gave her money at Christmas. I thought: I won't have to worry about forgetting her birthday, and I won't have to worry about sending her a Christmas present. I won't have to worry, period. It went like clockwork for a long time.

Then last year she asked me – it was in between money times, it was in March, or maybe April – for a radio. A radio, she said, would make a difference to her.

What she wanted was a little clock radio. She could put it in her kitchen and have it out there to listen to while she was fixing something to eat in the evening. And she'd have the clock to look at too, so she'd know when something was supposed to come out of the oven, or how long it was until one of her programs started.

A little clock radio.

She hinted around at first. She said, "I'd sure like to have a radio. But I can't afford one. I guess I'll have to wait for my birthday. That little radio I had, it fell and broke. I miss a radio." *I miss a radio*. That's what she said when we talked on the phone, or else she'd bring it up when she'd write.

Finally — what'd I say? I said to her over the phone that I couldn't afford any radios. I said it in a letter too, so she'd be sure and understand. *I can't afford any radios*, is what I wrote. I can't do any more, I said, than I'm doing. Those were my very words.

But it wasn't true! I could have done more. I just said I couldn't. I could have afforded to buy a radio for her. What would it have cost me? Thirty-five dollars? Forty dollars or less, including tax. I could have sent her a radio through the mail. I could have had somebody in the store do it, if I didn't want to go to the trouble myself. Or else I could have sent her a forty-dollar check along with a note saying, *This money is for your radio, Mother*.

I could have handled it in any case. Forty dollars — are you kidding? But I didn't. I wouldn't part with it. It seemed there was a *principle* involved. That's what I told myself anyway — there's a principle involved here.

Ha.

Then what happened? She died. She *died*. She was walking home from the grocery store, back to her apartment, carrying her sack of groceries, and she fell into somebody's bushes and died.

I took a flight out there to make the arrangements. She was still at the coroner's, and they had her purse and her groceries behind the desk in the office. I didn't bother to look in the purse they handed me. But what she had from the grocery store was a jar of Metamucil, two grapefruits, a carton of cottage cheese, a quart of buttermilk, some potatoes and onions, and a package of ground meat that was beginning to change color.

Boy! I cried when I saw those things. I couldn't stop. I didn't

think I'd ever quit crying. The woman who worked at the desk
was embarrassed and brought me a glass of water. They gave
me a bag for my mother's groceries and another bag for her
personal effects – her purse and her dentures. Later, I put the
dentures in my coat pocket and drove them down in a rental car
and gave them to somebody at the funeral home.

The light in Amanda's kitchen is still on. It's a bright light that spills
out on to all those leaves. Maybe she's like I am, and she's scared.
Maybe she left that light burning as a night-light. Or maybe she's
still awake and is at the kitchen table, under the light, writing me
a letter. Amanda is writing me a letter, and somehow she'll get it
into my hands later on when the real day starts.

Come to think of it, I've never had a letter from her since
we've known each other. All the time we've been involved – six
months, eight months – and I've never once seen a scrap of her
handwriting. I don't even know if she's *literate* that way.

I think she is. Sure, she is. She talks about books, doesn't she?
It doesn't matter, of course. Well, a little, I suppose. I love her
in any case, right?

But I've never written anything to her, either. We always
talked on the phone or else face to face.

Molly, she was the letter writer. She used to write me even
after we weren't living together. Vicky would bring her letters
in from the box and leave them on the kitchen table without a
word. Finally the letters dwindled away, became more and more
infrequent and bizarre. When she did write, the letters gave me
a chill. They were full of talk about "auras" and "signs".
Occasionally she reported a voice that was telling her something
she ought to do or some place she should go. And once she told
me that no matter what happened, we were still "on the same
frequency". She always knew exactly what I felt, she said. She
"beamed in on me", she said, from time to time. Reading those
letters of hers, the hair on the back of my neck would tingle. She
also had a new word for destiny: *Karma*. "I'm following out my
karma," she wrote. "Your karma has taken a bad turn."

*

I'd like to go to sleep, but what's the point? People will be getting up soon. Vicky's alarm will go off before much longer. I wish I could go upstairs and get back in bed with my wife, tell her I'm sorry, there's been a mistake, let's forget all this – then go to sleep and wake up with her in my arms. But I've forfeited that right. I'm outside all that now, and I can't get back inside! But say I did that. Say I went upstairs and slid into bed with Vicky as I'd like to do. She might wake up and say, *You bastard. Don't you dare touch me, son of a bitch.*

What's she talking about, anyway? I wouldn't touch her. Not in that way, I wouldn't.

After I left Molly, after I'd pulled out on her, about two months after, then Molly really did it. She had her real collapse then, the one that'd been coming on. Her sister saw to it that she got the care she needed. What am I saying? *They put her away.* They had to, they said. They put my wife away. By then I was living with Vicky, and trying not to drink whiskey. I couldn't do anything for Molly. I mean, she was there, I was here, and I couldn't have gotten her out of that place if I'd wanted to. But the fact is, I didn't want to. She was in there, they said, because she *needed* to be in there. Nobody said anything about destiny. Things had gone beyond that.

And I didn't even go visit her – not once! At the time, I didn't think I could stand seeing her in there. But, Christ, what was I? A fair-weather friend? We'd been through plenty. But what on earth would I have said to her? *I'm sorry about all this, honey.* I could have said that, I guess. I intended to write, but I didn't. Not a word. Anyway, when you get right down to it, what could I have said in a letter? *How are they treating you, baby? I'm sorry you're where you are, but don't give up. Remember all the good times? Remember when we were happy together? Hey, I'm sorry they've done this to you. I'm sorry it turned out this way. I'm sorry everything is just garbage now.* I'm sorry, Molly.

I didn't write. I think I was trying to forget about her, to pretend she didn't exist. Molly who?

I left my wife and took somebody else's: Vicky. Now I think maybe I've lost Vicky, too. But Vicky won't be going away to any summer camp for the mentally disabled. She's a hard case. She left her former husband, Joe Kraft, and didn't bat an eye; I don't think she ever lost a night's sleep over it.

Vicky Kraft-Hughes. Amanda Porter. This is where my destiny has brought me? To this street in this neighborhood, messing up the lives of these women?

Amanda's kitchen light went off when I wasn't looking. The room that was there is gone now, like the others. Only the porch light is still burning. Amanda must have forgotten it, I guess. Hey, Amanda.

Once, when Molly was away in that place and I wasn't in my right mind – let's face it, I was crazy too – one night I was at my friend Alfredo's house, a bunch of us drinking and listening to records. I didn't care any longer what happened to me. Everything, I thought, that could happen had happened. I felt unbalanced. I felt lost. Anyway, there I was at Alfredo's. His paintings of tropical birds and animals hung on every wall in his house, and there were paintings standing around in the rooms, leaning against things – table-legs, say, or his brick-and-board bookcase, as well as being stacked on his back porch. The kitchen served as his studio, and I was sitting at the kitchen table with a drink in front of me. An easel stood off to one side in front of the window that overlooked the alley, and there were crumpled tubes of paint, a palette, and some brushes lying at one end of the table. Alfredo was making himself a drink at the counter a few feet away. I loved the shabby economy of that little room. The stereo music that came from the living room was turned up, filling the house with so much sound the kitchen windows rattled in their frames. Suddenly I began to shake. First my hands began to shake, and then my arms and shoulders, too. My teeth started to chatter. I couldn't hold the glass.

"What's going on, man?" Alfredo said, when he turned and saw the state I was in. "Hey, what is it? What's going on with you?"

I couldn't tell him. What could I say? I thought I was having some kind of an attack. I managed to raise my shoulders and let them drop.

Then Alfredo came over, took a chair and sat down beside me at the kitchen table. He put his big painter's hand on my shoulder. I went on shaking. He could feel me shaking.

"What's wrong with you, man? I'm real sorry about everything, man. I know it's real hard right now." Then he said he was going to fix *menudo* for me. He said it would be good for what ailed me. "Help your nerves, man," he said. "Calm you right down." He had all the ingredients for *menudo*, he said, and he'd been wanting to make some anyway.

"You listen to me. Listen to what I say, man. I'm your family now," Alfredo said.

It was two in the morning, we were drunk, there were these other drunk people in the house and the stereo was going full blast. But Alfredo went to his fridge and opened it and took some stuff out. He closed the fridge door and looked in his freezer compartment. He found something in a package. Then he looked around in his cupboards. He took a big pan from the cabinet under the sink, and he was ready.

Tripe. He started with tripe and about a gallon of water. Then he chopped onions and added them to the water, which had started to boil. He put *chorizo* sausage in the pot. After that, he dropped peppercorns into the boiling water and sprinkled in some chili powder. Then came the olive oil. He opened a big can of tomato sauce and poured that in. He added cloves of garlic, some slices of white bread, salt, and lemon juice. He opened another can – it was hominy – and poured that in the pot, too. He put it all in, and then he turned the heat down and put a lid on the pot.

I watched him. I sat there shaking while Alfredo stood at the stove making *menudo*, talking – I didn't have any idea what he was saying – and, from time to time, he'd shake his head, or else start whistling to himself. Now and then people drifted into the kitchen for beer. But all the while Alfredo went on very seriously looking after his *menudo*. He could have been home, in Morelia, making *menudo* for his family on New Year's day.

People hung around in the kitchen for a while, joking, but Alfredo didn't joke back when they kidded him about cooking *menudo* in the middle of the night. Pretty soon they left us alone. Finally, while Alfredo stood at the stove with a spoon in his hand, watching me, I got up slowly from the table. I walked out of the kitchen into the bathroom, and then opened another door off the bathroom to the spare room – where I lay down on the bed and fell asleep. When I woke it was mid-afternoon. The *menudo* was gone. The pot was in the sink, soaking. Those other people must have eaten it! They must have eaten it and grown calm. Everyone was gone, and the house was quiet.

I never saw Alfredo more than once or twice afterward. After that night, our lives took us in separate directions. And those other people who were there – who knows where they went? I'll probably die without ever tasting *menudo*. But who can say?

Is this what it all comes down to then? A middle-aged man involved with his neighbor's wife, linked to an angry ultimatum? What kind of destiny is that? A week, Oliver said. Three or four days now.

A car passes outside with its lights on. The sky is turning gray, and I hear some birds starting up. I decide I can't wait any longer. I can't just sit here, doing nothing – that's all there is to it. I can't keep waiting. I've waited and waited and where's it gotten me? Vicky's alarm will go off soon, Beth will get up and dress for school, Amanda will wake up, too. The entire neighborhood.

On the back porch I find some old jeans and a sweatshirt, and I change out of my pajamas. Then I put on my white canvas shoes – "wino" shoes, Alfredo would have called them. Alfredo, where are you?

I go outside to the garage and find the rake and some lawn bags. By the time I get around to the front of the house with the rake, ready to begin, I feel I don't have a choice in the matter any longer. It's light out – light enough at any rate for what I have to do. And then, without thinking about it any more, I start to rake. I rake our yard, every inch of it. It's important it be done right, too. I set the rake right down into the turf and pull hard.

It must feel to the grass like it does whenever someone gives your hair a hard jerk. Now and then a car passes in the street and slows, but I don't look up from my work. I know what the people in the cars must be thinking, but they're dead wrong – they don't know the half of it. How could they? I'm happy, raking.

I finish our yard and put the bag out next to the curb. Then I begin next door on the Baxters' yard. In a few minutes Mrs Baxter comes out on her porch, wearing her bathrobe. I don't acknowledge her. I'm not embarrassed, and I don't want to appear unfriendly. I just want to keep on with what I'm doing.

She doesn't say anything for a while, and then she says, "Good morning, Mr Hughes. How are you this morning?"

I stop what I'm doing and run my arm across my forehead. "I'll be through in a little while," I say. "I hope you don't mind."

"We don't mind," Mrs Baxter says. "Go right ahead, I guess." I see Mr Baxter standing in the doorway behind her. He's already dressed for work in his slacks and sports coat and tie. But he doesn't venture onto the porch. Then Mrs Baxter turns and looks at Mr Baxter, who shrugs.

It's okay, I've finished here anyway. There are other yards, more important yards for that matter. I kneel, and, taking a grip low down on the rake handle, I pull the last of the leaves into my bag and tie off the top. Then, I can't help it, I just stay there, kneeling on the grass with the rake in my hand. When I look up, I see the Baxters come down the porch steps together and move slowly toward me through the wet, sweet-smelling grass. They stop a few feet away and look at me closely.

"There now," I hear Mrs Baxter say. She's still in her robe and slippers. It's nippy out; she holds her robe at the throat. "You did a real fine job for us, yes, you did."

I don't say anything. I don't even say, "You're welcome."

They stand in front of me a while longer, and none of us says anything more. It's as if we've come to an agreement on something. In a minute, they turn around and go back to their house. High over my head, in the branches of the old maple –

the place where these leaves come from – birds call out to each other. At least I think they're calling to each other.

Suddenly a car door slams. Mr Baxter is in his car in the drive with the window rolled down. Mrs Baxter says something to him from the front porch which causes Mr Baxter to nod slowly and turn his head in my direction. He sees me kneeling there with the rake, and a look crosses his face. He frowns. In his better moments, Mr Baxter is a decent, ordinary guy – a guy you wouldn't mistake for anyone special. But he *is* special. In my book, he is. For one thing he has a full night's sleep behind him, and he's just embraced his wife before leaving for work. But even before he goes, he's already expected home a set number of hours later. True, in the grander scheme of things, his return will be an event of small moment – but an event nonetheless.

Baxter starts his car and races the engine. Then he backs effortlessly out of the drive, brakes, and changes gears. As he passes on the street, he slows and looks briefly in my direction. He lifts his hand off the steering wheel. It could be a salute or a sign of dismissal. It's a sign, in any case. And then he looks away toward the city. I get up and raise my hand, too – not a wave, exactly, but close to it. Some other cars drive past. One of the drivers must think he knows me because he gives his horn a friendly little tap. I look both ways and then cross the street.

Elephant

I knew it was a mistake to let my brother have the money. I didn't need anybody else owing me. But when he called and said he couldn't make the payment on his house, what could I do? I'd never been inside his house – he lived a thousand miles away, in California; I'd never even *seen* his house – but I didn't want him to lose it. He cried over the phone and said he was losing everything he'd worked for. He said he'd pay me back. February, he said. Maybe sooner. No later, anyway, than March. He said his income-tax refund was on the way. Plus, he said, he had a little investment that would mature in February. He acted secretive about the investment thing, so I didn't press for details.

"Trust me on this," he said. "I won't let you down."

He'd lost his job last July, when the company he worked for, a fiberglass-insulation plant, decided to lay off two hundred employees. He'd been living on his unemployment since then, but now the unemployment was gone, and his savings were gone, too. And he didn't have health insurance any longer. When his job went, the insurance went. His wife, who was ten years older, was diabetic and needed treatment. He'd had to sell the other car – her car, an old station wagon – and a week ago he'd pawned his TV. He told me he'd hurt his back carrying the TV up and down the street where the pawnshops did business. He went from place to place, he said, trying to get the best offer. Somebody finally gave him a hundred dollars for it, this big Sony TV. He told me about the TV, and then about throwing his back out, as if this ought to cinch it with me, unless I had a stone in place of a heart.

"I've gone belly up," he said. "But you can help me pull out of it."

"How much?" I said.

386

"Five hundred. I could use more, sure, who couldn't?" he said. "But I want to be realistic. I can pay back five hundred. More than that, I'll tell you the truth, I'm not so sure. Brother, I hate to ask. But you're my last resort. Irma Jean and I are going to be on the street before long. I won't let you down," he said. That's what he said. Those were his exact words.

We talked a little more – mostly about our mother and her problems – but, to make a long story short, I sent him the money. I had to. I felt I had to, at any rate – which amounts to the same thing. I wrote him a letter when I sent the check and said he should pay the money back to our mother, who lived in the same town he lived in and who was poor and greedy. I'd been mailing checks to her every month, rain or shine, for three years. But I was thinking that if he paid her the money he owed me it might take me off the hook there and let me breathe for a while. I wouldn't have to worry on that score for a couple of months, anyway. Also, and this is the truth, I thought maybe he'd be more likely to pay her, since they lived right there in the same town and he saw her from time to time. All I was doing was trying to cover myself some way. The thing is, he might have the best intentions of paying me back, but things happen sometimes. Things get in the way of best intentions. Out of sight, out of mind, as they say. But he wouldn't stiff his own mother. Nobody would do that.

I spent hours writing letters, trying to make sure everybody knew what could be expected and what was required. I even phoned out there to my mother several times, trying to explain it to her. But she was suspicious over the whole deal. I went through it with her on the phone step by step, but she was still suspicious. I told her the money that was supposed to come from me on the first of March and on the first of April would instead come from Billy, who owed the money to me. She'd get her money, and she didn't have to worry. The only difference was that Billy would pay it to her those two months instead of me. He'd pay her the money I'd normally be sending to her, but instead of him mailing it to me and then me having to turn around and send it to her he'd pay it to her directly. On any account, she didn't have to worry. She'd get her money, but for those two months it'd come from him – from the money he owed me. My God, I don't know how much I spent on phone calls. And I wish I had fifty cents for every letter I wrote, telling him what I'd told her and telling her what to expect from him – that sort of thing.

But my mother didn't trust Billy. "What if he can't come up with it?" she said to me over the phone. "What then? He's in bad shape, and I'm sorry for him," she said. "But, son, what I want to know is, what if he isn't able to pay me? What if he can't? Then what?"

"Then I'll pay you myself," I said. "Just like always. If he doesn't pay you, I'll pay you. But he'll pay you. Don't worry. He says he will, and he will."

"I don't want to worry," she said. "But I worry anyway. I worry about my boys, and after that I worry about myself. I never thought I'd see one of my boys in this shape. I'm just glad your dad isn't alive to see it."

In three months my brother gave her fifty dollars of what he owed me and was supposed to pay to her. Or maybe it was seventy-five dollars he gave her. There are conflicting stories – two conflicting stories, his and hers. But that's all he paid her of the five hundred – fifty dollars or else seventy-five dollars, according to whose story you want to listen to. I had to make up the rest to her. I had to keep shelling out, same as always. My brother was finished. That's what he told me – that he was finished – when I called to see what was up, after my mother had phoned, looking for her money.

My mother said, "I made the mailman go back and check inside his truck, to see if your letter might have fallen down behind the seat. Then I went around and asked the neighbors did they get any of my mail by mistake. I'm going crazy with worry about this situation, honey." Then she said, "What's a mother supposed to think?" Who was looking out for her best interests in this business? She wanted to know that, and she wanted to know when she could expect her money.

So that's when I got on the phone to my brother to see if this was just a simple delay or a full-fledged collapse. But, according to Billy, he was a goner. He was absolutely done for. He was putting his house on the market immediately. He just hoped he hadn't waited too long to try and move it. And there wasn't anything left inside the house that he could sell. He'd sold off everything except the kitchen table and chairs. "I wish I could sell my blood," he said. "But who'd buy it? With my luck, I probably have an incurable disease." And, naturally, the invest- ment thing hadn't worked out. When I asked him about it over the phone, all he said was that it hadn't materialized. His tax refund didn't make it, either – the I.R.S. had some kind of lien on his return. "When it rains it pours," he said. "I'm sorry, brother. I didn't mean for this to happen."

"I understand," I said. And I did. But it didn't make it any easier. Anyway, one thing and the other, I didn't get my money from him, and neither did my mother. I had to keep on sending her money every month.

I was sore, yes. Who wouldn't be? My heart went out to him, and I wished trouble hadn't knocked on his door. But my own back was against the wall now. At least, though, whatever hap- pens to him from here on, he won't come back to me for more money – seeing as how he still owes me. Nobody would do that to you. That's how I figured, anyway. But that's how little I knew.

I kept my nose to the grindstone. I got up early every morning and went to work and worked hard all day. When I came home I plopped into the big chair and just sat there. I was so tired it took me a while to get around to unlacing my shoes. Then I just went on sitting there. I was too tired to even get up and turn on the TV.

I was sorry about my brother's troubles. But I had troubles of my own. In addition to my mother, I had several other people on my payroll. I had a former wife I was sending money to every month. I had to do that. I didn't want to, but the court said I had to. And I had a daughter with two kids in Bellingham, and I had to send her something every month. Her kids had to eat, didn't they? She was living with a swine who wouldn't even *look* for work, a guy who couldn't hold a job if they handed him one. The time or two he did find something, he overslept, or his car broke down on the way in to work, or else he'd just be let go, no explanation, and that was that.

Once, long ago, when I used to think like a man about these things, I threatened to kill that guy. But that's neither here nor there. Besides, I was drinking in those days. In any case, the bastard is still hanging around.

My daughter would write these letters and say how they were living on oatmeal, she and her kids. (I guess he was starving, too, but she knew better than to mention that guy's name in her letters to me.) She'd tell me that if I could just carry her until summer things would pick up for her. Things would turn around for her, she was sure, in the summer. If nothing else worked out – but she was sure it would; she had several irons in the fire – she could always get a job in the fish cannery that was not far from where she lived. She'd wear rubber boots and rubber clothes and gloves and pack salmon into cans. Or else she might sell root beer from a vending stand beside the road to people who lined up in their cars at the border, waiting to get into Canada. People sitting in their cars in the middle of summer were going to be thirsty, right? They were going to be crying out for cold drinks. Anyway, one thing or the other, whatever line of work she decided on, she'd do fine in the summer. She just had to make it until then, and that's where I came in.

My daughter said she knew she had to change her life. She wanted to stand on her own two feet like everyone else. She wanted to quit looking at herself as a victim. "I'm not a victim," she said to me over the phone one night. "I'm just a young woman with two kids and a son-of-a-bitch bum who lives with me. No different from lots of other women. I'm not afraid of hard work. Just give me a chance. That's all I ask of the world." She said she could do without for herself. But until her break came, until opportunity knocked, it was the kids she worried about. The kids were always asking her when Grandpop was going to visit, she said. Right this minute they were drawing pictures of the swing sets and swimming pool at the motel I'd stayed in when I'd visited a year ago. But summer was the thing, she said. If she could make it until summer, her troubles would be over. Things would change then – she knew they would. And with a little help from me she could make it. "I don't know what I'd do without you, Dad." That's what she said. It nearly broke my heart. Sure I had to help her. I was glad to be even halfway in a position to help her. I had a job, didn't I? Compared to her and everyone else in my family, I had it made. Compared to the rest, I lived on Easy Street.

I sent the money she asked for. I sent money every time she asked. And then I told her I thought it'd be simpler if I just sent a sum of money, not a whole lot, but money even so, on the first of each month. It would be money she could count on, and it would be *her* money, no one else's – hers and the kids'. That's what I hoped for, anyway. I wished there was some way I could be sure the bastard who lived with her couldn't get his hands on so much as an orange or a piece of bread that my money bought. But I couldn't. I just had to go ahead and send the money and stop worrying about whether he'd soon be tucking into a plate of my eggs and biscuits.

My mother and my daughter and my former wife. That's three people on the payroll right there, not counting my brother. But my son needed money, too. After he graduated from high school, he packed his things, left his mother's house, and went to a college back East. A college in New Hampshire, of all places. Who's ever heard of New Hampshire? But he was the first kid in the family, on either side of the family, to even *want* to go to college, so everybody thought it was a good idea. I thought so, too, at first. How'd I know it was going to wind up costing me an arm and a leg? He borrowed left and right from the banks to keep himself going. He didn't want to have to work a job and go to school at the same time. That's what he said. And, sure, I guess I can understand it. In a way, I can even sympathize. Who likes to work? I don't. But after he'd borrowed everything he could, everything in sight, including enough to finance a junior year in Germany, I had to begin sending him money, and a lot of it. When, finally, I said I couldn't send any more, he wrote back and said if that was the case, if that was really the way I felt, he was going to deal drugs or else rob a bank – whatever he had to do to get money to live on. I'd be lucky if he wasn't shot or sent to prison.

I wrote back and said I'd changed my mind and I could send him a little more after all. What else could I do? I didn't want his blood on my hands. I didn't want to think of my kid being packed off to prison, or something even worse. I had plenty on my conscience as it was.

That's four people, right? Not counting my brother, who wasn't a regular yet. I was going crazy with it. I worried night and day. I couldn't sleep over it. I was paying out nearly as much money every month as I was bringing in. You don't have to be a genius, or know anything about economics, to understand that this state of affairs couldn't keep on. I had to get a loan to keep up my end of things. That was another monthly payment.

So I started cutting back. I had to quit eating out, for instance. Since I lived alone, eating out was something I liked to do, but it became a thing of the past. And I had to watch myself when it came to thinking about movies. I couldn't buy clothes or get my teeth fixed. The car was falling apart. I needed new shoes, but forget it.

Once in a while I'd get fed up with it and write letters to all of them, threatening to change my name and telling them I was going to quit my job. I'd tell them I was planning a move to Australia. And the thing was, I was serious when I'd say that about Australia, even though I didn't know the first thing about Australia. I just knew it was on the other side of the world, and that's where I wanted to be.

But when it came right down to it, none of them really believed I'd go to Australia. They had me, and they knew it. They knew I was desperate, and they were sorry and they said so. But they counted on it all blowing over before the first of the month, when I had to sit down and make out the checks.

After one of my letters where I talked about moving to Australia, my mother wrote that she didn't want to be a burden any longer. Just as soon as the swelling went down in her legs, she said, she was going out to look for work. She was seventy-five years old, but maybe she could go back to waitressing, she said. I wrote her back and told her not to be silly. I said I was glad I could help her. And I was. I was glad I could help. I just needed to win the lottery.

My daughter knew Australia was just a way of saying to everybody that I'd had it. She knew I needed a break and something to cheer me up. So she wrote that she was going to leave her kids with somebody and take the cannery job when the season rolled around. She was young and strong, she said. She thought she could work the twelve-to-fourteen-hour-a-day shifts, seven days a week, no problem. She'd just have to tell herself she could do it, get herself psyched up for it, and her body would listen. She just had to line up the right kind of baby-sitter. That'd be the big thing. It was going to require a special kind of sitter, seeing as how the hours would be long and the kids were hyper to begin with, because of all the Popsicles and Tootsie Rolls, M&M's, and the like that they put away every day. It's the stuff kids like to eat, right? Anyway, she thought she could find the right person if she kept looking. But she had to buy the boots and clothes for the work, and that's where I could help.

My son wrote that he was sorry for his part in things and thought he and I would both be better off if he ended it once and for all. For one thing, he'd discovered he was allergic to cocaine. It made his eyes stream and affected his breathing, he said. This meant he couldn't test the drugs in the transactions he'd need to make. So, before it could even begin, his career as a drug dealer was over. No, he said, better a bullet in the temple and end it all right here. Or maybe hanging. That would save him the trouble of borrowing a gun. And save us the price of bullets. That's actually what he said in his letter, if you can believe it. He enclosed a picture of himself that somebody had taken last summer when he was in the study-abroad program in Germany. He was standing under a big tree with thick limbs hanging down a few feet over his head. In the picture, he wasn't smiling.

My former wife didn't have anything to say on the matter.

She didn't have to. She knew she'd get her money the first of each month, even if it had to come all the way from Sydney. If she didn't get it, she just had to pick up the phone and call her lawyer.

This is where things stood when my brother called one Sunday afternoon in early May. I had the windows open, and a nice breeze moved through the house. The radio was playing. The hillside behind the house was in bloom. But I began to sweat when I heard his voice on the line. I hadn't heard from him since the dispute over the five hundred, so I couldn't believe he was going to try and touch me for more money now. But I began to sweat anyway. He asked how things stood with me, and I launched into the payroll thing and all. I talked about oatmeal, cocaine, fish canneries, suicide, bank jobs, and how I couldn't go to the movies or eat out. I said I had a hole in my shoe. I talked about the payments that went on and on to my former wife. He knew all about this, of course. He knew everything I was telling him. Still, he said he was sorry to hear it. I kept talking. It was his dime. But as he talked I started thinking, *How are you going to pay for this call, Billy?* Then it came to me that *I* was going to pay for it. It was only a matter of minutes, or seconds, until it was all decided.

I looked out the window. The sky was blue, with a few white clouds in it. Some birds clung to a telephone wire. I wiped my face on my sleeve. I didn't know what else I could say. So I suddenly stopped talking and just stared out the window at the mountains, and waited. And that's when my brother said, "I hate to ask you this, but –" When he said that, my heart did this sinking thing. And then he went ahead and asked.

This time it was a thousand. A thousand! He was worse off than when he'd called that other time. He let me have some details. The bill collectors were at the door – the door! he said – and the windows rattled, the house shook, when they hammered with their fists. *Blam, blam, blam*, he said. There was no place to hide from them. His house was about to be pulled out from under him. "Help me, brother," he said.

Where was I going to raise a thousand dollars? I took a good grip on the receiver, turned away from the window, and said, "But you didn't pay me back the last time you borrowed money. What about that?"

"I didn't?" he said, acting surprised. "I guess I thought I had. I wanted to, anyway. I tried to, so help me God."

"You were supposed to pay that money to Mom," I said. "But you didn't. I had to keep giving her money every month, same as always. There's no end to it, Billy. Listen, I take one step forward and I go two steps back. I'm going under. You're all going under, and you're pulling me down with you."

"I paid her *some* of it," he said. "I did pay her a little. Just for the record," he said, "I paid her something."

"She said you gave her fifty dollars and that was all."

"No," he said, "I gave her seventy-five. She forgot about the other twenty-five. I was over there one afternoon, and I gave her two tens and a five. I gave her some cash, and she just forgot about it. Her memory's going. Look," he said, "I promise I'll be good for it this time, I swear to God. Add up what I still owe you and add it to this money here I'm trying to borrow, and I'll send you a check. We'll exchange checks. Hold on to my check for two months, that's all I'm asking. I'll be out of the woods in two months' time. Then you'll have your money. July first, I promise, no later, and this time I *can* swear to it. We're in the process of selling this little piece of property that Irma Jean inherited a while back from her uncle. It's as good as sold. The deal has closed. It's just a question now of working out a couple of minor details and signing the papers. Plus, I've got this job lined up. It's definite. I'll have to drive fifty miles round trip every day, but that's no problem – hell, no. I'd drive a hundred and fifty if I had to, and be glad to do it. I'm saying I'll have money in the bank in two months' time. You'll get your money, all of it, by July first, and you can count on it."

"Billy, I love you," I said. "But I've got a load to carry. I'm carrying a very heavy load these days, in case you didn't know."

"That's why I won't let you down on this," he said. "You

395

have my word of honor. You can trust me on this absolutely. I promise you my check will be good in two months, no later. Two months is all I'm asking for. Brother, I don't know where else to turn. You're my last hope."

I did it, sure. To my surprise, I still had some credit with the bank, so I borrowed the money, and I sent it to him. Our checks crossed in the mail. I stuck a thumbtack through his check and put it up on the kitchen wall next to the calendar and the picture of my son standing under that tree. And then I waited.

I kept waiting. My brother wrote and asked me not to cash the check on the day we'd agreed to. Please wait a while longer is what he said. Some things had come up. The job he'd been promised had fallen through at the last minute. That was one thing that came up. And that little piece of property belonging to his wife hadn't sold after all. At the last minute, she'd had a change of heart about selling it. It had been in her family for generations. What could he do? It was her land, and she wouldn't listen to reason, he said.

My daughter telephoned around this time to say that somebody had broken into her trailer and ripped her off. Everything in the trailer. Every stick of furniture was gone when she came home from work after her first night at the cannery. There wasn't even a chair left for her to sit down on. Her bed had been stolen, too. They were going to have to sleep on the floor like gypsies, she said.

"Where was what's-his-name when this happened?" I said.

She said he'd been out looking for work earlier in the day. She guessed he was with friends. Actually, she didn't know his whereabouts at the time of the crime, or even right now, for that matter. "I hope he's at the bottom of the river," she said. The kids had been with the sitter when the ripoff happened. But, anyway, if she could just borrow enough from me to buy some secondhand furniture she'd pay me back, she said, when she got her first check. If she had some money from me before the end of the week – I could wire it, maybe – she could pick up some essentials. "Somebody's violated my space," she said. "I feel like I've been raped."

396

My son wrote from New Hampshire that it was essential he go back to Europe. His life hung in the balance, he said. He was graduating at the end of summer session, but he couldn't stand to live in America a day longer after that. This was a materialist society, and he simply couldn't take it anymore. People over here, in the U.S., couldn't hold a conversation unless *money* figured in it some way, and he was sick of it. He wasn't a Yuppie, and didn't want to become a Yuppie. That wasn't his thing. He'd get out of my hair, he said, if he could just borrow enough from me, this one last time, to buy a ticket to Germany.

I didn't hear anything from my former wife. I didn't have to. We both knew how things stood there.

My mother wrote that she was having to do without support hose and wasn't able to have her hair tinted. She'd thought this would be the year she could put some money back for the rainy days ahead, but it wasn't working out that way. She could see it wasn't in the cards. "How are you?" she wanted to know. "How's everybody else? I hope you're okay."

I put more checks in the mail. Then I held my breath and waited.

While I was waiting, I had this dream one night. Two dreams, really. I dreamt them on the same night. In the first dream, my dad was alive once more, and he was giving me a ride on his shoulders. I was this little kid, maybe five or six years old. *Get up here*, he said, and he took me by the hands and swung me onto his shoulders. I was high off the ground, but I wasn't afraid. He was holding on to me. We were holding on to each other. Then he began to move down the sidewalk. I brought my hands up from his shoulders and put them around his forehead. *Don't muss my hair*, he said. *You can let go*, he said, *I've got you. You won't fall.* When he said that, I became aware of the strong grip of his hands around my ankles. Then I did let go. I turned loose and held my arms out on either side of me. I kept them out there like that for balance. My dad went on walking while I rode on his shoulders. I pretended he was an elephant. I don't know where we were going. Maybe we were going to the store, or else to the park so he could push me in the swing.

397

I woke up then, got out of bed, and used the bathroom. It was starting to get light out, and it was only an hour or so until I had to get up. I thought about making coffee and getting dressed. But then I decided to go back to bed. I didn't plan to sleep, though. I thought I'd just lie there for a while with my hands behind my neck and watch it turn light out and maybe think about my dad a little, since I hadn't thought about him in a long time. He just wasn't a part of my life any longer, waking or sleeping. Anyway, I got back in bed. But it couldn't have been more than a minute before I fell asleep once more, and when I did I got into this other dream. My former wife was in it, though she wasn't my former wife in the dream. She was still my wife. My kids were in it, too. They were little, and they were eating potato chips. In my dream, I thought I could smell the potato chips and hear them being eaten. We were on a blanket, and we were close to some water. There was a sense of satisfaction and well-being in the dream. Then, suddenly, I found myself in the company of some other people – people I didn't know – and the next thing that happened was that I was kicking the window out of my son's car and threatening his life, as I did once, a long time ago. He was inside the car as my shoe smashed through the glass. That's when my eyes flew open, and I woke up. The alarm was going off. I reached over and pushed the switch and lay there for a few minutes more, my heart racing. In the second dream, somebody had offered me some whiskey, and I drank it. Drinking that whiskey was the thing that scared me. That was the worst thing that could have happened. That was rock bottom. Compared to that, everything else was a picnic. I lay there for a minute longer, trying to calm down. Then I got up.

I made coffee and sat at the kitchen table in front of the window. I pushed my cup back and forth in little circles on the table and began to think seriously about Australia again. And then, all of a sudden, I could imagine how it must have sounded to my family when I'd threatened them with a move to Australia. They would have been shocked at first, and even a little scared. Then, because they knew me, they'd probably started laughing. Now, thinking about their laughter, I had to laugh, too. *Ha, ha, ha.*

That was exactly the sound I made there at the table – *ha, ha, ha* – as if I'd read somewhere how to laugh.

What was it I planned to do in Australia, anyway? The truth was, I wouldn't be going there any more than I'd be going to Timbuktu, the moon, or the North Pole. Hell, I didn't want to go to Australia. But once I understood this, once I understood I wouldn't be going there – or anywhere else, for that matter – I began to feel better. I lit another cigarette and poured some more coffee. There wasn't any milk for the coffee, but I didn't care. I could skip having milk in my coffee for a day and it wouldn't kill me. Pretty soon I packed the lunch and filled the thermos and put the thermos in the lunch pail. Then I went outside.

It was a fine morning. The sun lay over the mountains behind the town, and a flock of birds was moving from one part of the valley to another. I didn't bother to lock the door. I remembered what had happened to my daughter, but decided I didn't have anything worth stealing anyway. There was nothing in the house I couldn't live without. I had the TV, but I was sick of watching TV. They'd be doing me a favor if they broke in and took it off my hands.

I felt pretty good, all things considered, and I decided to walk to work. It wasn't all that far, and I had time to spare. I'd save a little gas, sure, but that wasn't the main consideration. It was summer, after all, and before long summer would be over. Summer, I couldn't help thinking, had been the time everybody's luck had been going to change.

I started walking alongside the road, and it was then, for some reason, I began to think about my son. I wished him well, wherever he was. If he'd made it back to Germany by now – and he should have – I hoped he was happy. He hadn't written yet to give me his address, but I was sure I'd hear something before long. And my daughter, God love her and keep her. I hoped she was doing okay. I decided to write her a letter that evening and tell her I was rooting for her. My mother was alive and more or less in good health, and I felt lucky there, too. If all went well, I'd have her for several more years.

Birds were calling, and some cars passed me on the highway. Good luck to you, too, brother, I thought. I hope your ship comes in. Pay me back when you get it. And my former wife, the woman I used to love so much. She was alive, and she was well, too – so far as I knew, anyway. I wished her happiness. When all was said and done, I decided things could be a lot worse. Just now, of course, things were hard for everyone. People's luck had gone south on them was all. But things were bound to change soon. Things would pick up in the fall maybe. There was lots to hope for.

I kept on walking. Then I began to whistle. I felt I had the right to whistle if I wanted to. I let my arms swing as I walked. But the lunch pail kept throwing me off balance. I had sandwiches, an apple, and some cookies in there, not to mention the thermos. I stopped in front of Smitty's, an old café that had gravel in the parking area and boards over the windows. The place had been boarded up for as long as I could remember. I decided to put the lunch pail down for a minute. I did that, and then I raised my arms – raised them up level with my shoulders. I was standing there like that, like a goof, when somebody tooted a car horn and pulled off the highway into the parking area. I picked up my lunch pail and went over to the car. It was a guy I knew from work whose name was George. He reached over and opened the door on the passenger's side. "Hey, get in, buddy," he said.

"Hello, George," I said. I got in and shut the door, and the car sped off, throwing gravel from under the tires.

"I saw you," George said. "Yeah, I did, I saw you. You're in training for something, but I don't know what." He looked at me and then looked at the road again. He was going fast. "You always walk down the road with your arms out like that?" He laughed – *ha, ha, ha* – and stepped on the gas.

"Sometimes," I said. "It depends, I guess. Actually, I was standing," I said. I lit a cigarette and leaned back in the seat.

"So what's new?" George said. He put a cigar in his mouth, but he didn't light it.

"Nothing's new," I said. "What's new with you?"

George shrugged. Then he grinned. He was going very fast now. Wind buffeted the car and whistled by outside the windows. He was driving as if we were late for work. But we weren't late. We had lots of time, and I told him so.

Nevertheless, he cranked it up. We passed the turnoff and kept going. We were moving by then, heading straight toward the mountains. He took the cigar out of his mouth and put it in his shirt pocket. "I borrowed some money and had this baby overhauled," he said. Then he said he wanted me to see something. He punched it and gave it everything he could. I fastened my seat belt and held on.

"*Go*," I said. "What are you waiting for, George?" And that's when we really flew. Wind howled outside the windows. He had it floored, and we were going flat out. We streaked down that road in his big unpaid-for car.

Blackbird Pie

I was in my room one night when I heard something in the corridor. I looked up from my work and saw an envelope slide under the door. It was a thick envelope, but not so thick it couldn't be pushed under the door. My name was written on the envelope, and what was inside purported to be a letter from my wife. I say "purported" because even though the grievances could only have come from someone who'd spent twenty-three years observing me on an intimate, day-to-day basis, the charges were outrageous and completely out of keeping with my wife's character. Most important, however, the handwriting was not my wife's handwriting. But if it wasn't her handwriting, then whose was it?

I wish now I'd kept the letter, so I could reproduce it down to the last comma, the last uncharitable exclamation point. The tone is what I'm talking about now, not just the content. But I didn't keep it, I'm sorry to say. I lost it, or else misplaced it. Later, after the sorry business I'm about to relate, I was cleaning out my desk and may have accidentally thrown it away – which is uncharacteristic of *me*, since I usually don't throw anything away.

In any case, I have a good memory. I can recall every word of what I read. My memory is such that I used to win prizes in school because of my ability to remember names and dates, inventions, battles, treaties, alliances, and the like. I always scored highest on factual tests, and in later years, in the "real world", as it's called, my memory stood me in good stead. For instance, if I were asked right now to give the details of the Council of Trent or the Treaty of Utrecht, or to talk about Carthage, that city razed by the Romans after Hannibal's defeat (the Roman soldiers plowed salt into the ground so that Carthage could never

402

be called Carthage again), I could do so. If called upon to talk about the Seven Years' War, the Thirty Years', or the Hundred Years' War, or simply the First Silesian War, I could hold forth with the greatest enthusiasm and confidence. Ask me anything about the Tartars, the Renaissance popes, or the rise and fall of the Ottoman Empire. Thermopylae, Shiloh, or the Maxim gun. Easy. Tannenberg? Simple as blackbird pie. The famous four and twenty that were set before the king. At Agincourt, English longbows carried the day. And here's something else. Everyone has heard of the Battle of Lepanto, the last great sea battle fought in ships powered by galley slaves. This fracas took place in 1571 in the eastern Mediterranean, when the combined naval forces of the Christian nations of Europe turned back the Arab hordes under the infamous Ali Muezzin Zade, a man who was fond of personally cutting off the noses of his prisoners before calling in the executioners. But does anyone remember that Cervantes was involved in this affair and had his left hand lopped off in the battle? Something else. The combined French and Russian losses in one day at Borodino were seventy-five thousand men – the equivalent in fatalities of a fully loaded jumbo jet crashing every three minutes from breakfast to sundown. Kutuzov pulled his forces back toward Moscow. Napoleon drew breath, marshaled his troops, and continued his advance. He entered the downtown area of Moscow, where he stayed for a month waiting for Kutuzov, who never showed his face again. The Russian generalissimo was waiting for snow and ice, for Napoleon to begin his retreat to France.

Things stick in my head. I remember. So when I say I can re-create the letter – the portion that I read, which catalogues the charges against me – I mean what I say.

In part, the letter went as follows:

Dear,
Things are not good. Things, in fact, are bad. Things have gone from bad to worse. And you know what I'm talking about. We've come to the end of the line. It's over with us. Still, I find myself wishing we could have talked about it.

403

It's been such a long time now since we've talked. I mean really *talked*. Even after we were married we used to talk and talk, exchanging news and ideas. When the children were little, or even after they were more grown-up, we still found time to talk. It was more difficult then, naturally, but we managed, we found time. We *made* time. We'd have to wait until after they were asleep, or else when they were playing outside, or with a sitter. But we managed. Sometimes we'd engage a sitter just so we *could* talk. On occasion we talked the night away, talked until the sun came up. Well. Things happen, I know. Things change. Bill had that trouble with the police, and Linda found herself pregnant, etc. Our quiet time together flew out the window. And gradually your responsibilities backed up on you. Your work became more important, and our time together was squeezed out. Then, once the children left home, our time for talking was back. We had each other again, only we had less and less to talk about. "It happens," I can hear some wise man saying. And he's right. *It happens*. But it happened to us. In any case, no blame. *No blame*. That's not what this letter is about. *I want to talk about us*. I want to talk about *now*. The time has come, you see, to admit that *the impossible* has happened. To cry *Uncle*. To beg off. To –

I read this far and stopped. Something was wrong. Something was fishy in Denmark. The sentiments expressed in the letter may have belonged to my wife. (Maybe they did. Say they did, grant that the sentiments expressed *were* hers.) But the handwriting *was not her handwriting*. And I ought to know. I consider myself an expert in this matter of her handwriting. And yet if it wasn't her handwriting, who on earth *had* written these lines?

I should say a little something about ourselves and our life here. During the time I'm writing about we were living in a house we'd taken for the summer. I'd just recovered from an illness that had set me back in most things I'd hoped to accomplish that spring. We were surrounded on three sides by meadows, birch woods, and some low, rolling hills – a "territorial view", as the realtor had called it when he described it to us over the phone. In front of the house was a lawn that had grown shaggy, owing to lack of interest on my part, and a long graveled drive that led to the road. Behind the road we could see the distant peaks of mountains. Thus the phrase "territorial view" – having to do with a vista appreciated only at a distance.

My wife had no friends here in the country, and no one came to visit. Frankly, I was glad for the solitude. But she was a woman who was used to having friends, used to dealing with shopkeepers and tradesmen. Out here, it was just the two of us, thrown back on our resources. Once upon a time a house in the country would have been our ideal – we would have *coveted* such an arrangement. Now I can see it wasn't such a good idea. No, it wasn't.

Both our children had left home long ago. Now and then a letter came from one of them. And once in a blue moon, on a holiday, say, one of them might telephone – a collect call, naturally, my wife being only too happy to accept the charges. This seeming indifference on their part was, I believe, a major cause of my wife's sadness and general discontent – a discontent, I have to admit, I'd been vaguely aware of before our move to the country. In any case, to find herself in the country after so many years of living close to a shopping mall and bus service, with a taxi no farther away than the telephone in the hall – it must have been hard on her, very hard. I think her *decline*, as a historian might put it, was accelerated by our move to the country. I think she slipped a cog after that. I'm speaking from hindsight, of course, which always tends to confirm the obvious.

I don't know what else to say in regard to this matter of the handwriting. How much more can I say and still retain credibility? We were alone in the house. No one else – to my knowledge, anyway – was in the house and could have penned the letter. Yet I remain convinced to this day that it was not her handwriting that covered the pages of the letter. After all, I'd been reading my wife's handwriting since before she was my wife. As far back as what might be called our pre-history days – the time she went away to school as a girl, wearing a gray-and-white school uniform. She wrote letters to me every day that she was away, and she was away for two years, not counting holidays and summer vacations. Altogether, in the course of our relationship, I would estimate (a conservative estimate, too), counting our separations and the short periods of time I was away on business or in the hospital, etc. – I would estimate, as I say, that I received seventeen hundred or possibly eighteen hundred and fifty handwritten letters from her, not to mention hundreds, maybe thousands, more informal notes ("On your way home, please pick up dry cleaning, and some spinach pasta from Corti Bros"). I could recognize her handwriting anywhere in the world. Give me a few words. I'm confident that if I were in Jaffa, or Marrakech, and picked up a note in the marketplace, I would recognize it if it was my wife's handwriting. A word, even. Take this word "*talked*", for instance. That simply isn't the way she'd write "talked"! Yet I'm the first to admit I don't know *whose* handwriting it is if it isn't hers.

Secondly, my wife *never* underlined her words for emphasis. Never. I don't recall a single instance of her doing this – not once in our entire married life, not to mention the letters I received from her before we were married. It would be reasonable enough, I suppose, to point out that it could happen to anyone. That is, anyone could find himself in a situation that is completely atypical and, *given the pressure of the moment*, do something totally out of character and draw a line, the merest *line*, under a word, or maybe under an entire sentence.

I would go so far as to say that every word of this entire letter, so-called (though I haven't read it through in its entirety, and won't, since I can't find it now), is utterly false. I don't mean false in the sense of "untrue", necessarily. There is some truth, perhaps, to the charges. I don't want to quibble. I don't want to appear small in this matter; things are bad enough already in this department. No. What I want to say, all I want to say, is that while the sentiments expressed in the letter may be my wife's, may even hold *some* truth – be legitimate, so to speak – the force of the accusations leveled against me is diminished, if not entirely undermined, even discredited, because she *did not* in fact write the letter. Or, if she *did* write it, then discredited by the fact that she didn't write it in her own handwriting! Such evasion is what makes men hunger for facts. As always, there are some.

On the evening in question, we ate dinner rather silently but not unpleasantly, as was our custom. From time to time I looked up and smiled across the table as a way of showing my gratitude for the delicious meal – poached salmon, fresh asparagus, rice pilaf with almonds. The radio played softly in the other room; it was a little suite by Poulenc that I'd first heard on a digital recording five years before in an apartment on Van Ness, in San Francisco, during a thunderstorm.

When we'd finished eating, and after we'd had our coffee and dessert, my wife said something that startled me. "Are you planning to be in your room this evening?" she said.

"I am," I said. "What did you have in mind?"

"I simply wanted to know." She picked up her cup and drank some coffee. But she avoided looking at me, even though I tried to catch her eye.

Are you planning to be in your room this evening? Such a question was altogether out of character for her. I wonder now why on earth I didn't pursue this at the time. She knows my habits, if anyone does. But I think her mind was made up even then. I think she was concealing something even as she spoke.

"Of course I'll be in my room this evening," I repeated, perhaps a trifle impatiently. She didn't say anything else, and neither did I. I drank the last of my coffee and cleared my throat.

She glanced up and held my eyes a moment. Then she nodded, as if we had agreed on something. (But we hadn't, of course.) She got up and began to clear the table.

I felt as if dinner had somehow ended on an unsatisfactory note. Something else – a few words maybe – was needed to round things off and put the situation right again.

"There's a fog coming in," I said.

"Is there? I hadn't noticed," she said.

She wiped away a place on the window over the sink with a dish towel and looked out. For a minute she didn't say anything. Then she said – again mysteriously, or so it seems to me now – "There

407

is. Yes, it's very foggy. It's a heavy fog, isn't it?" That's all she said. Then she lowered her eyes and began to wash the dishes.

I sat at the table a while longer before I said, "I think I'll go to my room now."

She took her hands out of the water and rested them against the counter. I thought she might proffer a word or two of encouragement for the work I was engaged in, but she didn't. Not a peep. It was as if she were waiting for me to leave the kitchen so she could enjoy her privacy.

Remember, I was at work in my room at the time the letter was slipped under the door. I read enough to question the handwriting and to wonder how it was that my wife had presumably been busy somewhere in the house and writing me a letter at the same time. Before reading further in the letter, I got up and went over to the door, unlocked it, and checked the corridor.

It was dark at this end of the house. But when I cautiously put my head out I could see light from the living room at the end of the hallway. The radio was playing quietly, as usual. Why did I hesitate? Except for the fog, it was a night very much like any other we had spent together in the house. But there was *something else afoot* tonight. At that moment I found myself afraid – afraid, if you can believe it, in my own house! – to walk down the hall and satisfy myself that all was well. Or if something was wrong, if my wife was experiencing – how should I put it? – difficulties of any sort, hadn't I best confront the situation before letting it go any further, before losing any more time on this stupid business of reading her words in somebody else's handwriting!

But I didn't investigate. Perhaps I wanted to avoid a frontal attack. In any case, I drew back and shut and locked the door before returning to the letter. But I was angry now as I saw the evening sliding away in this foolish and incomprehensible business. I was beginning to feel *uneasy*. (No other word will do.) I could feel my gorge rising as I picked up the letter purporting to be from my wife and once more began to read.

The time has come and gone for us – us, you and me – to put all our cards on the table. Thee and me. Lancelot and

Guinevere. Abélard and Héloïse. Troilus and Cressida. Pyramus and Thisbe. JAJ and Nora Barnacle, etc. You know what I'm saying, honey. We've been together a long time – thick and thin, illness and health, stomach distress, eye-ear-nose-and-throat trouble, high times and low. Now? Well, I don't know what I can say now except the truth: I can't go it another step.

At this point, I threw down the letter and went to the door again, deciding to settle this once and for all. I wanted an accounting, and I wanted it now. I was, I think, *in a rage.* But at this point, just as I opened the door, I heard a low murmuring from the living room. It was as if somebody were trying to say something over the phone and this somebody were taking pains not to be overheard. Then I heard the receiver being replaced. Just this. Then everything was *as before* – the radio playing softly, the house otherwise quiet. But I had heard a voice.

In place of anger, I began to feel panic. I grew afraid as I looked down the corridor. Things were the same as before – the light was on in the living room, the radio played softly. I took a few steps and listened. I hoped I might hear the comforting, rhythmic clicking of her knitting needles, or the sound of a page being turned, but there was nothing of the sort. I took a few steps toward the living room and then – what should I say? – I lost my nerve, or maybe my curiosity. It was at that moment I heard *the muted sound of a doorknob being turned*, and afterward the unmistakable sound of a door opening and closing quietly.

My impulse was to walk rapidly down the corridor and into the living room and get to the bottom of this thing once and for all. But I didn't want to act impulsively and possibly discredit myself. I'm not impulsive, so I waited. But there *was* activity of some sort in the house – something was afoot, I was sure of it – and of course it was my duty, for my own peace of mind, not to mention the possible safety and well-being of my wife, to act. But I didn't. I couldn't. The moment was there, but I hesitated. Suddenly it was too late for any decisive action. The moment had come and gone, and could not be called back. Just so did

Darius hesitate and then fail to act at the Battle of Granicus, and the day was lost, Alexander the Great rolling him up on every side and giving him a real walloping.

I went back to my room and closed the door. But *my heart was racing*. I sat in my chair and, trembling, picked up the pages of the letter once more.

But now here's the curious thing. Instead of beginning to read the letter through, from start to finish, or even starting at the point where I'd stopped earlier, I took pages at random and held them under the table lamp, picking out a line here and a line there. This allowed me to juxtapose the charges made against me until the entire indictment (for that's what it was) took on quite another character – one more acceptable, since it had lost its chronology and, with it, a little of its punch.

So. Well. In this manner, going from page to page, here a line, there a line, I read in snatches the following – which might under different circumstances serve as a kind of abstract:

> . . . withdrawing farther into . . . a small enough thing, but . . . talcum powder sprayed over the bathroom, including walls and baseboards . . . a shell . . . not to mention the insane asylum . . . until finally . . . a balanced view . . . the grave. Your "work" . . . Please! Give me a break . . . No one, not even . . . Not another word on the subject! . . . The children . . . but the real issue . . . not to mention the loneliness . . . Jesus H. Christ! Really! I mean . . .

At this point I distinctly heard the front door close. I dropped the pages of the letter onto the desk and hurried to the living room. It didn't take long to see that my wife wasn't in the house. (The house is small – two bedrooms, one of which we refer to as my room or, on occasion, as my study.) But let the record show: *every light in the house was burning*.

A heavy fog lay outside the windows, a fog so dense I could scarcely see the driveway. The porch light was on and a suitcase stood outside on the porch. It was my wife's suitcase, the one she'd brought packed full of her things when we moved here. What on earth was going on? I opened the door. Suddenly – I don't know how to say this other than how it was – a horse stepped out of the fog, and then, an instant later, as I watched, dumbfounded, another horse. These horses were grazing in our front yard. I saw my wife alongside one of the horses, and I called her name.

"Come on out here," she said. "Look at this. Doesn't this beat anything?"

She was standing beside this big horse, patting its flank. She was dressed in her best clothes and had on heels and was wearing a hat. (I hadn't seen her in a hat since her mother's funeral, three years before.) Then she moved forward and put her face against the horse's mane.

"Where did you come from, you big baby?" she said. "Where did you come from, sweetheart?" Then, as I watched, she began to cry into the horse's mane.

"There, there," I said and started down the steps. I went over and patted the horse, and then I touched my wife's shoulder. She drew back. The horse snorted, raised its head a moment, and then went to cropping the grass once more. "What is it?" I said to my wife. "For God's sake, what's happening here, anyway?"

She didn't answer. The horse moved a few steps but continued pulling and eating the grass. The other horse was munching grass as well. My wife moved with the horse, hanging on to its mane. I put my hand against the horse's neck and felt a surge of power run up my arm to the shoulder. I shivered. My wife was still crying. I felt helpless, but I was scared, too.

"Can you tell me what's going on?" I said. "Why are you dressed like this? What's that suitcase doing on the front porch? Where did these horses come from? For God's sake, can you tell me what's happening?"

My wife began to croon to the horse. Croon! Then she stopped and said, "You didn't read my letter, did you? You might have skimmed it, but you didn't read it. Admit it!"

"I did read it," I said. I was lying, yes, but it was a white lie. A partial untruth. But he who is blameless, let him throw out the first stone. "But tell me what is going on anyway," I said.

My wife turned her head from side to side. She pushed her face into the horse's dark wet mane. I could hear the horse *chomp, chomp, chomp.* Then it snorted as it took in air through its nostrils.

She said, "There was this girl, you see. Are you listening? And this girl loved this boy so much. She loved him even more than herself. But the boy – well, he grew up. I don't know what happened to him. Something, anyway. He got cruel without meaning to be cruel and he –"

I didn't catch the rest, because just then a car appeared out of the fog, in the drive, with its headlights on and a flashing blue light on its roof. It was followed, a minute later, by a pickup truck pulling what looked like a horse trailer, though with the fog it was hard to tell. It could have been anything – a big portable oven, say. The car pulled right up onto the lawn and stopped. Then the pickup drove alongside the car and stopped, too. Both vehicles kept their headlights on and their engines running, which contributed to the eerie, bizarre aspect of things. A man wearing a cowboy hat – a rancher, I supposed – stepped down from the pickup. He raised the collar of his sheepskin coat and whistled to the horses. Then a big man in a raincoat got out of the car. He was a much bigger man than the rancher, and he, too, was wearing a cowboy hat. But his raincoat was open, and I could see a pistol strapped to his waist. He had to be a deputy sheriff. Despite everything that was going on, and the anxiety I felt, I found it *worth noting* that both men were wearing hats. I ran my hand through my hair, and was sorry I wasn't wearing a hat of my own.

"I called the sheriff's department a while ago," my wife said. "When I first saw the horses." She waited a minute and then she said something else. "Now you won't need to give me a ride into town after all. I mentioned that in my letter, the letter you read. I said I'd need a ride into town. I can get a ride – at least, I think I can – with one of these gentlemen. And I'm not changing my mind about anything, either. I'm saying this decision is irrevocable. Look at me!" she said.

I'd been watching them round up the horses. The deputy was

holding his flashlight while the rancher walked a horse up a little ramp into the trailer. I turned to look at this woman I didn't know any longer.

"I'm leaving you," she said. "That's what's happening. I'm heading for town tonight. I'm striking out on my own. It's all in the letter you read." Whereas, as I said earlier, my wife never underlined words in her letters, she was now speaking (having dried her tears) as if virtually every other word out of her mouth ought to be emphasized.

"What's gotten *into* you?" I heard myself say. It was almost as if I couldn't help adding pressure to some of my own words. "Why are you *doing* this?"

She shook her head. The rancher was loading the second horse into the trailer now, whistling sharply, clapping his hands and shouting an occasional "Whoa! Whoa, damn you! Back up now. Back up!"

The deputy came over to us with a clipboard under his arm. He was holding a big flashlight. "Who called?" he said.

"I did," my wife said.

The deputy looked her over for a minute. He flashed the light onto her high heels and then up to her hat. "You're all dressed up," he said.

"I'm leaving my husband," she said.

The deputy nodded, as if he understood. (But he didn't, he couldn't!) "He's not going to give you any trouble, is he?" the deputy said, shining his light into my face and moving the light up and down rapidly. "You're not, are you?"

"No," I said. "No trouble. But I resent — "

"Good," the deputy said. "Enough said, then."

The rancher closed and latched the door to his trailer. Then he walked toward us through the wet grass, which, I noticed, reached to the tops of his boots.

"I want to thank you folks for calling," he said. "Much obliged. That's one heavy fog. If they'd wandered onto the main road, they could have raised hob out there."

"The lady placed the call," the deputy said. "Frank, she needs a ride into town. She's leaving home. I don't know who the injured party is here, but she's the one leaving." He turned then to my wife. "You sure about this, are you?" he said to her.

She nodded. "I'm sure."

"Okay," the deputy said. "That's settled, anyway. Frank, you listening? I can't drive her to town. I've got another stop to make. So can you help her out and take her into town? She probably wants to go to the bus station or else to the hotel. That's where they usually go. Is that where you want to go to?" the deputy said to my wife. "Frank needs to know."

"He can drop me off at the bus station," my wife said. "That's my suitcase on the porch."

"What about it, Frank?" the deputy said.

"I guess I can, sure," Frank said, taking off his hat and putting it back on again. "I'd be glad to, I guess. But I don't want to interfere in anything."

"Not in the least," my wife said. "I don't want to be any trouble, but I'm – well, I'm distressed just now. Yes, I'm distressed. But it'll be all right once I'm away from here. Away from this awful place. I'll just check and make doubly sure I haven't left anything behind. Anything *important*," she added. She hesitated and then she said, "This isn't as sudden as it looks. It's been coming for a long, long time. We've been married for a good many years. Good times and bad, up times and down. We've had them all. But it's time I was on my own. Yes, it's time. Do you know what I'm saying, gentlemen?"

Frank took off his hat again and turned it around in his hands as if examining the brim. Then he put it back on his head.

The deputy said, "These things happen. Lord knows none of us is perfect. We weren't made perfect. The only angels is to be found in Heaven."

My wife moved toward the house, picking her way through the wet, shaggy grass in her high heels. She opened the front door and went inside. I could see her moving behind the lighted windows, and something came to me then. *I might never see her again.* That's what crossed my mind, and it staggered me.

The rancher, the deputy, and I stood around waiting, not saying anything. The damp fog drifted between us and the lights from their vehicles. I could hear the horses shifting in the trailer. We were all uncomfortable, I think. But I'm speaking only for myself, of course. I don't know what they felt. Maybe they saw things like this happen every night – saw people's lives flying apart. The deputy did, maybe. But Frank, the rancher, he kept his eyes lowered. He put his hands in his front pockets and then took them out again. He kicked at something in the grass. I folded my arms and went on standing there, not knowing what was going to happen next. The deputy kept turning off his flashlight and then turning it on again. Every so often he'd reach out and swat the fog with it. One of the horses whinnied from the trailer, and then the other horse whinnied, too.

"A fellow can't see anything in this fog," Frank said.

I knew he was saying it to make conversation.

"It's as bad as I've ever seen it," the deputy said. Then he looked over at me. He didn't shine the light in my eyes this time, but he said something. He said, "Why's she leaving you? You hit her or something? Give her a smack, did you?"

"I've never hit her," I said. "Not in all the time we've been married. There was reason enough a few times, but I didn't. She hit me once," I said.

"Now, don't get started," the deputy said. "I don't want to hear any crap tonight. Don't say anything, and there won't be anything. No rough stuff. Don't even think it. There isn't going to be any trouble here tonight, is there?"

The deputy and Frank were watching me. I could tell Frank was embarrassed. He took out his makings and began to roll a cigarette.

"No," I said. "No trouble."

My wife came onto the porch and picked up her suitcase. I had the feeling that not only had she taken a last look around but she'd used the opportunity to freshen herself up, put on new lipstick, etc. The deputy held his flashlight for her as she came down the steps. "Right this way, ma'am," he said. "Watch your step, now – it's slippery."

"I'm ready to go," she said.

"Right," Frank said. "Well, just to make sure we got this all straight now." He took off his hat once more and held it. "I'll carry you into town and I'll drop you off at the bus station. But, you understand, I don't want to be in the middle of something. You know what I mean." He looked at my wife, and then he looked at me.

"That's right," the deputy said. "You said a mouthful. Statistics show that your domestic dispute is, time and again, potentially the most dangerous situation a person, especially a law-enforcement officer, can get himself involved in. But I think this situation is going to be the shining exception. Right, folks?"

My wife looked at me and said, "I don't think I'll kiss you. No, I won't kiss you good-bye. I'll just say so long. Take care of yourself."

"That's right," the deputy said. "Kissing – who knows what that'll lead to, right?" He laughed.

I had the feeling they were all waiting for me to say something. But for the first time in my life I felt at a loss for words. Then *I took heart* and said to my wife, "The last time you wore that hat, you wore a veil with it and I held your arm. You were in mourning for your mother. And you wore a dark dress, not the dress you're wearing tonight. But those are the same high heels, I remember. Don't leave me like this," I said. "I don't know what I'll do."

"I have to," she said. "It's all in the letter – everything's spelled out in the letter. The rest is in the area of – I don't know. Mystery or speculation, I guess. In any case, there's nothing in the letter you don't already know." Then she turned to Frank and said, "Let's go, Frank. I can call you Frank, can't I?"

"Call him anything you want," the deputy said, "long as you call him in time for supper." He laughed again – a big, hearty laugh.

"Right," Frank said. "Sure you can. Well, okay. Let's go, then." He took the suitcase from my wife and went over to his pickup and put the suitcase into the cab. Then he stood by the door on the passenger's side, holding it open.

"I'll write after I'm settled," my wife said. "I think I will, anyway. But first things first. We'll have to see."

416

"Now you're talking," the deputy said. "Keep all lines of communication open. Good luck, pardee," the deputy said to me. Then he went over to his car and got in.

The pickup made a wide, slow turn with the trailer across the lawn. One of the horses whinnied. The last image I have of my wife was when a match flared in the cab of the pickup, and I saw her lean over with a cigarette to accept the light the rancher was offering. Her hands were cupped around the hand that held the match. The deputy waited until the pickup and trailer had gone past him and then he swung his car around, slipping in the wet grass until he found purchase on the driveway, throwing gravel from under his tires. As he headed for the road, he tooted his horn. *Tooted.* Historians should use more words like "tooted" or "beeped" or "blasted" – especially at serious moments such as after a massacre or when an awful occurrence has cast a pall on the future of an entire nation. That's when a word like "tooted" is necessary, is gold in a brass age.

I'd like to say it was at this moment, as I stood in the fog watching her drive off, that I remembered a black-and-white photograph of my wife holding her wedding bouquet. She was eighteen years old – *a mere girl*, her mother had shouted at me only a month before the wedding. A few minutes before the photo, she'd got married. She's smiling. She's just finished, or is just about to begin, laughing. In either case, her mouth is open in amazed happiness as she looks into the camera. She is three months pregnant, though the camera doesn't show that, of course. But what if she *is* pregnant? So what? Wasn't everybody pregnant in those days? She's happy, in any case. I was happy, too – I know I was. We were both happy. I'm not in that particular picture, but I was close – only a few steps away, as I remember, shaking hands with someone offering me good wishes. My wife knew Latin and German and chemistry and physics and history and Shakespeare and all those other things they teach you in private school. She knew how to properly hold a teacup. She also knew how to cook and to make love. She was a prize.

But I found this photograph, along with several others, a few days after the horse business, when I was going through my wife's belongings, trying to see what I could throw out and what I should keep. I was packing to move, and I looked at the photograph for a minute and then I threw it away. I was ruthless. I told myself I didn't care. Why should I care?

If I know anything – and I do – if I know the slightest thing about human nature, I know she won't be able to live without me. She'll come back to me. And soon. Let it be soon.

No, I don't know anything about anything, and I never did. She's gone for good. She is. I can feel it. Gone and never coming back. Period. Not ever. I won't see her again, unless we run into each other on the street somewhere.

There's still the question of the handwriting. That's a bewilderment. But the handwriting business isn't the important thing, of course. How could it be after the consequences of the letter? Not the letter itself but the things I can't forget that were *in* the letter. No, the letter is not paramount at all – there's far more to this than somebody's handwriting. The "far more" has to do with subtle things. It could be said, for instance, that to take a wife is to take a history. And if that's so, then I understand that I'm outside history now – like horses and fog. Or you could say that my history has left me. Or that I'm having to go on *without history*. Or that history will now have to do without me – unless my wife writes more letters, or tells a friend who keeps a diary, say. Then, years later, someone can look back on this time, interpret it according to the record, its scraps and tirades, its silences and innuendos. That's when it dawns on me that autobiography is the poor man's history. And that I am saying good-bye to history. Good-bye, my darling.

Errand

Chekhov. On the evening of 22 March 1897, he went to dinner in Moscow with his friend and confidant Alexei Suvorin. This Suvorin was a very rich newspaper and book publisher, a reactionary, a self-made man whose father was a private at the battle of Borodino. Like Chekhov, he was the grandson of a serf. They had that in common: each had peasant's blood in his veins. Otherwise, politically and temperamentally, they were miles apart. Nevertheless, Suvorin was one of Chekhov's few intimates, and Chekhov enjoyed his company.

Naturally, they went to the best restaurant in the city, a former town house called the Hermitage – a place where it could take hours, half the night even, to get through a ten-course meal that would, of course, include several wines, liqueurs, and coffee. Chekhov was impeccably dressed, as always – a dark suit and waistcoat, his usual pince-nez. He looked that night very much as he looks in the photographs taken of him during this period. He was relaxed, jovial. He shook hands with the maître d', and with a glance took in the large dining room. It was brilliantly illuminated by ornate chandeliers, the tables occupied by elegantly dressed men and women. Waiters came and went ceaselessly. He had just been seated across the table from Suvorin when suddenly, without warning, blood began gushing from his mouth. Suvorin and two waiters helped him to the gentlemen's room and tried to stanch the flow of blood with ice packs. Suvorin saw him back to his own hotel and had a bed prepared for Chekhov in one of the rooms of the suite. Later, after another hemorrhage, Chekhov allowed himself to be moved to a clinic that specialized in the treatment of tuberculosis and related respiratory infections. When Suvorin visited him there, Chekhov apologized for the "scandal" at the restaurant three nights earlier but continued to insist there was nothing seriously wrong. "He laughed and jested as usual," Suvorin noted in his diary, "while spitting blood into a large vessel."

Maria Chekhov, his younger sister, visited Chekhov in the clinic during the last days of March. The weather was miserable; a sleet storm was in progress, and frozen heaps of snow lay everywhere. It was hard for her to wave down a carriage to take her to the hospital. By the time she arrived she was filled with dread and anxiety.

"Anton Pavlovich lay on his back," Maria wrote in her *Memoirs*. "He was not allowed to speak. After greeting him, I went over to the table to hide my emotions." There, among bottles of champagne, jars of caviar, bouquets of flowers from well-wishers, she saw something that terrified her: a freehand drawing, obviously done by a specialist in these matters, of Chekhov's lungs. It was the kind of sketch a doctor often makes in order to show his patient what he thinks is taking place. The lungs were outlined in blue, but the upper parts were filled in with red. "I realized they were diseased," Maria wrote.

Leo Tolstoy was another visitor. The hospital staff were awed to find themselves in the presence of the country's greatest writer. The most famous man in Russia? Of course they had to let him in to see Chekhov, even though "nonessential" visitors were forbidden. With much obsequiousness on the part of the nurses and resident doctors, the bearded, fierce-looking old man was shown into Chekhov's room. Despite his low opinion of Chekhov's abilities as a playwright (Tolstoy felt the plays were static and lacking in any moral vision. "Where do your characters take you?" he once demanded of Chekhov. "From the sofa to the junk room and back"), Tolstoy liked Chekhov's short stories. Furthermore, and quite simply, he loved the man. He told Gorky, "What a beautiful, magnificent man: modest and quiet, like a girl. He even walks like a girl. He's simply wonderful." And Tolstoy wrote in his journal (everyone kept a journal or a diary in those days), "I am glad I love . . . Chekhov."

Tolstoy removed his woollen scarf and bearskin coat, then lowered himself into a chair next to Chekhov's bed. Never mind that Chekhov was taking medication and not permitted to talk, much less carry on a conversation. He had to listen, amazedly, as the Count began to discourse on his theories of the immortality of the soul. Concerning that visit, Chekhov later wrote, "Tolstoy assumes that all of us (humans and animals alike) will live on in a principle (such as reason or love) the essence and goals of which are a mystery to us. . . . I have no use for that kind of immortality. I don't understand it, and Lev Nikolayevich was astonished I didn't."

Nevertheless, Chekhov was impressed with the solicitude shown by Tolstoy's visit. But, unlike Tolstoy, Chekhov didn't believe in an afterlife and never had. He didn't believe in anything that couldn't be apprehended by one or more of his five senses. And as far as his outlook on life and writing went, he once told someone that he lacked "a political, religious, and philosophical world view. I change it every month, so I'll have to limit myself to the description of how my heroes love, marry, give birth, die, and how they speak."

Earlier, before his TB was diagnosed, Chekhov had remarked, "When a peasant has consumption, he says, 'There's nothing I can do. I'll go off in the spring with the melting of the snows.'" (Chekhov himself died in the summer, during a heat wave.) But once Chekhov's own tuberculosis was discovered he continually tried to minimize the seriousness of his condition. To all appearances, it was as if he felt, right up to the end, that he might be able to throw off the disease as he would a lingering catarrh. Well into his final days, he spoke with seeming conviction of the possibility of an improvement. In fact, in a letter written shortly before his end, he went so far as to tell his sister that he was "getting fat" and felt much better now that he was in Badenweiler.

Badenweiler is a spa and resort city in the western area of the Black Forest, not far from Basel. The Vosges are visible from nearly anywhere in the city, and in those days the air was pure and invigorating. Russians had been going there for years to soak in the hot mineral baths and promenade on the boulevards. In June, 1904, Chekhov went there to die.

Earlier that month, he'd made a difficult journey by train from Moscow to Berlin. He traveled with his wife, the actress Olga Knipper, a woman he'd met in 1898 during rehearsals for *The Seagull*. Her contemporaries describe her as an excellent actress. She was talented, pretty, and almost ten years younger than the playwright. Chekhov had been immediately attracted to her, but was slow to act on his feelings. As always, he preferred a flirtation to marriage. Finally, after a three-year courtship involving many separations, letters, and the inevitable misunderstandings, they were at last married, in a private ceremony in Moscow, on 25 May 1901. Chekhov was enormously happy. He called Olga his "pony", and sometimes "dog" or "puppy". He was also fond of addressing her as "little turkey" or simply as "my joy".

In Berlin, Chekhov consulted with a renowned specialist in pulmonary disorders, a Dr Karl Ewald. But, according to an eyewitness, after the doctor examined Chekhov he threw up his hands and left the room without a word. Chekhov was too far gone for help: this Dr Ewald was furious with himself for not being able to work miracles, and with Chekhov for being so ill.

A Russian journalist happened to visit the Chekhovs at their hotel and sent back this dispatch to his editor: "Chekhov's days are numbered. He seems mortally ill, is terribly thin, coughs all the time, gasps for breath at the slightest movement, and is running a high temperature." This same journalist saw the Chekhovs off at Potsdam Station when they boarded their train for Badenweiler. According to his account, "Chekhov had trouble making his way up the small staircase at the station. He had to sit down for several minutes to catch his breath." In fact, it was painful for Chekhov to move: his legs ached continually and his insides hurt. The disease had attacked his intestines and spinal cord. At this point he had less than a month to live. When Chekhov spoke of his condition now, it was, according to Olga, "with an almost reckless indifference".

Dr Schwöhrer was one of the many Badenweiler physicians who earned a good living by treating the well-to-do who came to the spa seeking relief from various maladies. Some of his patients were ill and infirm, others simply old and hypochondriacal. But Chekhov's was a special case: he was clearly beyond help and in his last days. He was also very famous. Even Dr Schwöhrer knew his name: he'd read some of Chekhov's stories in a German magazine. When he examined the writer early in June, he voiced his appreciation of Chekhov's art but kept his medical opinions to himself. Instead, he prescribed a diet of cocoa, oatmeal drenched in butter, and strawberry tea. This last was supposed to help Chekhov sleep at night.

On 13 June, less than three weeks before he died, Chekhov wrote a letter to his mother in which he told her his health was on the mend. In it he said, "It's likely that I'll be completely cured in a week." Who knows why he said this? What could he have been thinking? He was a doctor himself, and he knew better. He was dying, it was as simple and as unavoidable as that. Nevertheless, he sat out on the balcony of his hotel room and read railway timetables. He asked for information on sailings of boats bound for Odessa from Marseilles. But he *knew*. At this stage he had to have known. Yet in one of the last letters he ever wrote he told his sister he was growing stronger by the day.

He no longer had any appetite for literary work, and hadn't for a long time. In fact, he had very nearly failed to complete *The Cherry Orchard* the year before. Writing that play was the hardest thing he'd ever done in his life. Toward the end, he was able to manage only six or seven lines a day. "I've started losing heart," he wrote Olga. "I feel I'm finished as a writer, and every sentence strikes me as worthless and of no use whatever." But he didn't stop. He finished his play in October 1903. It was the last thing he ever wrote, except for letters and a few entries in his notebook.

A little after midnight on 2 July 1904, Olga sent someone to fetch Dr Schwöhrer. It was an emergency: Chekhov was delirious. Two young Russians on holiday happened to have the adjacent room, and Olga hurried next door to explain what was happening. One of the youths was in his bed asleep, but the other was still awake, smoking and reading. He left the hotel at a run to find Dr Schwöhrer. "I can still hear the sound of the gravel under his shoes in the silence of that stifling July night," Olga wrote later on in her memoirs. Chekhov was hallucinating, talking about sailors, and there were snatches of something about the Japanese. "You don't put ice on an empty stomach," he said when she tried to place an ice pack on his chest.

Dr Schwöhrer arrived and unpacked his bag, all the while keeping his gaze fastened on Chekhov, who lay gasping in the bed. The sick man's pupils were dilated and his temples glistened with sweat. Dr Schwöhrer's face didn't register anything. He was not an emotional man, but he knew Chekhov's end was near. Still, he was a doctor, sworn to do his utmost, and Chekhov held on to life, however tenuously. Dr Schwöhrer prepared a hypodermic and administered an injection of camphor, something that was supposed to speed up the heart. But the injection didn't help – nothing, of course, could have helped. Nevertheless, the doctor made known to Olga his intention of sending for oxygen. Suddenly, Chekhov roused himself, became lucid, and said quietly, "What's the use? Before it arrives I'll be a corpse."

Dr Schwöhrer pulled on his big moustache and stared at Chekhov. The writer's cheeks were sunken and gray, his complexion waxen; his breath was raspy. Dr Schwöhrer knew the time could be reckoned in minutes. Without a word, without conferring with Olga, he went over to an alcove where there was a telephone on the wall. He read the instructions for using the device. If he activated it by holding his finger on a button and turning a handle on the side of the phone, he could reach the lower regions of the hotel – the kitchen. He picked up the receiver, held it to his ear, and did as the instructions told him. When someone finally answered, Dr Schwöhrer ordered a bottle of the hotel's best champagne. "How many glasses?" he was asked. "Three glasses!" the doctor shouted into the mouthpiece. "And hurry, do you hear?" It was one of those rare moments of inspiration that can easily enough be overlooked later on, because the action is so entirely appropriate it seems inevitable.

The champagne was brought to the door by a tired-looking young man whose blond hair was standing up. The trousers of his uniform were wrinkled, the creases gone, and in his haste he'd missed a loop while buttoning his jacket. His appearance was that of someone who'd been resting (slumped in a chair, say, dozing a little), when off in the distance the phone had clamored in the early-morning hours – great God in Heaven! – and the next thing he knew he was being shaken awake by a superior and told to deliver a bottle of Moët to Room 211. "And hurry, do you hear?"

The young man entered the room carrying a silver ice bucket with the champagne in it and a silver tray with three cut-crystal glasses. He found a place on the table for the bucket and glasses, all the while craning his neck, trying to see into the other room, where someone panted ferociously for breath. It was a dreadful, harrowing sound, and the young man lowered his chin into his collar and turned away as the ratchety breathing worsened. Forgetting himself, he stared out the open window toward the darkened city. Then this big imposing man with a thick moustache pressed some coins into his hand – a large tip, by the feel of it – and suddenly the young man saw the door open. He took some steps and found himself on the landing, where he opened his hand and looked at the coins in amazement.

Methodically, the way he did everything, the doctor went about the business of working the cork out of the bottle. He did it in such a way as to minimize, as much as possible, the festive explosion. He poured three glasses and, out of habit, pushed the cork back into the neck of the bottle. He then took the glasses of champagne over to the bed. Olga momentarily released her grip on Chekhov's hand – a hand, she said later, that burned her fingers. She arranged another pillow behind his head. Then she put the cool glass of champagne against Chekhov's palm and made sure his fingers closed around the stem. They exchanged looks – Chekhov, Olga, Dr Schwöhrer. They didn't touch glasses. There was no toast. What on earth was there to drink to? To death? Chekhov summoned his remaining strength and said, "It's been so long since I've had champagne." He brought the glass to his lips and drank. In a minute or two Olga took the empty glass from his hand and set it on the nightstand. Then

Chekhov turned onto his side. He closed his eyes and sighed. A minute later, his breathing stopped.

Dr Schwöhrer picked up Chekhov's hand from the bedsheet. He held his fingers to Chekhov's wrist and drew a gold watch from his vest pocket, opening the lid of the watch as he did so. The second hand on the watch moved slowly, very slowly. He let it move around the face of the watch three times while he waited for signs of a pulse. It was three o'clock in the morning and still sultry in the room. Badenweiler was in the grip of its worst heat wave in years. All the windows in both rooms stood open, but there was no sign of a breeze. A large, black-winged moth flew through a window and banged wildly against the electric lamp. Dr Schwöhrer let go of Chekhov's wrist. "It's over," he said. He closed the lid of his watch and returned it to his vest pocket.

At once Olga dried her eyes and set about composing herself. She thanked the doctor for coming. He asked if she wanted some medication – laudanum, perhaps, or a few drops of valerian. She shook her head. She did have one request, though: before the authorities were notified and the newspapers found out, before the time came when Chekhov was no longer in her keeping, she wanted to be alone with him for a while. Could the doctor help with this? Could he withhold, for a while anyway, news of what had just occurred?

Dr Schwöhrer stroked his moustache with the back of a finger. Why not? After all, what difference would it make to anyone whether this matter became known now or a few hours from now? The only detail that remained was to fill out a death certificate, and this could be done at his office later on in the morning, after he'd slept a few hours. Dr Schwöhrer nodded his agreement and prepared to leave. He murmured a few words of condolence. Olga inclined her head. "An honor," Dr Schwöhrer said. He picked up his bag and left the room and, for that matter, history.

It was at this moment that the cork popped out of the champagne bottle; foam spilled down onto the table. Olga went back to Chekhov's bedside. She sat on a footstool, holding his hand, from time to time stroking his face. "There were no human voices, no everyday sounds," she wrote. "There was only beauty, peace, and the grandeur of death."

She stayed with Chekhov until daybreak, when thrushes began to call from the garden below. Then came the sound of tables and chairs being moved about down there. Before long, voices carried up to her. It was then a knock sounded at the door. Of course she thought it must be an official of some sort – the medical examiner, say, or someone from the police who had questions to ask and forms for her to fill out, or maybe, just maybe, it could be Dr Schwöhrer returning with a mortician to render assistance in embalming and transporting Chekhov's remains back to Russia.

But, instead, it was the same blond young man who'd brought the champagne a few hours earlier. This time, however, his uniform trousers were neatly pressed, with stiff creases in front, and every button on his snug green jacket was fastened. He seemed quite another person. Not only was he wide awake but his plump cheeks were smooth-shaven, his hair was in place, and he appeared anxious to please. He was holding a porcelain vase with three long-stemmed yellow roses. He presented these to Olga with a smart click of his heels. She stepped back and let him into the room. He was there, he said, to collect the glasses, ice bucket, and tray, yes. But he also wanted to say that, because of the extreme heat, breakfast would be served in the garden this morning. He hoped this weather wasn't too bothersome; he apologized for it.

The woman seemed distracted. While he talked, she turned her eyes away and looked down at something in the carpet. She crossed her arms and held her elbows. Meanwhile, still holding his vase, waiting for a sign, the young man took in the details of the room. Bright sunlight flooded through the open windows. The room was tidy and seemed undisturbed, almost untouched. No garments were flung over chairs, no shoes, stockings, braces, or stays were in evidence, no open suitcases. In short, there was no clutter, nothing but the usual heavy pieces of hotel-room furniture. Then, because the woman was still looking down, he looked down, too, and at once spied a cork near the toe of his shoe. The woman did not see it – she was looking somewhere else. The young man wanted to bend over and pick up the cork, but he was still holding the roses and was afraid of seeming to intrude even more by drawing any further attention to himself. Reluctantly, he left the cork where it was and raised his eyes. Everything was in order except for the uncorked, half-empty bottle of champagne that stood alongside two crystal glasses over on the little table. He cast his gaze about once more. Through an open door he saw that the third glass was in the bedroom, on the nightstand. But someone still occupied the bed! He couldn't see a face, but the figure under the covers lay perfectly motionless and quiet. He noted the figure and looked elsewhere. Then, for a reason he couldn't understand, a feeling of uneasiness took hold of him. He cleared his throat and moved his weight to the other leg. The woman still didn't look up or break her silence. The young man felt his cheeks grow warm. It occurred to him, quite without his having thought it through, that he should perhaps suggest an alternative to breakfast in the garden. He coughed, hoping to focus the woman's attention, but she didn't look at him. The distinguished foreign guests could, he said, take breakfast in their rooms this morning if they wished. The young man (his name hasn't survived, and it's likely he perished in the Great War) said he would be happy to bring up a tray. Two trays, he added, glancing uncertainly once again in the direction of the bedroom.

He fell silent and ran a finger around the inside of his collar. He didn't understand. He wasn't even sure the woman had been listening. He didn't know what else to do now; he was still holding the vase. The sweet odor of the roses filled his nostrils and inexplicably caused a pang of regret. The entire time he'd been waiting, the woman had apparently been lost in thought. It was as if all the while he'd been standing there, talking, shifting his weight, holding his flowers, she had been someplace else, somewhere far from Badenweiler. But now she came back to herself, and her face assumed another expression. She raised her eyes, looked at him, and then shook her head. She seemed to be struggling to understand what on earth this young man could be doing there in the room holding a vase with three yellow roses. Flowers? She hadn't ordered flowers.

The moment passed. She went over to her handbag and scooped up some coins. She drew out a number of banknotes as well. The young man touched his lips with his tongue; another large tip was forthcoming, but for what? What did she want him to do? He'd never before waited on such guests. He cleared his throat once more.

No breakfast, the woman said. Not yet, at any rate. Breakfast wasn't the important thing this morning. She required something else. She needed him to go out and bring back a mortician. Did he understand her? Herr Chekhov was dead, you see. *Comprenez-vous?* Young man? Anton Chekhov was dead. Now listen carefully to me, she said. She wanted him to go downstairs and ask someone at the front desk where he could go to find the most respected mortician in the city. Someone reliable, who took great pains in his work and whose manner was appropriately reserved. A mortician, in short, worthy of a great artist. Here, she said, and pressed the money on him. Tell them downstairs that I have specifically requested you to perform this duty for me. Are you listening? Do you understand what I'm saying to you?

The young man grappled to take in what she was saying. He chose not to look again in the direction of the other room. He had sensed that something was not right. He became aware of his heart beating rapidly under his jacket, and he felt perspiration break out on his forehead. He didn't know where he should turn his eyes. He wanted to put the vase down.

Please do this for me, the woman said. I'll remember you with gratitude. Tell them downstairs that I insist. Say that. But don't call any unnecessary attention to yourself or to the situation. Just say that this is necessary, that I request it – and that's all. Do you hear me? Nod if you understand. Above all, don't raise an alarm. Everything else, all the rest, the commotion – that'll come soon enough. The worst is over. Do we understand each other?

The young man's face had grown pale. He stood rigid, clasping the vase. He managed to nod his head.

After securing permission to leave the hotel he was to proceed quietly and resolutely, though without any unbecoming haste, to the mortician's. He was to behave exactly as if he were engaged on a very important errand, nothing more. He *was* engaged on an important errand, she said. And if it would help keep his movements purposeful he should imagine himself as someone moving down the busy sidewalk carrying in his arms a porcelain vase of roses that he had to deliver to an important man. (She spoke quietly, almost confidentially, as if to a relative or a friend.) He could even tell himself that the man he was going to see was expecting him, was perhaps impatient for him to arrive with his flowers. Nevertheless, the young man was not to become excited and run, or otherwise break his stride. Remember the vase he was carrying! He was to walk briskly, comporting himself at all times in as dignified a manner as possible. He should keep walking until he came to the mortician's house and stood before the door. He would then raise the brass knocker and let it fall, once, twice, three times. In a minute the mortician himself would answer.

This mortician would be in his forties, no doubt, or maybe early fifties – bald, solidly built, wearing steel-frame spectacles set very low on his nose. He would be modest, unassuming, a man who would ask only the most direct and necessary questions. An apron. Probably he would be wearing an apron. He might even be wiping his hands on a dark towel while he listened to what was being said. There'd be a faint whiff of formaldehyde on his clothes. But it was all right, and the young man shouldn't worry. He was nearly a grown-up now and shouldn't be frightened or repelled by any of this. The mortician would hear him out. He was a man of restraint and bearing, this mortician, someone who could help allay people's fears in this situation, not increase them. Long ago he'd acquainted himself with death in all its various guises and forms; death held no surprises for him any longer, no hidden secrets. It was this man whose services were required this morning.

The mortician takes the vase of roses. Only once while the young man is speaking does the mortician betray the least flicker of interest, or indicate that he's heard anything out of the ordinary. But the one time the young man mentions the name of the deceased, the mortician's eyebrows rise just a little. Chekhov, you say? Just a minute, and I'll be with you.

Do you understand what I'm saying, Olga said to the young man. Leave the glasses. Don't worry about them. Forget about crystal wineglasses and such. Leave the room as it is. Everything is ready now. We're ready. Will you go?

But at that moment the young man was thinking of the cork still resting near the toe of his shoe. To retrieve it he would have to bend over, still gripping the vase. He would do this. He leaned over. Without looking down, he reached out and closed it into his hand.